P9-CNB-663

When the
Cypress
Whispers

MUSKOKA LAKES PUBLIC LIBRARY
P.O. BOX 189; 69 JOSEPH STREET
PORT CARLING, ON P0B 1J0
705-765-5650
www.muskoka.com/library

When the Cypress Whispers

YVETTE MANESSIS CORPORON

HARPER

www.harpercollins.com

WHEN THE CYPRESS WHISPERS. Copyright © 2014 by Yvette Manessis Corporon. All rights reserved. Printed in the United States of America. No part of this book may be used or reproduced in any manner whatsoever without written permission except in the case of brief quotations embodied in critical articles and reviews. For information, address HarperCollins Publishers, 10 East 53rd Street, New York, NY 10022.

HarperCollins books may be purchased for educational, business, or sales promotional use. For information, please e-mail the Special Markets Department at SPsales@harpercollins.com.

FIRST EDITION

Library of Congress Cataloging-in-Publication Data
    Corporon, Yvette Manessis.
        When the cypress whispers / Yvette Manessis Corporon.—First edition.
        pages   cm
        ISBN 978-0-06-226758-0 (hardback)—ISBN 978-0-06-226759-7 (electronic) 1. Greek American women—Fiction. 2. Fiancés—Fiction. 3. Grandmothers—
Fiction. 4. Greece—Fiction. 5. Domestic fiction. I. Title.
    PS3603.O7713W54   2014
    813'.6—dc23   2013019676

ISBN 978-0-06-232266-1 (International Edition)

14 15 16 17 18   OV/RRD   10 9 8 7 6 5 4 3 2 1

For my mother and my yia-yias

Saved when I neither hoped nor thought I'd be,
I owe the Gods a mighty debt of thanks.

—SOPHOCLES

Prologue

"*Yia sou*, Yia-yia," Daphne called out as she raced down the ancient stone steps. It was just a quarter mile down the dirt road to the beach, but to the anxious twelve-year-old, the trip felt like forever. She ran the entire way, stopping only once and only for a moment, fingers reaching out to pluck a blackberry from a roadside bush whose giant fruit looked too dark, heavy, and sweet to pass up—even for a girl on a mission.

Daphne dropped her towel the instant her feet reached the caramel-colored sand. Not even stopping to kick off her white Keds, she slipped out of them as she ran to the water. First right, then left, the laceless sneakers littered the pristine beach. Daphne had discovered long ago that laces on shoes only got in her way.

She finally slowed her pace, stepping gingerly, arms out for balance, as she navigated the black rocks that pocked the shoreline. She let out a little gasp as her bare feet first felt the cooling welcome of the Ionian Sea.

Daphne trekked ahead until the lower half of her slender thighs was underwater. She raised both arms above her head, fingers tapping together in anticipation, bent her knees, then sprang up on her toes, propelling her body forward in a perfect arc. Finally fully submerged in the calm, clear water, she opened her eyes.

There they were, just as she had left them last summer—her silent underwater companions. Daphne smiled as she spotted the spiky black sea urchins and then waved her arms and kicked her legs to turn and catch a glimpse of the knuckle-size barnacles that clung to the submerged rocks. Everywhere she looked there were fish, so many fish in different shapes and sizes, whose names she only knew in Greek. *Tsipoura. Barbounia.* She had never once considered learning their English names; why would she? It wasn't as if any of the kids back home ever stopped to ask how she spent her summers or what the fish were called. In fact, they never stopped to speak to her at all.

She stayed in the sea for hours, diving, swimming, and daydreaming, never once feeling lonely or scared in the water all by herself. She wasn't like some of the other girls, afraid of what might lurk under the surface. She loved being out here, solitary and silent in her little cove. The sea never judged her; it only welcomed her, even invited her. The sea didn't care that Daphne's hand-me-down swimsuit was too big, its elastic stretched beyond repair by cousin Popi's newfound curves. It didn't care that even now, even thousands of miles away from the diner, Daphne's hair still had the faint, stubborn scent of grease.

None of that mattered here. The sea christened her again each summer, making everything new, fresh, and clean. Daphne always imagined the earth and rocks that jutted out on either side of the cove as protective arms, caressing her and forming a safe little pool for her to swim in. Here she felt safe from the secrets of the open sea and from the stares of girls whose freckled skin smelled of strawberry lotion.

Even when her muscles began to spasm and her lungs ached from always holding her breath just a few seconds too long, she still wasn't ready to leave her watery playground. She simply flipped over on her back, floated, and stared up at the sky, impossibly blue and sprinkled with light, wispy clouds—clouds that to Daphne looked like delicate silk threads embellishing the perfection of the heavens.

No wonder Athena was mad. I bet that's what Arachne's silk looked like, she thought, remembering the story Yia-yia had told her about the vain girl who was turned into a spider because she dared to boast that her weaving skills were greater than the goddess's. Daphne smiled, retelling the story to herself as her fingers paddled the water and the incoming tide lapped against her weightless body.

Finally Daphne looked down at herself and noticed the telltale signs that she had done it again, stayed in the water too long. As much as she'd have liked to believe that she was one of the legendary sea nymphs who swam and frolicked in these waters, the sad reality was that she was merely a mortal. Her normally olive-colored fingers had turned grayish white, and her skin was puckered and pruned. It was time to get back to dry land.

As Daphne gathered everything she'd tossed about the beach, she looked at her watch and saw that it was 1:45, even later than she thought. She knew Yia-yia had prepared lunch and would be pacing the patio by now, waiting for her beloved granddaughter to return.

"Yia-yia's gonna kill me," Daphne said, though no one was there to hear her. Or was there? She looked around the small beach as she stood dripping on the sand. She had the strangest feeling, as if someone was watching her, as if she could hear someone in the distance. It sounded like a woman's voice singing . . . soft and familiar, yet so faint and fleeting that Daphne couldn't be sure what it was.

She turned again toward the sea and lifted her towel to shake it out. Closing her eyes against the barrage of sand, Daphne waved her arms up and down, the towel floating on the breeze like a gull in flight. Suddenly the wind picked up and an unexpectedly cool gust sliced against her wet skin. She dug her heels into the sand to keep from falling and tightened her grip on the towel, which was now slapping like a flag on a blustery winter day.

Eyes still closed against the sand, which stung as it struck her face, she heard the nearby cypress trees rustle as the wind tore through their branches and rattled their leaves. She froze. There . . . there it was. She heard it. She was certain this time. It had to be. Her fingers released the towel, and she opened her eyes to watch as the zephyr carried it down the beach. She knew she'd heard it this time.

Daphne's heart raced faster. Could it be? Could it really and finally be? As far back as she could remember, Yia-yia had told her the legend of the cypress whispers. In hushed, reverent tones, Yia-yia insisted that the cypresses had their own secret language that traveled between the trees on the gentle morning breeze and quieted down again as the afternoon stillness set in. Time and again the old woman had pulled Daphne close and asked her to listen. Time and again Daphne had tried to hear the truths that Yia-yia swore they spoke of, to hear the answers they whispered on the wind, but she could not.

Please, please speak to me, Daphne pleaded. Her eyes widened with possibility and hope. She clutched her hands to her heart and held her breath to be certain, to listen once more with no distractions. She turned her face toward where she thought the voice had come from, the farthest reaches of the cove, where the cluster of trees and thicket was so dense that not even she dared take that shortcut home. Feeling faint from holding her breath, Daphne waited and prayed.

This time she heard nothing, only the hollow churning of her empty stomach.

Finally she exhaled, her small shoulders slumped forward with the weight of yet another disappointment.

She sighed, shaking her black curls and sending droplets of water everywhere. It was no use. There was no singing. No story. No beautiful woman's voice serenading her. No answers to life's mysteries waiting to be plucked from the breeze like a blackberry. All she could hear was the ordinary sound of branches rattling and leaves trembling in the wind.

But even though they maintained their stubborn silence, Daphne knew that the shivering leaves had one thing to say to her.

They're telling me it's time to go home.

She slid her sand-coated feet into her sneakers.

Yia-yia is waiting for me. It's time to go home.

One

CORFU

PRESENT DAY

"There you are!" Popi's accented English echoed through the air-port as she threw her arms out and ran across the terminal. Push-ing aside a handful of newly arrived tourists, she barreled her ample body across the crowded terminal to greet her favorite cousin properly. "Oh my god, just look at you! How did you get so skinny? I ate a chicken bigger than you for dinner last night."

Daphne dropped her bags right there, in the middle of the exit ramp for the arriving flight. She heard the shouts and curses of the other passengers as they maneuvered around her luggage, but Daphne didn't care. Not in the least. It had been six years since Daphne had been here, six years since she was last in Greece, and she was not about to wait a moment longer to fall into the warm, welcoming embrace of her cousin, despite the protests of her fellow passengers. Like their *yia-yias*, who were sisters, Popi and Daphne had always been especially close. Popi's own grandmother had died when she was a baby. From that moment, Yia-yia had stepped in, raised Popi and loved her like her own granddaughter.

"It's so good to see you," Daphne cried. She opened her thin, toned arms and felt herself submerged in Popi's soft flesh.

Popi squealed. They held each other for just a few moments longer before Popi finally let go and shuffled back to get a better look at Daphne.

"Skinny, yes—but also beautiful. Ah, Daphne, your Stephen is a lucky man. What a beautiful bride you will make." Popi clapped her hands happily, suddenly stopping to cock her head to the right and narrow her eyes, leaning in for a closer look. "You look different."

"I've lost some weight."

"No. *Different*," Popi insisted as she pointed at Daphne's face.

Daphne touched her hand to her newly refined nose. She had laughed with Stephen about the procedure, calling it the cosmetic surgeon's version of ethnic cleansing. "Oh, yeah. My nose. I had it fixed."

"Fixed? Was it broken?"

"No, just big." Daphne laughed now too. Popi touched her finger to her own Greek nose as Daphne spoke.

"I was having problems breathing at night, and the doctor said this would help."

Popi didn't bother waiting for a further explanation. "My own cousin, marrying a rich *Amerikanos*. You can buy anything you want, even a new nose." She chuckled. "I am so happy for you, Daphne *mou*. Ah, Daphne . . . pinch your favorite cousin so some luck rubs off on me, eh? There are no men left in Greece for me." Popi spat at the floor in disgust.

Daphne was amused by her cousin's dramatics, but she knew her complaint was steeped in truth. Still single at thirty-four, Popi was an old maid by traditional Greek standards. She had dated a few men here and there, but no one had held her interest for more than a few weeks. But as much as Popi loved to complain about the lack of men in her life, she wasn't like the other island women, who would lower their standards and settle on a husband. Popi, like her cousin Daphne, had always wanted more.

Daphne reached behind her legs and pulled five-year-old Evie out from where she was hiding behind her mother's skirt. "Popi, this is Evie."

"*Ahooo*. What an angel you are!" Popi shrieked even louder this time. She dug her hands into her purse, searching as she bent down in front of Evie. "Oh, where is it? I know it's in here somewhere," she muttered while sorting through the keys, cigarette packs, and candy wrappers that littered her cavernous brown leather satchel.

Evie didn't say a word. She just looked at this stranger, who looked an awful lot like her mother, just bigger in every way. The little girl held on to her mother's hand while trying to maneuver herself back behind Daphne again.

"Okay, you're a little shy. That's all right," Popi told her. She finally found what she'd been looking for and pulled out a little stuffed dog. "I thought you might like this."

Evie's demeanor changed the moment she saw the little dog. Her reticence seemed to evaporate as she crept out toward Popi.

The little girl smiled as she took her new toy and hugged it to her chest.

"What do you say, Evie?" Daphne prompted.

"Thank you," Evie said dutifully.

"Evie, I'm your mother's cousin Penelope, but you can call me Thea Popi." Though in the United States, Popi would have been regarded as Evie's cousin, in Greece she was considered Evie's aunt. It was that way with the Greeks; the generational divide was always respected and never to be crossed. Calling someone *thea* or *theo*—aunt or uncle—was often more a sign of respect than familial ties.

"I know, it is a funny name," Popi continued. "But your mother gave it to me. Shame on you, Daphne." Popi looked up and shook her stubby finger at her cousin before turning back to Evie.

"When your mother and I were little girls just like you"—Popi tapped Evie's nose with the tip of her finger—"my family came to live in New York for a few years. Your mother and I were very, very close. Like sisters." Popi beamed. "Your mother tried and tried, but no matter how hard she tried, she just could not say my name. *Pee-ne-lo-pee*. Can you say *Penelope*?"

"*Pee-ne-lo-pee*," Evie repeated.

"That is perfect." Evie's spine straightened as the word left Popi's lips. The child seemed to grow inches before their eyes.

"But your mother"—Popi inched closer to Evie as she spoke—"ah, your mother, she was not so perfect. She just could not say it. So she started calling me Popi. Now everybody calls me that."

Evie looked up at her mother. "Mommy, you were a little girl once?"

"Yes, Evie. I was, but that was a long, long time ago." Daphne looked down at her daughter, remembering when she too was this young, this innocent, this eager to hear the stories the adults would share with her.

"Come, let's go." Popi slapped the gray Corfu Airport dust off of her black skirt as she stood. "We'll go straight to the apartment so you can take a shower and rest for a little while. Are you tired, Evie?"

Evie shook her head no. She reached for her small pink suitcase.

"We actually slept really well on the plane," Daphne said as she began to gather their bags. "We were in first class. They have seats that turn into beds. I mean, real beds that lie all the way flat." She wrapped her fingers around the handles of the two large black rolling suitcases, and tucked the white garment bag that held her wedding dress under her arm.

"Let me help. I'll take that," Popi said as she took the garment bag from Daphne.

"What a difference from when we were kids, huh, Popi?"

"What a difference a rich American husband makes." Popi snorted. She held out her hand to Evie. The little girl hesitated, but then lifted her delicate hand to lock fingers with her aunt.

As they walked through the terminal, Popi said, "I need to find a husband, too. A rich *Amerikanos*. And you're going to help me, okay?"

"Like Stephen?" Evie asked.

Popi nodded. "Yes, just like Stephen. I want a handsome, rich *Amerikanos* to make me happy and make me laugh all the time." Popi tickled Evie's palm with her fingernails.

Then Popi and Evie walked on hand in hand. Daphne stood still in the airless terminal, twirling her diamond ring, watching her daughter and cousin pass through the sliding doors and into the

Corfu sunshine. As Daphne began to follow, she heard a ring tone coming from somewhere deep in her handbag. She fumbled for a few moments, but finally located the phone just before the call went to voice mail.

"*Yia sou*, greetings from Corfu."

"Well, I see you've arrived. Safe and sound, I hope." It was Stephen, calling from New York.

"Safe and sound and dying for you to get here," she replied as she tucked the phone under her ear, readjusted her fingers around the handles of the suitcase, tilted it on its wheels, and walked out of the terminal into the dry heat of the island afternoon.

DAPHNE AND EVIE GAZED CONTENTEDLY at the scenery for the ten-minute trip to Popi's apartment in Kerkyra, the main city of Corfu, as they pointed out special places to Evie.

"You see that tiny little green island out there in the water?" Daphne asked as she pointed out the window.

"Yes, I see it," Evie answered.

"That's Pontikonisi."

"What does that mean?"

Popi interrupted. "Cousin, I know she's not fluent, but don't tell me she doesn't know *any* Greek?" She took her eyes off the road just long enough to look at her cousin.

Daphne ignored Popi's question and answered Evie's instead.

"It means Mouse Island in Greek, honey. You see that long white path that leads to the old monastery? People say that path looks like a mouse's tail."

Daphne laughed, remembering how as a young girl she thought

the island's name meant that it was home to giant mice. But as a teenager, she had been delighted to learn that instead it was where Odysseus had been shipwrecked in *The Odyssey*. She had loved visiting the island, walking its ancient paths, daydreaming under its majestic cypress trees—wondering if they would finally whisper their secrets to her. But the cypress whispers, like the story of Odysseus's travels, proved to be nothing more than another island legend.

"And over there, that is my café." Popi pointed to a sprawling outdoor café located along the water's edge where she had worked as a waitress for the past ten years. The tables were packed with tourists and locals. "Evie, you will come, and I will serve you the biggest and best ice cream in all of Corfu. It will be as large as your head and topped with not one but two sparklers for you."

"Really, as big as my head?" Evie touched her hands to the side of her head to measure just how big this special ice cream would be.

"If not bigger." Popi laughed as she glanced at Evie in the rearview mirror.

"Is that a castle up there?" Evie bounced in her seat, pointing up at Corfu's old fort on top of its craggy gray peninsula.

"Yes, it is our Frourio," Popi answered. "It was built many, many years ago to protect our island from pirates."

"Pirates!" Evie shouted, her long dark lashes fluttering. "Are there pirates here?"

"No, there are no more pirates, Evie *mou*," Popi told her. "But a long, long time ago my mama told me that if you walk through the Frourio at night, sometimes you can hear the ghosts."

Daphne coughed in an effort to get her cousin to stop, but it was no use. Popi continued with her story.

"She said that sometimes you can hear souls crying for mercy, begging for their lives. Even little children crying out for their mothers."

Evie whimpered.

"Evie, honey, those are just silly old island stories," Daphne said. "Don't worry." She was already concerned that jet lag would keep Evie awake all hours. And now, thanks to Popi's eagerness to tell ghost stories, she'd probably have nightmares to contend with as well.

Daphne had never told Popi about the nightmares that had haunted Evie's sleep these past few years. How could she, a single woman, understand what it was like to comfort a frightened child each night? How could she understand the loneliness of having no one to nudge awake and murmur, "It's your turn to go to her"? Daphne had longed for someone to share her bed and keep Evie's as well as her own nightmares at bay. For the longest time, when she heard Evie's nightly cries, she'd reach her arm across the bed, but she felt only emptiness and the faintest dip in the mattress where Alex used to sleep.

It still didn't seem real—one night Alex and Daphne had been standing side by side, holding hands over their daughter's bassinet, and the next, he was gone. Taken too soon. Daphne found herself alone, wondering how she would ever survive, how she would ever raise Evie without him. But she had managed somehow. The past few years had been so lonely and difficult. But that was then. She was getting married now. She would soon become Mrs. Stephen Heatherton. Daphne prayed that the nightmares and tears would finally be behind them.

"We got rid of all of the pirates long, long ago," Popi told Evie as Daphne left her reverie behind. "Now we only have giant sea monsters to worry about." Popi laughed, but Evie whimpered again.

"Popi, stop!" Daphne pleaded. "It's not funny." The hint of desperation in her voice made it clear that Daphne wasn't joking.

"Evie, *mou*," Popi began, "Thea Popi was only joking. There are no sea monsters here, I promise." Popi looked at Evie in the rearview mirror before turning to face Daphne.

"*Daphne mou, ti eheis?*"—What's wrong?—Popi asked in Greek, knowing Evie could not understand.

Daphne knew there was no way Popi could grasp what she had been through and how much things had changed, how much she had changed. When Alex died, there was no more laughter in Daphne's world, only a demanding, inconsolable baby, a growing stack of bills, and a persistent fear that she wouldn't be able to manage it all herself.

Daphne put her hand on her cousin's leg. "I'm sorry, Popi. I'm just nervous about everything," was all she told Popi now. Perhaps there would be another time to tell her more, or perhaps it was better to leave all the heartache in the past.

Popi took her hand from the wheel and waved the misunderstanding away. "Darling, it's all right. But I am starting to wonder what you've done with my cousin. In our family we always find a way to laugh, even through our tears."

The two women locked fingers, just as they had as children skipping down island paths. Daphne turned her face away and leaned out the window, as if the island air could cleanse away the misunderstanding and the all-too-familiar sadness.

Soon they were at Popi's.

"Just like you remember it, eh, Daphne?" Popi said as they

parked and got out of the car. "Come on, Evie. Let me take you inside." Popi opened the back door, grabbed Evie's bag, and once again tucked the garment bag under her arm before taking Evie's hand. "This is where your mother used to come when she visited. We had so much fun together. We really do have to find me a husband so I can give you cousins to play with, like your mother and I did. Maybe Mr. Stephen will bring some handsome *Amerikanos* to the wedding. What do you think?"

Evie smiled, giggling softly as they stepped up the white marble staircase and into the cool dimness of the lobby.

"If you meet a boy, you might have to kiss him."

"You think so?" Popi leaned in, happy to take the delicious bait Evie had just dangled before her.

"Does your mommy kiss Stephen?"

"No! Ewwwwwwww!" Evie shrieked as she ran up the curved stairs, her laughter reverberating around the marble lobby.

Daphne rode the creaky elevator to the second floor and wheeled the suitcases into the sunlit foyer of the apartment.

When everything had been brought inside, Popi led everyone into the living room. She smiled at the little girl and said, "*Ella*, Evie. Your mother and I could use a nice cup of *kafe* and I'm too tired to make it. Will you make a nice cup of *kafe* for us? I bet you are a great chef like your mama."

"I don't even know what that is," Evie replied as she shrugged her shoulders.

"Come on, Evie." Popi placed her hands on her hips. "Every Greek must know how to make *kafes*, even the little ones like you."

"But I'm not Greek. I'm from New York," Evie replied.

Popi put her hands together as if in prayer. A soft moan escaped her lips. "Evie, promise me you will never let Yia-yia hear you say that." She turned to Daphne. "Cousin, Yia-yia is going to kill you if she hears this." Popi made the sign of the cross and muttered just loud enough for Daphne to hear, "No Greek at all, this child. Nothing."

Daphne twirled her engagement ring round and round on her finger. She had never imagined that Evie would grow up like this. She had always intended to speak to Evie in Greek, knowing it was the only way she would grow up bilingual, as Daphne had. But Greek-speaking nannies are a rare commodity in Manhattan. And with Daphne out of the house twelve hours a day, getting home in time to say *kali nichta* instead of *good night* didn't seem like it would make much of a difference anyway. After a while, she stopped trying.

"Come." Popi narrowed her eyes and motioned for Evie to follow her into the large, bright kitchen. "Your Thea will teach you. Now you will become an expert in making frappe."

"I thought we were making coffee."

"Frappe is coffee. It's cold and delicious and very fun to make. You'll see."

Popi tugged at the handles of a hulking cabinet whose glass front was covered in a pristine white doily, and the doors opened with a jingle of glass. She took three tall glasses from the top shelf and placed them on the table, which was covered with a plastic tablecloth. Then she took out a container of Nescafé and two dome-covered plastic tumblers and handed them to Evie, one at a time.

"Here, put these on the table for me."

Finally, she waddled over to the icebox and took out a bucket of ice and a large bottle of filtered water.

"Your mother may be a famous chef, Evie, but I am famous for frappe. I will show you my secret recipe."

Daphne had stayed behind to organize the luggage, but Evie's frappe lesson was too entertaining to miss. She removed her black slingbacks, not wanting the click of her heels to give her away as she tiptoed down the hall to the kitchen. She made it to the doorway and stood hidden under the wooden archway as Popi directed Evie to place a teaspoonful of the Nescafé into each of the plastic containers along with water, ice, and a little bit of sugar.

"Now, put the cover on the cups and make sure they are on really, really tight. We don't want any accidents in my nice clean kitchen," Popi commanded.

Evie did as she was told, then pressed down on the lids with her little pink painted fingernails. She lifted the cups toward Thea Popi for inspection.

"Good. Perfect. Nice and tight. Now comes the fun part. Now we shake."

Popi took one cup in each hand and shook them, like a volcanic eruption of feminine flesh, arms, feet, hips, legs, black curls, and breasts moving up and down and around in every direction. Evie's face lit up.

"Evie *mou*, the secret to great frappe is to shake it properly." Then to please her willing audience she held her arms up in the air, hoisted the plastic frappe cups toward the ceiling, and gyrated and shook and shimmied as if she were the main act at a bouzouki nightclub. Evie was delighted.

Daphne attempted to stifle her laughter as she watched Popi's frappe frenzy. She was glad to see that twenty years and twenty pounds had not slowed Popi down. Daphne could not remember the last time she had felt that uninhibited.

It was time to jump in. "That's not how you make frappe," she challenged. "*This* is how you make frappe." She took a container from Popi's hand, then took her daughter's hand and twirled her little girl and the cup around and around until Evie fell on the floor in a heap of giggles. She turned to Popi and held out her hand as the cousins snapped their fingers, circled their wrists, and rotated their hips as expertly as they had done the night they had worked a group of Italian tourists into a belly-dance-induced trance.

"*Opa*, Cousin," Popi shouted, clapping her hands over her head.

"*Opa*, Popi *mou*," Daphne cried. Already she felt freer, happier, and more full of life than she had in years.

Two

As she was falling asleep, Daphne remembered a night just a few short months ago. The dream that Yia-yia was with her had felt so real. Yia-yia had been so close that Daphne could see her face and smell the lingering scent of the kitchen fire on her clothes. When Stephen shook her awake, she had been sitting up in bed, arms stretched out into the darkness as if she were reaching out to stroke Yia-yia's weathered skin. Even in the madness of the dinner rush the next night at the restaurant, Daphne had felt at peace just thinking Yia-yia had been with her. She knew it seemed silly, but it was as if she could feel Yia-yia's hand guiding every slice of her knife, each sprinkle of seasoning and toss of her pan.

Daphne knew in her bones what she had to do. She didn't understand why, but she just couldn't shake the need to go home to Yia-yia. She had always been a diligent, responsible granddaughter, calling Yia-yia weekly and never missing a monthly trip to the post office, hiding wads of twenty-dollar bills between cards and photos. She was startled to realize it had been six years since she'd visited Yia-yia. She'd always meant to come back, to bring Evie home. But between the demands of being a single mother and running a restaurant on her own, the time had slipped by.

It had taken a bit of convincing to get Stephen onboard with canceling the formal wedding for two hundred and trading it for a simple island affair on Erikousa, but now she was here.

They had circled around the conversation for days. Stephen always appeared to listen patiently, to understand Daphne's need to go to Yia-yia, but he was adamant about not wanting to trade New England pomp and circumstance for a peasant island wedding. Finally, he agreed. It was the caldera that did it. Daphne had shown Stephen photos of spectacular Santorini sunsets taken from a gorgeous private villa perched on whitewashed cliffs above the sea, overlooking the island's caldera. During Minoan times, a catastrophic volcanic eruption had decimated the island, transforming it into the stunning crescent-shaped tourist favorite of today. When she told him they could rent the villa for their honeymoon, and that her cousin Popi would be available to keep Evie so they could actually honeymoon alone, he finally agreed to move the wedding to Greece. Stephen got what he wanted—precious time alone with his new wife—and Daphne got to go home to Yia-yia. Everyone won.

Despite the threadbare mattress in the sparse back bedroom of Popi's apartment and the clanging dishes from the restaurant below, Daphne had slept better and sounder than she had in years.

She would have slept even later had the familiar ring tone of Stephen's call not awakened her.

"Good morning, honey." She rubbed the sleep from her eyes.

"I'm sorry I woke you. You must be exhausted." She could hear him typing at his computer as he spoke.

"No, I'm good—great, actually. How are things in New York?"

"Busy. Lonely. I hate sleeping in that big bed without you. I'm trying to wrap things up here so I can come make an honest woman of you already. Is there anything you've forgotten, or want me to bring? Anything you need?"

"Nothing but you. I can't wait for you to get here and meet everyone."

Popi entered the bedroom carrying a tray holding frappe, fresh figs, and *tsoureki*, the sweet braided bread that Daphne adored but hadn't indulged in since the nutritionist she hired ordered her to cut out anything white from her diet. Daphne noticed the ease with which her cousin balanced the heavy tray with one hand and served Daphne her coffee with the other. Popi's movements were smooth, seemingly effortless, but Daphne knew better. There was nothing effortless or easy about the years of backbreaking restaurant work it took to develop those skills.

"I'll call you once we get to Erikousa. I love you," Daphne added before hanging up the phone and sitting up in bed. She patted the space beside her.

"What did my new cousin have to say?" Popi asked, placing the tray on the bed.

"He was just checking in, making sure we're okay." Daphne took a bite of the *tsoureki* as Popi sat down next to her. "And wondering which of his very rich, very handsome, and very single friends to introduce you to," Daphne joked as she brushed crumbs from her lap.

"Come, *ella*, Daphne. This is not a joke, eh," Popi said.

"Hmm, who's lost her sense of humor now?" Daphne laughed as Evie came into the room, clutching her stuffed dog.

"*Ella*, Evie. Come to your Thea." Popi patted the bed for the little girl to join her. "There are a few things you must learn about Erikousa before we go there. Our tiny island is just a few miles from here, but it is very different."

Daphne had always described Yia-yia's island as a beautiful and magical place, and Evie was eager to hear what Popi had to say about it. She looked up at her aunt expectantly.

"First of all, you must watch out for the black widows," Popi warned.

"I hate spiders." Evie's nails dug into the dog's fur as she pulled it closer.

"Not spiders!" Daphne laughed. "Popi means the slobber sisters." She turned to Popi. "Are they still around?"

"Yes, of course they are," Popi told her. "Evie, you must always have a napkin in your pocket. This is very important."

"Why, Thea Popi?"

"When you get off the boat in Erikousa, you will see many *yia-yias* waiting at the port. They all come out of their houses when the ferryboat arrives so they can see who is coming and who is going. Now this is so they can go home and gossip about everyone later. They like to welcome everyone who comes to the island by kissing them two times on the cheek." Popi leaned over and kissed each of Evie's soft pink cheeks. "Like that. But, unlike your Thea Popi, many of the *yia-yias* give juicy wet kisses." Evie made the appropriate face as Popi continued. "That is why you need a napkin, to wipe the wet *yia-yia* kisses off. Okay?"

"That's gross," Evie crinkled her nose. "I'm going to watch TV," she announced before skipping out of the room. Daphne and Popi heard the television come on. Evie giggled as Bugs Bunny chomped on *karrota* instead of carrots.

"That's one way to get her to learn the language. What her mother doesn't do, maybe Bugs Bunny can." Popi smiled one of her wicked grins.

Daphne just shook her head and managed a slight, tight smile back. To change the subject, she jumped out of bed and sprang over to the white garment bag, which was hanging above the closet door. "I can't believe I haven't shown you my dress yet," she said as she unzipped the bag and revealed the cream silk and lace gown. She turned to her cousin for approval.

"Oh, Daphne, it's the most beautiful dress I have ever seen."

Daphne removed the gown from the garment bag and laid it on the bed. "Do you really think so? It's not a bit much?" Daphne bit her lip as she carefully fanned out the fabric so Popi could inspect every detail of the strapless lace bodice, lightly corseted waist, and straight silk skirt, which was adorned with the slightest spray of tiny sea pearls and crystal beads.

"Too much?" Popi asked. "Too much for what? It's your wedding dress. It should be special. And this"—Popi glanced up at Daphne as she ran her fingers along the dress's delicate lace trim—"this is very, very special."

"Oh, good." Daphne brought her left hand to her throat in relief. "I was hoping you'd say that."

Wearing a floor-length designer dress to a black-tie country club wedding was one thing; wearing it to a dirt-road island wedding was quite another. Daphne had never intended to wear such an elaborate gown, even before the wedding plans changed. But Stephen had surprised her with a trip to an elegant Fifth Avenue bridal salon. He took her by the hand, walked her into the salon, and asked the meticulously attired ladies to help his fiancée select a gown befitting her beauty. Then he handed the shop girl his credit card, kissed Daphne good-bye, and left her with a glass of champagne in hand and many beautiful dresses to choose from.

The morning sunshine caught her diamond ring, sending rainbow-hued flecks of light dancing across the white walls of the room. "Let me show you the back." Daphne gently turned the dress over to show Popi the double row of tiny pearl-encrusted buttons that decorated the entire length of the gown.

Popi made the sign of the cross. "This is too much! It is too beautiful! But there is only one problem." A glimmer of mischief returned to her face as she looked into her cousin's eyes.

"What problem?" Daphne asked as she scanned the dress, looking for a stain or a tear.

"The problem is that no man will wait for all those buttons to be undone on his wedding day. Your beautiful gown will be ripped to pieces as he tries to get at what is underneath the dress."

Daphne laughed. "Very funny, Popi. But Stephen is a patient man. I don't think I have to worry about that."

"You are crazy. No man is patient on his wedding night."

"Well, he waited two years before I even agreed to go out with him." Daphne moved the dress slightly and sat down on the bed next to Popi.

"Was it really that long? I don't know which one of you is crazier—you for waiting so long to say yes, or him for waiting around so long when I was right here and ready the whole time you were playing hard to get."

Daphne plucked a pillow off the bed and tossed it at her cousin. "I wasn't *playing* hard to get. I *was* hard to get. I wasn't ready. I didn't think I ever would be."

It was true. After losing Alex, Daphne never imagined that she would one day find love again. But somehow, despite her initial reluctance, despite all of the obstacles and complications, somehow, in some miraculous way, she had.

She remembered the first time she saw him across the expansive desk of the loan officer in the bank, where she sat fidgeting in her chair. She was desperate for the loan and for the paperwork to be filled out quickly, knowing that she couldn't afford to pay the babysitter extra hours. Walking into the bank that day, Daphne knew the reality of the situation. If the man behind the desk didn't see the potential of her business plan, her fate would be sealed, the legacy would continue, and she too would be condemned to a life working in diners.

As she sat pleading her case, she tried without success to read the face of the man behind the desk. There were moments of hope, when he nodded as she explained her business plan, and moments of terror as he stared back like a blank canvas. She had no idea how things were progressing; only that she was running out of time. She was annoyed at first when the door opened and the tall, immaculately dressed man with the pocket square walked into the room, apologized for the interruption, and walked over to the loan officer's desk, handing him a stack of papers. He smiled down at Daphne, at first noticing her legs twitching under her skirt and then her black-olive eyes.

"Hi, I'm Stephen," he said, asking for her name. She told him why she was there, praying this man in the perfectly tailored suit could help her in some way. He wished her good luck and walked

out of the room. She didn't know why, but the deep whisky baritone of his voice had instantly put her at ease.

When the phone rang a few days later and the words "You're
approved" rang in her ear, she thought of the immaculately
dressed man and wondered for a fleeting moment if he had helped.

The next months flew by in a blur; planning, constructing, dec-
orating, cooking . . . She put her heart and soul into launching the
restaurant, and the man was soon forgotten—until the night he
walked into her newly opened restaurant alone.

He sat in the back, savoring his lamb fricassee and taking in every nuance of the dining room. When she came out of the kitchen
at the end of dinner service, she spotted him and immediately went
over to welcome him to Koukla. He asked her to join him for a
glass of wine and they ended up talking for hours, his intoxicating
voice simultaneously transfixing and relaxing her. He proved to
be a wonderful conversationalist as well as an ally. Nothing went
unnoticed. He told her which waiters took too long with service
and which dishes left the diners wanting more.

Night after night for almost two years they ended evenings together over a glass of wine. Gradually, it became clear that Stephen had indeed helped to sway the loan officer. It also became
clear that he wanted more from Daphne than just a meal and a
glass of wine. Daphne wasn't sure at first, not certain if she was
ready to share more with this man, with any man. But that deep
whisky voice had a way of putting her at ease, of making it easier
to say yes.

The first yes was the hardest, then he made it so much easier to
say it again . . . and again and again and again.

Three

"Come on, Daphne. Let's go. We'll miss the ferry if you don't hurry up," Popi yelled as she piled the luggage back in the car for the short drive to the port.

"A ten a.m. ferryboat, too," Daphne said as she reached the car. "How civilized! I can't believe we don't have to get up at the crack of dawn anymore to catch the *kaiki*." She handed Popi the last piece of luggage and closed the trunk of the car.

It had been a yearly tradition to wake up at 6:00 a.m. (or, as the girls got older, to stay out all night in the discos) for the one-hour drive to the small northern Corfu town of Sidari, where passengers bound for Erikousa boarded the primitive and cramped *kaiki* for the sixty-minute trip to the island. There was no upgrade to first class on the *kaiki*, where everyone was squeezed in among the groceries, farming supplies, livestock, and *yia-yias* who'd lived on the water their entire lives but couldn't set foot on a boat without getting seasick and throwing up in the bucket that was passed around for all to use. Daphne always believed it was the vile stench from that communal bucket that made the *yia-yias* sick, not the choppy seas.

"It still runs, just not as often. Now we have Big Al, the Alexandros ferryboat," Popi said as she started the car for the ten-minute drive to the port. "It doesn't run every day, but I'd rather wait for Big Al than pile on to that old *kaiki* with the chickens."

"But what about Ari? Don't tell me Ari is gone?!" Daphne cried. Ari was the infamous islander who tended goats on Erikousa and traveled to Corfu to sell his homemade cheese. As proficient as Ari was in haggling the best price for his feta, he was equally pathetic in his hunt for a wife. Ari's lecherous stares and inappropriate comments were summer rites of passage for the girls. When he wasn't milking goats, he was spying on them as they sunbathed or "accidentally" brushing up against them as he walked along the beach. He seemed harmless enough, or so they hoped. But there was always a sense of uncertainty, discomfort, and even a hint of danger whenever he came slithering by. It wasn't until she reached her late teens that Daphne realized why she sometimes felt as if she were being watched as she swam alone in the cove. She spotted him there once, hiding behind a tree as she emerged from the water. He didn't come nearer or speak to her, just stood and stared.

Daphne ran all the way home that day and made the mistake of telling Yia-yia about it. Daphne couldn't believe her eyes as she watched the old woman move like she had been injected with youth serum. There were no signs of bunions, brittle bones, or arthritic joints as Yia-yia grabbed her gardening machete and literally ran down the hillside. She finally found Ari having a smoke and a frappe on the terrace of the only café in town. Yia-yia didn't care that the entire lunchtime crowd would hear what she had to say. In fact, she rather enjoyed the fact that she had many witnesses to her promise to cut off his manhood if he dared come near her granddaughter again.

Popi broke into her thoughts. "Don't worry, Daphne, Ari is still around, and he is still looking for a wife. So you can visit him if you like. Maybe you'll even change your mind and become Kyria Ari instead of Mrs. American Banker." Popi slapped the steering wheel, amused by the thought of her elegant cousin shacking up in a one-room house and making a living milking goats.

"That's certainly something to think about." Daphne laughed as they pulled up to the port.

The ferry ride was simply glorious. Gone were the cramped conditions and crates from the days of the *kaiki*. Big Al was elegantly appointed, with rows of real seats, a working toilet, and even a snack bar belowdecks. They sat on the upper deck talking and taking in the scenery, both the natural and the human variety.

Evie was entranced by the dolphins that swam and jumped alongside the boat. She leaned on the railing, absorbed by their beautifully synchronized choreography as they leaped out of the water. Daphne couldn't take her eyes off the kaleidoscope of sunlight and water that glistened on the walls of the caves and grottoes long ago etched into the colossal cliffs of Corfu by the persistent Ionian Sea. She held her breath as they passed the Canal d'Amour, where over thousands of years the sea had carved a tunnel through a towering rock. She strained her eyes to look into the canal, biting her lip as she saw the clusters of couples swimming there, remembering how Alex insisted that they swim the canal together so theirs would be an everlasting love, as the legend promised. Daphne wondered if the swimming lovers would one day learn, as she had, that the story was only an old wives' tale, another empty island promise.

"Daphne, look." Popi tugged at Daphne's sleeve. She tilted her head to the left toward a young couple sitting on the far end of the deck. They were tanned, blond, and beautiful in that disheveled backpacker way. He was tall, with shoulder-length hair streaked by the sun and piercing blue eyes. She was even fairer, slim and stunning. He leaned against their backpacks, stroking her hair as she lay against his bare chest.

"Can you imagine being so young and so in love?" Popi whispered.

Daphne watched as the young man leaned down and kissed the girl's forehead. Her eyes fluttered open, and she lifted his hand to her mouth and covered it with a blanket of soft kisses. He kissed her once more before standing up and going downstairs, leaving his beautiful partner to sun herself. Daphne didn't say anything, but the longing, almost mournful look in her eyes made it quite clear that yes, she could imagine being so young and so in love. In fact, she could remember it quite clearly. But that, like so many other aspects of her life, was simply a memory from a lifetime long ago.

The trance was shattered when Popi jumped from her seat. "Oh. My. God. Daphne, look. Look who it is!"

Daphne followed Popi's gaze to the stairwell and could not believe her eyes when she spotted Ari. It was as if time had stood still. He still wore a faded denim shirt unbuttoned to his navel, the same frayed cut-off jean shorts and plastic flip-flop *sayonares*, and his hair was still a mass of waves meticulously combed and gelled into a mullet. The only difference Daphne noticed was the generous sprinkling of gray that had invaded his once jet-black hair.

The cousins watched him as he stood at the top of the stairwell, a frappe in his hand and a cigarette dangling from his mouth. He squinted against the bright sunshine and surveyed the deck before making his move.

Ari turned to his left and began to walk along the railing, intermittently puffing on his cigarette and sipping his drink. Daphne was amused to see that his infamous swagger, in which his hips seemed to roll while his feet shuffled, had also been unchanged by the years. The girls knew that his tour of the upper deck was more than just an aimless stroll. His small black eyes soon found their target in a long-legged German beauty who had no clue her quiet ride was about to be rocked by the legendary lothario.

"He hasn't changed one bit, has he?" Daphne whispered.

Ari reached the spot where the young woman was lying, leaning against the backpacks with her eyes closed and face turned up toward the sun. There was plenty of room around her, but instead of stepping aside to avoid her golden brown legs, he stepped over them. As he lifted his leg over, he deliberately rubbed his foot against her thigh, his jagged toenails leaving a thin white scratch on her skin. He stumbled a bit to make it appear as if he had tripped and then tipped the frappe. The young girl shot upright.

"*Signomi, signomi,*" Ari muttered and bent down, using his dirty hands to wipe the liquid from the young girl's legs. "Sorry. *Desole. Traurig.*" Ari went down his repertoire of languages, apologizing as the girl snatched her legs to her chest.

The boyfriend emerged from the snack bar below to find his

love being molested before his eyes. He dropped the beers he was carrying and ran to confront the man who had dared to put his hands on her.

The lanky German towered above the soft and stocky Greek and surprised him with a violent shove.

"I am sorry. Accident. Accident," Ari muttered in broken English as he jumped up.

The tourist pushed him until he was pinned against the ship's railing. "Do not touch her!" he shouted. His English was as perfect as his aim: the first punch landed squarely in Ari's bloated gut. It knocked the wind out of him, and Daphne and Popi gasped as they watched him jackknife forward. But the boyfriend was not finished. The next punch produced a sharp cracking sound as it connected with Ari's jaw, snapping his head back as his body leaned back over the railing precariously.

"*Bitte, Anschlag,*" the girl pleaded with her boyfriend, terrified that his temper would land them in a Greek jail.

"He's going to kill him," Daphne cried as she attempted to shield Evie's eyes from the carnage. Evie nuzzled into her mother's chest and began to cry as the passengers continued to shout. But no one stepped forward.

By this point dozens had gathered round to watch the spectacle. Several of the men yelled for the German to stop but their cries did no good. Many of them had dreamed of doing the same thing to Ari at one time or another. Had Ari's attacker been one of their own, they might not have protested so loudly.

But it all had no effect on the young man, who was set on making this dark stranger pay for dishonoring his girlfriend, although Ari was already bloodied and in pain.

"This is crazy!" Daphne shouted. Kissing the top of Evie's head and putting her on Popi's lap, she stood up and walked toward the chaos. The salty Greek air had gotten under her skin and rekindled the spitfire that had dulled with the years. Chin held high, Daphne marched up to the German.

"Stop it," she demanded, "you'll kill him." She used all her strength to pull at his arms and stop him from throwing another punch, but it was no use.

"*Stamata!*" she yelled as she tugged at him again.

All eyes were on Daphne. The passengers stood silently, watching as she tried to pull the men apart. Finally, shamed by the fact that a woman dared to do what they had not, the men one by one began to step forward.

"That's enough now." A gray-haired man in a fisherman's cap was the first to speak.

The German ignored the stranger and turned once more to Ari.

"I said enough," the man growled. He stepped behind the German, wrapped his arms around the man in a bear hug, lifted him off the deck, and—although the young man flailed and kicked—calmly carried him to the other side of the deck and dropped him.

The German held his bloodied knuckles in the palm of his left hand. "He deserved it."

"I know he did," the Greek replied. He turned his back on the young tourist and walked back to where a disheveled Ari sat crumpled on the floor.

"*Malaka,*" the man spat at Ari.

Daphne made her way back to Evie and Popi. "Nice try, cousin," Popi said as Daphne took her seat. "Did you really think you were going to stop that man?"

Daphne lifted her trembling arms and pulled Evie close, then buried her head in the girl's lavender-scented hair. "Are you okay, honey? That was just a silly man behaving very badly. Don't let it upset you, all right?" Daphne leaned in to speak to Popi. "I couldn't just sit here and do nothing. Look at all those guys sitting over there. None of them did anything until I tried to."

"Isn't that the way it is, Daphne?" Popi said. "They think they are the braver, stronger sex, but we know the truth, don't we?"

"Yes, yes, we do." Daphne hugged Evie tighter and looked across the water. She could finally see the port of Erikousa getting closer.

Four

ERIKOUSA

SUMMER 1992

Daphne had been gone since morning, and she knew that now, as the sun began to set, Yia-yia was beginning to worry. She could picture her grandmother waiting at home on the flower-filled patio, pacing the outdoor kitchen back and forth under the shade of the lemon and olive trees. Mama had always told Daphne that since the Lord had chosen to bless them with only one child, it was Mama and Baba's divine obligation to keep Daphne safe. Back home in New York, even at fourteen years old, Daphne was never let out of the sight of her overprotective parents, let alone allowed to disappear for an entire day. But this was different. This was Erikousa. This was the island paradise where Daphne could spend her summer exploring, swimming, and doing exactly as she wished, as long as she made it home in time to share a meal with Yia-yia.

"Yia-yia! Yia-yia!" Daphne shouted as she reached the bottom of the steps leading up to the patio where her grandmother waited.

Yia-yia stood on the lush patio, her petite body overwhelmed by the shapeless black dress that was her uniform, her salt-and-pepper braids obscured by the black headscarf knotted under her chin. She looked down and scanned the garden path. A wide smile crossed her wrinkled face as she spotted her granddaughter.

"There you are. Come. Come now. I'm making your supper," Yia-yia said as she waved her arms up toward the sky.

Daphne bounded up the steps two by two. Not bothering to change out of her wet swimsuit, she just wrapped her towel around her body and sat on a rickety old chair next to her grandmother. Daphne watched as Yia-yia dipped her wooden spoon into a pan of boiling olive oil and removed a perfectly browned batch of fries. The young girl snatched a crispy specimen from the steaming pile and nibbled as Yia-yia peeled and cut more potatoes with her small, sharp knife. It was incredible to Daphne how her fingers sliced and diced so quickly and effortlessly. Even after all these years of being indulged by Yia-yia's cooking, Daphne was still amazed by the perfection of Yia-yia's delicious round fried potatoes. They were divine, so much better than the greasy stick fries sold back home. Making perfect fries was just one of Yia-yia's many talents.

"How was the beach?" Yia-yia asked as she carried twigs to the outdoor cooking fire. She knew the oil needed to reach just the right temperature for the fries to come out crispy on the outside and slightly soft on the inside, the way Daphne liked them.

"It was nice. Quiet. I went to the cove again. I like it when no one's around," Daphne replied as she reached over and grabbed another.

"Why don't you try the beach tomorrow? The other girls usually go swimming in the afternoon. It would be nice for you to have some friends to spend your day with, instead of always being alone or talking to an old woman like me. Okay, *koukla*?" Daphne was Yia-yia's *koukla*—her little Greek doll.

Yia-yia knew that Daphne wasn't like the other American girls who came for the summer and traveled in a pack, sunbathing, swimming, and flirting with the boys. But as much as she craved every moment shared with her granddaughter, Yia-yia didn't want Daphne to withdraw completely into the rituals and world that they had created these past few years. She wanted more for her *koukla*.

"Don't worry, Yia-yia. I'd much rather hang out with you. You're more fun anyway." She gave Yia-yia a wink. "And no one makes potatoes like this." She popped another in her mouth. In addition to the fries, they would be feasting on one of Daphne's favorite dishes, fried eggs with fresh tomatoes.

The young girl watched Yia-yia coat another pan with olive oil and add the freshly chopped tomatoes she had picked from the garden that morning. The bright red mixture sizzled, simmered, and popped until the tomatoes reached the perfect consistency, losing their firm texture and giving way to a sweet, thick paste. With her slightly burned and battle-scarred wooden spoon, Yia-yia cleared four little round holes in the simmering sauce. Daphne knew this was her cue. She reached over to the basket of freshly hatched eggs and cracked them one by one into the holes that Yia-yia had made.

Then Yia-yia rubbed her finger along the large green leaves of the basil sprig she had just picked. "Here, you've never smelled *basilico* like this." Yia-yia waved her basil-oil-infused fingers under Daphne's nose, and they shook their heads in unison.

"It's amazing." Daphne smiled at her grandmother.

"Let the Parisians have their fancy perfumeries. We know that this is the most priceless scent on earth. And it grows free, right here in my garden." With her bent fingers she ripped some of the green leaves into delicate ribbons.

Yia-yia dropped the torn basil into the pan and waited a few moments for the verdant leaves to wilt. She sprinkled the mixture with salt and then divided the eggs and tomatoes between two plates.

"Daphne!" Yia-yia cried as she saw Daphne reach for another potato. "Leave some for the meal." She leaned over and swatted Daphne with the basil leaves.

"Sorry, Yia-yia. I guess it's all this fresh air. It makes me hungry."

"Oh, *koukla*, it's okay. Those were all for you. Now eat, eat before your eggs get cold." Yia-yia handed Daphne her plate along with a thick crusty slice of peasant bread, perfect for dipping into the thick and savory tomato sauce.

They sat right there, next to the fire, and ate their simple meal. Yia-yia had long given up on the formality of setting a pretty table or eating indoors. She and Daphne knew that food tasted much better out here, in the clean, salty island breeze.

"Yia-yia—" Daphne shoveled another forkful of eggs in her mouth.

"Yes, *koukla mou*."

"Yia-yia, tell me about Persephone."

"Oh, Persephone. Poor, poor Persephone. What a sin, what happened to Persephone," Yia-yia replied in the mournful sing-song voice the island women instinctively reverted to when talk turned to death or anything remotely tragic. The myth of Persephone had always had a special meaning in the old woman's heart, and even more so now that she was able to share it with Daphne, this beautiful child she loved more than life itself.

Daphne clapped her hands in anticipation. "Tell me again. What happened to her?"

Yia-yia balanced her plate on her knee, wiped her hands on her apron, and then smoothed her headscarf with her sinewy and spotted hands. Slowly and deliberately, she began to speak.

"There was once a beautiful maiden whose name was Persephone. Her mother was Demeter, the great goddess of grain and crops. One day Persephone and her friends were in the field, picking wildflowers, when she was spotted by Hades, the king of the underworld. Demeter had warned Persephone not to wander away from the other girls. But Persephone was so consumed with finding the best, most perfect flowers for a wreath she was weaving that she forgot her mother's words of warning and wandered just a little too far down the meadow. Hades saw beautiful Persephone and fell instantly in love. He decided then and there that this maiden would be his queen, the queen of the underworld. In an instant, Hades rode up in his chariot from the bowels of the earth and snatched young Persephone from the earth, taking the sobbing girl back down to the darkness he ruled."

Daphne leaned in closer, rubbing her hands up and down her arms as if to ward off Hades' cold grip.

Yia-yia continued. "Demeter heard her daughter's cries and

hurried to the meadow, but all she found when she got there was the unfinished wreath that had fallen from Persephone's fingers. Demeter was inconsolable. She roamed the earth for months and months looking for her daughter. The goddess was so distraught that she refused to allow the crops to grow. The earth lay barren and the people were starving. But Demeter vowed that nothing would grow until Persephone was returned. Zeus looked down from Mount Olympus, and when he saw that the great famine threatened the existence of mankind, he ordered Hades to return Persephone to her mother. Hades did as he was told, but before he allowed Persephone to go, he laid a great feast before her and told her to eat to prepare for her long journey home. Young Persephone looked at the feast of food before her but managed to eat only six pomegranate seeds. It was those six tiny, blood-red seeds that sealed her fate and that of every human on earth. According to the laws of the underworld, once you feast at the table of Hades, you are bound to return to his dark kingdom. Because she ate six seeds, Persephone would be forever bound to spend six months as Hades' dark queen. The remainder of the year would be spent on earth with her mother."

Yia-yia leaned in closer. "And that is why the earth is cold and barren during the months of winter, Daphne *mou*. That is when Persephone sits beside Hades in the underworld while Demeter roams the earth, lonely and sad, refusing to allow anything to grow until Persephone is returned to her embrace."

Daphne and Yia-yia sat quietly after Yia-yia had finished her story. They both stared into the fire, replaying the myth in their minds. But Daphne and Yia-yia knew this was more than just another myth, fable, or story; it was their story.

Daphne broke the silence. "I don't want the summer to end. I wish it wouldn't end."

Yia-yia didn't answer. She couldn't. She turned her head away and stared out across the lush green island, listening as the leaves of the cypress trees danced upon the breeze and filled the evening air with their own hushed lament. As she cocked her head toward the rustling trees, Yia-yia nodded in agreement.

She knew they sang for her, that only they could understand the anguish of another winter without her Daphne. Yia-yia lifted her weathered hand to her face and wiped away the tears that one by one began to fall.

Five

Daphne leaned out over the railing as the ferry approached Erikousa's port. She couldn't believe her eyes. It was as if a sea of bodies awaited them onshore, as if the whole island had turned out to welcome the bride-to-be and her little girl. She grasped Evie's soft little hand in her own as they prepared to disembark from the boat and make their way through the throngs of relatives and well-wishers and the black sea of elderly widows who clogged the dock's narrow concrete road.

It felt good to be back. As she held Evie's hand and looked out over the landscape Daphne marveled at how green it was, how pristine, clean, and undeveloped. There were no tall buildings, skyscrapers, or concrete structures to break up the natural patina of the island. Deep rich colors flowed one into the next, as if a rainbow had fallen from the sky and infused the land and sea with vibrancy normally reserved only for the gods. The cobalt sea spilled rhythmically into the taupe sand, which gave way to the lush greenery of ancient bent olive trees. Shiny lemon trees were dotted with giant golden sunbursts, while blackberry bushes dripped with wine-colored orbs. And of course the tall, slim hunter-green cypresses stood regal sentinel above everything else.

She took a deep breath and filled her lungs with sea air once again, knowing the salty moistness would soon give way to the island's signature perfume of rosemary, basil, and roses.

"Oh, Mommy, it's so pretty," Evie cooed beside her.

"Yes, honey. Yes, it is," Daphne agreed.

"Hey, Evie, here you go." Popi nudged the little girl and slid a tissue into the back pocket of her jeans. "For the slobber sisters. They're all here," she said with a wink.

Evie giggled. She wrinkled her nose, stuck out her tongue, and again mumbled "Ewwwww." She held tightly to Daphne's hand as they took the short walk down the boat's ramp, into the waiting crowd.

The moment Daphne and Evie's feet hit the ground, they were surrounded. Dozens of aunts, uncles, cousins, neighbors, friends, and even strangers came at them from all directions; hugging, kissing, pinching, slobbering, and fawning over them. Daphne was overcome by emotion as well as several waves of nausea. The late-morning heat mixed with the often overwhelming and famil-iar island fragrance of elders who, even in these modern times, still didn't use deodorant.

"Daphne, I missed you."

"It's so wonderful to see you."

"Evie, look at you. You are beautiful."

"Daphne, poor, poor Daphne. I am a widow too. Only I can understand your pain."

"Daphne, I'm so happy for you. You are going to make a beautiful bride."

"Daphne, are you sick? Why are you so skinny?"

The salutations were warm, welcoming, endearing, and endless. Daphne made sure to greet each and every well-wisher with a hug and a kiss, even if she had no idea who her greeter was. The last thing she wanted was to appear aloof or ungrateful when really, it felt wonderful to feel so welcomed and so loved.

She greeted every older woman with a warm "*Yia sou, Thea*," and every older man with a joyous "*Yia sou, Theo*." "*Yia sou, Ksalthelfi*" and "*Yia sou, Ksalthelfi*" were reserved for the younger islanders whose names escaped her. That was the beauty of being from Erikousa—everyone was related somehow, so even if you had no idea who you were speaking to, you could always get away with simply aunt, uncle, or cousin, and no one was ever the wiser.

After scanning the crowd between the bobbing heads and bodies that were constantly coming at them, it was Daphne who spotted her first. "Yia-yia, Yia-yia!"

She held tight to Evie's hand and led her to the other side of the port, where Yia-yia waited. She wore her baggy black dress, headscarf, and black tights, even though it must have been ninety degrees outside already. She stood alone, slightly apart from the rest of the crowd, leaning on her bamboo walking stick and holding the reins of Jack—short for Jackass—the donkey that Daphne had named so many summers ago.

"Yia-yia, oh, Yia-yia," Daphne sobbed as she clung to her beloved grandmother. The old woman threw down her walking stick and even the reins of her prized donkey and grabbed Daphne as if she would never again let go. They stood there for several moments crying uncontrollably, heaving up and down with each sob—faded and stained black polyester pressed against delicate white linen.

"Here, Mommy." Daphne felt a tug at her white eyelet skirt and looked down to see Evie smiling up at her, offering her the tissue that Popi had earlier placed in Evie's back pocket.

"Thank you, honey." Daphne took the tissue from Evie's hand and wiped her mascara-streaked face. "Evie, this is Yia-yia." Daphne beamed.

Without any prompting from Daphne, Evie took two steps forward toward Yia-yia. "*Yia sou*, Yia-yia. *S'agapo*." Evie wrapped her little arms around Yia-yia's legs and gave the old woman a hug.

Yia-yia bent down and touched Evie's angelic face. She lowered her hollow cheek onto her great-granddaughter's head and stroked Evie's hair, her tears falling like a sun shower into the dark soil of Evie's curls. "I love you, Evie *mou*," Yia-yia responded, exhausting the extent of her English vocabulary.

Daphne stared at her daughter and grandmother in amazement. She had been so concerned about Evie's nervousness around new people. At home, Evie was so withdrawn that Daphne had worried about how she would handle her new, sometimes overbearing family. Evie had always been an introverted child, afraid of new experiences and new people. In fact, it had taken weeks of conniving and cajoling before Evie would even look Stephen in the eye, let alone speak to him. Daphne couldn't believe it yesterday when Evie took to Popi so quickly in Corfu. But seeing her warm up to Yia-yia immediately like this, taking it upon herself to use the one Greek phrase that she knew by heart, Daphne wondered if the Erikousa air was working its magic on Evie as well.

"Daphne," Yia-yia said. "Daphne, this is not a child. This is an angel sent from the heavens." Yia-yia placed her arthritic fingers under Evie's chin. The old woman's hand trembled slightly, but it steadied as it touched Evie's face.

"Yes, she is an angel. And so are you," Daphne said as she bent down to hand Yia-yia her walking stick.

"You told me on the telephone that she is shy. This child isn't shy. This child is full of life. Look at her." Yia-yia clucked and continued to gaze at Evie.

"Back home she is. But here, ever since we got here, she's like a different child."

"She's not a different child," Yia-yia insisted. "She's the same wonderful child both here and there, Daphne *mou*. The difference is love. She knows how much love there is for her here."

The two women watched as Evie reached her hand out to pet Jack.

"Children know when they are surrounded by love, Daphne *mou*," Yia-yia continued. "They can feel the difference. This child has a gift, Daphne, I can feel it."

"A gift?"

"Yes, she is blessed, Daphne *mou*. I can see it in her eyes." Yia-yia lifted her face and smiled as a delicate, almost undetectable breeze wafted through the port. "I can hear it on the breeze." Yia-yia looked out across the treetops, as if she could hear the cypress whispers serenading them right then and there.

Daphne inched closer to her grandmother and rested her head on Yia-yia's shoulder. It had been so long since she had heard Yia-yia profess that the cypress whispers existed, that she could hear the voices of the island. For the longest time, Daphne had believed

Yia-yia's claims; she had begged, prayed, and dreamed that she too would one day hear them. But the whispers never did materialize for Daphne, her hope eventually replaced by the fading echo of Yia-yia's insistence. After a while, Daphne simply stopped wishing, stopped believing.

After making a plan to meet for frappe later that afternoon, Popi went off to the small house she had inherited when her father passed away, on the other side of the port. Daphne and Yia-yia loaded the luggage on Jack's back, making sure to leave room for Evie to ride up there as well. Cars were a rare commodity on the island, where the roads were still for the most part unpaved and too narrow for a car to pass. Daphne was thrilled to see that donkeys were still a mainstay of transportation. She and her old friend Jack had had many adventures together, and she knew Evie was looking forward to creating some of her own.

Their little caravan slowly made its way along the main paved road that leads from the port, past the tiny downtown area of the island. The three of them were quite a sight; the black shrouded old woman hunched over and leading the way as she held on to Jack's reins with one hand and tightly gripped her walking stick with the other. A beaming Evie sat on Jack's luggage-saddled back, continually patting his neck as he lumbered along the cracked, uneven pavement. Daphne walked right beside Jack and Evie, never taking her eyes off her little girl, arms poised and ready just in case Evie somehow slipped from her happy perch.

As soon as they reached the white-and-blue-painted sign that read "Welcome to Hotel Nitsa," Yia-yia stopped and turned to Daphne.

"Daphne, *mou*. Do you want to go and say hello to Nitsa? To

tell her you are here. She asks me every day when you will be arriving. You should see her, Daphne, the way she buzzes around
like she is planning her own daughter's wedding." Yia-yia shook
her head. The tone of her voice changed as she sighed deeply.

Daphne knew what was coming next. She braced herself for the
lament song she knew would follow. Listening to the wailing and
moaning of the island women had always been Daphne's very own
version of fingernails scratching on a chalkboard.

"Ahhhhaaaa." Yia-yia shook her head and began to half speak,
half sing. "Ahh, poor Nitsa, poor widowed and childless Nitsa. It
is as if she is planning her own daughter's wedding, the daughter
she never knew, never could have. Poor lonely and childless
Nitsa."

Nitsa was the lovely grandmotherly woman who ran the small
rustic hotel with more care than if it was a Ritz-Carlton resort. It
was the only hotel on the island and the simplest of accommoda-
tions. But what Hotel Nitsa lacked in luxury, it more than made up
for in cleanliness and hospitality. Inside the lobby, the small recep-
tion/bar area opened to a flower-filled terrace that Daphne knew
would be the perfect location for her wedding reception.

Nitsa had been thrilled when Daphne called with the news and
a request to book the entire hotel for the celebration. Business had
been slow lately, and this windfall was a lifesaver to Nitsa, who
was a widow herself and relied on the fickle tourist trade to make
ends meet.

Daphne looked from Yia-yia to the hotel's front doors. As much
as she was looking forward to seeing Nitsa, Daphne didn't really
want to talk business right now. All she wanted to do was get
home, kick off her shoes, sit under the lemon tree, and dive into
whatever feast Yia-yia had prepared.

"Let's just go home, Yia-yia. I can go visit Nitsa later."

"All right," Yia-yia replied. "You must be tired and hungry, let's get home. I have many wonderful surprises waiting for you. We can see Nitsa later. Jack, *ella*, let's go." Yia-yia clicked her tongue several times as a signal to her four-legged companion to get moving again. But just as Yia-yia was about to lift her walking stick and take her first step, the doors to the hotel burst open.

He was tall, deeply tanned, and bearded—handsome, but not in the traditional sense of the word. There was something unkempt about his appearance: the crooked nose that looked as if it might have been broken in a bar brawl, the weathered face with its dense, gray-streaked facial hair, which made him attractive in the most primal way. Daphne had never seen him before.

He rushed down the stairs and into Yia-yia's path.

"Yianni *mou*!" Yia-yia shouted, lifting her walking stick into the air.

"Thea Evangelia." A warm smile spread across his face as he spotted her. He stepped into her arms and kissed her on each cheek.

"Yianni *mou*. I was worried about you. I have not seen you in days. I thought you forgot about me," Yia-yia teased.

"Thea Evangelia, how could I possibly forget about you, the most unforgettable woman on the island? I am so sorry, I didn't mean to leave without saying good-bye, but I didn't think I would be gone this long. I had to pick up a part for my boat in Kerkyra. That *malaka* sent me the wrong propeller last time, and I lost two days collecting my nets. But now—" Yianni held up a plain brown paper package in his hand as if it were a trophy. "Now I can get back to my nets and my boat." Yianni never looked away from Yia-yia's face as she held his hand to her cheek.

Daphne stood there and stared at Yianni and Yia-yia. She had no idea who this man was; she had never even heard Yia-yia utter his name.

"Yianni *mou*." Yia-yia used her walking stick to gesture behind her, never letting go of Yianni's hand. "This is my great-granddaughter Evie—isn't she beautiful?" Yia-yia glowed as she gestured to Jack's back, where Evie was perched, petting and caressing Jack as if he were a new kitten.

"Yes, she is very beautiful," Yianni agreed. He looked over at Evie but never once made eye contact or even acknowledged Daphne's presence.

"And this . . . ," Yia-yia announced. "This is my Daphne, my granddaughter. She is the one, the very famous chef in New York that I have been telling you about."

"Yes," he said, still never glancing her way. "The *Amerikanida*."

Daphne stared at him, confused. It was the way he said the word *Amerikanida*. Her parents had struggled for her to wear that title, and she wore it proudly. But the way the word had slithered across his tongue had nothing to do with pride. The way he said it sounded more like an accusation.

Yia-yia continued, "Yes, she is my *Amerikanida*. And a smart one, too. The same things we give to our friends and family for free here, she charges hundreds of dollars for in New York."

It usually made Daphne uncomfortable when Yia-yia bragged about her so openly, but she didn't care this time. She wanted this man to know exactly who she was and what she was, the *Amerikanida*.

"Yes, I know how they are in New York, Thea Evangelia."

Yianni snorted. "You could put a piece of shit on a stick, give it a fancy name, and people would line up down the street to pay for the privilege of eating it. They have so much but know so little," Yianni continued, reaching once again for Yia-yia's shoulder and giving her a gentle squeeze, as if they were sharing some sort of private joke that Daphne didn't find funny in the least.

"Actually, New York is known for its excellent restaurants," Daphne snapped. "But I imagine you must not know much about fine dining, or New York." Even as the words came out of her mouth, Daphne couldn't believe she had actually said them out loud. It was so unlike her to be downright rude like this.

"You are mistaken, American chef. I know more about New York than you think." Yianni finally turned to look at Daphne. "And I also know that the people who claim to be the most cosmopolitan are often the most ignorant."

His verbal assault hit its mark with exacting precision. Daphne inhaled sharply, the words literally taking her breath away. She searched for a worthy retort, but Yia-yia spoke before Daphne could summon the appropriate insult.

"Ah, Yianni, you always have such a way with words. I agree with you. I have no need for those big cities full of strangers when everything I want and everyone I love is right here." Yia-yia laughed, throwing her head back, her headscarf slipping off her hair and to her shoulders, revealing the braids that she perpetually wore hanging down her back.

"Yianni, I will say a special prayer to ensure your nets are full." Yia-yia turned to face Daphne. "Yianni is a gifted fisherman, Daphne. He is somewhat new to Erikousa, but he loves our island like we do. Be extra nice to him, as he will be the one feeding your wedding guests with his gifts from the sea." Yia-yia linked her arm with his.

Daphne couldn't believe what she was witnessing as Yia-yia continued to giggle and beam at Yianni. This man had so casually insulted Daphne right in front of Yia-yia, the one person Daphne would expect to always fiercely come to her defense. It was as if the laws of nature were being rewritten before her very eyes.

"*Ella*, Yianni. We are going home to eat. Will you join us? I made *boureki* and *spourthopita*. I know how you love them both," Yia-yia said temptingly as she lightly tapped his legs with her walking stick.

Daphne could not wait to get home and dive into Yia-yia's rich and creamy chicken *boureki* pie, or sweet pumpkin *spourthopita*. But the thought of this rude man intruding on their meal was simply too much. She had come thousands of miles to sit and feast with Yia-yia, not this ill-mannered stranger. But before she had the chance to protest, Yianni stepped in.

"Thea, thank you. No, I have to go. But save me a piece of *spourthopita*. You know I could eat a whole pan of it myself." Yianni kissed Yia-yia's cheek and turned to walk away.

"All right, Yianni. But promise me you'll come tomorrow for lunch. I'll make something special for you," Yia-yia called out.

"*Entaksi*, yes, Thea. I promise I will come." Yianni waved good-bye to Yia-yia before turning and walking directly toward Daphne on the narrow road.

There was barely room for him to pass. Reason told her to step aside, to make way and avoid another awkward confrontation. But anger and frustration had shoved reason right out of the way. Daphne stood her ground.

Let him move. She didn't budge as he walked toward her, directly into her path.

He walked right past her, skimming by so close that the wiry hairs on his arm brushed against hers—close enough to smell the Greek coffee on his breath and the scent of seawater and sweat on his skin. Once he was several feet clear of Daphne he finally turned and looked at her, a smile etched across his face.

"I'll see you tomorrow at lunch, stubborn *Amerikanida*," he announced as he placed a sun-bleached old fisherman's cap on his head and began his walk back to the port.

Daphne watched him walk away. She could feel the telltale burning in her cheeks, as if they were on fire. *"Malaka,"* she muttered, loud enough for him to hear.

But there was no reply from the fisherman, just the rustling of the cypress trees in the early-afternoon breeze.

Six

As she ascended the cracked stone steps to Yia-yia's house and closed the creaky patio gate behind her, Daphne was expecting to be comforted by the familiar sights—the large lemon tree whose branches bent downward with the weight of their fruit, the glazed blue-and-white-painted pots that housed Yia-yia's overgrown basil plants and the old wooden carved stools that still sat by the fire as if they were anticipating another one of Yia-yia's all-night storytelling sessions.

From the time she was a little girl, Daphne had burst through this gate in a fit of excited giggles. But as happy and excited as she was to be here again, this time it was different.

Their encounter had not lasted long, but it was as if with each second she was in Yianni's presence, with each exasperating moment, her frustration had grown incrementally stronger. Daphne felt as if she had stepped back into ancient times, when the winged furies would buzz about and torment mortals. She remembered trying to imagine what the tiny beasts might look like as she read Aeschylus's *Oresteia* over and over again as a teenager.

Is this what Orestes felt like? she wondered.

Unlike Orestes, Daphne knew she had committed no sin, no offense against the gods or nature. This wasn't the fabled and fallen house of Agamemnon, and she was not a mythological hero, or even a young maiden whose marriage or sacrifice could turn the tide of war. Daphne was merely a mortal—a lonely woman who had lost the love of her life far too young and finally, after years of mourning, was ready to open her heart again. This place was supposed to be her refuge, her reward. Daphne felt she had earned the right to come back here, to remember and maybe even in some way relive the pure and simple pleasures of her youth.

As she walked along the patio, she reached out and skimmed the basil plant's gargantuan leaves as she passed. When she reached the last plant, she lifted her fingers to her nose and inhaled the deep, familiar scent. Leaning in, she snapped off a branch and waved the leaves back and forth under her nose. In ancient times, it was believed that a basil sprig was powerful enough to open the gates of heaven.

Enough. That's enough, Daphne thought to herself as she exhaled deeply, opened her eyes, and held her hand out to Evie.

"Come on, Evie." Right then and there Daphne promised herself that although that man had managed to ruin her morning, she would not allow him to ruin her entire day, or Evie's for that matter.

"Come on, *koukla*, let me show you around before we have lunch," she announced, surprising herself with just how chipper and cheerful she managed to sound.

Hand in hand, Evie and Daphne walked through the garden, past endless rows of tomato vines covered with earth-scented globes that looked ready to burst. They continued down the back stairs, past a wall of honeysuckle whose tiny blossoms blanketed the area with a chorus of buzzing bees. They made their way to where Yia-yia kept Jack tied, under a hulking olive tree with plenty of lush branches to keep her old friend shaded and cool.

As if on cue, Jack once again bent his head as Evie approached. Evie reached her little arm forward to pat the soft spot right above the donkey's nose. As she did, Jack leaned in even farther and gave Evie a little nuzzle just under her neck.

"Oh, Mommy, he just gave me a kiss. He likes me." Evie giggled.

"Yes, honey. He sure does." They had only been in Erikousa for less than two hours, and it seemed Evie had already made a dear friend.

"Come on, sweetie, I want to show you something else." Daphne pried her daughter's hands from around Jack's neck.

She led Evie past the back patio, through the garden, and down the back stone staircase toward the chaos and cacophony of Yia-yia's bustling chicken coop. Daphne opened the wire lattice gate and ushered Evie inside before slamming the gate shut behind them. Once inside, Evie looked down, and her feet froze in place as she spotted half a dozen tiny yellow baby chicks running around like little drunken sailors at her feet. Daphne slowly bent down, picked up a newly hatched chick, and placed it in Evie's cupped hands. She stood there silently watching Evie's face, contorted with delight as she reached her tiny fingers out to stroke the baby bird's downy fur.

Daphne didn't dare budge. She just stood there watching as Evie made it her mission to nuzzle each and every one of the chicks. It seemed as if her little girl wanted to make sure all of the little baby birds felt loved, that none felt slighted or left out.

"*Elllla ellllla*. Daphne, Evie. *Elllllla*." Yia-yia's singsong cry could barely be heard over the clamor of wings flapping, chickens clucking, and Evie's squeals of delight.

Daphne lifted her head and squinted into the sun.

"Daphhneeee, Evieeeeee . . . *Ellllaaaaaa*," Yia-yia sang again.

Daphne held her hand up just above her forehead to shield her eyes from the blazing sunshine. But it was no use. With the sun directly above the house, all she could see was Yia-yia's backlit silhouette high above them on the terrace as she raised her trusty old wooden spoon toward the sky and sang out for her grand-daughter and great-granddaughter to join her at the table.

"Coming, Yia-yia. *Erhomaste*," Daphne replied.

"Can I bring her with me?" Evie begged as her mother held open the gate for her to pass. "Please. Oh, please, Mommy," she pleaded as she softly nuzzled the baby chick, which she still held cupped in her hands.

"No, honey. You have to leave her here. But you can come back and play after lunch," Daphne assured her.

"Promise? Do you really, really promise?" Evie asked with an almost imperceptible accusatory tone in her voice. No one else listening to the conversation between mother and daughter would have picked up on it, but it was there. Daphne knew it was. She had heard it many times before, and it broke her heart just a little bit more each and every time she did.

"Yes, I promise," Daphne said as she crouched down to look

Evie directly in the eyes. She reached both hands out and planted them on Evie's deliciously rosy and plump cheeks. "This is your house, honey. These are your baby chicks. You can come here whenever you like and play here as much as you want. Okay?" She placed a delicate kiss on the tip of Evie's nose. "Okay?" she repeated as she squeezed her hands just a little tighter on Evie's cheeks.

Daphne did her best to reassure her little girl, and outwardly, anyway, it seemed to be working. For a child who usually spent her days holed up in an apartment playing alone with her stuffed animals, having free rein here in the outdoors—in a chicken coop with real live chickens, no less—was like a dream come true. It was a taste of fresh air and freedom that Daphne knew her daughter craved. And it was a craving that Daphne wanted nothing more than to satisfy.

Daphne had always had the best intentions when it came to Evie; she was constantly planning trips to the Bronx Zoo and picnics in Central Park. But Daphne's best intentions were never enough to compensate for the bad timing when the sous chef at Koukla would call in sick or when the health inspector would show up for a surprise visit. There was always some reason for Daphne to once again put her plans with Evie on hold and race to the restaurant with a disappointed Evie in tow.

Daphne felt that familiar ache in her heart every time she glanced over to see her disappointed little girl fidgeting at a back table. Each time she caught a glimpse of her Evie sitting there alone, it so clearly reminded her of all the times her parents had done the same to her. On the surface a four-star *estiatorio* in Manhattan sounded a whole lot different than a little greasy spoon in

Yonkers. But Daphne knew that to a lonely little girl, they were really one and the same.

Yia-yia had shooed Daphne away from the kitchen when they first arrived at the house and refused any offer to help with lunch. Now, as she stood on the patio watching Yia-yia's final preparations, Daphne's mouth began to water as she spotted the banquet that Yia-yia had prepared. There were mountains of food: platters of spanakopita, *spourthopita*, a freshly baked chicken doused with lemon and sprinkled with oregano, an overflowing platter of Yia-yia's signature fried potatoes, a deep bowl of glorious Greek *horiatiki* salad of ruby-red chopped tomatoes, freshly cut cucumbers, and newly unearthed red onions so intense that Daphne felt her eyes sting.

"Daphne *mou*. What's wrong? I made your favorite dishes, yet you still cannot manage a smile for your *yia-yia*," Yia-yia said as she piled the last of the steaming potatoes on the platter. "Sit down. Eat, *koukla mou*. Eat. Men like a little something to hold on to. You are skin and bones," Yia-yia teased as she leaned across the table and set a plate before Daphne.

"I'm fine, Yia-yia. Just hungry, I guess." Not wanting to worry Yia-yia, Daphne began piling her plate high. As much as she didn't want to admit out loud how Yianni had gotten under her skin, she knew she had to come clean. If she could be honest with anyone, she could be honest with Yia-yia.

"It's just that man," Daphne finally blurted out. She let out a deep sigh before reaching over, picking up a plump, slick olive, and popping it into her mouth.

"What man, *koukla*?" Yia-yia asked, clearly confused. "Stephen? Your Stephen? What has he done to you? Is there a problem?" Yia-yia straightened herself and leaned on the table as if to brace for bad news.

"No, not Stephen." Daphne shook away the suggestion with a wave of her hand. "There's no problem with Stephen." She reached across the table and grabbed another slippery olive.

"Ah, *entaksi*. All right."

"It's that Yianni," Daphne blurted out.

"Yianni?"

"Yes, Yianni. That stupid fisherman. He was so rude to me, Yia-yia. He doesn't even know me. It's like he's judging me because I live in New York and make my living cooking for what he calls rich Americans. Like staying here catching fish from a damn boat automatically makes him a better person."

"Ah, Yianni." Yia-yia smiled as his name escaped her lips. "Don't be so hard on Yianni. He is a good man, Daphne. He has been a good friend to me. Talk to him some more, and you'll see for yourself."

"Talk to him? Yia-yia, did you see how rude he was to me? I don't want to talk to him, I want to slap him." As the words came out of her mouth, Daphne heard the front gate creak open. She felt the blood draining from her face as she snapped her face toward the gate to see who had come to join them for lunch and in doing so had witnessed her little tirade.

"Who, who are you going to slap? How exciting." Popi hurried to the table, kissing everyone on the cheek before grabbing a chair and settling in next to Daphne. She reached over the table and grabbed a handful of Yia-yia's fries. "I see I came just in time. So, who are we slapping?"

Oh, thank God it's just Popi. Daphne reached out and squeezed Popi's soft, round thigh.

"Yianni," Yia-yia announced as she placed an empty plate in front of Popi without waiting to hear if Popi had already eaten. "Your cousin wants to slap Yianni."

"Ah yes, the sexy fisherman." Popi nodded in agreement, the corners of her lips curling up. "I'd like to slap him a few times myself, but not on those cheeks." Popi leaned over the table and helped herself to a generous serving of spanakopita while Daphne and Yia-yia erupted in uncontrollable laughter.

"*Ella, ella*. Enough talk of spanking and silliness. The food is getting cold. Come on, eat." With that, Yia-yia began to unfold a square packet of aluminum foil that sat in the middle of the table. Her bent fingers unwrapped each of the layers until the contents of the pouch were revealed. Daphne watched as a thin stream of smoke escaped from the foil and then fanned out, gently lifting, swaying, and finally disappearing into the afternoon air.

"Yia-yia, your baked feta," Daphne cried. Inside the aluminum pouch, the one-inch-thick slab of cheese had been generously drizzled with olive oil and smoky paprika, then topped with just a few slivers of fresh peppers.

Daphne couldn't be bothered to wait for the feta to be served on plates. She reached over the table, dipped into the pouch, and shoved a forkful of the soft, savory cheese into her mouth. As she felt the cheese slowly melt away on her tongue, so did the stress she felt throughout her body. She dug her fork back into the dish again and again. As always, Yia-yia's cooking began to work its magic. With each exquisite bite, Daphne slowly but surely began to feel the knot in her stomach unravel and the pain in her temple dull.

"Daphne *mou*. When is Stephen arriving? When do I get to meet this man?" Yia-yia leaned over and squeezed half of a lemon on to the succulent chicken breast she had placed on Daphne's plate.

"He'll be here next week, Yia-yia. He wanted to come sooner, but he just can't get away from work for that long. It's a busy time for him right now." Daphne lifted the chicken breast to her mouth and tore away at the juicy flesh with her teeth.

"And a busy time for us, with a wedding to plan," Popi added as she reached for more fries.

"Ahh, Daphne *mou*. Daphne, Daphne *mou*." Yia-yia swayed and sang as the mournful singsong escaped from her lips.

Daphne cringed with the first syllable.

"I never thought you would find love again, Daphne. I never thought you would look for love again. Even though he was not a Greek, Alex was a beautiful man. I never thought you would replace him." Yia-yia dabbed at her eyes with the hem of her white apron.

Yia-yia's words stunned Daphne. She'd never felt like she was replacing Alex; no one knew more than Daphne how utterly irreplaceable Alex was. When Alex died, it had been as if Daphne had lost a part of herself. But like an amputee, Daphne had learned to live with a missing piece of her heart. She had no choice. Emptiness had replaced Alex as her constant companion.

"I'm not replacing anybody." The words came out harsher than she had intended them to.

"Ah, all right then. Yes, you know best. Of course." Yia-yia waved her hand in surrender. It was the standard Yia-yia reply on the rare occasions when granddaughter and grandmother disagreed. But until now their minor squabbles had usually been a clash of culinary culture, like why an old broom handle was better for rolling out filo than the expensive marble rollers Daphne's French pastry teachers insisted on using.

"*Kafes, ella*. I'll make *kafes*," Yia-yia announced.

"Yes, *kafes*. Perfect. I'd love some, Yia-yia," Daphne agreed—eager for both the coffee and the change of subject.

"Thea Popi, will you come with me to see the baby chicks?" Evie jumped up and down as she pulled at Popi's arm. The question was more a formality than anything else; by the way Evie was tugging at Popi, it was clear she wasn't going to take no for an answer.

Daphne attempted to intervene. "Come on, Evie. Wait just a few moments, let Popi have her *kafe*."

"No, cousin. That's all right," Popi insisted as she held Evie's face between her hands. "How can I resist such a sweet girl?"

Evie looked up at her aunt. She smiled sweetly for just a moment, then stuck her tongue out and crossed her eyes before breaking free and running toward the chicken coup. "*Ella*, Thea Popi," she called out as she ran. "*Ella*."

"How can I resist? It is impossible." Popi shrugged her broad shoulders at Daphne and turned to follow Evie toward the chicken coup. "I'm coming, Evie *mou*," she shouted as she barreled down the stairs.

Yia-yia returned with two demitasse cups of her thick Greek coffee. Despite the afternoon heat, which was now rising to the point of sticky discomfort, the coffee tasted wonderful. In four generous sips, Daphne had drained the cup and placed it on the table in front of her.

"Yia-yia . . ." Daphne gazed into the mud that remained at the bottom of the tiny cup. "Yia-yia, read my cup for me. Read my cup like you used to do when I was a little girl."

It was another of Yia-yia and Daphne's treasured traditions. They would sit together, side by side, draining cup after cup of thick black coffee just so Yia-yia could read the grounds and tell Daphne what the future held for her. Time and time again, Daphne would try as well. She would lift the cup to her face, turning it this way and that. But where Yia-yia saw birds in flight, long winding roads, and pure young hearts, Daphne never saw anything more than a sloppy, drippy mess.

"*Ne*, Daphne, *mou*. Let's see what we have." Yia-yia smiled as Daphne took her cue and lifted the cup. She swirled the grounds three times in a clockwise direction, just as Yia-yia had taught her to do as a child, then quickly turned the cup upside down and placed it back in the saucer, where it would sit for a few moments as the mud settled to reveal her fate.

After two or three minutes, Daphne lifted the cup and handed it to Yia-yia. Yia-yia stared into the muck as she twirled it in her wrinkled fingers.

"Well," Daphne asked, leaning in to get a closer look, "what do you see?"

Seven

YONKERS
MAY 1995

Daphne watched as they stumbled through the doorway of the diner; a tangle of wrinkled taffeta, smudged lipstick, and pale, lean limbs. A sinkhole opened in her stomach, and she prayed that she would drop dead right then and there, behind the counter cash register.

"Table for six," the tall blond girl announced to no one in particular. "I'm starving." She moaned as she tripped on the hem of her yellow prom dress and wrapped her arms around her broad-chested date, running her fingers along the lapel of his tuxedo as she attempted to steady herself.

"Daphne, *ksipna*. Wake up." Baba leaned through the grill opening and waved his spatula at her. "Come on, *koukla*." His bushy mustache didn't quite conceal the space left vacant in his smile by two missing molars. "Customers."

"*Ne Baba*. I'm going." Obedient, as always, she counted out six menus.

Of all the diners in town, why, lord, did they have to pick this one? Why her?

Daphne ran down her mental wish list. She wished she were anyplace else but here; she wished she didn't have to spend her weekends working at the diner; she wished that she too could know what it felt like to rest her tipsy head on the lapel of a rumpled tuxedo.

But Daphne knew those luxuries were not for girls like her. Prom dates and drunken diner breakfasts were not an option for girls trapped between old traditions and a new world.

She approached the group of teens. "Right this way." Her words were no more than a whisper.

Chin to her chest, she led them toward the back of the diner. She motioned to the largest corner booth, hoping they wouldn't notice the gash in the vinyl seat or that they knew their waitress from homeroom.

They slid into the booth, buttered by the afterglow of a perfect prom and the easy laughter of lifelong friends.

"Coffee," they said in unison, never bothering to look up at the girl whose job it was to serve them.

"Oh, and water," the blond girl added as she scanned the menu. She finally looked up at Daphne, never recognizing the girl who sat next to her in chemistry, seeing nothing more than a waitress. "Lots of ice. I'm dying for something cold."

Daphne didn't know which hurt worse, being different or being invisible.

She walked back to the counter, grateful that her back was now to the table. She pulled the lever on the silver coffee server, but her hand was shaking so badly that the hot liquid spilled all over the saucer and burned her skin as it splattered on her arm.

"Come on, honey, what's eatin' you?" Dina, Daphne's favorite waitress, was on her. Dina's pink talon nails scratched Daphne's hand as she leaned in to steady the cup and saucer. She flipped the lever to stop the coffee's flow.

"Those kids say somethin' to you?" She motioned to the teens in the corner booth.

"No." Daphne shook her head. "They didn't say anything to me."

Dina narrowed her kohl-lined eyes and poked at her black bun with the tip of her pencil. "You sure now?" She looked again at the teens. "I'm here if you need me."

"I know, Dina." She nodded. "I know."

"Well, you just say the word. And I'll take care of them." Dina turned to grab the cheese omelet and fries from the pass-through and tossed the dish on the counter in front of a hungry customer.

"It's fine. I've got it." Daphne nodded.

She filled the cups with steaming coffee and the glasses with ice water. Placing them all on her tray, she carried it to the table. Daphne bit her lower lip as she served the drinks and pulled her pad from the pocket of her black polyester apron. She looked down at her pencil and paper as she wrote, taking their breakfast orders without daring to look up. Trying in vain to stop the pencil from shaking, she scribbled while the teens giggled and kissed. Finally, when the last order was placed, she walked back to the kitchen pass-through and handed the paper to Baba.

"Here you go." She forced a smile as he took the paper from her hand. "Dina, can you cover the front, please? I've got to use the ladies' room."

"Sure, Daph. I've gotcha covered," Dina shouted from the counter where she was refilling the napkin holders.

Daphne walked to the back of the diner, away from the noise of the dining room and the manic preparations of the grill. She opened the door to the supply closet, stepped inside, and immediately fell to the floor in a heap of tears. She wept quietly, shoulders and stomach convulsing with each muffled sob.

She would have stayed hidden in the closet longer had the ringing phone not interrupted her bacchanal of pity and self-loathing. She dried her tears on the hem of her apron, opened the closet door, and reached for the wall phone.

"Plaza Diner." Despite her best efforts, her voice sounded hoarse and scratchy.

The line crackled with static, the voice distant yet distinct. "*Ella*, Daphne *mou*."

"Yia-yia!" Daphne screamed while attempting to rub the tears from her eyes. "Yia-yia, what's wrong? Are you all right?" Panic crept into Daphne's voice. "You never call us here."

"I know, *koukla mou*. But I needed to hear your voice. I wanted to know if you were all right."

"Of course I'm all right." Daphne sniffled. "I'm fine."

"You can tell me, *koukla*. You don't have to be brave for me."

"Oh, Yia-yia . . ." Daphne couldn't hold back any longer. Sobbing into the phone, she couldn't speak for several moments. "How . . . how did you know?"

"There, there, my sweet girl. I knew something was wrong," Yia-yia replied. "I could hear you crying."

Eight

"Evie, come on. There's nothing to be afraid of," Daphne pleaded. "The water's not even deep. Come on, Evie, you're going to love this."

"No."

"Come on, Evie. You don't know what you're missing."

"No."

"Evie, come on. I promise to hold on to you. I won't let go."

"No. I don't want to," Evie said as she turned her back on her mother and marched from the shoreline back to her blanket in the sand.

Daphne stood waist-deep in the water, hands planted on her hips, staring at her little girl. How is this possible? she thought. How could a child who comes from a family of fishermen be so afraid of the water? Daphne wasn't kidding herself. She knew the answer as well as she knew the mantra of *if only* that she repeated over and over in her mind.

If only . . . she had taken some time off, made the effort to come here and visit every summer. If only . . . it hadn't been so much easier to just lose herself in work, then she might not have already lost so much of Evie. If only . . . Alex hadn't taken that late-night overtime assignment to help pay for the pastry class she so desperately wanted to take. If only . . . the truck driver had not been drinking the night he crossed the divider and crashed into Alex's car. If only . . . her parents had not been in the diner that night it was robbed. If only . . . Baba had just shut up and opened the cash register for the junkie with the gun. If only . . . Mama had listened, not run to Baba's side, to hold and comfort him as he lay dying on the linoleum floor. If only . . . the junkie had noticed the picture locket around Mama's neck, the photos of Daphne and baby Evie, and realized that she had so much to live for, that she was needed, and that she was loved. If only . . . he could have known the pain he would cause when he pulled the trigger again and took her too.

If only she hadn't lost everyone she ever loved.

If only . . .

There was no changing what had happened. There was no bringing Mama, Baba, or Alex back to help her raise Evie and shower her with the love and attention she so deserved and craved. Daphne was only thirty-five years old, but she felt as if she had lived a lifetime of loss, that she too was shrouded in black mourning like the chorus of widows at the port. But songs of lament and black headscarves are not acceptable in the culture of Manhattan. Daphne learned to wear her mourning internally.

She knew she could not change the past. But watching Evie walk away from her, Daphne knew that from this point on she could and would change the future. Now that she was going to marry Stephen, she would have the free time, as well as the financial freedom, to give Evie everything she wanted and deserved. She had to. She had lost too much already; her husband, her father, and her mother. And now Daphne realized that in many ways, her own child was growing up without a mother as well. She would be damned if she would lose Evie too.

Standing there in the cool, clear water, watching Evie play on the sand as the gentle waves lapped against her thighs, Daphne made a vow. She would be there for Evie, in ways she had never been able to before. She would open up new worlds for her daughter. Evie had no idea what she was missing. How could Evie understand the exhilaration of charging into the water at full speed when she watched her own mother take nothing but careful, measured steps through life?

"Evie. Evie, honey," Daphne shouted. "I'm just going to swim for a few minutes and then we'll go up to the house, okay?"

"Okay, Mommy."

Daphne turned and faced the open sea. She bent her knees, raised her arms above her head, and took a deep breath.

Still sitting on the beach, Evie stopped digging her castle. She stood and turned toward the thicket. "Mommy, why are those ladies crying? What's wrong with them?"

But Daphne didn't hear her daughter. Just as the first faint cry reached Evie, Daphne sprang up and out, breaking under the water with a quick, crisp *whoosh*. She opened her eyes. *Barbounia, tsipoura*. They were all there. Six years later, and nothing had changed.

Six years later, and so much had changed.

Nine

"Go to the garden and pick some fresh dill for me, *koukla mou*. I don't think I have enough," Yia-yia said as she sprinkled flour on the indoor kitchen table. Feeling refreshed after her early-morning swim, Daphne practically ran down the back steps and snipped a generous helping of dill from the garden.

She smiled as she waved the dill under her nose. Its delicate featherlike leaves tickled as they danced across her lips. "It's so nice to actually pick fresh herbs from the earth and not a big icebox."

"I wouldn't know, Daphne *mou*. I've never done this any other way." Yia-yia took the dill from Daphne and placed it on the olive wood chopping board. She picked up her large knife and began chopping the green leaves into tiny threadlike pieces. Years ago, Yia-yia had taught Daphne the importance of finely dicing herbs. She insisted that they were meant to infuse a dish with flavor, not be bitten into like a piece of souvlaki.

"Yia-yia," Daphne cried as she spotted her old pink cassette player on the shelf above the sink.

"*Ne*, Daphne *mou*."

"Yia-yia, my old radio," Daphne squealed, remembering how she would sit and listen to Greek folk music for hours.

"Your old cassettes are in the drawer." Yia-yia motioned to the old wooden cabinet behind the kitchen table.

With both hands, Daphne grabbed the cabinet handles and pulled. There, on the bottom shelf, was a treasure trove of classic Greek music. Parios, Dalaras, Hatzis, Vissi—they were all there. Daphne searched through the bag and pulled out a white cassette, its black letters faded and rubbed off. It was Marinella, her favorite.

"I haven't listened to this in so long." Daphne sat down and pressed play. She leaned her elbows on the table, chin cradled in her palms—and closed her eyes. A smile spread across her face as the first notes escaped from the radio's tiny speakers.

"Daphne *mou*, come on—why are you listening to that sad music? It's depressing," Yia-yia chided as she crumbled cooled boiled potatoes into a pan.

Like her parents, Daphne had always loved Marinella's melodrama, her stories of all-consuming love affairs and aching black heartbreak. After Alex died, Daphne found herself swallowed up in her grief, listening to this music over and over again, but everything changed the night she finally said yes to Stephen.

"*Ella*, Daphne," Yia-yia said. "We have guests coming for lunch. Enough of lost love affairs; we have a lot to do."

"I know, Yia-yia." Daphne stood up and lifted the cassette player from the table. She placed it on a chair in the corner but didn't turn it off, just lowered the volume a bit.

For the rest of the morning, Yia-yia and Daphne worked side by side. As Yia-yia finished chopping the dill, Daphne grabbed a generous handful of the chopped leaves and tossed them into the pan. She then added the rice and boiled potatoes, which Yia-yia had already crumbled.

"I'll do the feta." Yia-yia reached into the refrigerator and pulled out a large white tub.

"Yes, you can do the feta." Daphne laughed, nodding.

"So, still?" Yia-yia shook her head. She pulled back the lid from the tub and reached into the milky brine with her bare hands. She pulled out a large chunk of white feta cheese. Yia-yia's hands glistened and dripped with the pungent white juice.

Daphne turned away and gagged. She could clean a whole fish, butcher any type of meat, and even impale a baby lamb on a roasting spit, but there was something about a tub of feta brine that had always made her stomach turn.

"So what do you do in the restaurant?" Yia-yia asked.

"I get someone to do it for me."

"Ah, you are so modern." Yia-yia nodded.

"Yes, I'm very modern." Daphne giggled as she cracked the first egg. A dozen more followed that Daphne scrambled until the liquid turned a pale yellow with just a few frothy bubbles on top. She poured the eggs into the mixture and used a dinner plate to mix the ingredients together, fanning the small dish up and down the length of the pan, making sure the crumbled potatoes, feta, rice, and eggs were all evenly distributed. Several flies buzzed around the kitchen. Daphne did her best to shoo them away, but it was no use.

Yia-yia was almost finished with the filo. She worked the old broom handle quickly and effortlessly, back and forth across the small balls of dough until they spread out paper-thin across the table. Daphne watched as Yia-yia lifted sheet after sheet of filo and draped it over each of the half dozen pans that were scattered over every available surface in the kitchen.

Not one hole, Daphne marveled, thinking of how she was constantly using her wet fingers to mend the tears that always sprang up whenever she rolled out her own filo.

"*Entaksi*," Yia-yia said as the last pan was filled with the rich *patatopita* mixture and topped with a sprinkling of sugar. She placed her hands on her hips, her black dress covered in a film of white flour. "*Ella*, Daphne *mou*, let's have some *kafe* before we clean this up. I'll read your cup again."

"No, Yia-yia. No more *kafe* for me." Daphne raised her hand, thinking of the three frappes Evie had insisted on making her before they headed to the cove that morning. "Besides, I like what you saw in my cup yesterday. I don't want to take a chance that you'll see something different today." She darted around the kitchen, sweeping dried bits of dough out the door.

Yia-yia took her *kafe* and walked outside to her chair under the shade of the olive tree. She drank her coffee, enjoying the occasional breeze and watching as Evie chased salamanders into the patio's crevices. The day before, when Yia-yia had looked into Daphne's cup, she had seen that the bottom was covered in deep black mud while the sides of the cup were only thinly streaked with grounds.

"What does that mean?" Daphne had asked.

"The bottom is your past; it shows you had a heavy heart. But see here—" Yia-yia leaned in to show Daphne. "See, you can see how the white of the cup shows through on the sides. That means your skies are clearing. Your heartache will clear."

Daphne had hugged her arms around her chest and leaned in closer. She sucked in her cheeks as she waited for Yia-yia to continue.

"I see one line toward the top of the cup. That is you. But here—" Yia-yia turned the cup and pointed to a fresh line that appeared halfway down the side. "This is your life's journey. And you see here, there is another line that appears here with you. The lines suddenly shift to the right. And look how they get clearer, stronger."

Yia-yia tilted the cup again. She winced as she pulled her shoulders back and straightened her spine. "You see, Daphne, there is someone who will change the course of your life. You'll be making a journey, a new trip, and he will join you on your journey. He makes you stronger and mends your broken heart. He will walk side by side with you for the rest of your life and show you love like you have never known."

The words made Daphne glow. In just a few days, Stephen would be arriving, and they would begin their new journey together—their new life, putting the darkness behind her once and for all.

In the past, Daphne had thought these readings were merely another way to pass the hot afternoons. But not this time. This time she needed to believe the cup's readings could in fact ring true. This time it was too important.

"All right, put your right index finger here, at the bottom of the cup. This is the deepest part of your heart, where all of your dreams are."

Yia-yia had gestured toward the very bottom of the cup, where the mud was the thickest. Daphne did as she was told. She took her left index finger, the one closest to the heart, and pressed it down.

"Now lift your finger," Yia-yia commanded.

Daphne removed her finger and turned it toward her. Daphne and Yia-yia both leaned in and looked into the mud. There, smack in the center, was a clear white imprint where her finger had been.

Daphne exhaled.

"See, Daphne *mou*. You left a clean mark. Your heart is pure, and your deepest wish will come true."

Now, sitting here on the patio as Evie played at her feet, Yia-yia stared into her own cup. She could hear Daphne singing an old, familiar song in the kitchen. It was the very lullaby that her own daughter, Daphne's mother, quietly sang years ago as Daphne slept in her cradle under the shade of the very same lemon tree. It was the very song that Yia-yia herself would sing over and over again as she bounced Daphne on her knee, praying the gods would listen to the words and understand what this child meant to her. And now it was Daphne's turn to sing the same words, to feel their meaning and understand just how they resonated. It was Daphne's turn to fully understand just how magical and transformative the power of a woman's love can be.

> *I love you like no other . . .*
> *I have no gifts to shower upon you*
> *No gold or jewels or riches*
> *But still, I give you all I have*
> *And that, my sweet child, is all my love*

I promise you this,
You will always have my love

Yia-yia turned her cup round and round. Staring into the darkness, she thought how she too would give all she had for her Daphne. She was a poor woman, and she had nothing to give her grandchild but some old stories and a glimpse into a muddy coffee cup. Daphne had been so happy with the reading yesterday that Yia-yia just couldn't tell her. She didn't have the heart.

Soon it would be Daphne's turn to take her place among their ancestors, to hear the voices that had kept Yia-yia company all these years. But it was too soon; Yia-yia knew her granddaughter still was not ready.

"*Ohi tora*, not now," Yia-yia said out loud, although she was alone on the patio. The old woman looked across the island, out toward the horizon as she spoke. "Just a little more time, please." She paused to listen. "She needs more time."

Yia-yia nodded as she heard the island's response. The wind picked up and the cypress trees rustled in the wind. The sound carried across the island and across the patio, the muffled sound of women whispering hidden between the vibrations of the leaves. It was the answer she had been waiting for, the answer Yia-yia knew that, for now, she alone could hear.

Yia-yia looked out across the sea and thanked the island for giving her this gift of time. She would keep what she saw to herself, at least a bit longer. She was an old, uneducated woman, but Yia-yia could read a coffee cup like a scholar reads a textbook. She knew that the clean white line that suddenly appeared halfway down the cup indeed meant that Daphne would be going on a journey; but that was not all she saw revealed in Daphne's grounds.

I have no gifts to shower upon you
No gold or jewels or riches
But still, I give you all I have

For now, Yia-yia chose the gift of silence.

Ten

Later that afternoon Daphne, Evie, Yianni, and Popi all sat under the olive tree on old wooden chairs, feasting on Yia-yia's *patato-pita*. Daphne had spent the entire morning hoping that Yianni might somehow have forgotten about Yia-yia's lunch invitation and his promise to join them. But she was not so lucky.

Yianni had shown up right on time, his tales of excruciating hunger sending Yia-yia into a fit of giggles and Daphne running to the kitchen to escape this man who had come to devour the pita along with the peace and tranquillity of her day. She had decided that the best way to deal with Yianni was to simply ignore him.

It appeared that Yianni entered the lunch with the same strategy.

He burst through the gate, holding in one hand a beautiful large *tsipoura* wrapped in newspaper, fresh from his nets. In the other hand was a large chocolate bar filled with chopped hazelnuts.

"*Yia sou* Thea!" he shouted as he entered the patio, bending down slightly to kiss Yia-yia on both cheeks and handing her the newspaper-wrapped fish.

"And for you, little Evie," he said in perfect but heavily accented English as he patted Evie's dark curls and handed her the chocolate bar. He had nothing for Daphne; no gift, no words, no acknowledgment.

Evie climbed into Daphne's lap and nuzzled into her shoulder. As Daphne wrapped her arms around her little girl, she marveled at the therapeutic powers of Evie's skin against her own. She had never been happier to have Evie crawl into her lap and cuddle. She needed Evie's innocence and affection right now. It was a stark contrast to the cold presence of Yianni, who sat just inches away.

Evie continued to sit there, enjoying the indulgence of Daphne's time and attention. With the majority of the conversation taking place in Greek, the little girl had quickly lost interest in trying to decipher what the adults were saying and instead turned her attention to twirling her mother's corkscrew curls around and around her fingers. As Evie lay draped across her mother's lap, one arm dangling down to the patio, the other tugging, playing with, and twirling Daphne's dark ringlets, she suddenly jumped out of Daphne's lap and began to scream.

"Mommy, Mommy. Get it off of me, Mommy."

"Evie, honey. What is it, what's wrong?" Daphne cried as she scanned Evie's body top to bottom.

"It's a spider, a huge spider, crawling on my arm. Eww . . . Mommy, help."

There it was, tiny black body and eight spindly legs meandering down the length of Evie's arm. With one *whoosh* of her hand, Daphne sent the spider flying off the terrified young girl.

"It's all right, honey, it was only a spider, nothing to be afraid of." But of course, knowing her daughter, Daphne knew her words were useless.

"Evie, it is just a spider," Popi chimed in.

"Yes, honey. It's nothing," Daphne agreed as she pulled the little girl back onto her lap, running her hands up and down Evie's arm as if to wipe away the spider's tiny footsteps.

"Ah, Evie *mou*, do not be afraid—it is good luck for a spider to kiss a child. Daphne *mou*, tell her it is Arachne's kiss," Yia-yia added.

Still holding Evie in her lap, Daphne leaned in to her little girl's ear and explained what Yia-yia had said. "So you see, honey, a visit from a spider is nothing to be afraid of; it's a gift from Arachne."

"But who's Arachne?" the little girl asked. "Is she another cousin? Mommy, why do I have so many cousins with weird names?" Evie huffed. "Why don't people here have normal names?"

"No, Evie." Daphne laughed. "Arachne is not a cousin. She's a spider."

"Mommy, now you're just being silly." Evie planted her hands on her hips and pursed her lips. The sight of her like that, confused and indignant, was enough to send the adults into a fit of laughter.

"Evie"—Daphne leaned in closer to explain.—"Arachne *is* a spider. When I was a little girl, just about your age, Yia-yia told me the story of Arachne and Athena. Arachne was a young girl who was too proud and far too vain. She was known throughout Greece for her skill at taking different-colored threads and weaving them into beautiful pictures on her loom. She had the nerve to brag that she was better at weaving than the goddess Athena herself. Now Athena got really mad and challenged Arachne to a contest, to see who could weave a better picture. They sat side by side and worked, and finally the contest was finished. Both looms were perfect. But Arachne still had the nerve to insist that hers was better than Athena's. The goddess got so angry that she cast a spell on Arachne. Athena turned Arachne into the first spider. From that moment on, Arachne would weave forever, and she would forever be attached to her loom."

"Do you see, Evie?" Popi added as she took another bite of *patatopita*. She opened her mouth to speak again, crumbs flying out of her mouth as she did. "Athena made Arachne into the first spider because she was a very naughty girl."

"But why was she so naughty, Thea Popi? All she did was make a picture. So what?" Evie asked.

"Well, Evie . . . ummmm . . . you see . . ." Popi looked up at Daphne for help. "Um, the reason is . . . because . . ." For once Popi seemed to be at a loss for words. It was clear from her stuttering and stammering that she had no idea how to answer her inquisitive little niece.

Daphne sat back in her chair, lifted another piece of *patatopita* to her mouth, and remained quiet. She was rather enjoying this little exchange between her curious, high-spirited daughter and her know-it-all cousin who just the other day had had the nerve to question Daphne's parenting.

"Yes, Popi," Daphne finally spoke. "Tell us, why did Arachne get in trouble?" Daphne broke off a piece of the *patatopita*'s crust with her thumb and forefinger.

"I will tell you, Evie." Yianni inched his chair closer to Evie. He leaned in, eye to eye with the little girl.

Yianni's offer took Daphne by surprise. She glanced over at him. It was the first time she'd dared look straight at him since he arrived for lunch. But now, seated here on the patio, there was no ignoring the ignorant fisherman as he now offered to help Evie. She turned once again and caught another glimpse of his profile: the slightly hooked nose, creased eyes, and scruffy beard, which appeared even more heavily flecked with gray than she had remembered.

"Evie, Arachne got into trouble because she thought she was better than everyone else," Yianni said. "She had too much pride. In mythology we call this hubris."

"Yes, that's right, Evie *mou*," Daphne added. "Yianni seems to know this myth very well. It's clear he's well versed in hubris."

For the first time since he arrived, Yianni turned to look at Daphne. The gentle ease with which he spoke to Evie dissolved as he locked eyes with the *Amerikanida*. For Daphne he reserved a cocky stare that reeked of challenge. Daphne felt the urge to look away, to escape his black eyes, which felt colder than the dead fish that now lay on a bed of ice on the kitchen counter. But Daphne didn't look away; she couldn't and wouldn't concede defeat—not again.

"Yes," Yianni said, turning his attention from Daphne back to Evie. "Evie. The ancient Greeks called it hubris. It's a big word, but it means that someone is too proud. It is never good to be too proud." He turned toward Daphne as he spoke the words "too proud."

"Okay," Evie said as she jumped off her seat to chase a salamander across the patio, clearly finished with hubris and this entire conversation.

"Well, Daphne. You really got her attention that time." Popi laughed.

"I know." Daphne shook her head. "She's not exactly a captive audience, is she?"

"She's a beautiful little girl," Yianni added, his eyes following Evie as she skipped away. "It's no wonder Evie is so beautiful. She is named for Thea Evangelia, isn't she? She is beautiful like her great-grandmother."

"Yes, she is." Popi refilled her glass with beer and clinked glasses with Yianni. "Isn't that right, Daphne? Isn't Evie named for your *yia-yia*?"

Daphne nodded. She turned toward Yianni, who was now watching Evie skip across the patio and flip rocks over with a stick in search of salamanders. Once Evie reached the old cellar door, its blue paint peeling and chipping away, Evie stopped in her tracks. Her mouth dropped and her eyes opened wide when she spotted a spider spinning her web in the corner of the door frame.

"Thea Evangelia, look at Evie. She's found Arachne." Yianni pointed to where Evie stood, watching the spider spin her web.

"Just one more piece." Popi leaned across the table and lifted the last piece of pita from the platter, leaving nothing but a few crumbs on the large white serving dish.

"Ah, everyone is hungry today. I'll get some more pita." Yia-yia lifted the empty platter from the table and shuffled back into the kitchen.

"To Yia-yia," Popi exclaimed, her words beginning to slur.

"To Thea Evangelia," Yianni shouted.

"Yes, to Yia-yia," Daphne concurred, surprised that there was actually something that she and Yianni agreed on.

"There is no one like Thea Evangelia," Yianni said, shaking his head from side to side. "And there never will be another like her," he added as he drained his beer, his fourth of the afternoon.

"Daphne," Popi said as she lifted her glass to her lips. "Daphne, I never asked you this. Why did you name Evie after Yia-yia, and not your own mother? Angeliki is a beautiful name. And that's our tradition, to name children after their grandmothers, not great-grandmothers. Just like you are named for your father's mother, Daphne."

Yianni looked at Daphne, waiting for her to reply.

"I don't know. I thought about it. But I guess I wanted to honor Yia-yia somehow. To let her know how much she means to me. She was like a second mother to me." Daphne shivered as she thought of her mother, killed so senselessly, taken from them too soon, just as Evie had begun to toddle her first steps.

"There are many ways to honor someone," Yianni said as he refilled his beer glass. "And I for one don't see the great honor in naming a child after someone who is kept separated from this child. One who dreams night and day that she may one day finally meet her. That to me is not honor—that is torture."

"Excuse me?" Daphne spun to face him.

Popi sat up straighter in her seat, ready for the fireworks that were sure to ensue.

"What the hell is that supposed to mean?" Daphne demanded.

"It means you might be wiser to think of some other ways to *honor* your *yia-yia*, as you call it." Yianni shrugged.

"You don't know anything about us, about me." Daphne could

feel the rage simmering to the surface. She felt as red as the tomatoes hanging on the vines and as hot as the Greek coffee Yia-yia
was brewing on the stove. This man knew nothing about her,
nothing about Yia-yia. How dare he presume to know their story,
their history? How dare he presume to have any grasp of the depth
of emotion Daphne felt for her *yia-yia*?

"I know more than you think, Daphne," Yianni replied. "You
think naming a child after an old woman is an honor. What good
is that honor when the same old woman sits alone day after day
and night after night, praying that she might one day be lucky
enough to meet this child which carries her name? What good is a
name to an old woman who sings songs of lament morning and
night and cries that child's name, all the time knowing her voice is
too far away to be heard by the two little ears she longs to caress
and kiss?"

"Who the hell do you think you are?" Daphne hissed. "What
the hell do you know?"

"But I do know," Yianni replied, unfazed by her anger. "I know
things that you don't, Daphne. I see things you can't see. I know
how she misses you. How alone she feels. I know how many times
I come to visit her, and I find her staring into the fire, crying. How
she pores over the photos you send. I've come here silently at night
to check on her, and I've watched and seen how she sits alone and
talks to your photos, whispers your favorite stories into the photos, praying you might somehow still be able to hear them."

"Stop it." Daphne jumped from her seat, knocking over the
rickety wooden chair. "What is it with you? Haven't we had
enough myths for one day?"

"Me?" Yianni shrugged his shoulders. "I've done nothing but

speak the truth. Whether you like it or not, it is the truth. I see it, Daphne. I know. I may like to tease about how ignorant you Americans can be, but don't sit here pretending to be blind as well."

With one shaky hand, Daphne grabbed the table to steady herself. "You don't know anything," she growled as she looked him dead in the eyes, expecting to once again be confronted by his cold, callous gaze. But when her eyes found his, Daphne was shocked to catch a fleeting glimpse of what might pass for compassion.

"I take care of her," she insisted. "I send money. I work from early morning to late at night every single day just so I can take care of Evie and Yia-yia. There's been no one to help me, no one. I've done it all alone, supported us all. You have no right to say those things." Daphne turned her back on Yianni just as she felt her eyes well up. She would be damned if he was going to see her cry.

"What good is your money, Daphne?" he continued, his voice just a bit softer now. "Do you think your *yia-yia* cares about your money? Do you think that money keeps her company at night when she is lonely? When she is afraid? Do you think it buys her comfort? Speaks to her when she is starved for company?"

Daphne couldn't listen anymore. Her head was spinning, as if instead of one small glass of Mythos, she had kept pace with Yianni and Popi. She began to walk toward the house.

"I told her once that my boat was giving me trouble, and that I could not afford a new engine. She took me by the hand and brought me into the house. Your *yia-yia* pulled a box filled with dollars from under her bed and told me to take what I needed, that she had no use for it. I took nothing. She keeps it all in that box. That's where your money goes. See what good it does there." He grabbed his fisherman's cap from the back of the chair, placed it on his head, and stomped toward the gate. "*Yia sou*, Thea Evangelia. I have to go. Thank you for lunch."

The gate slammed shut behind Yianni just as Yia-yia emerged from the kitchen with a tray carrying more pita.

"Popi, where is everyone? What happened?" Yia-yia asked as she placed the tray on the wooden table.

"I have no idea," Popi replied, shaking her head from side to side, draining her glass of the last few drops of beer.

Daphne opened the door to the small house and walked inside. She closed the door behind her and steadied herself against the door frame, her legs shaking and uncertain. She lifted her head and looked out across the room. It was a tiny home, just two small bedrooms and a sparsely furnished living room. The pounding inside her temples was so strong that it blurred her vision.

There was nothing in the room but an old, uncomfortable green sofa and a table with four chairs whose red satin seats were covered in plastic slipcovers—to protect from the guests who never come, Daphne thought, sighing.

Behind the table, up against the wall, was a long glass cabinet covered in family photos. There was a black-and-white photo of Daphne's parents on their wedding day; Mama's hair teased, sprayed, and curled elaborately. There was a faded black-and-white photo of Papou from his days in the Greek navy, handsome in his pressed uniform and squat mustache. Next to Papou was a rare photo of Yia-yia as a young mother, standing at the port, holding Mama's tiny hand, a stern expression on her face, as was the standard back then—no one of that generation ever smiled for photographs. The rest of the photos were all of Daphne—Daphne at her christening, Daphne taking her first steps out on the patio under the olive tree, Daphne looking awkward and buck-toothed in her third-grade school portrait, Daphne and Alex kissing on their wedding day, Daphne looking far more ethnic with her familial Greek nose still intact, Daphne and Evie blowing kisses to Yia-yia from their Manhattan apartment, and Daphne in her chef's whites waving to Yia-yia from the kitchen at Koukla. It was Daphne's entire life played out in cheaply framed, dusty photos.

She felt a bit steadier now, away from the burning afternoon sun and the burning vitriol of Yianni's accusations. When she was certain she could stand on her own, without holding the wall for support, Daphne walked toward Yia-yia's bedroom. She knew what she would find, but she had to see it for herself.

The bed creaked as she sat down, her hands beside her body fingering the crochet bedspread and dipping in and out of the web-like pattern. After a few moments, she leaned forward and reached down under the bed, her hands finding and grasping it almost instantly. Daphne lifted the box on to her lap. She placed her hands on top of the dusty shoe box, her chipped fingernails tapping the lid for a few seconds before she lifted the top off the box and looked inside.

There they were, just like Yianni said they would be. There in the box were stacks of dollars, piles of green bills, thousands of dollars—all of the money Daphne had been sending Yia-yia for the past several years.

Daphne stared into the box and looked down on the result of all those hours spent away from home, away from Evie, away from

Yia-yia. She put her hands in the box and lifted out the result of all those hours spent on her feet, fighting with suppliers, arguing with her staff, and crying from bone-aching exhaustion. She fanned out the bills, the result of the awards, accolades, and full reservation book that she had fought so hard to earn.

There it all was, all stuffed in a shoe box shoved under Yia-yia's bed. And it was all meaningless.

Eleven

Manhattan
January 1998

Daphne wrapped the crochet scarf once more around her neck as she exited the Eighth Street subway station near New York University. She burrowed her face deeper into the scratchy wool and braced herself against the biting wind that whipped up Broadway. Another icy gust slammed against her body as a wind-induced tear rolled down her face.

Damn it. She buried her face even deeper in the brown material. There was no escaping it. Even the brand-new scarf that Yia-yia had made, which had just arrived yesterday from Greece, was already infused with the scent of diner grease.

Damn damn damn.

Daphne shivered uncontrollably, even under the arsenal of layers that Mama made sure she put on before she walked out into the single-digit cold. As her muscles vibrated and twitched, Daphne felt as if she were lying on one of those ridiculous twenty-five-cent massage beds that Baba became obsessed with a few years back during their big family getaway to Niagara Falls.

It had always been a dream of Baba's to see the legendary falls in person. After all, he had seen them on a Seven Wonders of the World list, right there alongside the Parthenon. As much as she knew her father wanted to see the falls for himself, Daphne was shocked when her parents actually left Theo Spiro in charge of the diner, packed up the Buick, and headed north for a two-day get-away. Baba never left the diner, never.

But as impressed as Baba was with the ferocious beauty of the falls, it seemed he was even more taken with the vibrating beds at the Howard Johnson's. Daphne had fed quarter after quarter into the tiny slot and watched as Baba smiled peacefully, his enormous belly shaking and jiggling like the giant bowls of cream-colored tapioca Mama served every Sunday. Daphne knew that for Baba, this twenty-five-cent indulgence was the epitome of luxury and success. For him, a man accustomed to standing on his feet behind a hot grill, flipping burgers for sixteen hours a day, a pulsating bed in a $69.99-a-night motel room decorated in a palate of Nathan's mustard yellow meant he had indeed made it, that he was finally living the American dream.

Daphne reached the lecture hall a good thirty minutes before the start of class. She hated getting here so early, but since the train from Yonkers to Manhattan ran only twice an hour, Daphne often found herself sitting alone in lecture halls, waiting. Some of the other commuter students often met for coffee and cigarettes in the cafeteria across the street, but Daphne hated their gossipy small talk and crude flirtations. She preferred to just sit alone and wait.

Grateful to be out of the cold, she began the process, unpeeling layer after layer. First, the bulky black down coat came off. Then she removed the yellow cardigan, followed by a brown cotton sweater, and finally the diner-scented scarf. There was no way Daphne could fit it all on the back of her small lecture-hall chair; she had to pile everything on the floor next to her aisle seat. She detested doing this, but with no place else to stash her winter wardrobe, she had no choice. Nothing screamed *commuter student* like a pile of warm winter clothes and an entire day's worth of books lugged around in a backpack.

Daphne knew she wasn't like many of the students who lived on campus in a haze of bong hits, dorm parties, and guilt-free sexual exploration. But sometimes, sitting alone in a lecture hall, she liked to pretend that she was. Maybe it was really possible? Maybe she could be mistaken for a tousle-haired co-ed who had just raced out of her boyfriend's bed and sprinted across the street to make it to class in time. Daphne relished her daydreams of being like the other students. But then, inevitably, her eyes would once again fall on the telltale pile of clothes and books beside her. She was again reminded that instead of an intoxicating mixture of incense, patchouli, and morning sex, Daphne's signature scent was diner grease.

Daphne would never forget that day in her History of Theater class. It wasn't the bone-chilling temperatures that made the day memorable. It was him. It was Alex.

She had seen him around campus a few times, but she never really thought much about him other than a fleeting notice of his all-American good looks. But that day, when Alex stood up in their theater class to give his oral presentation, Daphne realized that appearances could be very deceiving. This was not the one-dimensional privileged American boy "who only wants one thing from a nice Greek girl like you" that her mother had so fiercely warned her about. The moment he began to speak, Daphne knew there was so much more behind those cornflower blue eyes than football, keg parties, and the latest sorority girl conquest.

Daphne would never forget how his voice cracked and his hands shook as he stood in front of the class, holding his paper. His shirt was worn and wrinkled, and his khakis were creased in all the wrong places.

"In my opinion, Christopher Marlowe's *Doctor Faustus* contains one of the greatest, if not the greatest, passage in theatrical history," Alex began. He paused for a moment and looked around the classroom, then lifted the paper slightly closer to his face and once again began to speak. But as he began to read the passage, Daphne noticed that his hands had stopped shaking, and his voice took on a steady calm.

> *Was this the face that launched a thousand ships*
> *And burnt the topless towers of Ilium?*
> *Sweet Helen, make me immortal with a kiss.*
> *Her lips suck forth my soul; see where it flies!—*
> *Come, Helen, come, give me my soul again.*
> *Here will I dwell, for Heaven is in these lips,*
> *And all is dross that is not Helena.*
> *I will be Paris, and for love of thee,*
> *Instead of Troy, shall Wittenberg be sack'd*

And I will combat with weak Menelaus,
And wear thy colours on my plumed crest;
Yea, I will wound Achilles in the heel,
And then return to Helen for a kiss.
Oh, thou art fairer than the evening air
Clad in the beauty of a thousand stars;
Brighter art thou than flaming Jupiter
When he appear'd to hapless Semele:
More lovely than the monarch of the sky
In wanton Arethusa's azur'd arms:
And none but thou shalt be my paramour.

As he finished the passage, Alex once again looked up from his paper. He planted a slight, crooked smile on his face as he scanned the room for some sort of encouragement or reaction from his fellow students, but all he met was bloodshot blank stares—until he glanced at the girl with the pile of books and clothing beside her. Daphne locked eyes with the disheveled American boy and shyly but knowingly smiled back.

"Very well chosen, young man," the professor remarked. "Now, tell me what this all means to you."

"To me, this passage is art," Alex began. He stared into the paper, which he clenched with both hands. "For me, true art evokes emotion. Love, hatred, joy, passion, compassion, sadness. Whatever form it takes on, art makes you feel something. It makes you know that you're alive."

Alex stopped to take a breath. He looked up from his paper and made eye contact with Daphne once again. She squirmed just a little in her seat and felt a knot form in her stomach.

"This passage makes me think of the power and possibility that exists between two people," Alex continued. "It makes me think of what it might be like to love someone so deeply and completely that you would go to war for her, risk the lives of your friends for her—as Paris did for Helen. If art evokes emotion, then this passage haunts me. I feel haunted by it, by the possibility that a mere kiss can make the angels sing and make a person immortal . . . that the gates of heaven can be opened by a kiss."

On the surface, it made no sense. This was a class assignment, homework, nothing more. But despite the immigrant's cardinal rule, "Keep to your own kind," as Daphne watched Alex give his five-minute presentation, she knew that everything had changed.

"Thank you, Alex. Well done." The professor dismissed Alex with a nod of his head.

Alex gathered his papers and prepared to return to his seat, starting up the stairs that led to the multitude of empty chairs in the cavernous lecture hall. Daphne forced herself to look away, to stare instead at the mosaic pattern of the lecture hall carpet. It hurt too much to watch him, to know that boys like him were not meant for girls like her. But then her solitary contemplation was interrupted by a whisper from above.

"Excuse me, is this seat taken?"

She knew it was him before she even glanced up. As Daphne stared up at him, he didn't wait for an answer. They both knew he didn't have to. With his long, muscular legs and frayed-at-the-hem khakis, he climbed over the pile of Daphne's clothes and slid into the seat beside her—and into her life.

"Hi, I'm Alex," he said as he extended his hand. Her long lashes fluttered before her big black-olive eyes locked in on his once more.

They went for coffee after the lecture, both uncharacteristically cutting classes for the rest of the day. The entire afternoon was spent walking and talking and holding hands under the coffee shop table; just their fingertips touching at first, but by sunset, he cradled her hand in his. By nightfall she knew it was time to go, that Mama and Baba would worry if she were late. He asked her to stay, to come back to his room. She wanted nothing more than to do just that, to nestle against his chest, to smell him and feel his heart beating against hers. But Daphne said no.

They walked hand-in-hand to the subway, neither one complaining about the bitter cold or even seeming to notice it. There, at the entrance to the Eighth Street subway station, he lifted her chin with his fingers and kissed her for the first time.

When she finally opened her eyes, she found his, electric blue and staring back. From that moment on, Daphne loved staring into those eyes.

She missed those eyes.

Twelve

Thankful Evie had finally fallen asleep easily, Daphne grabbed her white cardigan from the back of one of the plastic-covered chairs. She held tight, wringing the soft material around and around with her hands as she stepped out into the breezy moonlit night.

"*Ella*, Daphne *mou*. *Katse etho*. Sit here," Yia-yia said as she patted the chair beside her, the dark spots and bulging veins of her hands illuminated by the golden glow of the fire.

Daphne joined Yia-yia in their usual spots by the outdoor oven. Neither spoke at first. They sat side by side and watched as the flames jumped from the burning logs, sending white-hot embers floating and tumbling into the evening breeze like the circus acrobats Daphne perpetually promised to take Evie to see, but had never quite found the time for.

"Are you cold, Daphne *mou*?" Yia-yia asked as she reached out to grab her own shawl, which hung on the back of her chair, and draped the fringed black fabric around her hunched shoulders.

"No, I'm fine."

"Do you want something to eat, Daphne *mou*?"

"No, Yia-yia, I'm not hungry."

"You didn't eat very much at dinner. I told you, you need to put on some weight. You don't want to look like a skeleton in that gown, now do you?" Yia-yia teased.

Daphne didn't even have the ability to fake a smile. She just kept looking into the fire, mesmerized by the smoldering embers. She felt drained.

In the few hours since their heated conversation, Daphne had played the scene over and over again in her head, her temples throbbing. But eventually something odd struck Daphne, something she'd never expected. At first she didn't realize it, but once she'd caught a glimmer, there was no escaping it. As hateful as Daphne thought Yianni's words were, she couldn't help but feel that she had caught a glimpse of concern under the heap of insults he had piled on her. No matter how misguided his accusations were, there was an underlying theme to them. There was no question; this fisherman seemed to care deeply for Yia-yia. Even though Daphne wanted to despise him, to hate him, to make him suffer for causing such chaos in the short time she had known him, she felt conflicted. How could she hate someone who loved and cared for Yia-yia so deeply?

Daphne turned and looked at her grandmother. Each line, each wrinkle and dark spot, on the old woman's face was awash in the soft amber light of the fire. Reaching out her hand, Daphne lifted Yia-yia's hand to her mouth. She kissed Yia-yia's rough knuckles before holding the old woman's hand against her own cheek.

Does she really think I've abandoned her? Does she really think I'm not there for her? Daphne felt her eyes well up again. She squeezed her eyelids shut, trying to stave off the tears that were certain to come again. Yia-yia studied her granddaughter's face for a moment as Daphne held her hand so tenderly. They both had so much they wanted to say, but for a little while longer, neither said a word. Finally, Daphne spoke.

"Yia-yia."

"*Ne*, Daphne *mou*?"

"Yia-yia. Are you lonely here?" The words spilled out of Daphne's mouth like the guts of a sacrificed lamb.

"Daphne, what do you mean?"

"Are you lonely here? I know it's been a while since I've visited, and with Mama and Baba gone . . ."

Yia-yia lifted her hand from Daphne's lap. With both hands now free, she raised them to straighten her scarf, untying and then retying the knot under her chin.

"I need to know," Daphne pleaded. "I know it's been a long time since I came to see you. But I was trying so hard to take care of everything. To make sure Evie and I, and you, would be all right."

"We are all right, *koukla mou*. We'll always be all right."

"I hate the thought of you here, by yourself, with so little, when we have so much back in New York."

"I am not alone. I am never alone. As long as I am here, in my home, surrounded by the sea, the wind, and the trees, I will always be surrounded by those who love me."

"But you are alone, Yia-yia. We've all gone. Isn't that why Mama and Baba left here, to make a better life for us all? It worked, Yia-yia. We finally have everything they hoped for us. I can finally give you and Evie the things Mama and Baba could only dream about giving me."

"What do you think Evie needs, Daphne? She's a little girl. Little girls need their imaginations and their mothers, nothing else. She needs your time. She needs you to whisper secrets with. She needs you to tell her stories, to kiss good night."

Daphne winced at the words. She couldn't remember the last time she had been home early enough to tuck Evie into her bed back home in New York. It had been weeks, months even.

Yia-yia looked away from Daphne for a moment. When she turned back, Daphne could see the fire's reflection in her grandmother's eyes.

"Nothing can replace a mother's love, Daphne. Nothing can replace a mother's time. Your own mother always knew that, even as she struggled to give you a new life." Yia-yia watched as Daphne squirmed in her seat, but it didn't deter the old woman from finishing what she had to say. "Did you see her tonight when she sat in your lap, purring like a small kitten? It's because you didn't push her away this time."

"I don't push my daughter away," Daphne protested, struggling not to raise her voice.

"Tonight when Evie sat in your lap, you didn't run off to take care of something else more important. You were still. Finally, you were still long enough for Evie to catch you, to hold you, and to feel you hold her back. For that sweet moment, Evie felt like she was the most important thing in your life. And for that moment, that child was happy."

Daphne felt the tingle in her eyes once more. *Damn it*. She had not seen Yia-yia in years, yet it was still true; Yia-yia could read Daphne with one glance.

"Daphne *mou*." Yia-yia spoke again. "I see how you go through the motions, but the life has gone out of you. Whittled away like your modern new nose. Beautiful, yes, but where is the character, the very thing that makes you different, special—alive? You've forgotten how to live, and even more so, you've forgotten why to live."

Daphne gazed into the fire. "Yia-yia . . . ," she said, speaking directly into the flames, "didn't you ever wish your life had turned out differently? How if you could change one moment, everything would have turned out so different . . ." The sound of her voice trailed off, "So much better . . ."

"Daphne *mou*," Yia-yia replied, "this is my life. No matter who is with me, who has been taken away from me or gone away in search of a better life, this is my life, the only one I have. This is the life that was written for me in countless coffee cups, decided for me in the heavens before I was born and then whispered about on the breeze as my mother gave birth to me, her screams mixing with the cypress whispers as I emerged from her womb. A person cannot change what has been whispered about, Daphne. A person cannot change her fate. And this is mine—just as you have yours."

There was nothing more for Daphne to say. She just sat there next to Yia-yia, watching as the last smoldering log collapsed on the ever-growing pile of ashes.

Thirteen

At five a.m., Daphne had enough. She had been staring at the cracks in the ceiling and reliving the fireside conversation with Yia-yia again and again in her mind. How was it possible that a woman who had never been educated, was technically illiterate, had never set foot outside Greece, and rarely even left her home had managed to read Daphne more thoroughly and precisely than the expensive therapist Daphne visited once a week back home?

Daphne thought that she had become a master of reinventing herself—successful entrepreneur, fiancée of a wealthy bank executive. It was what she wanted, what she thought would make her happy again. On paper, she was living the life so many others dreamed of and envied. But now, at one glance from Yia-yia, the cracks in her carefully cultivated foundation were beginning to show.

Daphne swung her legs over the side of the bed, careful not to awaken the irritable old bedsprings or Evie. She slipped her cardigan over her long white nightgown and crept across the room, reaching over to the bureau and grabbing her cell phone from the corner, where it sat blinking with the pulsating red reminder of unheard messages.

As soon as she opened the door, Daphne felt soothed by the island's early-morning symphony; the clear serenade of crickets, the rustling of the trees in the predawn air, and the distant rhythmic crash of the tide as it continued its predawn call to the fisherman. As she closed the door behind her, Daphne also closed her eyes and listened for a moment, knowing that the first rooster call would soon welcome daybreak.

The air was cooler than she had anticipated, so Daphne snatched Yia-yia's fringed woolen shawl from the back of the chair where Yia-yia had left it before going to bed. Stepping gingerly in her bare feet to avoid the many cracks and crevices of the pavement, Daphne shuffled across the patio and dialed Stephen's number on her cell phone. It was 11:00 p.m. in New York. She knew she would likely wake him; he often went to bed early and was up before dawn to get a jump on the overseas markets. But Daphne dialed anyway; she needed to hear his voice.

"Hello," he answered after five long rings.

"Hi. Did I wake you?" she asked, knowing full well that she had.

"Daphne? No, honey, its okay. I'm glad you called." Stephen let out a long, loud yawn into the phone. "I've been trying to reach you. I left you a message on your cell phone earlier today. We really need to do something about the phone situation there. The phone lines were down all day, and your cell phone service seems spotty at best. Can't you get the phone company out there to take a look, maybe replace those antiquated lines or something? I hate not being able to get hold of you, especially after you told me there's no police on this island of yours. Not exactly comforting knowing that, Daphne."

"We're fine. We've never had police stationed on the island. There's never been a need. But we finally have a doctor living here. That's progress." She laughed, knowing how utterly provincial this must sound to Stephen.

"Very funny, Daphne. Just look into the phone thing, please. For me."

"Oh, Stephen." Daphne tried her best to muffle her laugh. "Things don't work that way here. It would take weeks, months even, to get those guys out here." She gathered the fabric of her nightgown under her legs and sat on the stone wall. Shortly, with the sunrise's first light, she would have a perfect view of the beach and the port.

Daphne knew her answer would not sit well with Stephen, a man accustomed to making things happen. But life on this island was regulated by different rules and had a very different rhythm from that on the island of Manhattan. Everything here took longer. This was a place decades behind the rest of the world and even years behind the mainland of Corfu, a mere seven miles away. But to Daphne, that was the beauty of the island.

"Well, see what you can do anyway."

"Yes, I'll see what I can do." Daphne knew full well that for Stephen, "fixing it" meant paying someone to make the problem go away.

"Oh, hey, Stephen. What was the mystery message, anyway?" she asked.

"I wrapped things up at work and managed to book an earlier flight. I get in to Corfu at two p.m. on Tuesday. I can't wait to see you. I miss you."

"I miss you too. And that's great news!" Daphne shouted as she jumped up from the wall, momentarily forgetting that it wasn't quite six in the morning yet, and that most of the island was still asleep.

"My family is still coming next week, but I wanted to get in as soon as I could. I can't stand being away from you this long. I want to help you, to make sure everything is just as you dreamed it would be. I want you to be happy."

"It will be. I know it will." She took a deep breath, allowing the dawn's mist to fill her lungs. "I'll see you at the airport. I love you," Daphne said as she hung up the phone. She put it down on the wall as she looked out toward the beach below.

Stephen was coming on Tuesday. It really was happening. They really were going to get married. There was still so much left to do, but for some reason, Daphne wasn't at all stressed out by her massive to-do list the way she had been back at home. Maybe it was the clean sea air, or maybe it was the comfort of having Yia-yia so close by, or maybe it was the fact that perfection was not a requirement here, the way it was back at home. Here, imperfection was expected, celebrated. As much as Daphne wanted everything about the wedding to be just right, she didn't feel nearly as uptight about everything as she had just a few days before. I'll stop by and see Thea Nitsa later this morning to work out all the final details, she thought, taking a deep breath and stretching her arms out above her head. A loud yawn escaped her mouth, and she felt her eyelids flutter with the weight of her restless night.

She stretched, looking out to where the sea meets the sky, and watched as the first hint of light poked through the darkness, highlighting the sea's surface with broad metallic brushstrokes. Where she stood on the patio, just under the largest olive tree on the property, she knew she would have the best view of the awakening port and beach below. That was the thing about Yia-yia's modest little house. Many of the other homes on the island were larger and far more modern, with their new appliances, perfect terra-cotta roofs, and colorful new exteriors, but none of them could boast a perfect, unobstructed view of the port like the one from Yia-yia's terrace. Yia-yia had always joked that for a poor woman, she owned a priceless view. As Daphne stood under the olive tree, predawn shadows turning into a colorful sunlit landscape before her eyes, she realized Yia-yia was right.

As the first light began to infiltrate the darkness, Daphne looked down on what seemed like a scene from a Hollywood zombie movie. There below, on every crudely paved road and dirt path that led to the port, the sun revealed the silhouettes of fishermen embarking on their morning ritual. Some were old, their bodies hunched over from years of hard living, hauling their heavy nets morning and night. Others, still young, strong, and upright, virtually sprinted toward the port. A few of the men walked with reams of nets slung over their shoulders, no doubt having spent the better part of their evening crouched over the thick twine, mending them by the fire as they smoked cigarettes and drank licorice-scented ouzo while their wives prepared dinner. Young or old, tired or energized, each of the men made his way toward the port in the dim light, preparing to climb aboard his fishing boat and wondering what that morning's nets might reveal.

Daphne was so busy watching the fishermen below that she didn't hear Yia-yia, who had made her way outside to begin the day's chores.

"*Ella*, Daphne *mou*," Yia-yia called from the other side of the patio. "*Koukla mou*, I didn't expect you to be up so early."

"Neither did I, Yia-yia, but I couldn't sleep." Daphne turned her back on the port and walked toward Yia-yia, who was already dressed and bent over the outdoor stove, lighting the first fire of the day.

"Ah, wedding nerves." Yia-yia chuckled as she piled several slim twigs under a large log. Reaching over to the pile of old yellowed newspapers that she kept in a basket beside the fire, she shoved them into the pile as well, struck a long wooden match along the worn black strip of a matchbox, and leaned in to set the kindling ablaze.

"Yes, I guess it is wedding nerves." Daphne smiled at Yia-yia as she removed the black shawl from her own shoulders and wrapped it around Yia-yia. The old woman's lined face exploded into a broad, thankful smile.

"Yia-yia—" Daphne watched her grandmother reach for the small copper *briki*, sugar, coffee, and bottled water.

"*Ne*, Daphne *mou*." Yia-yia scooped out a spoonful of dark coffee grounds and stirred them into the small, shiny pot.

"Yia-yia, how do you know Yianni? How is it that I don't remember him at all? I know everyone on this island."

"*Ne, koukla*. There are not many of us left. Of course you know everyone here. But Yianni, ah, Yianni . . ." Yia-yia sighed as she gazed into the fire. "No, Daphne *mou*. You didn't know his family. But I did. I knew his *yia-yia* and his mama." Yia-yia added just a little sugar to the *briki* and stirred before placing it on a metal cooking grate over the open flame.

"But why didn't I ever meet them?" Daphne asked, bringing her knees to her chest under the gauzelike material of her nightgown, her red toenails dangling over the edge of her chair.

"Ah, Daphne *mou*, Yianni's family left here a long time ago. Yianni grew up in Athena, not here. That's why you don't remember him." Yia-yia snatched the bubbling coffee from the *briki* just as the boiling foam rose to the top of the pot and threatened to spill over the sides.

"Yianni never set foot on the island until a few years ago. He didn't spend his childhood here, like you did. But he loves this place as much as you do. As much as any of us." Yia-yia poured the thick coffee into two demitasse cups and handed one to Daphne.

"He's an educated man, Daphne, not a fisherman by birth like the other men on the island. He went to the best schools, went to college . . . just like you. But the island called to him."

Daphne lifted her cup to her lips and watched as Yia-yia held hers, the small cup cradled in her hands, warming her bent fingers.

"He came and found me that very first day. As soon as he set foot on the island, this was the first place he came. His *yia-yia* had told him stories about us, how we were wonderful friends a long, long time ago. He walked in through the gate that first day, and we sat down together and I made him *kafe* and we drank it together, just as we are doing now. When he was finished, I asked him for his cup. I looked inside, and I saw the heavy black sorrow that weighed him down. But then I turned the cup and saw his heart. It was pure and clean—unlike the hearts of so many men whose cups I have gazed into.

"And I saw something else that day, something I never expected," Yia-yia continued. "I saw his heart and his mind, each pictured clear as day. Each of them at the end of a bold, straight line that met in one place. This place. I looked into his cup, and then I told him that this was where his search ended. That this was where his heart and mind would finally join as one."

"Do you see him often—Yianni, I mean?" Daphne asked, twirling the coffee in her cup. "Yesterday at lunch, he told me he comes here and spends a lot of time with you, that he brings you fish. Does he?"

"Yes, Daphne. He does. He comes almost every day to see if he can help me, or if there is anything I need. But every day I tell him, just as I tell you, there is nothing I need. So he sits here with me, and we talk. We talk about the old times with his *yia-yia*, his life in Athens, all of the wonderful things he studied at university. And many nights, we talk about you."

Daphne shifted in her seat, uncomfortable with the thought that Yianni sat here, in her own chair no doubt, and spent evenings listening to Yia-yia talk about her. "What do you tell him about me?" she couldn't help but ask.

"Ahh, I tell him all of the incredible things you are doing in New York," Yia-yia said, her face glowing with pride. "I show him your pictures; I tell him about Koukla and how proud I am that you have managed to turn our simple recipes and traditions into a big business."

Daphne shifted again in her seat.

"We talk about things that others don't seem to understand,"

Yia-yia continued. "We talk about things others don't want to know about or believe, but Yianni does. He understands them, Daphne, he believes in them. I have shared with him the story of the cypress whispers, and how the island speaks to me and shares with me her secrets."

"And what does he say?"

"Even if he can't hear them, he understands. He knows that ours is a magical island, my love. He knows that he too is connected to this place, that the island never forgets those who love her."

Daphne was growing impatient. She usually loved hearing Yia-yia's stories of the magical and mysterious ways of the island, but this time she needed facts, not fantasy. "But I don't understand. If he is so wonderful, so caring—why has he been so horribly rude to me?"

Yia-yia smiled just a bit, just enough to show a glimmer of her silver eyetooth, a remnant of a trip to a mainland dentist many years ago. "I know, *koukla*. Perhaps he was a little too hard on you," she admitted, unsuccessfully attempting to stifle a small giggle that escaped like a tiny air bubble into the morning mist.

"A little? Did you hear what he said?"

"Daphne, I know, but you have to understand. I think Yianni misunderstands sometimes. He has become very protective of me. He knows how I have missed you, so he is angry that you have not come sooner."

"But Yia-yia, that is between you and me, not for some strange man to discuss. And besides, you know he's wrong, really wrong—" Daphne practically sprang from her seat.

"I know everything, Daphne," Yia-yia reassured her. "I may

not have telephones and computers, but I learn things even without those modern gadgets. I understand more than you think." Yia-yia looked past Daphne to the silvery olive trees and the cypresses that dotted the landscape as far as the eye could see.

"Before he left Athens, Yianni's grandmother made him promise that he would come find me here, in the place that saved us both, even when we were both beyond salvation. His *yia-yia* and I helped each other, Daphne, when the war made things here very difficult, more difficult than you could imagine. By the laws of man, neither of us should have survived. We would sit here night after night asking each other the same question: Why were we chosen? Why had we been saved?" As she spoke, Yia-yia's red eyes glazed over. But just as she had snatched the *briki* from the brink of boiling over, she controlled her emotions.

"Sometimes the laws of man do not apply, Daphne *mou*. Sometimes there are greater laws and powers at work. Yianni made a promise to come here and honor his grandmother's memory, her dying wish. He never expected that promise to change his life the way it did. But it did. He learned quickly what a special place we have been blessed with, Daphne, how our island changes us all. And if he is hard on you, I think it's because he can't understand why you have chosen to stay away. But I do." Yia-yia reached out and patted Daphne's knee.

"*Entaksi, koukla mou.* Talk to him. You'll see. You are not so different, you two. You have much in common." As she finished speaking, Yia-yia glanced up at the morning sun. From its position just over the mountain peak beyond the port, she could tell that it was already past seven—midmorning, by Yia-yia's standards.

"It's late already. You must be hungry." She clapped her hands several times, signaling that their cozy heart-to-heart was about to come to an abrupt end. "Sit, I'll get us something to eat." In an instant, Yia-yia was up and hurrying toward the kitchen.

Daphne took her feet down off the chair and placed them on the cool concrete. She reached across the table and grabbed the *briki*, only to find that she had already drained it of its last drop of coffee.

"Ah, this is more like it. How are we expected to get our work done if we have no energy?" Yia-yia returned from the kitchen, carrying a large tray loaded down with the makings of their breakfast.

Daphne leaned in to get a better look as Yia-yia strained to place the heavy tray on the table. There on the platter Yia-yia had assembled all of Daphne's favorites; olives, cheese, crusty bread, salami, and crumbly sesame halva, dotted with almonds. Unlike other cultures that view breakfast as a time for sweet, sticky breads and jams, Greeks prefer their breakfast simple and salty.

"Yia-yia, I can never find olives as juicy as these back in New York," Daphne said as she picked up a perfect specimen and tossed it in her mouth. Her teeth pressed down on the protective skin, breaking through to the soft, juicy flesh with an explosion of juice, vinegar, and salt that felt like a Mediterranean sunburst in her mouth. Daphne closed her eyes and swallowed. She could feel the briny bits sliding down her throat. She wished she could develop taste buds down her gullet and into her stomach, just to prolong the multilayered sensory experience of each perfect olive.

"*Ne*, I know. Some things you cannot buy, *koukla mou*. Our old tree and barrel serve us well." Yia-yia gestured around them to the canopy of olive trees that sheltered the property. It was a yearly ritual for Yia-yia to harvest the olives and brine them in the tremendous barrel that sat in the kitchen.

Daphne devoured several more of Yia-yia's olives, watching as the old woman sliced several paper-thin pieces of *kasseri* cheese and placed them in a small, shallow baking pan. Yia-yia put the pan directly on top of the smoldering embers and scurried to the other side of the patio, where she plucked a huge, round lemon from the lemon tree. Daphne kept her eyes fixed on the cheese-filled pan, watching as the sturdy edges of the thin sheets gradually wilted and melted together to form a golden mass of melted ambrosia.

Seated once again by the fire with her prized lemon on the table beside her, Yia-yia kept watch until the bubbles turned a deep, golden brown, forming a thin crispy crust that hid the delicious ooze underneath. Gathering the hem of her apron in her hand, Yia-yia removed the pan from the heat. With her sharp paring knife, she sliced through the giant lemon and, using both hands to squeeze, doused the still-bubbling cheese with a spray of lemon juice.

"Mmmm," Daphne moaned as she ripped off a generous helping of bread and dipped the crust into the melted *kasseri*. "It's been so long since I've had *saganaki*. I almost forgot how much I love this."

"What do you mean? You love *saganaki*, why don't you eat it?" Yia-yia asked.

"Remember—it's white. Well, off-white. I told you about that diet I went on."

"*Ne*, so silly, these diets. Foods are flavors, Daphne, not colors," Yia-yia chided.

"Oh, Yia-yia, I almost forgot. I spoke to Stephen this morning."

"I know, *koukla mou*, he's coming. I will finally get to meet this man."

"But how do you know that?" Daphne dredged another piece of bread through the *saganaki*. "I just hung up with him."

"I told you, *koukla mou*. The island shares her secrets with me."

Daphne shook her head. It was always this way with Yia-yia; somehow she always seemed to know things before they happened. As a teenager Daphne had begun to wonder if Yia-yia was more than just an intuitive old woman adept at reading coffee cups.

"I'm going to go meet him at the airport in Corfu. It's just for a day, so Evie can stay here—she'll be happier here with you."

"*Entaksi*. Fine."

"What time does Big Al come? Is it today or tomorrow morning?" Daphne asked as she looked out over the water and put her plate down on the table.

"There is no more Alexandros until Wednesday. It just came last night. It does not run every day."

Daphne wiped her mouth with the back of her hand. "I guess I can take the *kaiki*."

"Stamati went to Athens for his niece's wedding. There's no *kaiki*."

Daphne looked out over the sea, as if miraculously her ride might appear on the horizon. "What am I supposed to do?" She turned to Yia-yia once more.

"Yianni."

Daphne flinched. "Yianni? Isn't there anyone else?"

"There's no one else, Daphne. Just Yianni," Yia-yia repeated. "We'll ask him to take you. His boat is fixed now. I'm sure he'll do it."

Daphne stared out across the horizon once again, but she could see nothing but sea and sky. There was no boat emerging in the distance, no ferry or *kaiki* miraculously appearing to save her from the dreaded thought of being stuck on Yianni's boat for the two-hour trip to Kerkyra. Daphne knew she had no choice.

"All right." Daphne inhaled. "Yianni."

It was like an emotional flashback. For the first time in years, Daphne felt as if she were once again stuck in the back booth of her parents' diner on a sunny Saturday afternoon or crouched down, hiding and humiliated in the back seat of the Buick, as her parents scoured the off-ramp to the Bronx River Parkway for dandelion greens that they would pluck from the ground and take home to boil for dinner. Even now, as a grown woman so many years later, she once again felt trapped, as if there were nothing she could do to escape.

Fourteen

It was 10:00 a.m. before Evie emerged from her sleep, announcing that she had dreamed of challenging Arachne to a weaving contest. For a five-year-old American child used to waking at 7:00 a.m. for school, Evie had seamlessly adjusted to her new Greek island schedule of sleeping late and staying up past midnight with the adults. After breakfast, the mother and daughter raced down the stone steps to catch Nitsa before she was bogged down with lunchtime orders at the hotel's restaurant.

"Why are you taking that?" Evie asked as Daphne grabbed the long bamboo stick that was propped against the stone wall at the bottom of the stairs.

As they walked, with each step, Daphne tapped the side of the unpaved road just where the loosely packed dirt met the brush. *Tap tap tap tap*, side to side she wielded the bamboo stick in the oppressive heat as the cicada choir filled the air.

"It's for the snakes," Daphne answered as she held Evie's hand, swinging it back and forth as they walked.

"Snakes?" Evie shrieked. She clutched Daphne's leg.

"Yes, snakes."

"Mommy, that's not funny, and it's not nice!" Evie shrieked, her giant eyes opening wide.

"Don't worry, honey, the snakes hear the tapping and get scared away. They won't come out as long as they hear the noise."

But Daphne's assurance wasn't enough for Evie. The little girl was terrified and didn't stop moaning and shaking until Daphne reluctantly hoisted Evie up on her back. With Evie clinging to her, Daphne continued tap-tap-tapping her bamboo stick along the dirt road as she walked.

They hadn't rounded the corner of the Hotel Nitsa sign before Daphne heard her booming voice echo off the freshly washed marble floor. "There she is . . . the beautiful bride. *Ella*, Daphne. *Ella*, give your Thea Nitsa a hug."

Nitsa waddled right up to them the moment they crossed the threshold of the hotel's lobby. With her long black skirt, black cotton T-shirt, and plastic *sayonares*, the seventy-eight-year-old moved faster than anyone would have imagined possible for an overweight woman with asthma, diabetes, and arthritic knees—who also happened to suck down two packs of Camel Lights a day.

Daphne always felt there was something special about Thea Nitsa. When her husband suffered a heart attack and there was no hospital or doctor on the island to save him—by the time Nitsa could summon help and their *kaiki* finally made it across the sea to Kerkyra, he was already dead—she had been left a widow at the tender age of twenty-three.

But as with everything else in life, Nitsa had faced her fate head-on, and always on her terms. Yes, she wore black day in and day out, as was the island's tradition for widows. But unlike the others,

Nitsa never covered her hair with a scarf. And although she had never remarried, or even looked at another man, Nitsa didn't sit home solemnly by the fire, waiting to be reunited with her dead husband in the afterlife. On any given night, when her work in the hotel was done, you could find Nitsa sitting at the hotel bar smoking her Camel Lights and knocking back Metaxa brandy with her clients.

Unlike the other widows, who could always rely on family to provide for them, Nitsa was childless. Too stubborn and proud to ask for handouts, Nitsa had taken her husband's life savings and bought the hotel at a time when it was unheard of for a woman to run a business on her own. But Nitsa had nurtured and raised the hotel to prosperity just as she would have raised children, if God had blessed her with them. For the longest time she ran the hotel singlehandedly, doing all the cooking, cleaning, and anything else that needed to be done. She had slowed down these past few years, her advancing age and declining health finally making her realize that she could no longer do it all on her own. But despite the addition of a young staff, Nitsa still insisted on doing all the cooking and serving of food herself. The hotel was more than Nitsa's business, it was her home, and she viewed each and every diner as her personal dinner guest.

"Thea Nitsa. It's so good to see you." Daphne leaned in for a kiss, first on Nitsa's left, then on her right cheek. Her fat, sun-tanned cheeks were dewy with perspiration, but Daphne resisted the temptation to wipe Nitsa's sweat off her own skin.

"*Ahooo . . . kita etho,*" Nitsa shouted in Greek as she gazed at Evie, still perched on her mother's back. Then, noticing Evie's blank stare and realizing that the little girl could not understand her, Nitsa switched effortlessly to English. "Look who we have here."

This was yet another way in which she differed from the other women on the island. Most of the other elderly women simply refused to learn English. They knew that by forcing their grandchildren to communicate in Greek, they would keep their language alive, clinging to their most prized and valuable possession— their heritage.

"Ah, Evie . . . little Evie, I have heard much about you, little one." Nitsa rubbed her hands together as if the friction of her calluses might start a fire. "*Ahooo*, let me see you. Like a Greek goddess, like Aphrodite . . . I tell you . . . ah, but with the nose of the *Amerikanos*." Nitsa laughed. "This is a good thing, *koukla mou*," she added with a knowing wink.

"Mommy . . ." Evie's voice trembled. "Mommy, am I going to be in trouble?" she whispered into Daphne's ear, wrapping her legs around Daphne's waist and holding her little arms tighter around her mother's neck.

"Honey—" Daphne pried Evie's hands from her throat. "Evie, honey. Why would you be in trouble? You haven't done anything, have you?"

"No," Evie whispered as she shook her head. "No, I haven't." Evie lifted her trembling finger and pointed it at Nitsa. "But she said I look like Aphrodite. Is that going to make Aphrodite mad? Is she going to turn me into a spider too?"

"No, honey. Not at all." Daphne did her best to stifle her laugh, thankful that she was somehow able to swallow at least most of it.

But Nitsa was not as adept at these things. Nitsa was used to a life lived out loud, on her terms and with no one to answer to but

God himself—the same God whom she worshipped down on her
fleshy knees at dawn every single day instead of hauling herself to
church and lighting a candle along with the other widows who
preferred to pray in public, placing their virtue on display for all to
admire. Nitsa deemed Evie's answer utterly adorable and thereby
worthy of a glorious, guttural belly laugh.

"*Ahooo*, you have been listening to your great-grandmother's
stories." Nitsa's entire body convulsed with laughter. Every bit of
her ample flesh—from her thick ruddy cheeks to her trunklike
calves to her droopy braless breasts, which hung down and
touched the top of her enormous gut—shook and jiggled as she
laughed.

"*Ella, koukla*." Thea Nitsa reached her dimpled arm out to Evie.
"Just to be safe, to make sure that you are protected from Aphrodite and anyone else who may be jealous of your beauty, I have
something for you. Ella, Thea Nitsa will protect you. We have
enough spiders on the island already; what we need are little girls
like you."

Evie hesitated.

"It's okay, Evie," Daphne assured. "Go ahead."

The little girl placed her delicate hand in Thea Nitsa's grip.
Daphne watched as they walked hand in hand to the bar area.
Nitsa hoisted Evie up on a stool and disappeared behind the bar,
opening and closing drawer after drawer as she searched for this
"very special thing."

"I know it was in here. Where did I put it?" Nitsa mumbled as
she continued to look in every drawer and crevice behind the towering wooden bar. "Ahhh, *nato*, here it is," she exclaimed, victori-
ous, as she pulled out a long, delicate chain.

Evie squirmed in her seat to get a better look.

"Here, put this on, and you will be safe," Thea Nitsa said as she clasped the chain around Evie's neck.

Evie looked down at her chest. There, attached to the delicate chain and lying just against her heart, was a small blue glass eye. She lifted it with her fingers to get a better look.

"*To mati*," Nitsa said. "The eye. It will protect you from the evil eye. *Ftoo, ftoo, ftoo*." Nitsa spit at Evie three times.

Evie flinched. She had actually started to grow fond of Thea Nitsa, but that was before she started spitting.

"It's okay, Evie." Daphne laughed. "Thea Nitsa is making sure that you'll be safe. The eye protects you from evil spirits and wishes. I had one of these pinned to your crib when you were a baby."

Evie looked closer at the eye, a wide smile spreading across her face. "Good. I don't want to be a spider. I want to stay a little girl."

"Well, good. Because I want you to stay a little girl, my little girl." Daphne scooped Evie up and off the bar stool. It felt good to see Evie's broad smile, to feel her arms tighten around Daphne's neck.

Reluctantly, Daphne pried the tiny fingers off her. "Now, Mommy and Thea Nitsa have some things to talk about—"

"*Ne*, Evie. My cat, Katerina, has new kittens; they are out on the patio. Do you want to see?" Nitsa motioned toward the patio.

Nitsa had found the magic words. Evie skipped out to the flower-covered patio, anxious to see the new kittens for herself.

"Bravo, Daphne *mou*." Nitsa clapped her hands together. "Now, what would you like to eat? Maybe some *yemista*—I remember how you love my stuffed peppers. I made them this morning with lots of raisins and mint, just the way you like it . . . *thelis ligo*, do you want some?"

Nitsa didn't wait for Daphne's response. She sprang up and disappeared into the kitchen, returning with a large plate filled with *yemista* before Daphne even had a chance to answer.

"Thank you, Thea." Daphne dug her fork into the green pepper. The taste was exquisite; light, fresh, and fragrant—just the way Daphne remembered it.

They spent the better part of the morning planning the menu. The women agreed that sticking with local delicacies and traditional fare would be the perfect way to celebrate the wedding feast. They decided on a variety of freshly caught local grilled fish embellished with nothing more than lemon, olive oil, oregano, and sea salt. Daphne did, however, insist that after displaying the fish whole, Nitsa would debone them tableside. She knew Stephen's family wouldn't know the first thing about filleting a fish and were liable to choke on a mouthful of fish bones if they even tried. The rest of the menu was just as superb in its simplicity. Besides the fish, Nitsa would also make endless platters of appetizers, cheeses, and dips. Once their business was done, Nitsa dove into the other business she was equally famous for—gossiping.

"Daphne, I tell you. That Sophia is something else."

Daphne clearly remembered Sophia, and she could not believe what she was hearing. When they were children Daphne had always felt bad for Sophia, who lived on the island year-round with her family. Sophia was stuck here, knowing she would never see the world, get a proper education, or marry anyone other than a local boy her parents determined to be an acceptable match. And indeed they had, marrying her off to a boy from the other side of the island when she was just sixteen years old.

"You should see her. She's not sitting home alone, waiting for her husband to return from America. Ha, it is the ones who play the innocent who are the guiltiest." Nitsa leaned in, legs apart, elbows on her knees, and lit another Camel Light, eager to share her thoughts on Sophia, who according to Nitsa, had turned into the island's resident *poutana*.

Nitsa took another long, deep drag and looked around to make sure no one was nearby to hear them. "And trust me, Sophia has not been lonely while her husband is in America working in the diners to make enough money to send for her. In the old days, when the men went away, it was they who would cheat. Now look how modern we are—the women cheat as well."

Nitsa slapped her knee and emitted yet another guttural laugh. She lit another Camel Light, the ashtray already overflowing with the cigarettes she had smoked just in the past hour with Daphne.

"Nitsa—" Daphne smiled, realizing that Nitsa might actually be able to shed some light on the mystery of Yianni. Daphne didn't feel that her prying was actual gossiping—she preferred to think of it as research. After all, she would be placing her life in his hands tomorrow morning on the trip to Kerkyra.

"Thea Nitsa—"

"*Ne*, Daphne."

"Thea, what about this Yianni . . . the fisherman? What do you know about him?"

"Ah, Yianni. Yes, for a man who did not grow up on the sea, he has become quite a magician with his nets. Daphne, I tell you, his catch is always the best of the day. I have become his best customer." Nitsa nodded as she scratched the inside of her thigh, cigarette dangling dangerously close to the fabric of her skirt.

"Yes, but what do you know about him? He seems to spend an awful lot of time with Yia-yia. We know he fishes, but what else does he do? He has no family here. He's not married. Does he have any friends?"

"Never." Nitsa shook her head. "I never see him with friends, just your *yia-yia*, of course. He is something of a mystery, Daphne *mou*. I remember his *yia-yia* from many years ago, but she was something of a mystery as well. She showed up here during the war with her daughters, but no husband. There were stories about her, you know. At first people said that her arrival was a bad omen; that your *yia-yia* never should have taken in more mouths to feed when our own people were starving. But your *yia-yia* wouldn't hear of it." Nitsa leaned in closer to Daphne and raised her right eyebrow. "Some say that a miracle happened here on the island during that time."

"A miracle?" Daphne asked. She had heard of miracles attributed to Saint Spyridon back on Corfu, but she had never heard of any here, on Erikousa.

"Yes, a miracle, Daphne *mou*." Nitsa bowed her head. She made the sign of the cross three times and dug her crucifix out from between her breasts, kissing it before continuing with her story.

"All around us, on Kerkyra and on the mainland, people were murdered, starved, and tortured. But not here. Here, no one was killed. The German soldiers were vicious, evil, I tell you, Daphne. They massacred many innocent people on Corfu. But none here." She nodded slowly, deliberately.

"Everyone expected the worst, but your *yia-yia*, she knew. She had faith. Even when others feared that there would not be enough food, that the soldiers would turn violent, or that in desperate times we would turn against each other—she knew better. Even when everyone on the island was panicked, she remained calm and insisted we would be rewarded for our acts of kindness, for helping each other as well as the young mother who came to live among us. And she was right. Your *yia-yia* knew, just like she always does."

"She never really talked to me about the war."

"They were difficult times, Daphne *mou*. Times best left forgotten, left in the past. We all have deep scars from that time. And as it is with scars, it is often best not to pick and prod at our wounds, but to try and forget they are there. We pray that somehow, eventually, over time we will heal. There is always a reminder, a permanent mark on our skin, on our soul—maybe they will fade with time, but they will never truly disappear—but sometimes it is best to try and pretend they do."

Nitsa slapped at the ashes that had dropped on her skirt. "*Ella*, you were asking me about Yianni, and I went on and on about old times and old women. Just like an old woman, eh? What did you want to know about Yianni?"

"Why is he here? I mean, if his family left after the war, why did he come back?"

"My girl, I have asked myself the same thing. He is an educated man. So what he's doing here, among the fishermen and the old women? I do not really know. But I do know that he never goes to church." Nitsa laughed as she picked a piece of tobacco from her tongue.

"No friends?"

"None. Just his nets and his books. That is all."

"His books?"

"Yes—when he is not working on his boat, he can be found here, at the bar." Nitsa motioned toward the bar area. "He comes in—sometimes it's frappe, sometimes brandy, but no matter what the drink, there is always a book. He inhales those books the way I do these." She laughed as she lit yet another cigarette.

"But there is one thing, Daphne," she continued. "A few weeks ago he was here, sitting at the end of the bar, with his brandy and a book." She laughed as she waved her lit cigarette in the air, leaving a series of smoke rings in its wake. "It was late, very late, and everyone had had a lot to drink, even me. I was a little drunk," she admitted with a chuckle, shrugging.

"I left to go to bed. But I forgot my glasses, and as I came down the stairs a few minutes later to get them, I saw Yianni with his arms around Sophia. He was holding her very, very tight. He stood holding her for a moment, and then he put his arm around her waist and she buried her neck in his shoulder and they walked out into the night together. So while I don't know if you could call them friends"—Nitsa chortled—"I think Yianni did more than read his book that night."

So Yianni's not as wonderful as Yia-yia would like to believe, Daphne thought to herself. There's nothing different or special about him at all. She sighed.

She didn't quite understand it; as of this morning she'd had nothing but contempt for the man. But now, sitting here as Nitsa divulged this rare glimpse into Yianni's true character, Daphne was surprised to realize that she actually felt somewhat disappointed. But in what exactly, she wasn't so sure. Was she disappointed in Yianni, for being the kind of man who would bed a married woman? In Yia-yia, for so blindly having faith in this man who suddenly turned up on her door with nothing but a name and a story from long ago? Or was it in herself, for momentarily wavering, questioning the very strong and very negative first impression she had of the man?

"Daphne, come tonight for dinner." Nitsa stabbed her cigarette into the overflowing ashtray. "Come, as my guest. I want to give you a gift, a beautiful dinner with your family before your *Amerikanos* arrives." She rose from her seat and headed toward the kitchen.

"That would be wonderful, Thea. Let me just ask Yia-yia—"

"There is nothing to ask. I will call her for you." And with that, Thea Nitsa exited the hotel. She stood on the small marble stoop, cupped her hands around her mouth like a megaphone, and literally called Yia-yia across the island.

"Evan-ge-liaaaaa. Evan-ge-liaaa!" she shouted.

It took a few seconds, but the reply came loud and clear from above the olive trees. "*Ne?*"

"Evangelia, *ella* . . . You and Daphne will come to the hotel for dinner tonight, all right?"

"*Ne, entaksi.*"

"There, it is done." Thea Nitsa wiped her hands on her apron as she came back inside the hotel. "Ten o'clock, eh. This is Greece, we eat at civilized hours, not like your Americans who eat so early."

And with that, Nitsa was off to begin her lunch shift, mumbling the entire way as she did. "Eating dinner at five o'clock, what's wrong with those Americans?" She shook her head. "So uncivilized," she mumbled, leaning down, cigarette dangling from her fingers as she scratched at her inner thigh before disappearing into the kitchen.

Fifteen

ERIKOUSA

1999

The drying bundles of oregano hung on every surface, from every rafter of the root cellar. Wrapped in clusters of a dozen or so sprigs, the drying herbs peppered the air with their pungent scent. Daphne felt a tickle in her nose each time she reached up on her toes to pull down one of the fragrant packages. One by one she pulled them from the ceiling and tossed them into the giant white sheet she had laid on the floor.

Just two weeks ago, soon after Daphne arrived in Greece, Yia-yia had packed a lunch of cold *patatopita* and they had spent the day side by side on the mountain picking the wild oregano. Now Yia-yia had deemed the oregano sufficiently dried and ready for shredding.

"Daphne, *etho*. Bring them here. I'm ready," Yia-yia called out from the patio.

With folded towels placed under their knees to protect them from the hard patio below, Daphne and Yia-yia knelt side by side on a second clean white bedsheet. One by one, they placed each bundle on the mesh metal shredder. They rubbed their hands across the drum and watched as the dried tiny leaves fell to the sheet below like a fragrant rainfall.

The entire ritual took the better part of the morning, taking Daphne away from her customary solitary swim in the cove. But Daphne didn't mind one bit. She was in heaven right here, down on her knees, up to her elbows in dried oregano, and singing along with her pink radio, which blared Greek music from the kitchen.

"Daphne *mou*." Yia-yia shook her head as she watched Daphne sing along with yet another old, melodramatic love song. "Sometimes I think you were born in the wrong time. You, so modern and American, yet you're drawn to that drama as if you were a lonely old woman reflecting back on her life, or perhaps an ancient longingly watching the sea for her love to return. These are songs for lonely old women, not beautiful young girls."

"Did you do that, Yia-yia?" Daphne reached her hand out and placed it on Yia-yia's shoulder. She could feel her bones beneath the fabric. "Did you sit here and watch the sea for Papou to return?" Yia-yia rarely spoke of Papou, Daphne's grandfather, who had disappeared during the war. He had kissed his wife and infant daughter good-bye one morning and boarded a *kaiki* with eight other men. The plan was for them to pool their money and go to Kerkyra to buy enough supplies to last the winter. But Papou never did make it to Kerkyra. His boat was never found. Papou and the seven other men onboard were never heard from again.

"Ahhh, Daphne." Yia-yia sighed. It was a deep mournful sigh that Daphne thought might lead to a lament song, but it did not. "I did," she confirmed as she continued to sift through the oregano, shredding the leaves as she stared out toward the faraway horizon.

"I sat here, under the big olive tree, day in and day out, and I watched and waited. First there was hope, hope that he would return. I sat here with your mother at my breast, gazing out to the sea like Aegeus searching for Theseus's white sail. But no sail emerged from the horizon. No black sail, no white sail. Nothing. And unlike Aegeus, I could not throw myself into the sea below as I dreamed of doing so many times. I was a mother. And then, it seemed, a widow as well."

Yia-yia lifted her fingers to straighten her scarf and once again turned her full attention to the oregano. Now, as always, there was work to be done, tasks to be completed, preparations to make for the harsh winter ahead. Now, just as back then, there was no time for mourning the past, for what had happened and what might have been. Now, just as back then, self-pity was unwelcome here. They finished bottling the last of the oregano in silence, Yia-yia's fingers tightening the lids with no hint of the chronic arthritic pain that permeated each of her joints.

It had only been a few months since that day in the lecture hall when she first locked eyes with Alex. It had been merely weeks since their hand-holding and kissing were no longer enough, and she finally agreed to go back to the dorm with him, to lie with him in his twin bed and make love until the sun set and it was time to return home. Now that she knew what it was like to lie next to

him, twirling her fingers in his hair as he slept, she ached to think
of what it must have been like for Yia-yia, reaching her hand out in
the bed and finding no one, nothing but emptiness.

That day, under the olive tree, as her nose twitched from oregano dust, Daphne's heart broke for the first time. It broke not because of a boy. She was falling in love with Alex, and falling
hard—the only pain she felt right now was the reality of their sep-
aration.

That morning under the olive tree, Daphne's heart broke because she finally recognized that when Papou failed to come back,
Yia-yia had lost not only her husband but any chance of a better
life. Unlike the stories of brave Odysseus and stoic and patient Penelope that Yia-yia loved to repeat over and over again, there was
no epic myth or legend to be found in what had happened to Yia-
yia. When Papou was lost, her future prospects turned as dark as
the black uniform she was bound to wear for the rest of her life.

In that moment, Daphne made a promise to herself. She would
make it right somehow. She would make it easier for Yia-yia. She
vowed that she would finish her education, get a job, and work her
fingers to the bone to provide for Yia-yia. She would do what Papou never had the chance to do, and what her own mother was
desperately trying to do—working all the while against the harsh
realities of immigrant life.

After the assorted jars and bottles were safely stored in the
kitchen, Yia-yia prepared a simple lunch of broiled octopus and
salad. While they had been preparing the oregano, the octopus
had been simmering in a pot filled with beer, water, salt, and two
whole lemons. After several jabs with her serving fork, Yia-yia
finally deemed the octopus sufficiently tenderized. She slathered

it with olive oil and sea salt before placing it on the outdoor grill to char.

"Daphne *mou*, do you remember the story of Iphigenia?" Yia-yia began as she removed the octopus from the fire.

"Yes, I love Iphigenia, that poor girl. Can you imagine a father doing that to his own daughter? Tell it to me again, Yia-yia."

"Ah, *entaksi, koukla mou*. Iphigenia." Yia-yia removed her plate from her lap, placed it on the table, and wiped her mouth with the hem of her white apron. The old woman once again recited the tale of the tragic young girl whose father, King Agamemnon, sacrificed her to the gods in order to make the winds blow so his men could go off to battle. The king had lied to his wife and daughter, telling them the young princess was to be married to Achilles. Only when the bridal procession reached the altar did the young girl realize she was not to be married, but sacrificed instead.

Daphne shuddered as Yia-yia finished her story. Although it was another oppressively hot day, her flesh erupted in goose bumps. As far back as she could remember, Daphne had loved each and every one of Yia-yia's stories, but the myth of Iphigenia always lingered with Daphne in a way the others did not. Each time she heard the tale, a vivid picture of a young girl just about Daphne's age came into her mind. But now the picture was even clearer. Now with Alex in her life, she could feel the excitement Iphigenia must have felt with each step she took closer and closer to her groom. Daphne could picture herself walking to the altar, imagining Alex there waiting for her. She could see his iridescent eyes ablaze, his khakis frayed at the hem.

She could see Iphigenia, wearing a one-shouldered robe embroidered with gold and a wreath of wildflowers woven into her long black hair. She could feel the girl's anxious excitement as she clutched her mother's hand and walked through the city streets while the citizens tossed flower petals as she passed. And then, every time Yia-yia got to the part where Iphigenia realized she was to be not wed but murdered, Daphne felt the blood drain from her body, just as if it were her own delicate throat being slit in sacrifice.

"I can't believe they actually used to do that, Yia-yia. Kill their own children as a sacrifice to the gods. Why would they do that? Why would someone ask for that?"

"Ah, *koukla mou*. There are many things we can't understand. But don't be fooled— don't blame bloodlust solely on the gods. There was a time . . ." Yia-yia gazed at the coffee simmering on the fire. "There was a time when people consulted old soothsayers or young priestesses to decipher the will of the gods. But as is often the case, power corrupts. It is said that even the great soothsayer Calchas had his own motives for sending Iphigenia to her death." The thick black coffee in the *briki* erupted into a furious boil.

"But don't worry, my girl. Just as the furies were revealed to be benevolent, so were the gods. When they saw that their wishes were being twisted and translated for the selfishness of man, the great god Zeus became furious. From that moment on, the gods ordained that only older women with pure, open hearts were to translate the gods' wishes and be given the honor of oracle reader. They knew that only women who had truly known what it is to love another could be trusted, Daphne. Only these women could understand how precious life really is."

Daphne watched as Yia-yia swirled her coffee in her cup. Where are those supposed benevolent gods and furies now? Daphne wondered. If they had been so just, so fair, as Yia-yia claimed, then why had her own grandmother's life taken such a tragic turn? She wondered what Yia-yia's life might have been like if she didn't have the stigma of the word *widow* attached to her, like a scarlet letter emblazoned on her black dress.

Daphne knew she had been given a glorious gift in being born in America with its opportunities, equality, and dorm rooms to sneak away to. She knew she was lucky to have found Alex, and she wanted nothing more than to continue discovering the nuances of life and love with him. As she looked into her coffee cup, Daphne pictured herself walking through life not alone, as Yia-yia had. She pictured herself holding Alex's hand—side by side with him, instead of in his shadow. She twirled the cup around and around, imploring the grounds to reveal her life's journey.

But it was no use. As usual, Daphne could see nothing more than a muddy mess.

Sixteen

It had been a glorious, if exhausting, day—the kind of day Daphne
knew she and Evie would look back on and cherish. After leaving
Nitsa's, Evie once again climbed on her mother's back the moment
she saw Daphne grab the bamboo stick. They *tap-tap-tapped* their
way home to Yia-yia's, stopping only so Evie could pick the biggest, ripest, and blackest blackberries.

Once back at home, Daphne packed a bag with towels, their
swimsuits, water bottles, and the fatty mortadella sandwiches that
Daphne had loved as a little girl and now Evie had developed a
taste for as well. Off they went, with no plan other than to enjoy
the day and each other's company while exploring the island. But
as they left the house, Daphne did make sure they had just one
more addition to their explorers' party.

Knowing that Evie wouldn't soon forget her snake fixation and
that carrying Evie all day long, up and down the island's many
hills and rocky paths, would soon grow tiresome, Daphne untied

Jack from his post in the back garden and enlisted the gentle donkey's help.

"Think of him as our own little island taxicab." Daphne laughed as she placed Evie on his back and guided them down the stairs to begin their adventure.

Their first stop had been the island's tiny, picturesque church. With its overgrown cemetery, whitewashed walls, elaborate stained-glass windows, and trough of hand-dipped candles burning continually in its entrance, the church looked exactly as Daphne had remembered it, as if it had been frozen in time. At first Evie was petrified by the idea of dead people buried right there in the cemetery adjacent to the church and refused to get off Jack's back. Just as Daphne was about to coerce her down, Father Nikolaos spotted them from inside the graveyard, where he had been busy replenishing the olive oil and lighting the wicks of the eternal candles of the dead. With his flowing black robes gathered in his right hand and waving frantically with his left, Father Nikolaos came running out of the cemetery straight at them. This sent Evie into a fit of hysteria: she thought the bearded, black-robed person heading toward them was some sort of demon who had escaped from the grave.

Evie watched as her mother bent down to kiss the priest's hand. But it wasn't until Father Nikolaos's wife and children came running to see what the fuss was about that Evie actually believed there was nothing to be afraid of. Finally, after much coercion, Evie agreed to come down from the donkey's back. Hand in hand with the priest's thirteen-year-old daughter, she followed Daphne into the church.

Inside, standing on the altar before an icon of the Virgin Mary

and Baby Jesus, Father Nikolaos made the sign of the cross, blessing mother and daughter. Father's children stood watching, heads
bowed and quiet.

"Amen," Father said when the blessing was done.

Having witnessed this prayer hundreds of times before, the
priest's children knew this was their cue, as well as their escape.
"Ella, ella—" They tugged at Evie's arm and pulled her outside to
play, leaving the adults to discuss the wedding details.

It would be a simple, traditional ceremony, they all agreed. The
priest's wife, Presbytera, as all priests' wives are called, offered to
weave the betrothal crowns from local wildflowers. "So much
prettier and more symbolic than those store-bought ones," she insisted as she bounced her baby, the youngest of her five children,
on her knee.

"We received the baptismal certificate," Father Nikolaos added.
"Your young man is welcome in our church, and we are pleased
that you have chosen to be married in Christ's house." His wide
mouth erupted in a broad smile that peeked out from the thick
brush of his beard.

"Daphne," the priest's wife said, her long brown hair neatly
knotted at the nape of her neck. "Join us for lunch," Presbytera
insisted as the baby gurgled and lifted his arms toward his father.

Father Nikolaos swooped down and snatched the baby from
Presbytera's lap. Once safely snuggled in his father's arms, the
baby reached his chubby hand up and tugged at his father's beard,
eliciting deep belly laughs from both. Presbytera watched, a se-
rene smile on her face.

For a moment, Daphne was tempted to join them. There was
something about Father Nikolaos and Presbytera that drew

Daphne to them. On the surface, Daphne had absolutely nothing in common with the simple island priest and his lovely, yet haggard wife. Daphne's urban lifestyle and opinions were so far removed from those of the devout couple who lived and breathed according to the church's rules and customs. Daphne knew they would be horrified if they ever learned that back at home she rarely stepped inside a church and that Evie associated Easter Sunday with a visit from the Easter bunny rather than a glorious celebration of Christ's resurrection. And if Father and Presbytera had any idea that Evie had not received Holy Communion since her baptism, they would truly be horrified. Here, as in all Greek Orthodox churches around the world, each Sunday, like a weekly spiritual vitamin, parents made sure their children dutifully lined up before the priest to receive the bread and wine of communion. In and out, in and out, the priest dipped the same golden spoon in the chalice and then into each child's mouth. It's not that Daphne didn't want to believe that the communion was blessed and therefore would sanitize any germs; she did have faith, and she actually did want to partake in the ritual of the sacrament. But once again, the reality of her life as a single mother did not allow for any romanticism whatsoever. Whenever Evie got sick, even just with a cold that required her to stay home from school, Daphne's world was thrown into chaos. Daphne had decided long ago that until the practice was modernized and sanitized, communion was yet one more element of her own Greek childhood that would remain foreign to Evie's Americanized world.

Daphne watched as Presbytera took the baby from the priest's arms. Cooing in the baby's ear with each step, she walked to the altar and genuflected before the large icon of the Virgin Mary holding a chubby baby Jesus in her arms. Presbytera leaned closer to the icon and kissed the Virgin's feet before lifting her child to do the same, his drool leaving a streak of wet gloss across the pale blue folds of baby Jesus' swaddling.

As much as Daphne would have loved to spend more time in the company of the spiritual couple, she knew that once she and Stephen were married, there wouldn't be as many opportunities for her to spend an entire day alone with Evie. She politely declined with a promise to come back and visit.

From the church, Daphne, Evie, and Jack headed straight for the cove, where they spread a large blanket out just above the waterline and covered it with the food Daphne had brought from home. They didn't say much as they sat nibbling the sandwiches, just sat on the blanket; Daphne with her feet straight out in front of her and Evie nestled between her mother's legs, leaning her back against Daphne's slim torso, the little girl's curls cascading down Daphne's body like a dark waterfall. As they sat together, eating their lunch, they looked out toward the horizon and watched as the seabirds performed their soaring ballets, dipping, climbing, and gliding across the cloudless sky.

Daphne thought about telling Evie a story, one of Yia-yia's stories—maybe the one about Persephone, or perhaps even Cupid and Psyche. But as she opened her mouth to speak, Daphne looked down at Evie and was surprised by the quiet peacefulness of her face—her pink cheeks, her rosebud lips, the dark veil of her long lashes fluttering with each blink. Her little girl seemed happy— truly and honestly happy. Daphne felt a swell of emotion in her chest and an eruption of tears in her eyes.

Evie was happy. And it wasn't a gift or a toy or anything remotely material that was responsible for the joy she felt. It was this place. It was this moment. It was as Yia-yia had said: the mere fact that Daphne was sitting still long enough for Evie to catch her.

Daphne opened her mouth to speak, but as she did, a sudden gust of wind kicked up, blowing sand in her eyes and mouth. As she rubbed her stinging, burning eyes, she looked once again at Evie, who was now sitting straight up and looking behind them toward the veil of trees that lined the beach.

"What is it, honey?" Daphne asked as she rubbed her eyes.

"Did you hear that?" Evie asked as she looked back toward the trees.

"Hear what?"

"I thought I heard singing." Evie added as she stood, turning her back to Daphne, and looked down the beach. "A woman's voice." She took a few steps closer to the trees. "It was pretty and soft . . . and Greek."

Daphne stood and looked toward the thicket. Impossible, she thought as chills ran up and down her spine. She reached for Evie's hand. Daphne remembered standing here, on the very same spot, as a young girl herself, straining to hear the faintest whispers of a song on the breeze.

"You know, Evie," she said as she put her arm around the little girl and pulled her back to the blanket, "when I was a little girl, I would come here every day and swim alone in the cove. I was never afraid of being alone in the sea because Yia-yia told me the story about the cypress whispers. She told me that the island would look after me and speak to me in whispers and songs."

Evie's eyes widened as she clutched Daphne's hand. "Like

ghosts?" She shuddered. "You mean I heard a ghost?" She burrowed into her mother's lap.

"No, Evie, honey. There are no ghosts." Daphne laughed at the
irony—the same thought which terrified Evie now, was the one
thing which Daphne had prayed for herself as a child. It was the
one thing that she had wanted most of all, but like so many of
Daphne's dreams, it never had materialized.

"It's just another story like Persephone or Arachne," Daphne
continued, "an old myth for the old women to share by the evening fire. What you heard was just the radio at Nitsa's. People are
always complaining that she plays it too loud." Daphne watched as
the relief washed over Eve's face.

"But when you told me you heard singing, it reminded me of
when I was a little girl, of how many times I would sit here hour
after hour, waiting and wondering if I would ever hear the cypress
whispers myself."

"But you never did?"

"No, honey, I never did," Daphne said as she looked beyond the
thicket. "They don't exist. The cypress whispers don't exist."

AT ABOUT EIGHT IN THE evening, when the sun's rays began to lose
their dagger-like edge and the oppressive heat of the day finally
began to lift, Daphne glanced down at her watch. It was time to
gather their things and head for home. As she guided Jack and
Evie back home along the blackberry-lined paths, Daphne looked
back at her daughter and was once again filled with overpowering
emotion. Evie's face was still as bright and beaming as the midday
sun had been.

"That was fun, wasn't it, honey?" Daphne asked.

"Mommy, that was the most fun I've had in my whole entire life," Evie shouted as she leaned her little body forward and wrapped her arms around Jack's neck.

"Me, too—the most fun ever." Daphne nodded in agreement and smiled at her daughter, holding tightly to Jack's reins as they continued their walk home. *The most fun I've had in my entire life*, Daphne repeated to herself again and again.

It was true—she had forgotten how wonderful, how rewarding, a day spent doing virtually nothing could be. But now, Daphne realized, as long as Evie was beside her, there really was no such thing as a day filled with nothing. Even life's simplest pleasures—a picnic, a sandcastle, a ride on an old, tired donkey— were cause for celebration more joyous than any she could have ever imagined.

Seventeen

Sitting on the edge of the bed, Daphne flinched as she gingerly applied the *lemonita* lotion to her pink shoulders. As she dabbed the final drop of opaque liquid onto her burning skin, Daphne took a deep breath and summoned all the strength left in her aching body to stand up. Still wrapped in her towel, she walked over to the closet and flung it open, scanning the contents before she found what she was looking for. She slipped the strapless blue dress over her shoulders.

"Yia-yia, Evie. *Pame*, let's go. I'm ready," Daphne called as she reached across the bed to snatch a flashlight from the bureau, knowing they would need the additional light, since there were still no streetlights along the island's paths. As she rushed out the door, flashlight in hand, Daphne caught a final glimpse of herself in the mirror. Her feet froze in place as she did, and she turned her head once more to look more closely at her reflection. Gone were the dark circles under her eyes. Gone was the sallow, green-tinged complexion that greeted her when she looked into a mirror back at home. Gone was the frumpy, messy bun that she always wore when she was cooking. Tonight the woman who stared back was younger, happier, more alive and vibrant, than Daphne had felt or looked in years. With her sun-kissed skin, loose, bouncy curls, strapless summer dress, and, most importantly, relaxed, stress-free face, the woman in the mirror was not a bundle of worry and angst. This woman was happy. She was carefree. And she was beautiful. For the first time in a very long time, Daphne *felt* beautiful.

"*Ella*, Evie, Yia-yia, *pame*—let's go," she shouted again before she stole one last look in the mirror and practically skipped out the door.

At precisely 10:05 p.m., Daphne, Evie, and Yia-yia walked through the double doors of the Hotel Nitsa. As they stepped inside, they were immediately assaulted by the blaring bouzouki music that filled the reception area. But as loud as the music was, it was intermittently drowned out by a half dozen or so shaggy-haired French tourists who sat at the bar playing a drinking game that consisted of them shouting *"Opa!"* whenever someone did a shot of ouzo—which, from the looks of it, seemed to be every few seconds.

"Daphne!" Popi cried out from the bar stool where she sat between two of the young tourists, shot glass in hand. *"Ella*, come play. Meet my new friends." Popi brought her hand to her mouth and giggled before shouting, *"Opa!"* and downing the shot. Immediately, her new friends followed suit.

"Opa!" cried the Frenchmen.

Daphne, Yia-yia, who was shaking her head in disbelief, and even little Evie stood in the center of the room, staring at Popi.

Yia-yia brought her hands together in prayer, shaking them back and forth, an exasperated moan escaping from her mouth as she rocked them. Daphne looked at Yia-yia, knowing that this hand-shaking often led to singsonging, and she immediately made up her mind that she would have none of that tonight. As tired as she had been earlier in the evening, Daphne now felt energized. Maybe it was the bouzouki music, maybe it was the flattering glimpse of herself that she'd caught in the mirror, or maybe it was the remnants of a perfect day spent with Evie; whatever it was, she felt alive tonight, and she wasn't about to let a lament song bring her down. Before Yia-yia could begin her first verse, Daphne scurried over to Popi's side at the bar, grabbed her under the arm, and practically lifted her off the bar stool.

"Come on, Cousin," she insisted. "Say good-bye to your new friends."

"But Daphne . . . ," Popi protested and leaned in to whisper in Daphne's ear. "They're really cute."

"And they're about half your age." Daphne laughed as she pulled Popi away. "Besides, some solid food might do you good."

She struggled to keep Popi moving and away from a fresh line of shots that were already poured and waiting. With both arms now firmly planted around Popi, Daphne was completely focused on getting her cousin safely away from the bar. As she stumbled and shuffled along, struggling to divert Popi's attention, Daphne didn't even notice the person standing in her path with his back to her, immersed in conversation with Yia-yia.

"Owwww," she shouted as she bumped full force into the hulking back, still clinging to Popi lest her cousin use the collision as an opportunity to escape.

"*Malaka*," the annoyed man hissed as he turned to see who had jostled him and interrupted his conversation.

Daphne looked up from the strong back, her eyes wandering upward to a pair of broad shoulders. As the man turned, Daphne caught a glimpse of his expansive chest; shirt unbuttoned just enough to catch a glimpse of chest hair, sprinkled with a smattering of grays. Daphne's eyes continued to linger, wandering upward until they landed on his face.

Damn. It was Yianni.

"I didn't see you." It took restraint for Daphne to bite back the snide, sarcastic comment that she felt he strongly deserved for his past transgressions. But knowing that he was her only option for a ride to Kerkyra tomorrow, Daphne tamped down the impulse. Although she couldn't quite muster a smile, she did the next best thing. She gritted her teeth and held her tongue.

"You have your hands full, it seems." He snatched a thick, dog-eared book from the coffee table beside them, turned, and tipped his sailor's hat to Yia-yia before taking off for a small table at the other end of the reception area, away from the noise and the crowds.

After taking a deep breath and regaining her composure, Daphne led the way from the reception area to the small patio out back. Just as they rounded the corner to the flower-filled deck, Nitsa came bursting out of the kitchen doors balancing four dinner plates on her arm, a cigarette dangling from her lips.

"There she is, there's my *nifee*. Here's our beautiful bride," she bellowed as she shuffled past them and out into the courtyard with the steaming plates.

Daphne watched Nitsa sling the dishes on the table of a beautiful Italian couple and their two young children. Nitsa didn't bother asking who had what. She never forgot a face or an order.

"All right now, *kali orexi*," Nitsa ordered as she stood over the family, hand on her hip, puffing away at her cigarette. "I have a wonderful surprise for dessert, eh. You little ones will love it." She tousled the hair of the young boy and pinched the cheek of his younger sister.

"Evangelia, Daphne. *Etho*, come here." Nitsa waved her arms and motioned for them to join her. "Here, I have a special table ready for you right here." She shepherded them over to a round table at the very center of the patio, decorated with an overflowing basket of white-and-blue wildflowers.

"Thank you, Nitsa." Daphne kissed their host on both cheeks.

"Evangelia"—Nitsa laughed, wiping her hands on her apron and reaching into her pocket to pull out another cigarette—"I know that nothing can compare to your cooking, but tonight, I tried."

"Nitsa, *ella* . . . You are the better cook. I have learned so much from you," Yia-yia insisted as she took her seat. "Everyone knows that you are the best cook on the island."

"*Ella*, Evangelia. Come on." Nitsa flung her arms up into the air, cigarette ashes flurrying in their wake "*Ella*, I cannot begin to compare—"

"Don't be silly, Nitsa," Yia-yia insisted, her face nearly obscured by the large bottle of Nitsa's homemade wine that, along with the basket of flowers, was a staple on all of the tables.

"Enough," Daphne shouted, her head bobbing back and forth between the old women as if this were some sort of culinary tennis match. She crossed her arms. "Tonight, I'm judge and jury, and I'm starving."

"*Ahoooo*, the great American chef is calling for a challenge. I am ready for you, chef," Nitsa bellowed as she pointed her lit cigarette at Daphne. "By the end of this meal you will be begging me to come live in New York City with you and cook for all of your fancy friends."

"Well, Nitsa," Daphne said as she poured a little wine into Yia-yia's glass and then filled Popi's as well as her own. "All right then, consider this your audition." Daphne laughed as she lifted her glass toward Nitsa. "*Opa!*" she shouted as she downed the wine in one gulp.

"*Opa!*" Yia-yia and Popi replied. Popi chugged her glass as Yia-yia lifted her wine and took a small sip.

"*Opa!*" The French tourists echoed from inside the bar. Daphne and Popi looked at each other and dissolved into giggles. Daphne poured herself another glass of wine, and Nitsa scurried into the kitchen to begin her audition.

Within moments, Nitsa was once again beside the table, carrying the first of many courses. They began with an assortment of small meze plates; a tangy *melitzanosalata* of fire-roasted eggplants pureed with garlic and vinegar, *taramosalata*, *tzatziki*, succulent grape leaves stuffed with savory rice and pine nuts and Nitsa's soft and creamy homemade feta, which melted on Daphne's tongue the moment she put it in her mouth. Next came the *tiropites*—small triangular cheese pies filled with feta and spices, followed by stuffed zucchini flowers whose rice and pork filling were delicate enough not to overpower their slightly sweet casings.

The main course was a masterpiece. Instead of the traditional and expected grilled fish, Nitsa surprised both Yia-yia and Daphne with a large platter of *bakaliaro*, delicately fried medallions of cod along with a heaping bowl of pungent *skordalia* paste made from potatoes, garlic, and olive oil.

"Nitsa!" Daphne cried as she looked up at Nitsa, who was waiting for Daphne to taste the fish. "I haven't had fried *bakaliaro* in years."

"Yes, because it's white." Yia-yia laughed as she leaned over and pinched Daphne's arm. "*Ella*, Daphne *mou*. It's time to live again."

Daphne's lips parted to reveal a beautiful, bright smile. She was literally drooling as she placed a dollop of the *skordalia* on a small square of the fried fish, then popped the whole thing in her mouth. She closed her eyes and chewed slowly, savoring the complexity of the flavors and the surreal sensation of the smooth potato paste melting away on her tongue. Its hot, garlicky afterbite was then tempered again as she bit into the fish, its sweet crunchy batter breaking open like a vault to reveal the silky and savory flesh within.

"This, Daphne *mou*, is why I never again want to hear you say that you will not eat white food." Yia-yia laughed as she dabbed at her mouth with her paper napkin. "Family and food, Daphne *mou*. It's in your blood, you cannot escape it."

"I don't want to escape it. I want another helping." Daphne laughed as she stabbed another medallion with her fork and dragged it through the *skordalia*.

By the time the meal was over, everyone seemed to be sufficiently stuffed as well as slightly drunk. Evie had long abandoned the table of adults and was playing in the corner with the Italian children and the kittens. Their laughter mixed with the music, the chatter of well-fed diners, and the soft undercurrent of waves breaking in the distance. On the other side of the terrace, the French tourists had abandoned the bar for a large table covered with some of Nitsa's most famous dishes. Even as the last of the dinner dishes were cleared, everyone lingered, drinking, laughing, soaking in the island perfection of the little flower-filled patio.

The later the evening got, the louder the music became. Soon, the small space facing the tables was turned into an impromptu dance floor. The Italian couple were the first to get up, hanging on each other as if in a drunken lovers' trance, so clearly under the spell of this island paradise and thankful that their children were being kept busy by the basketful of purring kittens. All eyes were on the couple as they took the dance floor. There was something intoxicating about them, the way they moved together in the dim light, the way their hips fit together and followed one another in perfect rhythm, a rhythm clearly perfected by years of lovemaking, by years of spooning one another as they slept. Watching the couple, Daphne was mesmerized and slightly ashamed, as if she were a voyeur intruding on a private lover's moment. But the couple didn't seem to mind. They didn't even notice. They just continued their dance, lost in the magic of Erikousa.

"Look at them, Daphne. It gives you hope, doesn't it? That two people can be so in love after having children, after so many years together." Popi sighed, elbows resting on the table, her head in her hands.

"Yes. Yes, it does," Daphne replied, looking away toward the blackness of the beach. But unlike Popi, for Daphne, watching this couple was not some huge discovery that an epic love affair can actually exist. It was the way she had envisioned her life, the path she had planned.

"Come on, Daphne." Popi grabbed her cousin's hand. "Come on, let's show them how the natives do it."

"No, I don't think—"

"Come on. Think of this as your bachelorette party. Get up and dance with me." Popi tugged at Daphne's arm and dragged her toward the dance floor. After a few more futile attempts to sit this one out, Popi got her way, and they joined the couple on the tiny dance floor. The Italians glanced over and smiled when they saw the cousins, but quickly returned their full attention to each other. From the other side of the room, the Frenchmen erupted into raucous cheers as the cousins began their belly dance.

Daphne lifted her arms above her head, snapping her fingers and rotating her wrists with the droning beat of the bouzouki music. Popi followed suit, raising her arms and expertly moving her hips in time with the music. As she spun round and round, dancing, thrusting, and laughing with her cousin, Daphne threw her head back, her ringlets reaching to the middle of her back. Deep into her backbend, she shouted a hearty *"Opa!"*

Lifting her head again, laughing at the exhilaration of letting loose, Daphne felt lost in the moment, amazed at how young she felt, how sensual, how sexual. Her hips seemed to feel the rhythm, like they knew the next beat, the next strum of the bouzouki before it escaped the stereo speakers. There was always such drama in Greek music, and tonight Daphne reveled in it, lost in a haze of music, dance, cigarette smoke, and the cheers of a room full of drunken tourists.

As the music changed from bouzouki to a traditional sailor's dance, Daphne turned toward her cousin. Her eyes opened wide under the dark veil of hair that partially obscured her face as she danced. She caught Popi's eye, and the cousins nodded in unison, knowing what was next. They shuffled together, standing hip to hip, arms draped over each other's shoulders.

Darararum, darararum . . . The music called to them.

Snapping her fingers, Daphne dropped her head forward, tapping her toes as she waited for the right note to begin their dance.

Darra . . . darrararum. Daraaaa . . . darra. . . . darrarrarram. The music began slowly, each note lingering in the air, perfectly spaced to accentuate the drama of the song. For the tourists, this was Zorba's song, the dance they had seen Anthony Quinn perform countless times on television. But for the locals, the Greeks, this was the *sirtaki*, the dance performed at every happy occasion in their lives, every wedding, every christening, every Easter Sunday celebration as far back as they could remember. It was as if this song, this music, flowed through their veins like the DNA that linked them to each other and to this island.

First left, then right, the cousins stepped in unison. With deliberate steps they jumped forward, then back, then forward again. Daphne bent down on one knee, swiping her hand across the floor, then lifted it again in time for the next chord to call them back to both feet and begin the dance again. As the tempo picked up, so did the pace of the dance. Daphne looked over at Yia-yia as she shuffled left again and then right, and noticed that Yia-yia was waving to someone on the other end of the room to join her at the table.

DARARARAUMMMMM— The cousins jumped forward, higher and with more force this time as the music got faster. Daphne looked to her left as she jumped right to see Yianni taking a seat at the table beside Yia-yia.

DADADA—DADA—DADADA— Faster and faster Daphne and

Popi dove and stepped and jumped to keep time with the now-frenzied pace of the music. All eyes were on the cousins as everyone in the room clapped and cheered them on. Faster and faster they danced, Daphne and Popi leaping forward on one knee just as the first dish came crashing on to the dance floor, followed by another and then another. As her head whipped right and left with the dance, Daphne noticed that it was Nitsa who was lobbing dishes at them as she stood just off to the side with a pile of white dishes in her hand. Finally, just when the music was so fast that Daphne and Popi found it physically impossible to jump or dance any faster, the final dramatic note was hit: *DA RA RA RUM*. The dance ended with a flourish as the cousins fell into each other's arms, sweating and exhilarated.

"That was awesome." Daphne could barely get the words out. She dragged herself to Yia-yia's side, leaning her arms against the table and sucking down a tall glass of water.

"Popi, Daphne—beautiful!" Yia-yia cried as she held her hands together. "Yianni, did you see my girls, how beautiful they dance?" The old woman nudged Yianni with her elbow.

"Yes, it was a beautiful *sirtaki*, perfect in fact," he agreed, lifting his glass and nodding toward Yia-yia.

The compliment was lost on Popi, who was already beside the table of Frenchmen, accepting their congratulations as well as a glass of wine. But Yianni's words were not lost on Daphne. In fact, she could hardly believe what she was hearing.

"Thank you," she said as she wiped her damp forehead with the back of her hand. "I can't remember the last time I danced like that. I can't believe I even remember the steps."

"Some things stay in our memories forever, only to be reawakened when we need them most," he replied, looking over at Yia-yia, who was nodding in agreement.

Daphne looked back and forth from Yianni to Yia-yia. She wanted to tell them that she knew about Yianni's grandmother, that Nitsa had told her the story, but Yianni opened his mouth to speak before she had the chance.

"Daphne, your *yia-yia* tells me I am to take you to Kerkyra to-morrow."

"Yes." Daphne replied, still breathing heavily and glistening with sweat. "If it's not too much trouble for you." She was still un-settled by the thought of being alone with this man. But knowing she had no other option, she did her best to appear gracious.

"It is no trouble. I lift my nets at six a.m., and we should be ready to leave by seven thirty. We will go to Sidari. I have work to do there tomorrow. From Sidari you can take a taxi to Kerkyra."

"Yes, that's fine. Thank you," Daphne replied, relieved that Yi-anni was making the trip anyway and that she was merely tagging along for the ride. Despite what Yia-yia said about Yianni, Daphne still wasn't comfortable with the idea of being indebted to him for any reason. Before she could say another word, Daphne heard her name being called from the other side of the room.

"Daphne *mou*. Daphne," Nitsa called out to her. "Daphne, *ella*, dance. I dedicate this song to you." Nitsa pointed her finger at someone behind the bar, someone who clearly had control of the stereo. As the first notes erupted from the speaker, the entire room once again erupted into applause. The tourists had no idea what they were cheering and clapping for, but at this point they were too drunk to care.

"*Ella*, dance," Nitsa shouted and clapped.

"No, Nitsa, I can't." Daphne shook her head in protest. "Really, no."

"*Ella*, Daphne," Nitsa shouted.

"Come on, Daphne, do it," Popi commanded from across the room, standing up, ouzo in hand.

"Yia-yia . . ." Daphne looked to her grandmother with pleading eyes.

"Your host is calling you. *Pegene*—go, dance for us. You are young and beautiful. Dance," Yia-yia replied, nudging her head toward the now-empty dance floor.

Daphne looked at Yia-yia and forced a small smile. She knew there was no turning back now. Protocol called her to heed her host's wishes, even though she really didn't want to go out there and make a spectacle of herself. She reached over and grabbed her half-full glass of wine from the table. "*Yiamas* . . . to our health," she shouted as she tipped the glass back and downed it with one gulp before heading to the dance floor.

Once she was on the floor, the music took over as the final gulp of wine helped build her confidence. Round and round she spun, arms over her head, wrists rotating along with her hips. Daphne knew she wasn't the best dancer; Popi was far superior in that category. But that was the beauty of Greek dancing. It was more about living the music, expressing yourself through movement, than it was about technicalities. And tonight, despite her initial embarrassment, Daphne closed her eyes and felt every note work its way through her body.

"*Opa!*" Daphne heard someone cry just as she felt the first sprinkling of flower petals fall on her face and hair as she spun around and around. Eyes still closed, she lifted her chin toward the sky and felt the petals tickle her eyelids and lips, as if she were being kissed by tiny raindrops while running through a sun shower.

"*Opa!*" the voice repeated as Daphne felt another wave of petals dance across her body. They flitted across her shoulders and arms like a lover's gentle touch. She turned and spun again, opening her eyes wide and then wider still. There, standing directly in front of her, was Yianni.

"*Opa!*" he shouted again as he ripped the petals from the red carnation and tossed them at Daphne as she danced.

Eighteen

The next morning, as Daphne walked along the concrete path toward the port, she silently thanked God that she had listened to Yia-yia and forced herself to eat something before leaving the house. She had wanted to cry when she first opened her eyes before dawn and felt the brutal pounding in her head, the result of too much of Nitsa's homemade wine. Even more than that, Daphne wanted to cry at the thought of spending the morning on a *kaiki*—face-to-face and alone with Yianni—without Yia-yia, bouzouki music, or Nitsa's wine to serve as a buffer.

She did feel slightly better after a cold shower and a hot *briki* of Yia-yia's strong Greek coffee. Even so, eating was the last thing on Daphne's mind. The way her stomach burned and churned, she didn't think it would be possible to keep anything down. But despite Daphne's protests, Yia-yia insisted that Daphne could not leave without eating a chunk of crusty peasant bread along with a handful of home-cured black olives. Yia-yia was adamant that eaten together, the salty olives and dense bread were a reliable hangover cure, sure to settle her stomach and ease her pounding headache.

Daphne didn't buy it at first, nibbling on the bread and olives merely to appease Yia-yia, her stomach doing backflips with every bite. But after a few minutes, the bread and brine began to work their magic, just as Yia-yia had promised they would. She did feel better; her legs, while still somewhat shaky, were no longer in danger of crumbling beneath the weight of her body. Her stomach, while still tender, didn't feel like it was ready to empty its contents at a moment's notice. By the time she reached the port, Daphne had started to feel somewhat human again.

"Daphne, *etho* . . . over here." She heard Yianni's voice above the chattering of the other fishermen. He stood against the rail of the *kaiki*, laying his nets out to dry on the deck. He ran his hands along the rough, wet twine, making certain there were no holes.

"You are on time," Yianni said, stone-faced. "I expected you would be late. Americans are always late."

Both of his arms were fully extended as he lifted the wet nets into the air to examine them. Daphne looked up at Yianni's black outline framed against the blazing light. She imagined this is what Icarus might have looked like as well; his handcrafted wax wings awash in sunlight, silhouetted against the sky before his fateful and fatal plunge into the sea below—another victim of hubris. Surely Yianni's hubris would catch up with him too. But Daphne quietly said a little prayer, hoping the wrath of the gods would wait just a little longer—at least until he delivered her safely ashore in Sidari, anyway.

Daphne took a deep breath before responding, willing herself to remain calm and maintain peace.

"I'm always on time," she replied, lifting her hand to shield her eyes from the sun.

"*Ella*," he shouted as he leaned across the railing and held his brown arm out to Daphne. "It's time to leave—there's a *furtuna* coming, and we need to go before the winds kick up."

Daphne glanced up at Yianni's hand. Instinctively, she reached hers up, but not toward Yianni; she had other plans. Reaching her arm up and wrapping her fingers around the wooden railing, she lifted her right leg on deck and hoisted herself up. Once she was up and standing on the outer deck, Daphne swung her legs over the railing. She promptly took a seat along the inner ledge, folding her hands on her lap and smoothing her long, white skirt over her legs.

"Well, let's go." She stared at Yianni, who was still standing in the same spot, hand extended toward the dock, shaking his head at her. Daphne felt empowered. She chuckled as she ran her fingers through her hair, the damp curls springing to life in the morning breeze.

"Stubborn runs in your family," Yianni muttered as he withdrew his hand and leaned over the railing again, this time to pull up the anchor.

Just get to Kerkyra. Just stay calm. Daphne repeated the mantra to herself before lifting her head and responding to Yianni's sarcasm. "It runs deep in the Erikousa bloodline. You're just as guilty as I am."

"Don't be so sure." He snorted as he took his seat behind the large wooden steering wheel of the *kaiki*. With his fisherman's hat on his head, legs spread open in a broad V, and his giant hands gripping the dark brown wooden wheel, Yianni began maneuvering the boat out of the port and into the open sea.

They rode in silence for the first few minutes of the trip. Daphne never had been one for small talk, and she was certainly not about to change now, not for Yianni. She was looking forward to a quiet journey, a trip whose silence would only be broken by the hollow thud of waves crashing against the boat's side or the shrill cries of seabirds as they circled above.

Daphne leaned back against the railing. She stretched her legs out along the deck, back pressed up against a metal post and head tilted back as the light wind blanketed her in a film of salt and sea mist. There was so much on her mind at the moment. She had gotten so lost in the rhythm of island life, so absorbed in enjoying simple pleasures like a walk with Evie or a coffee with Yia-yia, that she had uncharacteristically fallen behind on her work: the wedding plans. There were still several details to arrange, lists to tackle, and fleeting moments of solitude, like this, to cherish. Soon her life would be changed forever; the loneliness that she had felt for all these years would be exorcised by Father Nikolaos as she walked three times around the altar holding her new husband's hand and wearing a crown of wildflowers.

"Are you hungry?" Yianni asked.

Daphne opened her eyes, startled by the sound of his voice interrupting her thoughts.

"I said, are you hungry?" Yianni repeated, his voice raised ever so slightly as he stood up, both hands still gripping the wheel.

"No, I'm good," she lied, despite the gnawing rumbling in her belly. "I'm not hungry."

"Well, I am." He grunted. "Come here and hold the wheel." He stood, one hand still on the wheel, the other lifted to his forehead as he scanned the surface of the sea.

The fact that he did not ask, but instead barked his command, was not lost on Daphne.

"I said, come here and hold the wheel."

"I'm a chef, not a deckhand."

"You're stubborn, is what you are. Just come here and hold the wheel. All you have to do is hold it straight. Any idiot can do it, even an American chef."

Daphne felt the blood rise in her cheeks again. Hands at her sides, she clenched them into tight balls, her fingernails cutting into the palms of her hands.

"Come on. I'm joking." Yianni laughed. "That was a joke, Daphne. You are so tense, you make an easy target. I hope that fiancé of yours knows what he's doing and can take care of that stress for you." Yianni slapped at the wheel as he laughed. "Ah, but Americans are not known for their romantic prowess like the Europeans are. Perhaps your American can ask Ari for some advice; he is a master with the ladies, you know."

Daphne just couldn't help herself. The laugh started like a private giggle in the quiet recesses of her mind, but the longer she thought about Stephen having anything to do with Ari, the more she found that there was no way to suppress her laughter. The quiet giggle soon erupted as Daphne's stomach and shoulders bobbed up and down, convulsing at the thought of Stephen and Ari together under any circumstances, let alone a master class on romance.

"Daphne," he repeated. "Come, take the wheel. I need to take care of something."

She didn't even stop to think this time, but stood up and made her way to the captain's seat. She grasped the rail with her right hand as she shuffled along toward the back of the boat, careful not to lose her footing. The waves as well as the wind had intensified in the short time that they had been on the sea, rocking the boat from side to side with increased frequency and force.

"What do you need me to do?"

"Here, grab the wheel." He positioned himself behind Daphne, lifted her hands in his own, and nudged her closer to the steering wheel. His chest pressed against her back. "Just hold it steady, here and here."

"So, any idiot can do this," Daphne mocked. "Even you."

She turned and stole a glimpse at the man who had with one perfectly absurd statement managed to soften her resolve and transform her from passenger to deckhand.

"Yes, any idiot at all." He nodded in agreement, looking away from Daphne and out into the now-choppy sea. "The tide is strong and against us—it will take longer to get to Sidari than normal. The sea has made me hungry, as it always does. I can't wait to eat. Are you sure you're not hungry?"

"Actually, I'm starving," she admitted.

She hadn't intended on sharing conversation with Yianni, let alone a meal; but there was something about being out here on the open sea that made her feel slightly more adventurous—as well as more ravenous than normal.

"Good. Just stay like this—I'll be right back." Before Daphne could ask where he could possibly be going, Yianni stripped off his shirt, grabbed a ratty old canvas bag from the deck, and draped it across his chest. He then stepped up on to the railing and propelled himself off the deck, diving straight down into the choppy water.

"What the hell—" Daphne watched him disappear under the whitecaps. She stood just as he had positioned her, clutching the captain's wheel and struggling to hold it straight against the current. She scanned the water in anticipation of Yianni's return. For someone who loved the sea and had never had any fear of being out in the water alone, Daphne felt surprisingly anxious. It wasn't as if she was drifting out in the middle of nowhere. From the deck she could clearly see the jagged cliffs of Kerkyra, the lush beaches of Erikousa, and the beautiful yet deserted beaches of Albania. But somehow, for some reason, the moment Yianni went over the side of the boat, Daphne felt nervous, uneasy, and unusually isolated.

Finally, after what seemed like an eternity but in reality could have been no more than a minute or two, Yianni broke through the surface.

"What are you doing?" Daphne demanded as she looked out into the sea where Yianni had emerged, about fifty yards away from the *kaiki*.

Yianni didn't answer. He just continued to swim toward her.

"Here," he said as he hoisted himself back on the boat.

He stepped over the railing, seawater cascading off his body, leaving pools of water on the deck with every step.

"Here," he repeated. "What is it you Americans call it? Oh yes, brunch." He smiled a long, broad grin. The muscles of his wet forearm bulged and flexed against the weight of the canvas bag that he now held out toward Daphne.

Not certain what to do, except for trying really hard not to stare at his glistening torso, Daphne reached out to take the bag from Yianni. She opened the sack and looked inside.

"*Heinea* . . . sea urchins." She laughed as she looked up from the bag to Yianni.

"Yes. There is bread, olive oil, and lemons belowdecks."

She didn't wait for him to ask this time; Daphne made her way belowdecks, holding the rail the entire way as insurance against the increasingly rocky sea. She stopped in the doorway, holding the door frame for support as she scanned the small cabin. The room was meticulously neat and immaculately clean, unlike any fishing boat she had ever seen. There was, of course, the standard utility kitchen, a small sink and hot plate, along with a small bed tucked up against the wall. But unlike any other fishing boat she had been on, there was a small desk in the corner, with a computer. And although the cabin was neat and tidy, everywhere she looked there were piles and piles of books.

My, how modern, not a vomit bucket in sight. She laughed as she scanned the room. There, in the corner, beside the hot plate and the *briki*, Daphne spotted the basket containing the oil, bread, and lemons, as well as a bottle of sea salt. She grabbed the basket and cradled it to her chest before heading back up to the deck.

As Daphne emerged from the cabin, she looked around in disbelief. How could that be? In the short time she'd been below, the winds had died down and the sea was suddenly less choppy, a glassy stillness replacing the whitecaps that had been developing just moments before.

Daphne took her seat along the deck and spread the makings of their meal out on a small crate that Yianni had dragged over between them. Yianni reached deep into the pockets of his wet jean shorts and pulled out a pair of worn yellow leather gloves. Squeezing them onto his hands, he reached into the bag and pulled out a black spike-covered sea urchin. Holding the sea urchin in one gloved hand, he picked up a large fishing knife with the other. Pressing the blade into the spiky protective covering, he cracked open the top of the shell as one might crack open the shell of a soft-boiled egg. Yianni handed Daphne the sea urchin, and she went to work, adding a squeeze of fresh lemon, sea salt, and a drizzle of olive oil to the soft brown flesh. When all of the urchins were opened and properly seasoned, Daphne ripped off a corner of the crusty bread and handed it to Yianni before tearing off another piece for herself.

"*Yia-mas,*" she said as she picked up a sea urchin and toasted Yianni with it.

"*Yia-mas,*" Yianni replied before tearing into his meal. "Hey, Daphne—so how much are you going to charge me for this meal? Maybe a hundred dollars, eh? Isn't that what you charge in your restaurant?"

Daphne looked up from her spiky bowl and looked Yianni squarely in the eyes. "Well, you get the *kaiki* discount. After all, you are giving me a ride. For you, only seventy-five."

"So generous," Yianni mocked. "Thea Evangelia did say you were quite the businesswoman."

"Yes, apparently you and my *yia-yia* spend quite a bit of time talking about me."

"Not just you, Daphne. We talk about everything." He handed her another sea urchin.

"Why is that? I can't figure it out." Daphne tossed her empty shell overboard and wiped her mouth with the back of her hand. "Honestly, what is it about you two? I've never laid eyes on you or even heard of you before this trip. And now, out of nowhere, here you are, like the son she never had. Exactly how am I supposed to welcome you to the family, when you've been obnoxious and rude since our first meeting?" She slammed the sea urchin on the crate, harder than she meant to.

Yianni looked at Daphne for a moment, as if contemplating what to say. As the wind picked up again, he tossed a crust of bread over the side of the boat. It floated on the breeze for a moment before falling into the sea and being pounced on by a seagull who had been circling above, following the boat in anticipation of its next meal.

"I owe her my life," he said, without a hint of his usual sarcasm or bravado. "I would not be sitting here if it were not for Thea Evangelia."

Daphne didn't understand. How could this big, burly man owe his life to frail Yia-yia? "What are you talking about?" She released the air from her lungs in a huff.

Here we go again, right back to square one, she thought. Since they'd shared a laugh as well as the sea urchins, Daphne had imagined that something had shifted between them. That perhaps he too had grown tired of this battle of wills they had engaged in since their first meeting. But now, with this latest grand, dramatic claim, it seemed Yianni was at it again, tainting a perfectly pleasant morning with his innate ability to summon the furies and, in turn, render Daphne furious.

"Don't look at me like that, Daphne." His dark eyes homed in on Daphne's face like the seabird to the discarded piece of bread.

"Are you always so dramatic?"

"This is not a joke, Daphne. I owe your *yia-yia* my life, and my mother's life, and my grandmother's as well. She saved them both.

She risked her own life to save theirs, and for that, I am eternally bonded to her."

Daphne sat still for a few moments, attempting to process what Yianni was getting at. She gnawed on her lips, her teeth tearing their pink flesh as her mind raced.

"You're serious?"

"I couldn't be more serious." He was devoid of sarcasm. "There's much you don't know about your *yia-yia*, Daphne. Things she never told you, things she wanted to protect you from."

She wanted nothing more than to spring from her seat and tell him that what he was proposing was absurd—crazy, in fact. It was impossible that he would be privy to Yia-yia's secrets while she, Yia-yia's own flesh and blood, was kept in the dark, protected from whatever dark past Yianni was alluding to. It was impossible. Or was it? Her mind raced back to the way Yia-yia greeted Yianni, the way she coddled him—the way he knew about the shoe box under Yia-yia's bed, the way they looked at each other as if they could read each other's minds, each other's secrets. As her mind flashed through the scenes, Daphne felt her heart beating faster and faster against her rib cage. She had been searching for answers, and now it seemed Yianni was willing to serve them up as readily as the sea urchin brunch he had produced. Daphne was desperate to hear what he had to say; whether or not she believed him would be another story.

"Tell me." She folded her hands on her lap, promising herself not to judge, just to sit and listen. "Tell me. I need to know."

Yianni began to speak before the words had even left her mouth.

Nineteen

"I was like you, Daphne," he began. "You see, we are more alike than you could ever imagine. I too loved nothing more than to sit and listen to my grandmother's stories. I, like you, lived for those stories."

Daphne nodded in agreement as well as surprise. He watched her face change, the muscles around her mouth finally unclenching.

"My own grandmother told me what happened many times when I was a child. I loved listening to her stories, but to be honest, I thought they were the hallucinations of an old, tired woman who could no longer separate fact from reality. But then I met Thea Evangelia, and it all finally made sense."

"What made sense—what did she tell you?" Daphne tucked her legs under her body and held the railing as if to brace herself for what might come next.

"She told me what had happened to them during the war. She

told me how in one moment, strangers changed each other's lives—saved each other's lives. She told me what it is like to face the devil himself . . . and to refuse him your soul."

This was indeed the story that Yia-yia and Nitsa had both mentioned to her. But Yianni's version seemed different, darker.

"Why am I only learning about this now?"

He smiled at her, as if he'd anticipated this question before he could begin the tale in earnest.

"She wanted to put the past behind her, to forget. She didn't want you weighed down by those old ghosts like she had been, like your mother was. She wanted you to be free of them, for you to know of only magic and beauty." His face softened, but Daphne could still see the vein in his temple bulging, throbbing blue under his translucent light brown skin.

"Tell me," she said. It was time she learned the truth.

"It started in Kerkyra," he began. "My grandmother, Dora, lived in the old town, in a second-floor apartment just under the Venetian arches. My grandfather was a tailor, the finest tailor in Kerkyra. His suits and shirts so perfectly fitted, his stitches so immaculately precise—people marveled at his garments. They would line up ten deep just for a chance to purchase his exquisite clothes, my grandmother would boast. . . ." His voice drifted for a moment.

"She said everyone, everyone marveled at his gift, agreeing that no machine could match the skill in his nimble fingers—that this gift was a blessing from God himself. His shop was located just below the family's apartment, on the ground floor in the Jewish quarter."

"The Jewish quarter?" Daphne had never heard of a Jewish neighborhood in Kerkyra.

"Yes, the Jewish quarter. My family was part of a thriving community of two thousand Jewish merchants and artisans. For generations, Kerkyra was their home, just as it was your family's home. They were a part of that island, as were your own ancestors. But that was before the war, before the Germans came and everything changed." He looked down at the floor and inhaled deeply. One hand gripped the wheel as he continued to direct the *kaiki* toward Sidari.

"It was 1943—the Italians were occupying Kerkyra, and there was an uneasy calm in the city. For the most part, the Italians left our people alone. The Italian soldiers were barbaric all across Greece, but not on Corfu. Here, with the islands so close to Italy, many of the men spoke Italian, and the soldiers looked kindly on the men who spoke their mother tongue, even warning them, telling them to flee as the Germans approached. The Italians were very aware of how this tragic script would play out should the Germans reach Corfu. But sadly, my grandparents and their community stayed rooted in the place they loved, the place they called home. My family had heard that the German troops were indeed getting closer, that they had decimated communities, massacred Greek resistance fighters and Jews across Greece. But my grandparents felt safe in Corfu, among these civilized and cultured people." He paused. "Among their friends.

"But when the Italians finally surrendered, so did civilization—so did the eyes of God, as my grandmother used to say." Daphne thought she saw dampness coat his eyes at the mention of his grandmother. Perhaps it was the sea mist—she couldn't be certain.

"It was June 8, 1944. Just two days after the Allied forces landed on the beach in Normandy. Salvation was close, so incredibly close. But just not close enough. The Germans issued an ordinance that all the Jews in Corfu present themselves in the town square the next morning at six a.m."

He shook his head and turned to look at Daphne. "Imagine someone coming into your home, the home where your own grandparents were born, where you cooked dinner every night and where your children played and slept. Imagine waking up one day and being told that you were nothing—that your family meant nothing. This is what was happening all across Greece. And it had finally reached Corfu. Many of their friends left that night, escaping to the mountains, to the tiny remote villages. But not my family. They stayed."

Daphne stared at him, not making sense of his story. "But why? Why would they stay, if they knew how dangerous it was?"

"They couldn't leave." He shook his head again. His eye caught a seabird in the distance. He watched her gliding, soaring, flying gracefully around and around before finally diving and plucking a fish from the sea. Only then did he continue.

"They couldn't leave. My grandmother, Dora, had gone to a clinic in Paleokastritsa. She took my mother, Ester, and her two-year-old sister, Rachel, with her, leaving my grandfather and their four-year-old son, David, at home. Rachel was a sickly child, and she had a fever once again that had not broken for days. The doctor in Paleokastritsa was truly skilled and knew the remedies that always made little Rachel better. Dora never thought twice about making the trip. The Germans were cruel and menacing, but the Jews had learned to avoid them, to stay quiet and out of their way. They lived like that for months, praying the Allied forces would get closer and that soon the Nazis would be expelled from their island. No one saw the trouble coming, but things changed overnight. Corfu became dangerous, and their whole world transformed overnight. My grandfather would never leave his wife and daughters behind. He chose to stay, to defy the order and wait for his wife and daughters to come home.

"The next morning," Yianni continued, "as Allied bombs fell on Corfu, the Germans gathered all the Jews on the *platia*, in the town square. They emptied the prisons, the hospitals, and even the mental institutions. All the Jews of Kerkyra—even expectant mothers waiting to give birth—everyone was rounded up in the square. The soldiers went house to house, hunting for anyone; men, women, children, the elderly . . . anyone who dared defy the order. One day they were a thriving community; the next, ripped from their homes as if they were nothing. Imagine being dragged from your home by strangers like an animal being plucked from his cage, plucked like a fish from the sea . . ." He turned and looked at Daphne. This time there was no mistaking the source of his red, wet eyes.

"They stood there in the blazing sun, all morning and all day and into the evening, not knowing what would happen, not willing to believe their fate. Finally the soldiers took them. They were thrown into prison, all of them. Almost two thousand Jews, herded into the Frourio. The same place where they would stroll with their families on the Sabbath became their prison. They were all kept there with no food or water, stripped of their possessions, their identity—their dignity." He finally looked away from her. His eyes closed, and his head sank to his chest. He sat silent and still for a few more moments before he could finally get the words out. "Before they were sent to Auschwitz."

His words stung like a slap across the face. "What?" she cried, thinking of the scenic fort, always a symbol of protection, of strength and safety. "What are you saying?"

Yianni ignored her question. "My grandfather and David . . ." He exhaled. Daphne could see his fingers tremble as he grabbed the wheel tighter. "They were in the shop, my grandfather and David, when the soldiers came. They looted stores, arrested everyone, and shot those who dared protest. My grandfather refused to go, refused to leave without his wife and daughters. The soldiers beat him for his disobedience and ordered him to line up with the rest of the men that had been herded like cattle, like sheep to the slaughter. But he refused to let his son watch him being led away like an animal." Yianni closed his eyes once again. "So they shot him."

Daphne brought both hands to her mouth, but there was no quieting the sob that escaped from between her fingers.

"They shot my grandfather in the head. Right there in front of his son. They left his lifeless body draped across his sewing table."

"Oh my god." Daphne sobbed, breathing deeply yet feeling as if she couldn't pull any oxygen into her lungs. If he heard Daphne's cries, Yianni didn't let on. It was as if he had waited so long to share this story that nothing would stop him now. The words continued to pour out of him, even faster now, even more devastating.

"My grandmother arrived back in the Jewish quarter to find the streets empty. She ran all the way home, clutching her daughters' hands. They ran into the store and found my grandfather there, cold and lifeless, and David—David, gone."

Daphne could no longer suppress her tears. She felt them well up and spill over, tears falling down her face; crying for this little boy, crying for his father, for his mother and sisters, crying that Kerkyra was not the paradise she always pictured it to be; that it too had a dark and tragic past.

"That's how your grandmother found them—my young mother and her sister, collapsed on the floor, caressing, cradling, their dead father's body as my grandmother ran shrieking through the alleys, searching for her son."

"Yia-yia found them? Yia-yia was there?" *How could this be?* It was impossible to imagine that her grandmother had witnessed this horrific scene. It made no sense to Daphne that Yia-yia was even there. She rarely left Erikousa. It was as if Yianni sensed that she had begun to doubt him. Before she could question the valid-ity of his story, he continued.

"Your grandmother had just come from Erikousa and had not yet heard about the raid and the arrests. She was merely coming to the Jewish quarter to pay a debt. She owed my grandfather money. It had been months and months, and Evangelia still could not pay her bill. She walked into the shop with a basket of eggs and a bottle of olive oil, hoping he would accept them as payment. Instead, she walked right into my family's hell. Thea Evangelia got down on her knees and pulled the children away from their father's stiff and bloody body."

It was as if Daphne could see the blood, smell it. She stopped breathing for a moment and listened, feeling as if she could hear their sobs still reverberating across the island.

"But David, what happened to David?"

"They took him away . . . but your *yia-yia* tried . . . She tried . . ." His voice trembled as he repeated the words.

"She dressed my grandmother as one of her own, placing her

own black headscarf on Dora and draping her in the black sweater taken off Evangelia's very own back. They took refuge in the church of Saint Spyridon, your *yia-yia* praying to the saint while my grandmother and her girls cried in each other's arms in a heap on the floor. Your *yia-yia* told them to stay and pray with her. She told them Agios Spyridon would protect them. And he did, he did protect them. They hid there in the church for more than a full day, listening to the gunfire and chaos just outside the church door. But no German entered the church, not one. Finally, when the screams and the shooting stopped, your *yia-yia* told Dora to stay in the church, not to move and not to speak to anyone. Evangelia stepped outside and ran all the way to the Frourio. She planned to speak to the police and claim that there was a mistake, to say that David was her own son, a Greek and not a Jew. But it was too late. The Frourio had already been emptied, and the *Juden*, as the soldiers called them, spitting in disgust as they said the word, had been taken away.

"That night, under the safety of darkness, your *yia-yia* took Dora, my mother, and little Rachel to Erikousa. At first my grandmother refused to go—she refused to leave until she found her son. She vowed to die before she abandoned hope of finding her boy. But your grandmother made it very clear that there was no hope of finding David. Her little boy, her David, had been taken away with all of her friends, all of her family—it was too late to save him. It was too late to save any of them."

Yianni brought his large, rough hand to his face and tugged at the whiskers of his beard. He turned to look at her. "Daphne, you are a mother. Imagine having to tell another mother to give up hope of finding her child. Imagine your Evie, the beautiful child you carried, gave birth to, nursed, and nurtured. Imagine walking away and leaving her for dead. Knowing that as you still live, breathe, and walk this earth, that you have left your baby in the hands of godless, soulless animals intent on making her suffer, intent on murdering her. Imagine your beautiful Evie discarded like a piece of trash. And now you can begin to imagine my grandmother's hell."

Daphne pictured her beautiful baby girl, her Evie— immediately willing the image of her daughter out of her head. She couldn't bear the thought. . . . It was too much to contemplate . . . even from the safe distance of decades gone by. All she could do was shake her head. No.

"And imagine your own grandmother, Daphne. Having to tell another mother to forget this child—to forget her own child in the hopes of saving the others."

"No, I can't." Her whisper was barely audible.

Yianni raised his head again and looked at Daphne dead on. "But your *yia-yia* did this, and it saved their lives. She saved my family's heritage, our legacy. That morning, as your *yia-yia* dragged them from the tailor's shop, Dora ran back in. She knew she could take nothing with her, that Evangelia was right, they needed to leave immediately, before the soldiers returned. But Dora grabbed one thing, the one thing that would bear proof that her family did indeed exist. It was her family menorah, the one her own father had carved of olive wood and given to her on her wedding day. Knowing they would be killed if anyone saw them carrying it through the streets, your *yia-yia* wrapped my grandmother's menorah in her apron and hid it under the folds of her own skirt.

"Evangelia traded the eggs and olive oil for the passage back to Erikousa. It was all she had, but she gave them to a fellow islander to keep quiet and take them in his *kaiki*. She risked everything to help my family. The Nazis knew that Jews had escaped, that they were being hidden by Greek families all around Corfu, in the villages and on the smaller islands. They issued a proclamation that any Christian found hiding or helping a Jew would be murdered. That they, and their entire families, would be shot and killed for defying the order and helping the *Juden*. But despite this, despite the risk, the threats, and the knowledge that she could be killed, Evangelia hid them, she protected them. She saved them." He paused. "She saved us."

Daphne stared at Yianni. She felt torn—torn between calling him a liar for daring to conjure up such a horrific fairy tale, or embracing him, clinging to him, and thanking him for finally sharing the truth.

"How?" was all she could manage.

"They lived like that until the war was over. The two widows and their children, scraping by on what little they had, living in Evangelia's house. Dora taught Evangelia the art of sewing, of making beautiful clothes from the few scraps they could find, and Evangelia taught Dora and her girls the ways and customs of the island women so they would blend in . . . so they would live. They spent night after night talking, teaching each other the stories, traditions, and culture of their people. They learned that despite what they had always heard in their lives, they were more similar than different—the Greeks and the Jews. Evangelia told everyone on the island that my grandmother was a cousin who had come to stay, but everyone knew better. Everyone on Erikousa knew who she was—*what* she was. They all knew my grandmother was hiding, that she and your grandmother and perhaps they themselves would be killed if the Nazis found them. But no one told. No one on the island gave away the secret. Despite the risk to themselves, to their families, and to the entire island, no one told the Nazis. Not one adult, not one child, Daphne, no one. At first, they stayed away and simply let the widows live in peace. But Dora said that as time moved on, the islanders embraced them. They helped them, protected them, and, along with Evangelia, made them feel like part of their island, part of their family."

Daphne wrung the white fabric of her skirt in her hands, the cotton twisted and knotted around and around and between her fingers. "But how—how did they manage to hide from the soldiers?"

Yianni stopped for a moment and smiled. "Your *yia-yia* is a brave and special woman, Daphne. Whenever my grandmother would tell me about her, it would always be in hushed tones, with respect and reverence."

"My *yia-yia* . . ." Daphne pictured her frail *yia-yia*, who seemed dwarfed even by her black uniform. The same Yia-yia who spoke no English, had never been formally educated, and had never stepped onto an airplane or even outside Greece. "How could she know what to do?"

"When I would ask that question, my grandmother would simply say she knew. She could feel it. She knew when the soldiers would come. She knew when they would leave. She would dress Dora and the girls in peasant skirts and blouses and send them off with a sack of bread and olives and water, and always my grandmother's cherished menorah wrapped in an apron and hidden in the folds of my grandmother's dress. They would hide in the hill-top caves on the wild, uninhabited side of the island until the sol-diers were gone again. She always knew when they would come, and she always knew when they would go. She was the only one who did. Somehow, she could hear them coming. At first it was just Evangelia who would make the dangerous trip to bring food and water when they were hiding. But then, one by one, the is-landers began to come. They brought food and supplies and even crudely made dolls from scraps of fabric and corn husks for the girls." He smiled at this, his eyes crinkling at the thought of little girls playing so innocently in such dangerous circumstances. But then the smile disappeared, as he remembered again what came next in the story.

"The Germans never occupied Erikousa, but they would visit, usually once a month, and stay for only a few days, always search-ing for Jews who had escaped. Those days always seemed endless and the Germans were brutal, beating even small children who dared not greet them with raised arms or whose *Heil Hitler*s were not loud enough for the soldiers' liking. But Dora, Evangelia, and the islanders had settled into somewhat of a routine, as routine as things can be in times of war. Everyone knew where Dora and the girls were hiding, and as difficult as it was for them on the moun-tainside, they never went hungry. Someone would always come and bring them what they needed . . . clothing, food, companion-ship and conversation to fill the scared and lonely hours. But one time, the Germans stayed longer than usual. It was the last days of summer, and a terrible and stubborn storm rolled in and would not leave. It rained for days upon days, and the sea rolled and churned. No fisherman's boat dared attempt to sail, and neither did the

Germans—even their big, modern boats were powerless against the angry sea. Dora said they waited and prayed for what seemed like an eternity to be told it was safe to return home, but that message did not come. It never came." He shook his head, his shoulders slumping farther and farther down, weighted by Dora's fear and desperation.

"The endless dampness was too much for Rachel's frail body. The coughing set in and got worse with each passing day. Even the precious medicine that Evangelia and the other islanders risked their lives to bring her was no match for the infection that took hold, the endless coughing that shook her battered little body. The sea finally calmed, and the Germans set sail for Kerkyra, but it was too late. Rachel's cough grew worse with each passing day, and then the fever set in. It was too much. The poor thing could fight no longer. She died, there in your *yia-yia*'s bed, as Dora and Evangelia held vigil, holding her tiny hand and cooling her burning forehead with wet rags. It was too much for Dora. How much can one woman be expected to bear? It was too much. She sat silent for weeks, catatonic with grief. Evangelia had listened to Dora's stories and knew what needed to be done. She washed Rachel's tiny body and ripped the sheets from her own bed, using them to make Rachel's funeral shroud. Since Rachel was Jewish, the priest would not allow her to be buried in the Christian cemetery. But Evangelia got down on her hands and knees, and with her bare hands she cleared the earth just outside the cemetery gate. They buried Rachel there, near the entrance. The priest stood with Dora, your *yia-yia*, and the other islanders, and although he did not know the Kaddish, the Jewish prayers for the dead, he said prayers from his heart and asked God to take this innocent child into his arms."

Daphne was silent. She opened her mouth to speak, but no words came. There were no words. But Yianni was still not finished. He still had more to say.

"I learned many stories of the war at university," he continued. "We studied the bravery of Athenian archbishop Damaskinos, who told his clergy to hide Jews in their very own homes and issued false baptismal certificates that saved thousands. When the Nazis threatened him with the firing squad for his actions, the archbishop boldly replied, 'According to the traditions of the Greek Orthodox Church, our prelates are hanged, not shot. Please respect our traditions.' " Yianni closed his eyes again. He sat motionless and silent, savoring the archbishop's words.

"I learned too of Bishop Chrysostomos and Mayor Loukas Karrer of Zakynthos. When ordered by the Germans to present a list of Jews living on the island, they handed over a list with only two names—their own. Beause of these men, not one Jew perished in Zakynthos, not one."

He took a deep breath, his chest expanding, his spine straightening.

"Evangelia is just as brave as these men, Daphne, just as deserving of acknowledgment and honor. You have been asking why I feel so close to your grandmother, Daphne. And that is why. I owe her everything, everything I have, everything I am. My whole life, I always promised that I would return to Erikousa and find Evangelia, to thank her. To hold her hand and kiss her cheek and look into the eyes of the woman who risked her own life to save my family. That is all Dora ever asked of me, and I promised I would do this for her. When I was younger, I never found the time, always too busy, running here and there. I spent my whole life studying, my head stuck in books, desperate to suck up knowledge and information. But in the end, it all meant nothing. I was filled with facts, but I was empty. That's when I realized it was time to fulfill my grandmother's wish, to come and meet the woman who saved her life, who saved my own mother as well. That's when I came and found your *yia-yia*."

"Why didn't anyone ever tell me?"

"She had always planned to tell you when you were a mother yourself. She felt then, and only then, could you truly understand what happened. But then you were struck by tragedy as well, another young widow with a child to raise. She didn't want to weigh you down with ghosts from the past when you were haunted by ghosts of your own."

There was no denying the truth in his words. Her eyes were closed as she listened to him speak, but Daphne could feel his gaze. What she saw when she opened them surprised her once again. Gone was the piercing and challenging intensity that had always stared back from Yianni's face. There was no challenge in his eyes this time, no contest to win, no riddle to unravel.

Gone was the straight-shouldered bravado that Yianni had worn just a few short hours ago as they boarded the fishing boat. His shoulders were now hunched as he leaned on the railing for support. This trip, this story, had exhausted him. He looked toward the dock; it was closer than he had anticipated—as if the shore had snuck up on them, their journey together too quickly coming to an end. He jumped up without another word and prepared to dock the boat.

No, don't go. We're not finished. She wanted him there with her, but she could not bring herself to say it, not out loud. *Come back. Come back and sit with me, tell me more.* But he could not hear her silent pleading.

"We're here." He leaped onto the dock, tying the *kaiki* with the expertise of a man who could fashion complex knots with his eyes closed.

"Wait!" she shouted. "Wait, don't go!" Daphne yelled as she jumped up from her seat. She reached her arm up to him. He pulled her up and guided her to shore with no hesitation. Daphne looked up again, knowing what she needed to do. *Just once more, just to be certain.*

Her eyes locked in on his. It was all the confirmation she needed.

There was no denying the pain in the black eyes that stared back at her. It was a look she knew well.

It was like looking in a mirror.

Twenty

Daphne ran into Stephen's arms the moment he emerged from the crowd of suntanned tourists at the Corfu Airport. As soon as she laid eyes on him, with his perfectly tailored pants and striped polo shirt, Daphne had anticipated feeling a sense of relief. Stephen had always had a calming and quieting effect on Daphne; it was the one thing that always stood out in her mind about her fiancé. When Stephen was nearby, it seemed that everything would always somehow be all right—every problem would have a solution, every minute detail would be taken care of.

There, in the middle of the hot, dusty airport terminal, as he greeted her with, "Hello gorgeous," he scooped her up into his arms and bent down to kiss her lips. But even Stephen's presence, his strong hands, the pull of his fingers stroking her hair, the anesthetic timbre of his voice, could not dull the lingering ache that Yianni's story had left. This time, even Stephen was powerless to fix what had happened. Even Stephen couldn't dull the impact of

Yianni's words, nor the impact of his eyes. As she leaned into Stephen's body, Daphne felt as if there were no strength left in her own, as if the trip across the Ionian Sea that morning had drained her too, leaving her as dry and empty as the black sea urchin shells that she and Yianni had left bobbing on the sea in their wake.

But Daphne knew this wasn't the time nor the place to tell Stephen what had happened, what she had learned. In the process of convincing him to move the wedding here, Daphne had painted a vision of an island paradise, a beautiful place filled with nothing but love and laughter. For her entire life, Daphne had believed this to be true. Only earlier in the day, onboard a simple *kaiki*, had a bearded fisherman shattered her fantasy.

"Honey, are you all right? What's wrong?" Stephen asked.

"Nothing," she replied. "I'm just so happy to see you. I guess I'm just . . ." She paused, making certain to choose her words carefully. "I guess I'm just overwhelmed."

And she was. As much as she had loved having Evie and Yiayia to herself for so many days, she'd also been anxious to move forward, to begin her new life. But something had changed for Daphne that morning in the terminal. When she laid eyes on Stephen, instead of sensing relief, Daphne was overcome with something else, something she'd never expected. When Daphne spotted Stephen as he emerged from the plane, she didn't stop to think how lucky she was to be with a man who had all the answers. Instead, Daphne realized that she, herself, had none.

Yes, she had success, she now had money, she even had the highest accolades; but it was all due to Stephen's help. She could never have done it without him. All these years, Daphne had imagined herself so advanced, so independent, so very modern and evolved from the peasant roots that tethered her to the dirt roads, chicken coops, and archaic customs of her family's homeland. But in that moment she realized that despite her education, her American upbringing, cosmopolitan outlook, and financial success, she was not the vanguard in her family. She was not the one whose accomplishments and life should be revered and regaled. After listening to Yianni's story, there was no doubt in Daphne's mind that that particular honor was reserved for Yiayia.

It was Yia-yia, not Daphne, who had proven what it was to be a woman; fearless, strong, unstoppable, and divine. As Daphne clutched Stephen's hand and walked with him toward the terminal exit, she didn't feel like any of those things. She felt like a coward.

"I'll be right back." Stephen kissed Daphne's cheek as he headed toward the bathroom to shower.

Daphne rolled over in bed. She clutched the white sheet to her chest and listened to the hotel's antiquated plumbing screech and groan as Stephen turned on the water in the white marble bathroom. Despite its four-star rating, the Corfu Palace hotel still maintained some of the quirks and characteristics of traditional Corfu life.

Even as a young girl, Daphne had always loved the majestic old hotel. Whenever she and Yia-yia made the trip from Erikousa to Kerkyra, either to stock up on supplies or for one of Yia-yia's doctor's visits, they would walk arm in arm along the sidewalks of Garitsa Bay, gazing up across the main road at the ornate hotel. Yia-yia would always cluck and coo over the lush gardens—the leafy palm trees, towering lilies, and seemingly endless rainbow of rosebushes. Daphne adored the hotel's meticulously maintained grounds, but she was fixated on the hotel's grand entrance.

More than anything, she loved the wide semicircular driveway, lined with an army of international flags that stood sentry as the bell captain greeted each guest. Daphne had loved standing across the street with Yia-yia, watching the flags dance to life in the bay breeze. For Yia-yia, this view was something to enjoy, appreciate from afar. But for Daphne, this hotel was more than something to admire; it was something to aspire to.

After all those years of gazing up at the hotel from the public park across the street, this was the first time Daphne had actually stayed at the Corfu Palace. It was the first time she could actually rationalize spending hundreds of dollars on a room when Popi's apartment sat empty just a few blocks away. She had thought about staying at the hotel when she arrived from New York with Evie, but despite the fact that Evie would have loved the large, shallow, and therefore unthreatening kiddie pool, Daphne knew that Popi and Evie would bond better in the apartment, without any outside distractions.

But now, on Stephen's first day in Kerkyra, Daphne knew it was the perfect time to make good her lifelong dream of driving up the flag-lined driveway and being greeted by the bell captain. She wanted Stephen's first impressions of Greece to be warm and positive ones. And if he stayed here, they no doubt would be. Confident she had made the right decision, Daphne rolled over once again and stepped out of bed, her toes sinking into the deep pile of the hotel suite's white carpet.

We'll save the reality of flies, chickens, and donkey poop for later.

Daphne laughed, thinking of the culture shock that awaited Stephen on Erikousa. *For now, we'll just let him think we're all about marble baths and room service.*

AS STEPHEN SHOWERED, DAPHNE WRAPPED herself in her makeshift toga and pushed open the terrace doors. The sheet lifted as it caught the breeze that kicked up from the shores of Garitsa Bay below. Daphne walked to the terrace's metal rail and leaned out, one hand grasping the sheet to her chest, the other clutching the rail to steady herself. She pushed her torso forward to take in every detail of the stunning view, looking straight down on the hotel's outdoor restaurant and pool area. The saltwater pool was lined with Corinthian columns and lush green plants, as if guests had turned the corner from the modern lobby and found themselves transported to a secret, ancient grotto. Daphne smiled as she realized that was kind of how she felt here, surrounded by the opulence of the Corfu Palace, just miles away but yet worlds from her family's life on Erikousa.

She looked up from the swimming pool and out across the bay. The water's glassy surface was dotted with grand yachts as well as the humble, weather-beaten fishing boats she knew so well from her childhood. There was something enchanting about the light this time of day. Daphne loved when the blinding light of midday began to fade, allowing the naked eye to see colors and details that the daylight often obscured with its intensity. She took it all in; the peeling pale blues of the fishing boats' hulls, the two-toned grain of the yachts' wooden rails, the rusty orange of the hibiscus plants that bordered the bay's pedestrian walkways, and of course, the last gold and purple flecks of the sun's dying rays skating across the water's surface.

She inhaled sharply as she spotted it, waves of grief washing over her again and again, mimicking the incoming tide lapping against the shore below. There it was. Just beyond the pool area, to the left of the bay, jutting out into the water and standing sentinel on a man-made island, there stood the old fort. Daphne shuddered to think of what had happened there, of what Yianni had told her. She still couldn't understand how a place built to protect the people of Kerkyra could have been used for such evil. She couldn't imagine the people, men, women, and children, dragged there, plucked from the quiet routine of their lives, terrified and uncertain of their fate. Their own lives and the lives of their children at the mercy of strangers with guns strapped to their waists. She imagined Yia-yia, a younger woman then, marching through the streets of the town to the fort, determined to save another woman's child. This all seemed more fantastical and surreal than any myth or fable Daphne had ever heard. But according to Yianni, it was all true, disturbingly and frighteningly true.

Daphne was so lost in her thoughts that she didn't notice that the noisy shower pipes had stopped squeaking or that Stephen had slid open the terrace door behind her. Not until he pressed his still-damp naked chest against her back did she snap out of her daydream with a startle.

"Are you cold?" he asked. "It feels like ninety degrees, and you're covered with goose bumps." He rubbed his hands up and down her shoulders.

"No, I'm good." Daphne turned to face him. "I'm good," she repeated, attempting to convince herself more than Stephen.

"Isn't this hotel beautiful?" She lifted her arm and swept it into the air around her. "That bed and those sheets are so comfortable. I could crawl back in and sleep for days." She hunched her shoulders, gripping the sheet with both hands and burrowing her face in the soft, white cotton.

"Yes, but not as beautiful as you." He leaned in and kissed her forehead. "Let's go. I'm starving, and I'm dying to see this island you've been bragging about for so long." He kissed her again and turned to go back inside.

Daphne watched as he unzipped his garment bag and pulled out a pair of perfectly pressed khaki pants and a polo shirt. As he began to dress, Daphne looked out once more across the water. It was now officially twilight; a pale gray and purple pallor had settled over the entire bay. The yachts bobbing on the water's surface had all turned their lights on, casting an eerie sheen across the bay. She looked down toward the park and watched as children whizzed ahead on their scooters while couples walking hand in hand trailed behind. Daphne closed her eyes and inhaled one last time. The fresh sea air was now permeated with the smoky scent of lamb roasting below on a spit, smothered in garlic, rosemary, and lemon.

Her stomach growled. Realizing that Stephen was probably dressed by now, she turned to go inside and get dressed herself. But then she spotted them, and felt compelled to stay and watch a bit longer.

There below, walking arm in arm along the bay, was a teenage girl in a miniskirt and an elderly woman in a shapeless black dress. Daphne's eyes followed them as they strolled along the bay. They talked and talked, giggling and smiling at each other, the old woman leaning on the young girl for support as they walked. Daphne leaned over just a bit, straining to hear what they were saying, but the terrace was too high, she could hear nothing. But then Daphne realized that it really didn't matter. She didn't need to hear the conversation between a *yia-yia* and a young girl as they walked in the twilight, surrounded on one side by the sea, and on the other by the siren call of a grand hotel. She didn't have to hear their words or wonder what they were talking about; Daphne remembered it all quite well.

Twenty-one

It was past nine when they finally made it out of the hotel, dressed, showered, and desperate for something to eat. As they walked hand in hand along the bay toward town, Daphne decided not to play tour guide. She originally had every intention of giving Stephen the grand treatment and pointing out all of the minute details that made Kerkyra special. But it was such a perfect night that this time Daphne thought it best to let the island speak for itself. She said nothing as they walked past the grand gazebo in the park where the Corfu Philharmonic was entertaining the crowd with a free concert, its lyrical strings and pounding drums offering the perfect background music for their walk. Linking arms, they continued to the edge of the park where the manicured grass met the old Venetian arches of Spianada Square. There, they stopped and watched the gypsies who lined the square haggling over everything they had to offer; balloons, toys, a ten-minute ride on a motorized car, roasted corn, and even spanakopita.

Daphne stopped directly in front of one old gypsy who had caught her eye. There was no real way of knowing just how old he was, maybe fifty, maybe ninety-five. His skin was dark, shiny, and thick, like leather, his face lined with deep crags. When he made a sale, his wide grin revealed a smattering of missing teeth. Despite the fact that it was still about eighty degrees outside, he wore an old, ill-fitting suit jacket with a scarf knotted around his neck.

They watched as he tended his corn. He lifted each ear with tarnished tongs, bringing them to his face for inspection and making certain they were caramelized and brown but never burned. When he was convinced that the corn was roasted to perfection, he placed it in another pan and sprinkled it with a generous coating of sea salt.

"Come on, let's get some." Daphne tugged Stephen closer to the corn gypsy.

"Are you kidding me?" He pulled away. "Daphne, he has no teeth. Did you see his fingernails? They're black. There's no way—"

But Daphne didn't wait to hear the rest of his protests. She dropped his arm and approached the corn seller with a broad smile. "Two, please," she said in Greek, reaching into her bag for her wallet.

The gypsy met Daphne's order with a broad grin, foamy spittle collecting at the corner of his mouth. "For you, pretty lady, two euro. A special price." He wrapped the ears in plain brown paper and handed them to Daphne.

"*Efharisto*," she replied, handing the man a twenty-euro bill and walking away before he could make change.

The old gypsy watched Daphne turn and walk away from him, then looked down at the bill lying faceup in his hand, his small, cloudy eyes wide with disbelief. Crumpling the bill in his fist, he looked around to make sure no one else was watching, then shoved the money into his jacket pocket before turning back to tend his corn.

"Here," she said as she held the corn out to Stephen. "Trust me. It's delicious." She sank her teeth into the sweet, succulent appetizer. Despite the fact that it had been roasted on hot coals, this corn wasn't dry. As Daphne bit down again, her mouth exploded with the sugary juice that escaped from each kernel, balanced by just the right amount of savory crunch from the sea salt.

Still holding the corn in his hands, Stephen continued staring at Daphne. "This from a woman who won't eat a hot dog from a Manhattan street cart. A *licensed* and *regulated* street cart." He shook his corn at Daphne.

"Yeah, but those dirty-water dogs are gross. I mean, who knows how long they sit in that rancid water before some sucker tourist comes along and buys them?" She laughed.

"All right, if you insist. When in Rome—" He bit down on his corn, smiling as the flavors burst in his mouth.

"May I remind you that this is Greece?" She once again linked her arm under his and continued their walk.

They stopped once more for something to eat, the next location just as unconventional, unassuming, and yet delicious as the first. Ninos Fast Food had always been a favorite of Daphne and Popi's. The greasy souvlaki sandwiches piled high with *tzatziki* sauce, onions, tomatoes, grilled pork cubes, and even French fries were always a staple when the cousins were in town together. Even

Yia-yia, who rarely ate out, would insist they bring her home a souvlaki from Ninos whenever she came to Kerkyra.

"Now this is good, really good," Stephen said as he took another bite of his souvlaki, *tzatziki* dripping down his chin. Daphne leaned in and wiped the juice from his face before using the same napkin to clean her own face. "You should serve this at Koukla. Seriously," he said through a mouthful of souvlaki.

"No, not at Koukla." She shook her head. "But something like this would be great downtown, near NYU. There was this little greasy falafel place that did great business when I was a student, but it was a dirty little hole-in-the-wall. Think what you could do with modern Greek fast food. You know, take the classics like this, the roasted corn and spanakopita, and dress them up for those downtown students with some cute packaging." She stopped talking and looked up at the exterior of Ninos, with its simple wooden sign and line of tourists and locals that went out the door and wound across the sidewalk. "You know, something like Ninos New York."

"That could work," Stephen agreed, sinking his teeth into the sandwich, his second.

"I know," Daphne replied, not certain if she should be pleased that Stephen liked her idea or afraid that he did. Yes, with Stephen's help Koukla had become a huge success, but it was also the genesis of her eighteen-hour workdays away from Evie. Daphne was well aware that success, like everything else, had its price.

"Come on," she said as she tugged at his arm, eager to change the subject. "There's something I want to show you."

As Stephen finished his souvlaki, Daphne led him down the narrow maze of alleyways that make up the town's historic shopping district. Finally, after turning down yet another alley, they came to a stop in a wide square.

"What's this?" Stephen asked, wiping the last of the souvlaki from his face.

"Oh, good, it's still open." Daphne sighed when she saw the open double doors. "I wasn't sure what time they close."

"When what closes?"

"It's Agios Spyridon, Saint Spyridon. Come on." She led the way to the old church.

The familiar scent of smoke and incense welcomed Daphne the moment she approached the church's wooden double doors. Everything was just as she had remembered it; the large room was dotted with black-clad widows and white-haired men wearing ill-fitting suit jackets and genuflecting toward the icon-adorned altar. She held Stephen's hand and took it all in, remembering the story Yianni had shared. She imagined Yia-yia, Dora, and the girls hiding here as the bloodthirsty death squads lurked just outside the doors. She tried to imagine the scene and found herself enveloped by grief again. Once again she willed the picture from her mind. Not now. It was too much for her to contemplate, too much to process. She had to will Dora and the girls out of her mind, even if it was just for tonight.

She turned her gaze to the trough of candles at the church's entrance, watching mothers hovering over children as their shaky little hands lit candles and placed them in the sand-lined troughs. Inside the church, a silvery glow filled the room. Daphne looked around as other mothers lifted little ones who were still too small to reach the icons. She watched as they whispered into their children's ears, instructing them to kiss the saint, as they planted the first seeds of tradition and faith in their children, and she realized just how much she missed Evie. She had only left her with Yia-yia for one night, but now, seeing the other mothers with their children, she wished Evie were here with her now.

She had meant to bring Evie to the church, to teach her about their beloved saint, but there just hadn't been enough time. *After the wedding*, she promised, lighting a candle and placing it with the others. She pinched the three fingers of her right hand together, made the sign of the cross three times, as she had been instructed by Yia-yia when she was a child, and held back her hair as she leaned forward to kiss the silver-framed icon of Saint Spyridon. But, unlike the other worshippers, Daphne was careful to plant her kiss away from any lip prints left behind by the faithful.

Stephen lingered in the doorway for a moment, taking in this mysteriously exotic scene. It was the antithesis of the pristine white Episcopal chapel attended by his family back home.

"This is some church," he whispered in her ear.

"I know." She nodded. "But this is nothing." She turned and smiled at him. "Here, come with me." She took his hand and led him across the church. There, just to the right of the altar, stood a second doorway covered in ornate icons. Stephen tried to get a better look, but dozens of people were filing in and out of the door, and he couldn't make out what was inside, what everyone was clamoring to see.

"It's the saint," Daphne whispered as she pointed to the open door.

Stephen craned his neck to see, but he still wasn't sure what it was he was supposed to be looking at.

"It's the saint," Daphne repeated. "Saint Spyridon, our patron saint."

"What is it, a shrine or something?"

"No, he's *in* there. His body is in there."

He pulled away from her.

"He's the protector of the island, our patron saint. He's very special to the people of Corfu. His body is centuries old, but still intact. He protects the island, protects us, performs miracles for us."

"For us?" He turned away from the altar and faced Daphne. "Come on, Daphne. You don't actually believe in this stuff?"

Daphne was taken aback. She had never really stopped to think about qualifying her beliefs before. Back home, she never made it to church or discussed religion, so it was no wonder Stephen was surprised by her connection to the saint. But belief in Agios Spyridon was not something anyone from Kerkyra ever questioned. There was no reason to. It was embedded in each and every child born with a connection to the island. It was as if the saint himself blessed every birth and took every step beside that child, protecting her and watching over her for the duration of her life. And yes, now, even more than ever, especially after hearing Yianni's story, there was no question that Daphne did in fact believe.

"Yes." Daphne looked Stephen directly in the eyes. "Yes, I do. I do believe."

"Come on, Daphne." He tilted his head and looked down at her. "Really?"

"Yes, really. I always have, and I always will."

The tiny room that held the saint's remains began to empty before she could say more. Several women and men filed out, some holding the hands of small children, while a few curious tourists straggled behind, confused by what they had just witnessed.

"Come on." Daphne linked her arm with Stephen's. "The service is over. Let's go in."

He seemed unsure, pulling back as Daphne drew him toward the door.

"Come on." She gave him a final tug.

The tiny room had emptied out. Two old women and a priest, deep in conversation, lingered over the open silver casket that held the saint's remains. Daphne smiled, knowing how lucky they were to find the casket open; it was only opened by the priests for special occasions and special prayer services. Daphne bowed her head at the bearded priest, who did the same in return. Clutching Stephen's hand, she led him around the small room, dripping in silver lamps and lined with paintings depicting the saint's life. She stopped first at the far end of the casket and pointed out the red velvet slippers that adorned Agios Spyridon's feet.

"Those are his shoes." Daphne leaned in closer to Stephen as she spoke, so as not to interrupt the other worshippers who had begun filing into the room. "Every year the priests put a new pair of those slippers on his feet," she whispered. "And at the end of the year they open the casket and find that the slippers are worn out."

Stephen squeezed her hand. Daphne knew he was having a hard time believing any of this, but she was determined to continue with her story. "They're worn because every night, the saint rises and walks the streets of Kerkyra, protecting the island and its people." She walked around to the other end of the casket. "Here. See."

In the dim light it was hard to make out the details, but there it was; the face of Agios Spyridon. His face was mummified, dark gray and dry. His eye sockets were sunken in, his cheeks hollow, a straight indentation where his mouth should be. Those without faith might have recoiled at the sight. But to Daphne and those who believed, the sight of their protector was comforting.

Daphne said a quick, silent prayer as Stephen continued pressing his face closer to the casket. When she had finished thanking the *agios* for her good fortune and the health of her daughter and Yia-yia, Daphne also thanked the *agios* for providing safe refuge for Yia-yia, Dora and the children.

I know your miracles are many, she prayed. *Thank you for always finding a way to help and protect our family. Please, Agios Spyridon*, she pleaded, *please walk beside me and guide me. Hold my hand and help me make the right decisions on my life. Please help me find strength, the same strength you gave Yia-yia. Please guide me as you have guided her, and help me lead Evie toward a happy and fulfilled life.*

When her prayer was finished, Daphne made the sign of the cross three more times. She knelt down and kissed the casket before taking Stephen's hand and leading him toward the door.

"Well. That was something." He ran his fingers through his hair. "So he gets up and walks around at night." He raised an eyebrow at Daphne. "In his slippers."

His attempt at humor was not lost on Daphne, but not finding it the least bit funny, she decided not to engage. She chose to simply ignore it.

"Come, we're not done." She led him to the main church area and picked up a pencil and a small square piece of paper from a basket left out on a bench.

"What are you doing?" he asked

"It's traditional to write the names of those you want the saint to protect on a piece of paper." Daphne wrote her list: Evie, Yia-yia, Popi, Nitsa, and Stephen. She kissed the paper, folded it in half, and placed it in another basket, which was quickly filling with the notes of the faithful.

Daphne turned. She smiled at her fiancé and lifted his hand to her lips for a kiss. She knew he didn't understand it, that he thought the whole idea of miracles and worshipping a mummified body was somewhat archaic and creepy. He was a man of reason—of facts, not blind faith. Daphne knew there were basic differences between them; their cultures and histories were worlds apart. But in the end, that really was all right. She had long ago given up on the ideal of a perfect companion who understood and adored her every nuance. Daphne had buried that dream the day they placed Alex's body in the earth.

"Come on, let's go." She tugged at his hand again. "There's a beautiful rooftop bar at the Hotel Cavalieri I want to show you."

"Now that's more like it. Let's get out of here. I could use a drink." He placed his arm around Daphne and led her toward the door.

"Yeah, me too." She turned once more before exiting the church. As she glanced back toward the saint's tomb, Daphne stopped.

"What is it?" Stephen asked.

There, standing at the entrance of the tomb, was Yianni. Daphne felt her stomach jump alive. She tried to swallow, but it seemed as if the butterflies had also gathered in her windpipe, their fluttering wings blocking her air passage. She stood there beside Stephen and watched as Yianni bowed his head before the icon. Daphne noticed how unlike the other worshippers, he did not perform the sign of the cross. *Of course not, he's Jewish.* But he did lean forward toward the base of the icon and kiss the feet of the saint who had helped save his mother and grandmother so many years ago. He walked through the door and disappeared into the small room where the *agios* slept.

"What is it?" Stephen asked again.

"Nothing." She smiled up at her fiancé. "Just a guy I know."

They walked arm in arm out of the church and into the cool night air of the cobblestone square. She looked back toward the church one last time. "He's just an old friend from Erikousa."

Twenty-two

NEW YORK
2001

"Never." Mama slammed her fist on the dining room table. "You will never see him again," she hissed through clenched teeth.

"But Mama, he is not what you think," Daphne cried. She reached her arms out to her mother, pleading. "Please, he's not what you think." Her voice quivered, as did her hands.

Mama stood. She stared down at Daphne. Her eyes narrowed and seemed to grow three shades darker as Daphne looked up at her.

Mama brought the knuckle of her right index finger to her mouth and bit down hard. Daphne had only seen Mama do that once before, the time she had dared give her phone number to the sweet, pale, and sweaty-palmed boy she met at the seventh-grade school dance. When he called the next morning and simply asked to speak with Daphne, Baba had hung up on him, slamming the phone down so hard and loud that Daphne came running out of her room to see what was the matter. Baba stormed off to the restaurant without speaking or looking at her. Daphne knew all too well the staggering depths and ramifications of Baba's temper. It had been twenty years since he had spoken to his own siblings after an argument about the inheritance of his parents' small garden plot on the neighboring island of Othoni. She wondered how long it would be before he spoke to her again. As the door banged closed behind him, Mama gnawed on her knuckle before slapping Daphne across the face. *"Poutana,"* she spat before banishing Daphne to her room.

That was the first and last school dance Daphne ever attended.

But that was then. She wasn't that scared and obedient thirteen-year-old anymore. Respectful, yes—but no longer scared. This was too important. This was Alex.

"Baba, please." His back was to her. She stood, placing her hand on his shoulder, willing him to turn around and see the honesty in her eyes. "You need to trust me. Alex is a good man."

Baba lifted his chin and swallowed hard.

"Just meet him. You'll see when you meet him."

He walked away from his daughter just as he had the morning after the dance, again—never meeting her eyes. Her limp arm fell to her side as she heard the click of the radio and Greek news blaring too loudly from the next room.

Mama stood from her seat at the head of the dining room table. She took three steps toward the kitchen, then stopped and turned to face Daphne, wringing her hands. Her black bun, normally so neatly pinned on top of her head, had come undone. Bobby pins are no match for the flailing, chest beating, and gesticulations of a Greek mother whose daughter dares defy her parents and her heritage.

"You will not do this to your father. You will not do this to me. We did not come to this country to stand on our feet sixteen hours a day, cleaning, cooking, serving, slaving—working like animals until we are so tired that even sleep does not soothe our exhausted bodies—we did not do this, Daphne, for you to be the whore of some American boy you met at school."

Her words hurt worse than the slap across her face had. Daphne straightened her spine and met her mother's glare without blinking and without backing down. "I am not his whore." She spoke slowly and deliberately. "I love him, and he loves me. And we are going to be together."

Mama did not say a word. She stormed out of the dining room and into the kitchen. Daphne heard the refrigerator slam shut. She shuddered as Mama's cleaver slammed down on the chopping board again and again, louder and harder and more deliberate than necessary.

End of discussion.

Beginning of Daphne and Alex's herculean mission.

SEATED BETWEEN HER PARENTS IN the pew, Daphne recited the Our Father first in Greek, and then in English, along with the rest of the congregation.

"*Pater emon, O en tis Ouranis, Agiastiste to onoma sou . . .*"

"Our father, who art in heaven, hallowed be thy name . . ."

She knew he was there. She didn't have to see him. She could feel him near. Knowing it was disrespectful to look behind you in church, she stared straight ahead, never daring to look back for confirmation.

Remember Orpheus and Eurydice, she reminded herself, knowing how close Orpheus had come to saving his beloved Eurydice. The young bride had stepped on a poisonous snake and died, taken away to become a shade in the underworld. Orpheus was distraught, playing his lute so mournfully that Queen Persephone and even King Hades himself had taken pity on the heartbroken lovers and promised to reunite them. They allowed Eurydice to follow Orpheus out of the underworld on one condition: that Orpheus never look back to see if she was there. But overcome with fear and doubt, Orpheus turned to look. Eurydice disappeared before his eyes.

Daphne would not make the same mistake.

"Lead us not into temptation . . ." She continued reciting the prayer a bit louder than usual.

When it was time for communion, she stood with her parents and walked to the altar. Father Anastasios dipped the communal spoon into the chalice of wine and bread and then slipped it into her mouth. She turned to go back to her seat, and finally she spotted him, seated toward the back, alone in a sea of families and *yia-yias*.

Her eyes lit up at the sight of him. He smiled back, keeping his head solemnly bowed, along with the rest of the parishioners.

Mama looked at Daphne and then followed her gaze to Alex. No introduction needed.

"What is he doing here? He is not Greek," she hissed under her breath as she grabbed Daphne's elbow, just a little too hard, and directed her back into their pew. Baba followed behind, lost in his thoughts, not noticing the drama playing out before him.

Daphne leaned over and pulled the red velvet-lined prayer kneeler down. She got down on her knees, made the sign of the cross, clasped her hands together, and said a silent prayer of thanks before turning to face her mother.

"He loves me." She smiled. That was all the explanation needed.

Mama got down on her knees and said a prayer of her own.

IT CONTINUED LIKE THAT FOR months. Each Sunday he sat at the back of the church, respectfully and solitary, never approaching Daphne or her family. Just smiling at Daphne and, when she dared look and acknowledge his presence, at Mama as well.

He was there on August 11, the litany of Saint Spyridon. From the corner of her eye, Mama watched as he lit the red glass offering candle and placed it on the altar by the feet of the saint's icon.

He was there again on August 15, the feast of the Dormition, at the celebration of the Holy Virgin Mother's assumption into heaven. Mama had just returned from the ladies' room when she spotted him lighting a candle and making the sign of the cross, not with three fingers as in the Greek Orthodox tradition, but a "cross of other churches," as Mama called it, using his entire hand.

He was there on Christmas Eve, carrying an armload of gifts for Saint Basil's orphanage collection. He smiled broadly as he approached the Ladies' Philoptochos Society table where Mama was volunteering for the toy drive.

"Merry Christmas, young man," one of the ladies greeted him

as he handed over the gifts. Mama busied herself with untying and retying a large green bow on a small square box.

"*Kala Hristougena, kyries,*" he replied; "Merry Christmas, ladies." The accent was off, but the vocabulary was perfect.

"Bravo, young man." The ladies clapped their hands and fussed over him.

Mama said nothing.

HE WAS THERE ON PALM Sunday. Alex bent down to kiss Father Anastasios's hand as the priest handed him his woven palm cross at the end of the service. Mama watched as Father welcomed Alex to the church family and invited him to stay for coffee hour. "Everyone is welcome in Christ's house," the priest said, slapping Alex's back.

Mama and Baba watched from across the church hall as Daphne approached Alex. They stood drinking coffee, talking and smiling at each other. They dared not kiss or touch, knowing that would be insolent and imprudent. Baba huffed as he watched them, taking one step forward to put an end to this shameful display. But Mama put her hand on his arm and stopped him from going farther.

"No," she said. "Everyone is welcome in Christ's house."

He was there every night of Holy Week, through every moment of every solemn service. He stood in line at the altar on Holy Wednesday and lifted his head toward Father Anastasios while the priest anointed his face with holy oil, first on his forehead, then chin and cheeks as well as his palms and hands. On Good Friday he joined the procession as the flower-covered *epi-*

taphios depicting Christ's tomb was carried around the church and the congregation followed solemnly behind. Daphne walked with her parents at first, but gradually found her way to Alex's side. Mama and Baba watched and shook their heads as their daughter slowly drifted away from them. But neither tried to stop her.

At the midnight Easter Anastasi Service of Christ's Resurrection, Alex was already seated as Daphne and her parents filed into the church just before midnight. They had run late, the diner busier than usual, making it impossible to get there in time to secure seats for the always crowded service. They stood in the back, just behind Alex, who knew better than to turn and confirm she was there. The packed church was quiet and still as the celebrants stood shoulder to shoulder, holding unlit candles and waiting for a joyous end to the mournful and reflective week.

Just before midnight all the lights were turned off. Father Anastasios emerged from behind the altar into the darkened church holding a single lit candle. He then turned to the altar boys lighting each of their candles. The boys walked into the congregation, and one by one, candle by candle, row by row, the light of Christ's resurrection spread through the church. The young mother seated in front of Alex turned to light his candle. Alex then turned around to share the flame and came face-to-face with Daphne and Mama. He smiled as he lit Daphne's wick. Mama stared at him and hesitated for a moment. But finally she leaned in and allowed Alex's light into her life. In that moment, the church erupted into the joyous hymn of Christ's resurrection.

"*Christos Anesti ek nekron. Thanato Thanaton patisas, Kai tis en tis mnimasi, Zoi, Harisamenos.*"

Daphne lifted her face toward the light and sang each word as if it were coming from her heart and not her mouth.

With one hand she held her candle, with the other she reached for her mother's hand. Mama didn't hesitate this time. She locked fingers with Daphne as they sang.

"Christ is risen from the dead, trampling down death by death, and to those in the tombs, granting new life."

And in that moment Daphne knew she had indeed been granted a new life.

Twenty-three

Evie ran across the dock as soon as she saw Daphne disembarking from Big Al. She let out a high-pitched screech and took a flying leap into her mother's arms.

"Mommy, I had so much fun," Evie squealed as she wrapped her legs around her mother's waist and cinched her arms around Daphne's neck.

"Well, did you miss me even a little bit?" Daphne kissed her little girl's neck. Evie smelled of sunblock and the giant red rose that she wore tucked behind her right ear.

"Yes, but Mommy. You won't believe it. Yia-yia showed me how to make pita, my very own pita dough. I used an old broom and everything, just like the one you have at home. It was so cool. Mommy, I loved it. How come you never cook with me back home, Mommy? How come? Promise me you'll cook with me, promise me, Mommy?"

"Honey, of course I'll cook with you." Daphne laughed.

"And you know what else?" the little girl continued. "Thea Popi told me a story. There was this guy, King Midas, and he was really greedy, Mommy. Everything he touched turned to gold—I mean everything."

"Sounds pretty good." Stephen chuckled.

"Yeah, until he touched his little girl." Daphne stroked Evie's hair and kissed her little pink cheek.

"And then she turned to gold, too," Evie shouted as she clapped.

"It's a great story, honey. One of my favorites. But aren't you forgetting something?" Daphne chided. "Aren't you going to say hello to Stephen? He came all this way to see you." Daphne unwrapped Evie's arms from around her neck and placed the little girl back on the ground.

"Hi." Evie fingered the glass eye that hung around her neck.

"Well, hello to you too. For you, Miss Evie," he said as he hugged her, then took a rainbow-colored lollipop out of his pocket and handed it to her.

"Thank you," Evie said as she took the treat, unwrapping it and placing it in her mouth before racing off with one of the stray dogs who lived at the port.

Popi, who had been standing off to the side watching the entire exchange, stepped forward. "Welcome back, Cousin." She hugged Daphne and kissed her on both cheeks.

"Popi, this is Stephen."

"Ah, finally we meet," Popi bellowed as she threw her arms around Stephen. He stood motionless for a moment, his arms straight at his side, not sure what to do with this much affection from a stranger. "Welcome, Stephen," Popi shouted as she squeezed one last time and released Stephen from her anaconda grip.

Daphne giggled. She had to admit, it was pretty funny. On one hand, there was Popi, red-cheeked, rotund, and bursting with unbridled energy and affection, swinging her hips and her arms as if she were performing some sort of ancient fertility dance. And then of course, there was Stephen; fit, self-contained, immaculately dressed and mannered, not a hair or gesture out of place.

"Where's Yia-yia?" Daphne asked as she looked around the port.

"She's back at the house, waiting for us. Ah, Cousin Stephen, you are in for a big surprise." Popi clucked as she linked her arm with Stephen's.

Daphne bit her lower lip to keep from laughing. There was Stephen, usually so in control, looking as if he were afraid Popi was going to eat him for breakfast.

"So what's the surprise?" Daphne asked.

"Ah, Cousin Stephen." Popi patted his forearm as they walked. "For you, Yia-yia has outdone herself. For you, *stifado*."

"Stif-what?"

"Stee-faa-do," Popi repeated.

"It's a stew," Daphne chimed in. "A really delicious, thick, rich stew."

"Then why haven't you made it for me before, if it's so delicious?" Stephen teased.

"I know, I've been holding out," Daphne admitted. "It's really, really labor-intensive, actually. It's a tangy beef stew simmered with tomatoes and vinegar and tiny little pearl onions. It takes hours to clean those little onions."

Daphne's mouth as well as her eyes watered, just thinking back to the last time she'd made *stifado*. It had been for Alex's birthday.

She was seven months pregnant at the time, and by the time she was done peeling the tiny pearl onions, her hands cramped and her back ached. The stew had turned out delicious, but Daphne spent two days lying in bed just to recover from its preparation. But she hadn't minded. It was worth seeing the sublime satisfaction on Alex's face when he dove into the dish and lapped up each last drop of sauce. That was the first and last time she had ever made *stifado*.

"Popi, how is Yia-yia making *stifado* with her arthritis?"

"She's been up since four a.m., that's how. It's slow, but she's determined to do it." Popi sashayed away from the port, her arm still linked with Stephen's. "Cousin Stephen, you are a lucky, lucky man." Popi gazed up at her new cousin and batted her thick lashes.

"Yes, I know." He looked at Daphne and a broad grin crossed his face. "Believe me, I know just how lucky I am." He released the suitcase, reached into his back pocket for the white cotton handkerchief that he always carried with him, and dabbed at the beads of sweat that had formed on his brow.

With Evie and the scrawny stray dog leading the way, they moved away from the port and toward Nitsa's inn, where Stephen would be staying.

It was a typical island morning, the soft breeze from the port at their backs, the cracked pavement of the makeshift roads at their feet, an infusion of sea spray, honeysuckle, and fresh rosemary bushes in their nostrils. And everywhere they turned, a swarm of *yia-yias* looking to kiss, hug, and pinch the newly arrived American. If Stephen didn't know what to make of Popi's bold display of affections, he certainly had no idea what to make of what was to come.

Damn, Daphne thought, suppressing the giggle in her throat. I forgot to warn him.

As the first black widow approached, Stephen had no idea that he was in fact the target she was homing in on. Thea Paraskevi circled her prey for a few moments, fanning her hands in the air and squealing and shrieking her congratulations. But unfortunately, instead of well wishes, all Stephen understood was that a shriveled-up old woman veiled in faded black was screaming at him while accosting him with wet kisses.

Daphne watched from the sidelines as one by one, every *thea*, *theo*, *ksadelfos*, and *ksadelfi* they crossed paths with made sure to bid a proper welcome to the immaculate *Amerikanos* who had arrived to marry their Daphne. With pleading eyes, Stephen shot Daphne a series of SOS signals, but Daphne was powerless to stop the surge of well-wishers. She just shrugged her shoulders and whispered, "I'm sorry, I know," while her fiancé repeatedly reached into his back pocket for a hankie to wipe the wet kisses from his cheeks.

Finally they arrived at Hotel Nitsa. Just as Stephen thought he was in the clear, safe from the overzealous gaggle of islanders, they entered the polished marble lobby, where Nitsa was waiting to pounce.

"*Ahoo*!" Nitsa's raspy voice could be heard echoing off the white marble. "There you are. Come here. Come to Thea Nitsa. Come let me see you and welcome you."

The wineglasses above the bar jingled with each waddle. Stephen dropped his suitcase right there in the lobby. He looked like he wanted to run and hide as he spotted Nitsa scurrying toward him in her white apron, hair net, and of course, lit cigarette held high in her right hand. She was half his height, three times his girth, and dead set on giving the American banker a proper Erikousa welcome.

"Look at him," Nitsa screeched as she held his face in both of her hands, the embedded scent of tobacco and garlic on her fingertips making Stephen gag. "Look at him. He looks like Kennedy. He's Kennedy, I tell you. Daphne, your man looks like President Kennedy." Nitsa pinched three plump fingers together and made the sign of the cross. "May God rest his soul."

"Thank you," Stephen stammered and smiled at Nitsa, not sure exactly what the appropriate response would be in a situation like this. He'd barely got the words out before Nitsa again sandwiched his face between her thick hands.

"Welcome to Hotel Nitsa," she announced, spinning and lifting her arms to the sky. "I—," she proclaimed, pounding her chest, "—am Nitsa."

"Nice to meet you," he replied.

"You are family now, and I will make certain you feel at home. *Ella*. You must be tired. I will show you to your room. It is the finest one we have to offer."

"I'll wait here with Evie," Popi shouted as she grabbed Evie's hand and headed toward the bar, where a new group of Australian tourists was settling in with frosty mugs of Mythos. "Take your time. I'll watch her."

Daphne and Stephen followed Thea Nitsa down a long white hallway and turned right at the very last door. Nitsa turned the unlocked doorknob and showed them into a bright, sparsely furnished but immaculate room. The bed, no larger than a full-size mattress, commanded most of the space in the compact room.

Starched and ironed sheets peeked out from beneath the holes of the delicate crochet blanket covering the bed. Daphne knew this tiny rosette pattern was one of the more complicated patterns, and that Nitsa reserved this coverlet for the most special of guests. Besides the bed, there really wasn't much else in the room, just a small dark wood bureau adorned with a small vase that held two perfect red roses. A single French door led to a tiny terrace that overlooked the sea.

"Here you are." Nitsa stood in the doorway, since there wasn't room for her in the room. She took a cigarette out of her apron pocket and lit it, blowing smoke directly into the tiny room. "It may not be fancy like other hotels you have stayed in. But it is the best we have on Erikousa, and I hope you like it and are happy here."

"Yes, it's perfect. Isn't it, Stephen?" Daphne said from the edge of the bed, where she was fingering the delicate strands of the rosette petals on the blanket. "Isn't it?" She got up from the bed and opened the terrace door in an attempt to clear the cigarette smoke from the room. There was nothing Stephen hated more than the smell of cigarette smoke.

"Yes. It's very nice. Thank you, Nitsa." He was examining the bathroom, and popped his head out to respond. "One thing, how late is the business center open?"

"The business center?" Nitsa laughed. "Why, *I* am the business center. I am here all the time. I am always open for my guests." She pounded on her chest again with her left hand, oblivious to the cigarette ashes that had fallen on her black T-shirt. "Any business you need, you tell Nitsa—and Nitsa will take care of it for you."

"So, there's no business center then?" He shot a glance at Daphne.

"No. No business center." Daphne spun her engagement ring.

"All right, then. I will leave you two alone to get settled. Again, welcome." Nitsa turned, starting to close the door. "Anything you need, you ask Nitsa, okay?"

"Thank you." He dismissed her with a nod.

As disappointed in the room as he was, Daphne knew Stephen's manners would never allow him to show that disappointment to Nitsa. One thing was certain about Daphne's fiancé; he was a gentleman. He waited at the door until the seismic vibrations from Nitsa's stomp grew softer and softer. Only when he heard Nitsa bellow from the bar area below, "Hello my new friend, would you like another Mythos?" did he deem it safe to speak.

"Well, it's not exactly the Four Seasons, is it?" The springs creaked as he sat down.

"I know it's not what you're used to. It's simple, but it's clean. And it's not like you'll be spending much time in the room anyway," she said. "Remember, that's what I told you. Simple island elegance. That's what we're about here."

"Well, you've got the simple part right."

He got up from the bed and unzipped his garment bag. Second only to cigarette smoke, Stephen hated unkempt and wrinkled clothing. He pulled open the door to the empty closet. "Hey, where's your stuff?"

"Back at Yia-yia's house. Where else would it be?"

"Here, with me, your fiancé." He paused. "Remember me?" He pointed to himself.

"Come on, Stephen, I explained this to you. We're not married yet, remember?" She lifted her engagement ring and wiggled it toward him.

"So you weren't joking then." He slid behind her and held her to him. "Are you sure we can't stay together, here"—he motioned around the room—"or anywhere else?"

"No, I'm not joking." She turned to face him, shaking her head and waving her finger, mockingly scolding him. "This place is very traditional, remember I told you? I can't stay here until we're married, honey. I just can't. Everyone will talk. I know it sounds silly, but that's how it goes here. And remember, when in Rome—"

"May I remind you that this is Greece." He grabbed her and threw her to the bed, hovering over her before kissing her gently on the lips. "Are you sure there's *nothing* I can do to convince you?"

"Don't make this harder for me than it already is." She narrowed her eyes and shook her head at him. "Things here are very traditional. I know it's hard to understand. But when I'm here, I respect those traditions."

She had explained this all to Stephen back at home, telling him how modern life had yet to change the way things are done on Erikousa even though Corfu, just seven miles away, was by comparison contemporary and cosmopolitan. But Erikousa had always been in its own provincial time warp. Certain traditions, prejudices, and customs never changed. To those who loved Erikousa, that was the charm of the island—the predictability and nostalgia of it all. But to outsiders, the culture of the island was difficult if not impossible to understand.

"It would mean a lot to me if you respected those traditions while we're here."

"I know, Daphne. And I will. If it makes you happy, you know I will." He kissed her again and stood up. He walked toward the closet but paused and turned again to face her. "But it just seems funny to me when for so long I've heard you talk about how hard all those traditions made things for you when you were a kid. Don't you think it's pretty ironic that you're going back to those same traditions now, as an adult—when you can make your own decisions?" His tone was not angry; he seemed truly confused by the contradiction.

"I know. I guess I never thought of it that way." She smiled at her fiancé. "But this isn't about me having to go to Greek school instead of Girl Scouts, Stephen. This is different. And no, a lot of things about this place don't make much sense. I think maybe I like that right now. I'm so tired of making so many decisions all the time. Maybe it's kind of nice to let tradition take over and make the decisions for me, at least for a little while." She smoothed her skirt and shrugged her shoulders.

He shook his head as he shook the wrinkles from his navy blazer.

"When in Greece—"

Twenty-four

"Yia-yia." Daphne opened the gate and was surprised when she did not immediately see Yia-yia sitting there by the fire. "Yia-yia?"

The door to the house squeaked open, and Yia-yia leaned against the door frame. "*Koukla mou*, you are back. I missed you."

"Yia-yia, *ella*, come meet Stephen. I've been waiting so long for you to meet him."

"*Ah, ne. O Amerikanos. Pou einai.* Where is he?" The old woman took Daphne's hand and walked toward Stephen. She wore no shoes, the outline of her bunions clearly visible through the thin fabric of her stockings.

As they walked together out of the doorway and onto the patio where Stephen stood, Daphne noticed how Yia-yia leaned on her a bit more than usual. Yia-yia was a slight woman, without the traditional heft of the other widows who spend their days indulging in a gluttonous cycle of cooking and eating. Although it was impossible that she could have gained any considerable weight in the past twenty-four hours, Daphne was certain that Yia-yia had never before felt this heavy on her arm.

As they approached, Stephen smiled politely and extended his hand.

"*Te einai afto?* What is that?" She looked from Stephen to Daphne. "Daphne *mou*. Please tell your young man that this is not a business meeting. This is our home."

"Stephen, honey." Daphne reached her free hand out and touched his shoulder with her fingertips. "People here hug and kiss hello, we don't shake hands. That's for business." She looked around and saw Yia-yia, Popi, and even Evie staring back. "This is family."

Without another word, Stephen nodded and stepped forward. He circled his arms around the old woman and gave her a hug. Yia-yia leaned in and kissed him on each cheek. As she pulled her face away, Stephen smiled at her, his perfect white teeth glowing in the sunlight. Yia-yia's eyes narrowed and focused in on his.

Daphne bit her lower lip and watched as Yia-yia stared deep into Stephen's eyes. She looked past his lashes, past the muddy blue of his irises, through the black pools of his pupils, and seemingly down into his very soul. Even the trees stopped their rustling so their soft whispers would not distract Yia-yia from her mission.

"*Ah, kala.* All right." It seemed she had seen what she needed to see.

As Daphne watched, she couldn't help but wonder what was running through the old woman's mind. Daphne knew Yia-yia well enough to know that she had been searching for something when she looked at Stephen that way. There were no coincidences when it came to Yia-yia. Everything about her—every word, every glance, every *briki* of coffee—was steeped in significance.

"Popi, Evie." Daphne stood, still holding on to Yia-yia. "Why don't you show Stephen around the garden and maybe even introduce him to Jack, okay? We'll get lunch ready." She turned toward Stephen and smiled. "It'll only be a few minutes, and it'll be nice to have some time with Evie, you know she always needs a little time to warm up."

"Sure." He looked around the patio for Evie, who had spotted another spider weaving her trap between the twisted branches of the lemon tree. "Come on, Evie," he called. "Where's this famous donkey I've heard so much about?"

"Look." She pointed to the web. "It's Arachne."

"Oh, a spider. Well, we have those back home in New York, you know. Come on. What we don't have are donkeys, or chickens, and from what I hear, you have plenty of those."

"No, she's not just a spider." Evie finally looked away from the web and up at Stephen. "It's Arachne. She's a girl who was too proud. Thea Popi taught me that. Athena punished her and turned her into a spider." She stared at him squarely in the face, her little arms crossed at her chest. "That's what you get when you think you're better than everyone else."

"Well, little Evie. You sure have learned a lot since you've been here." As he spoke, something small and black flew above their heads and into the arachnid's trap. "Well, look at that. See, she was smart enough to catch a little friend." Stephen leaned in closer.

Stephen and Evie both watched the fly struggle against the sticky threads, its small black body and wings twitching, fighting until there was seemingly nothing left to fight for. The spider didn't move. It sat perched on the opposite end of the web, as if waiting for dinner hour to approach.

"Do you know what happens next, Evie? That fly is going to be dinner. Spiders suck the blood of insects who are dumb enough to get caught in their traps. That's pretty cool, huh? If you ask me, those little eight-legged guys are pretty smart. They have every reason to be proud, no matter what Athena thinks."

"Not always." Evie turned toward Stephen, her catlike eyes ablaze. "Thea Popi says sometimes Arachne is still too proud for her own good. And Yianni told me that anyone who is too proud should watch out."

"Well, I'd say that sounds like pretty good advice," Stephen replied. "But don't forget, little girl, pride can be a good thing—it can push you to do more, be better, be the best. And there's nothing wrong with being the best—just look at your mom." But Evie's famously short attention span had gotten the best of her. She turned and skipped down the stairs and toward the chicken coop before the words were out of Stephen's mouth.

Just as Evie danced away, Popi was on Stephen like flies on honey cakes. She stroked his biceps with her thick fingers. "Come, I will show you everything. Daphne tells me how smart you are in business, how much she has learned from you. There is something I would like from you as well. After all, we are going to be cousins, and family helps each other, no? I have an idea, and there is no one else on these islands who can help me with it. If I wanted to learn how to gut a fish or make cheese, no problem, I would have all the help in the world. But business—" Popi took her right hand and scraped her fingers along her neck and chin, the Greek equivalent of someone giving the middle finger back in the States. "Business, *tipota . . . skata*. Shit."

"Well, you are a spitfire, like your cousin." Stephen shook his head and smiled at her.

"We are the same, Daphne and I. But she was the lucky one, raised in America. Here, we are not as lucky. We do not have so many opportunities, so many choices. I have worked in the café for many many years and I know I can do better. I have watched and stayed quiet and learned. I know I can do this. I want more than just to work for the *malakas* who water down the liquor, smoke their cigarettes, bed the tourists, and call themselves big businessmen. I have ideas, Stephen. I want to be like my cousin. I want to be like Daphne." She glanced over at Daphne, her eyes filled with both longing and love.

"So let's hear these ideas of yours," he said as they walked.

Daphne watched as Popi led Stephen away. She strained to hear what Popi was saying to him, but it was no use. They disappeared into the chicken coop before Daphne could make anything out. And perhaps, Daphne thought, it was better that way.

Daphne turned to Yia-yia once again and held her liver-spotted hand a bit tighter, careful not to squeeze too tight, knowing how painful Yia-yia's swollen joints could be. Yia-yia was the first to speak.

"So, this is your American."

"In another week he'll be *our* American."

"No, not mine, definitely not mine." Yia-yia shook her head.

"Why, what's wrong? Is something wrong?"

"Yes, there is. Something is very wrong, Daphne. He's too skinny, just like you. This man has so much money, yet he cannot afford to buy food. I do not understand Americans sometimes. *Tsk tsk tsk*. Come, let's check the stew. We don't want it to stick." And with that, it seemed Yia-yia's analysis of Stephen was finished.

Daphne desperately wanted to know what Yia-yia had seen when she looked into Stephen's eyes, but there was also so much more that Daphne wanted to speak to Yia-yia about, so much she wanted to ask. Why she had insisted on making *stifado* when she knew it would take days for her ailing body to recover from the strain? Why, after all these years of sharing stories and secrets, had she not shared with Daphne the story of Dora and what happened during the war? Daphne knew she could ask anything of her grandmother, and she would be met with the truth. But the more she thought about what the truth might actually reveal, the more anxious she grew. They walked together from one end of the patio to the other, Daphne running through the questions she would ask over and over again in her head, just how she would word them and what she thought the answers might be.

"Look, *koukla*." Daphne's internal dialogue was interrupted by Yia-yia pointing to the lemon tree. "Look, Daphne. See, it's as I told you. Just as I told Evie."

Yia-yia pointed to the spiderweb, the same one that Evie had spotted earlier. There, on one end of the ornate web, was a gaping hole where the fly had escaped.

"See, Daphne *mou*," Yia-yia said. "Hubris is a dangerous thing. Look away for a moment, and your prized possession may escape even the loveliest of traps."

Twenty-five

"Here, let me do it for you." Daphne leaned over the fire and lifted the heavy silver pot from the metal grate.

"*Entaksi*, all right, *koukla mou*. Be sure you don't break the seal." Still in her stocking feet, Yia-yia sat in her wooden chair.

"I know, I know." Daphne's muscles flexed from the weight of the stew. She swirled the pot around and around. She was careful to keep the lid securely fastened on top and not to disturb the tape that Yia-yia had placed around the lid to seal in the vapors. Although she herself had not made *stifado* in years, Daphne knew that the secret to a rich and savory stew was to seal in the vapors so the simmering vinegar would ensure a pungent sauce.

"There." She placed the pot back on the metal trivet.

"Do you want coffee?" Yia-yia asked as she lifted her hands to secure several long gray coils that had escaped the confines of her braids.

Daphne leaned over and tucked the strands behind Yia-yia's

ear. "If you like, I'll wash and braid your hair tonight for you."
She smiled at her grandmother, knowing that Yia-yia's brittle
joints made weaving her long hair into braids more and more difficult with each passing day.

"Thank you, *koukla mou*." Yia-yia nodded. "Are you hungry?"

"Yes, but I can wait for the *stifado*." Daphne pulled her chair
closer to Yia-yia and sat down. Evie's delighted squeals could be
heard from the garden below.

"What is it, Daphne *mou*? What's wrong?" Yia-yia could read
Daphne's face like the grounds at the bottom of a muddy cup.

"Yianni told me everything."

"Ah, *kala*, all right." She closed her eyes. "I thought he might."

"Why, Yia-yia? Why didn't you ever tell me? Why would you
keep that from me? I always thought we told each other everything. That we had no secrets between us."

Yia-yia's eyes were heavy and red. "This was not a secret,
Daphne *mou*. This was our history. You have your own." Yia-yia's
voice was soft, barely audible. "Daphne *mou*. *Koukla*. It is a terrible day when a person realizes that there is evil in the world. That
the devil walks this earth. I learned this the moment I looked into
the terrified black eyes of Dora and saw what those men did to her,
what they stole from her. Those animals thought it was within
their rights to extinguish people as one puts out an evening fire, a
church candle. They stole too many lives already, destroyed too
many families. I could not let them do it again. And why—because
Dora's people called their God by another name? God does not
judge us by what name we call him. This is not how we are judged."

Daphne took Yia-yia's hand and watched as the first tear slid
down her hollow cheek, navigating a slick path for the others that

would follow. But Yia-yia never let go of Daphne's hand to wipe her face; she just held on even tighter.

"Sometimes, it is not just blood which these monsters crave. They want a small piece of our souls—but that too is dangerous, sometimes even more so. Even that is too much to give." She finally lifted her index finger, crooked and scarred, and wiped clean the wet streak from under her eyes. "Had I not helped Dora that day, they would have succeeded in taking my soul too. I could not lose that, I would not lose that."

Yia-yia continued, her voice still shaky but gaining strength now, becoming clearer, more powerful and passionate. "Sometimes in facing those monsters, you find your strength, you find your purpose." She looked out toward the horizon. "I never even knew I had either. I wasn't supposed to have either, but I did. I found them in the Jewish quarter that terrible, terrible day, Daphne."

She pulled Daphne closer, and just as she had done earlier to Stephen, Yia-yia looked into the depths of her granddaughter's black-olive eyes, eyes that were as vibrant and clear yet as confused and searching as her own had once been. "Sometimes facing the devil makes us stronger, Daphne. You'll never know how strong you are, who you really are and what you are capable of, until you do."

"So that's why you and Yianni are so close. He feels indebted to you . . . for saving his family."

"No, I didn't save them." The conviction in Yia-yia's voice startled Daphne. "They saved me."

There was so much she did not know about her grandmother, so much she had never bothered to ask. All those years sitting in this very spot, listening to Yia-yia spin her tales of Hades, Medusa, and the unrelenting furies, Daphne had always assumed Yia-yia was repeating old myths for her amusement, a way to pass the evening. But now Daphne realized that there was more to these old stories. Like the greatest heroes in these tales, Yia-yia had come face-to-face with mythic evil herself.

"How did they save you?"

Yia-yia released Daphne's hands and leaned back in her chair. "How did they save me? How did they save me?" she repeated again and again.

Daphne could detect a melodious undertone to her voice. For a moment, it seemed as if Yia-yia was going to answer in a lament song. But Daphne didn't care. She just wanted answers. Daphne leaned in closer, wringing her hands together in anticipation of hearing the words that would unravel this great mystery for her. She had been consumed with learning more about this story from the moment Yianni had tossed out the first description of the vibrant Jewish quarter. Now she needed to hear Yia-yia's version, so she too could better understand the secrets of the island, the secret her grandmother had clung to for so many years—and hopefully, in some way, better understand how their lives and these legends were so inexplicably intertwined.

But as Daphne waited for Yia-yia to unravel this mystery, the voices from below grew louder. She could hear Evie's giggles more clearly now, and she could make out some of the words of Popi's prattle; words like *opportunity* and *investment* and *risk*. Words Daphne was shocked to realize that Popi even knew.

"How did they save you?" Daphne asked again, desperate to learn the answer before the others joined them. But it was too late.

The patter of Evie's ballet slippers was upon them as she bounded up the last few steps, raced across the patio, and dove into Yia-yia's lap.

"Be careful, Evie." Daphne lurched forward, frustrated that this conversation had come to such a sudden end. There was no way she would learn what Yia-yia was about to say now; it would have to wait for later this evening, when Yia-yia and Daphne were alone—then, and only then, would Daphne broach the subject again.

There were not many secrets on this island, not many whispered conversations. Everything here was shared and shouted across the treetops; news, recipes, weather reports, and gossip. As primal as this method of communication seemed, that was the reality of life here; people needed each other. They needed to know each other's business, not just for lack of other entertainment but in order to survive. But this conversation was different. Evie was too young, Popi too frivolous, and this culture and its customs were still so new to Stephen. No, this would be a conversation finished over the evening's last dying embers, reserved for Yia-yia and Daphne alone.

"Can I? Can I? Can I?" Evie asked again and again as she bounced up and down on Yia-yia's knees, the very knees that Daphne had noticed earlier seemed a bit more swollen than usual.

"Evie, be gentle. Stop it." Daphne reached her arm out to stop the little girl's acrobatics. "You'll hurt Yia-yia. Can you what?"

"It's all right, Daphne *mou*. This child cannot harm me. She is my best medicine." Yia-yia wove her crooked fingers through Evie's hair.

"So can I go for a ride on Jack?" Evie begged.

"Later, honey. I promise. Stephen just got here—it's not polite to leave him alone. He wants to spend time with you, he missed you."

"If he missed me so much, then why is he playing with Thea Popi and not me?"

Although Evie spoke in English, Yia-yia nodded in agreement. She didn't need to speak the language to understand what was happening. The old woman was fluent in reading the faces of those she loved.

"Now, Stephen, don't let Popi monopolize you, everyone wants to get to know you," Daphne called out.

"No, it's okay. Your cousin has some great ideas."

"Yes, yes. I'm sorry. I didn't mean to take up so much of your time. This is a wedding we are celebrating, after all. Daphne, I really am sorry, you are the bride, and this is your time. My time will come too, I know it will. And now that we are family, there will be plenty of time for business after the wedding. What's the word"— Popi scanned the recesses of her mind for the elusive word— "merger." She clapped in celebration of her verbal victory. "Yes, it is a family merger, and great things will come of this for all of us. *Ella*." Popi lifted her arms and clapped her hands again, this time above her head. "Come, let's eat."

Daphne watched Popi sashay to the table. She could swear she noticed a little extra olive oil lubricating her hips as they swung back and forth.

"Thanks for tolerating her. She's a little overbearing sometimes, but she's a good person. She means well." Daphne pulled Stephen closer.

"I'm not tolerating her. She's pretty amazing, actually." Stephen watched as Popi took her seat by the table. "She does have some good ideas. Really good ideas." He laughed as if surprised that this place could spawn more than just chickens, flies, and donkey dung. "She's a smart girl, Daphne, like you." He squeezed her hand. "This is going to be some wedding . . . like your cousin said, this is going to be some merger."

"Come on, it's time to eat. Enough business for one day." Daphne clapped her hands and shooed everyone toward the table. "One of the great things about this stew is the smell when you first open the pot lid. It's incredible. Come on, you're gonna love it." She smiled at Stephen and led him to his seat.

"I mean it, Daphne." He leaned in just inches from her face and placed his hands on her shoulders. "When I'm done, we'll be the biggest thing New York has ever seen. Hell, that Greece has ever seen. I have big plans for us."

For generations, as far back as people could remember, island weddings were celebrated for the joyous yet vital merger of two families. Nowhere did the phrase *strength in number*s ring more true than right here, where families joined by marriage would share their crops, their livestock, and all of the essentials of their lives. Daphne remembered attending so many of these festive celebrations with Popi and Yia-yia. There was the summer when Daphne was nine . . . she would never forget the pleasure of dancing along the dirt roads with a colorful parade of women; bundles of clothes, blankets, and towels balanced on their heads as they took part in the *rouha*, a beautiful ritual where the women of the island would carry a bride's possessions to her new husband's home. There was the mortification she felt the time, at twelve years old, the kilo of rice she cradled in her arms in anticipation of the bride and groom's emergence from church slipped out of her hands and down the back of Thea Anna, who had worn her one "good dress" for the occasion and dripped rice from her girdle all over the dance floor for the remainder of the evening. But there was no image of island marriage more seared in Daphne's memory than the stories Yia-yia had shared of when she was a girl and bloodstained white sheets would hang from an olive tree, billowing in the breeze, the morning after a young couple married.

There would be no dancing women balancing Daphne's possessions atop their heads, no kilo of rice to throw, since she had insisted on rose petals instead, and certainly no stained sheet to confirm her purity. No dowry, livestock, linens, or land would be changing hands. Hers was by no means a typical Erikousa wedding. It was to be modern and elegant—*Amerikanico*. But after watching Popi work her magic on Stephen, and hearing Stephen's excitement about the potential for new business ventures ahead, Daphne couldn't help but feel that in some ways she was far more traditional than she ever could have imagined, that she too was a measure of her dowry.

When the stew was finally ready, Yia-yia insisted they eat on the table under the large olive tree. But that would be Yia-yia's only concession to American formality. The round loaf of peasant bread was placed in the middle of the table, pieces to be torn away by hand, as was the usual custom. There would be no delicate china or serving dish either; the old, battered pot was placed straight from the fire right at the center of the table as Daphne stood to do the honors.

"It's ready, you can remove the tape," Yia-yia announced, signaling to Daphne that she could now peel the charred silver tape from the lid.

"Why are you doing that?" Stephen leaned in to get a better look. He had spent countless hours with Daphne in the kitchen at Koukla, but he had never before seen her prepare a dish using electrical tape.

"It is to keep the flavors in," Popi answered. "We know special tricks here, wonderful tricks." She stood, almost knocking over her chair with the sheer force of her hips. She bent forward, bottom pointed straight up, leaned her entire body across the table, grabbed the round, crusty loaf of bread, and shoved it into Stephen's face. "Here, smell," she commanded.

Stephen did as he was told. "That's wonderful."

"Yes, it is." Popi nodded furiously. "See, we take hospitality very seriously here, cousin Stephen. There is nothing we don't do for our guests."

"This is delicious. Absolutely delicious." He took a piece of bread and dipped it into the thick sauce. "And I love these little onions." He plunged his fork into the stew and pulled out a perfect little round pearl onion. "Delicious." Stephen devoured his stew and dabbed at his mouth with the paper napkin while Daphne refilled his bowl. "Daphne, seriously. You need to put this on the menu at Koukla. I mean it, as soon as you get back to work."

"Just eat, enjoy . . . okay?" Daphne filled his bowl again.

"Okay. But we have a lot to talk about once this little vacation is over."

Yia-yia watched as Stephen inhaled the stew that she had slaved over since before the sunrise. She leaned in and whispered into Daphne's ear. "Your young man has good taste. But have you warned him about those little onions that he loves so much?"

Daphne brought her hand to her face and laughed. She shook her head.

"Ah, *kala*. He'll have a nice souvenir from his first day in Eri-kousa," Yia-yia muttered under her breath.

That was all it took. In an attempt to keep from laughing, she pursed her lips inward, biting both her top and her lower lip. She tilted her head down, allowing her hair to fall in front of her face. The veil of black curls obscuring her features might have done the trick and hid the fact that she was laughing, but it was the way her entire body jiggled up and down that gave her away.

"What's so funny?" Stephen pierced another pearl onion and plucked it from his fork with his teeth.

"It's nothing." Daphne tried composing herself, but one look at Yia-yia had her dissolving into giggles again.

"Really, what's so funny?" he asked again.

"It's the onions," Popi offered as she filled her beer glass again.

"What's so funny about the onions?"

"They . . . how do you say . . ." Popi tapped her glass with her fork as she searched for the right word. "They, you know . . . make air."

"Huh." Stephen took another sip of beer.

"They make air." Popi waved her arms around her as if she might be able to capture the correct word from the passing breeze.

"They give you gas." Daphne took a very large sip of her Mythos, not certain how Stephen would react to where this con-versation was heading. As much as Stephen had a fine sense of hu-mor, these were unchartered waters for him. With Greeks, no conversation was ever off-limits; nothing was ever considered too gross, inappropriate, or even risqué for dinner table conversation. There was basic, primal humor to be found in body functions, and Greeks always seemed to value a good punch line over propriety.

"Farts!" Popi yelled, slamming the empty bottle of Mythos on the table. "Yes, that's the word. Farts."

Daphne hid under her hair once again.

Popi placed her hand on Stephen's shoulder and leaned in closer toward him. "Cousin, be glad you are here outside with us and not in one of your important meetings. *Stifado* is so good." She smacked her lips. "But not good for business."

And from the way Stephen squirmed in his seat and dabbed at his forehead with his handkerchief, it seemed it wasn't good for dinner-table conversation either.

Twenty-six

After everyone had stuffed themselves with the *stifado*, Daphne insisted Yia-yia stay seated so she alone could clear the table. Daphne knew how much work had gone into this lunch, and she didn't want Yia-yia to exhaust herself any further. She cleared the plates one by one, scraping what little bits were left into a large bowl to give to Nitsa so she could feed her pigs later that evening. Daphne noticed how little was left on each plate; the *stifado* had been too extraordinary to leave any morsel behind. She felt sorry for the pigs whose evening slop would be slighter than normal. As she lifted Stephen's plate, she laughed out loud, noticing how he had picked the bowl clean except for the tiny pearl onions, which had been left behind in a smattering of sauce.

"Daphne *mou*, I'll sit here and rest a moment. *Efharisto*." Yia-yia sat with her hands folded on her lap and watched as her newly extended family went about the business of getting to know each other. But like any good Greek hostess, she always had enough food to feed the entire village. And like any good Greek village, the villagers were more than happy to show up and enjoy the hospitality.

Nitsa was the first to arrive, her heavy footsteps heralding her arrival before the squeaky gate could do the honors. Nitsa was followed by Father Nikolaos and his entire family, as well as half a dozen or so *theas* and *theos* who were happy to indulge in Yia-yia's delicious *stifado* as well as the entertainment of getting to know Daphne's rich American.

"Stephen. How is your first day on our beautiful island?" Stephen braced himself as Nitsa approached. Cigarette in hand, Nitsa enveloped Stephen in her arms and hugged him close, pressing his face deep into her bosom.

"Great. Just great," he managed to spit out, despite the fact that Nitsa's humongous breasts were now blocking all of his air passages.

"Excuse me, Thea Nitsa." Daphne pulled Stephen away before the lack of oxygen could do any harm. "I need to borrow my fiancé. He still hasn't met Father Nikolaos and Presbytera."

"Thanks," he whispered, red faced, as she pulled him away.

"Don't mention it." Daphne laughed. She led him back to the table where Yia-yia still sat, now surrounded by Father Nikolaos, his wife, and their baby.

"Father." Daphne took the priest's hand and kissed it. "Father, this is my fiancé. This is Stephen."

"*Yia sou,*" Stephen said. The priest reached his hand out. Instead of kissing the priest's hand, as was the custom, Stephen shook Father's hand as if he were closing a deal. If Father was offended, he didn't show it. The priest simply smiled. He lifted his right hand and formed the sign of the cross in the air between Daphne and Stephen. "God bless you" was all he knew to say in English.

"Same to you," Stephen replied.

"Stephen, this is Presbytera. She was kind enough to offer to make our wedding crowns from local flowers. Isn't that wonderful? Now that is a true blessing."

"*Yia sou*, Stephen." Presbytera stood, her gurgling baby straddling her hip as she kissed Stephen on each cheek. "Daphne, tell your young man we are so happy and honored to welcome him to our island and to God's house. I pray Agios Spyridon watches over him and that God grants you both many children, and many years of health and happiness."

Daphne translated Presbytera's wishes for Stephen, who smiled politely in response.

As the sunlit afternoon gave way to a beautiful sunset, the welcome party thinned considerably. It had been a long afternoon filled with food, laughter, and a lot of translation as Daphne found herself interpreting well wishes the entire afternoon.

"Congratulations."

"Welcome to the family."

"Welcome to Greece."

"May God bless you."

"Why are you so skinny?"

"Is this why you are so rich, because you spend no money on food?"

"Exactly how rich are you?"

"My son wants to come to America. Can you give him a job?"

* * *

WHEN THE PLEASANTRIES AS WELL as the food were finally exhausted, Daphne stood alone on the edge of the patio and watched
as the sun tucked itself away behind the faraway shelf of the Ionian
Sea, reveling in the fleeting quiet and the magical golden light.
She looked around her and took in the moment. There was Yia-
yia, huddled over and making coffee by the fire. Evie played quietly in one corner of the patio with her favorite baby chick, her
kitten curled up in her lap. And there, huddled together under the
olive tree, were Popi and Stephen, once again deep in conversation.

Just as the final glimmer of the sun's orange orb disappeared
behind the horizon, Daphne was about to turn and join Yia-yia for
coffee, but the creaking of the gate made her turn instead toward
the noise.

"*Yia sou*, Thea Evangelia."

It was Yianni. He carried a brown net draped across one shoulder and a large white bucket in his hand. "Thea Evangelia . . ." He
dropped his net and bucket at Yia-yia's feet and bent down to kiss
the old woman on both of her cheeks. "Thea *mou*, tonight the sea
delivered many gifts. She was very generous as I lifted my nets. I
thought, with your family growing every day . . ." He looked
around the patio and saw that everyone—Daphne, Evie, Popi,
and even Stephen—had stopped what they were doing to watch
him. "I thought that you might like to share in her bounty."

"Ah, Yianni *mou*. You are always so good to me, so kind." Yia-
yia poured him a cup of coffee before he could ask for one.

Daphne felt the uneasiness return in her belly, the knot in her
neck tighten. After their time together on the *kaiki*, when he told
her the story of how their *yia-yias* had survived the war together,
she had seen another side to this man whom she had once so

strongly disliked. Daphne no longer saw Yianni as a danger. He was no longer a threat. When they had first met, the mere thought of Yianni unleashed the vicious furies in Daphne's mind. But from the moment he had opened up to her, had shared his *kaiki*, his stories, and the sea urchins, Daphne realized, that was no longer the case. There was nothing to fear about this mysterious man. And like the bloodthirsty furies who had their fill of vengeance and ultimately turned benevolent in the story of Orestes, Daphne felt a shift in their story as well.

"*Yia sou*, Yianni." It seemed the arrival of a single, eligible man was what it took to pry Popi away from Stephen. "Yianni, this is Stephen. This is my cousin, Daphne's fiancé. *O Amerikanos*," Popi announced.

"Welcome to Erikousa. I hope you will come to love our island as much as we do." Yianni spoke directly to Stephen and in perfect English.

"You speak English?" Stephen scanned Yianni head to toe. With his deep tan and frayed denim shorts, he wore the appearance of a man who spent his life on the open sea, not in a classroom learning proper English.

"Yes, I speak English." Yianni sipped his coffee. "I studied at Athens University before continuing my degree at Columbia."

"I didn't know that. You never said you lived in New York." Daphne stepped forward. She thought she had learned so much about him on their trip to Kerkyra. Now, once again, she felt she knew nothing.

"Yes. The classics. I was going to be a great professor, you know." He laughed, but it was a nervous laugh, the laugh of a man trying to convince himself as much as the others. This time

Daphne had no trouble reading Yianni. She could see the longing in his eyes, hear the disillusionment in the crack of his voice. Everything about this man was so foreign, yet so familiar.

"My plan was to come back to Athens and to open the minds of the younger generation to the lessons of our ancestors." Yianni laughed at how ambitious it all sounded, how futile. "But things didn't work out as planned. I studied at Columbia but left after a year." He looked from Daphne to Stephen. "Ivy League life was not for me. I prefer the simplicity of life here. I was like a fish out of water. A bad pun, I know." There was that laugh again. "But it is the truth."

"When were you there—when were you in New York, I mean? You could have gotten in touch with me, Yia-yia could have told you how." Daphne surprised herself with the sincerity of her words.

"It was years ago, Daphne. That was before I met your *yia-yia*, before I came to this island. It feels like a lifetime ago."

"That's too bad. We could have met each other a lifetime ago, as you said." It was Daphne's turn to laugh now, thinking how nice it would have been to have had some link to Erikousa back home in New York. Daphne always felt like she straddled two worlds, her Greek life and her American life. She had always wished there were a way to bridge the gap between the two. But once Mama and Baba died, there was nothing or no one to share her Greek self with; it was as if part of her identity had died along with her parents.

"Yes, it is too bad. I might have given New York another try had we met back then. Maybe I would have stayed longer, had reason to try harder. Things might have been different," Yianni replied, never taking his eyes off of Daphne.

"Well, it is beautiful. Amazing though, don't you think that in this day and age things can still stay so old-fashioned"—Stephen glanced around at the sloped and cracked patio, past the gate to the dirt path in front of the house—"so unchanged."

"This place is unlike any other, and so are its people." Yianni tugged at his beard. "But don't be fooled by our outward simplicity, my new American friend. There are many layers to the people of this island, and many incredible things here besides the sea and its natural beauty."

Yianni took his hand from Yia-yia's shoulder and leaned forward to grab Evie as she chased the chick across the patio. He plucked the little girl up and tossed her into the air, her laughter dancing across the treetops and across the island like a tender melody carried on the evening breeze. Yianni planted a gentle kiss on Evie's head before setting her down again. The little girl stood there for a moment, looking up at Yianni, her cheeks red from laughter, her eyes glistening with mischief. She reached her little hand up and tickled Yianni's belly with her tiny fingertips and was rewarded with a deep belly laugh. Evie stuck her tongue out at him and ran away, her giggles trailing behind like ribbons in the wind.

Perhaps this is one of the magical things Yianni was talking about, Daphne thought as she watched Evie skip away. Daphne had never seen her little girl so at ease with a man before. Having grown up without a father, she wasn't used to having men around; in fact, she was still getting used to Stephen.

"Well, I guess I'm just a New Yorker, like my fiancée, right, Daphne?" Stephen pulled her to him and kissed her on the lips. It was an unusual gesture from a man who rarely indulged in public displays of anything. This fact was not lost on Daphne.

"Well, then, my congratulations again for the happy couple. It seems you were meant for each other." He put his cap on his head, pulling the brim down so the black pools of his eyes were now shaded, almost obscured. "So, as I said, we may be simple people, but we are generous. What little we have, we share." Yianni lifted the bucket from the floor and dumped its contents on the patio. "I know the bride likes sea urchins. Consider this a wedding gift." About two dozen black and brown sea urchins spilled across the patio, the spiky creatures rolling in every direction along the uneven surface.

"*Kali nichta*—good to meet you, Stephen. I hope you enjoy your visit with us." Yianni kissed Yia-yia good-bye and tipped his hat to Popi and Daphne. He opened the gate and was hurtling down the stairs before the last of the sea urchins had settled into place.

As one of the urchins stopped at her feet, Daphne bent to pick it up. Maybe it was the beer, or maybe she was just tired. But whatever the reason, Daphne was a bit more careless than usual when she bent down to pick up the black spiked ball at her feet. She cupped her fingers around the barbs and pressed on the sea urchin just a little harder than she should. She flinched as the spike penetrated her skin, a tiny red drop of blood emerging where it had broken through. Daphne brought her finger to her mouth and sucked until the blood disappeared in her mouth, the copper taste spilling across her tongue as she watched the gate slam shut.

Twenty-seven

Daphne and Yia-yia sat and clapped in time to the strumming of the bouzouki that blared from the cassette recorder in the kitchen.

"*Opa*, Evie." Daphne beamed as she watched her little girl dance in time to the music.

"Bravo, *koukla mou*. Bravo, Evie," Yia-yia said as Evie twirled round and round, her pink nightgown filling with air as if it were a balloon.

"She likes a good party, just like her Thea Popi." Daphne giggled. It was no secret that even in their colorful extended family, Popi stood out as the most fun-loving of all.

And in fact that evening was no different. Even after a full day of festivities, dining, drinking, and gossiping with everyone who had come to welcome Stephen to Erikousa, Popi was still not content to call it a night. Popi suggested that she escort Stephen back to the hotel so Daphne could finish cleaning up and put Evie to bed. At first, Daphne resisted. After all, Stephen was her fiancé, and she knew he was already annoyed by the fact that she would not be staying at the hotel with him, that she instead chose to follow the island's strict moral code. But in the end, Stephen didn't seem to mind at all. He had been getting into the island spirit, first with several bottles of Mythos, then with the chilled shots of ouzo Popi insisted were yet another island tradition they must indulge in. In the end, all it took was Popi's promise that she would reveal the deepest, darkest, and most embarrassing secrets of Daphne's childhood once they reached the bar at the hotel. Stephen then kissed Evie, Yia-yia, and Daphne good night before linking arms with Popi for the dark walk back to the hotel.

"This is nice." Yia-yia put her hand on Daphne's knee while they continued to watch Evie dance. "I love having you here, having you both here. Even if it's for just a short while."

Evie bounced over to Yia-yia and gave her great-grandmother a hug. She lingered for a moment, just long enough for Yia-yia to feel the warmth of Evie's soft cheek against her own. But then, just as the next song began, Evie sprang back into position, ready for their final recital of the evening. On tiptoes this time, hands held high above her head, she danced between her mother and great-grandmother as the music blanketed the night like a luxurious cashmere shawl.

When her dance was finished, Evie again went to Yia-yia's side and gave her a hug. Yia-yia held tight this time, stroking Evie's hair as she leaned in and softly sang to her.

> *I love you like no other . . .*
> *I have no gifts to shower upon you*
> *No gold or jewels or riches*

But still, I give you all I have
And that, my sweet child, is all my love
I promise you this,
You will always have my love

When the song was finished, Evie kissed the tip of Yia-yia's nose and went off to play with her kitten.

"*Koukla mou*"—Yia-yia smiled at Daphne—"always remember me when you hear that song." Yia-yia lifted her hands to her chest and folded her spindly fingers over her heart. "Your mother and I would sing it to you over and over again as we watched you sleeping in your cradle, right here, where you are sitting now. We would stay here for hours, Daphne, just watching you breathe, just thanking the heavens for your perfection and praying to the *agios* that he walk beside you and keep you safe."

The olive and cypress trees around them vibrated in a subtle breeze. As their soft hum filled the air, Yia-yia spoke again. "Daphne *mou*, I will always sing for you. Even when you can't hear me, even in your new life so many miles away from me, I know that I will always be there for you, singing those words for you, reminding you that you are loved."

"I know that, Yia-yia. I've always known that." And she had. In a life filled with loss, Yia-yia had remained Daphne's one constant. Her rock. Yia-yia had always been the one person Daphne knew would love her unconditionally and completely.

With her wedding just days away, this was supposed to be a time of bliss for Daphne. But as happy as she was counting down the days until she and Stephen would become man and wife, along with the building excitement of each passing day came something

Daphne hadn't anticipated: a sense of melancholy. As the wedding approached, so did the reality that Daphne would soon be leaving the island to begin her new life—a life of luxury, financial security, and seemingly everything else she had struggled and prayed for through all the long, lonely years since Alex died. But in all the excitement of planning for the future, there was one thing Daphne had never stopped to think about. The beginning of a new life meant the end of another.

Twenty-eight

"Mommy, can I ask you something?" Evie climbed across the bed
on all fours before yanking down the sheet and plopping her head
on the pillow. She didn't pull the covers up over her body, just lay
there, straight and still, her slender tanned limbs naked to the
night air.

Daphne leaned forward and pulled the sheet to Evie's chest.
"Yes, honey. You can ask me anything."

"Can I bring my chick back to New York, Mommy?"

"No, honey, you can't. Our building doesn't allow baby chicks."

Evie wrinkled her nose. "Well, can we just stay here, then? I
don't want to leave her. Her name is Sunshine, you know, because
she's yellow like the sun."

"I'm sorry, honey—we're going to have to go back home, and
Sunshine will need to stay here."

"Mommy, can I ask you something else?"

"Of course, honey." Daphne fluffed the pillow beneath Evie's
head.

"Why didn't you tell me about Jack and Yia-yia and Erikousa? Why didn't you ever tell me that it was so much fun here?" Evie waved her arms and legs across the bed as if the white cotton sheet were freshly fallen snow and she were making a snow angel.

"But honey, I did tell you." Daphne pushed a curl away from Evie's face. "I did, remember. I told you all about Yia-yia and why we were coming here, so she could be at the wedding. Remember, honey?" She sat on the edge of the bed beside Evie, right where the angel's wings would have been.

Evie sat up in bed. "But you didn't tell me how much fun it was here, how great everyone here is. Even when I don't understand what they're saying, they're still really funny."

"Yes, honey. They are really funny."

"I wish we could come here all the time."

"I know, honey, I do too. I'm really happy we came. And we'll come back again." She leaned in and kissed Evie's little pink lips. "Good night, Evie."

"Mommy."

"Yes, Evie."

"There's one more thing I wanted to ask you."

"Yes, honey. What is it?"

"You had a lot of fun here when you were a little girl, right?"

Daphne thought back to the happiest times of her childhood. Evie was right, they had all taken place right here. "Yes, Evie, I had the most fun of my life here."

"But I don't understand, then, Mommy. You are always telling me to share my toys, that nice girls share. Why didn't you share this place with me?" Evie yawned, staring up at her mother, waiting for an answer, unaware of the magnitude of her words. "I really wish you had shared this with me."

Speechless, Daphne bit her lip. She winced at the pain but bit down harder still, teeth cutting into soft flesh. The pain was sharp and stinging, but no match for the pain Evie's words had caused.

"Good night, Mommy. I'm really tired." Evie rolled over on her side and was asleep instantly.

As Daphne stood up to leave the room, she glanced back at the sleeping child. Yes, Evie had been right. It seemed Yia-yia wasn't the only one in the family with secrets; Daphne had kept a few of her own.

"That was quick." Yia-yia handed Daphne a glass of homemade wine as she sat down.

"She was exhausted. It was a long, busy day." Daphne lifted the glass to her lips. The wine was perfect, slightly sweet and chilled. As she took her first sips, Daphne decided not to trouble Yia-yia with the details of Evie's indictment. She knew Yia-yia would be thrilled to hear how much Evie loved it here, but the rest of the conversation was something better left for mother and daughter to sort out. Yia-yia and Daphne had enough sorting out to do themselves.

"You must be tired too." Yia-yia nodded. "And what about your young man? Do you think Popi is still keeping him prisoner at the bar?"

"No, she probably dumped him in favor of a German tourist."

"Or Italian." Yia-yia smiled, her silver tooth glistening with saliva and firelight.

"This is my favorite time of day." Daphne brought the cool glass to her cheek, an instant respite from the warm night. "It always has been, you know. Even when I was a little girl, I loved nothing more than having you all to myself at night. Just the two of us and the fire and the breeze and your stories."

"You are wrong, Daphne *mou*. It's never just the two of us, my dear love. It never has been." She pulled her shawl tighter. Although the night air was thick and warm without the usual refreshing evening breeze, Yia-yia was chilled. She inched closer to the fire.

"What do you mean?" There was no one else there, just Evie inside curled up in her bed and Daphne and Yia-yia here, side by side by the fire. "There's no one else here." Daphne looked around just to be certain.

Yia-yia smiled as if she could somehow see the invisible guests that she spoke of. "Generations of our family, Daphne *mou*. They are all here. This is their home, and they have never left, just as I will never leave. They are all still here, all the women who have come before us, who guide us. We are not the first who know what it is to grieve, to have our men snatched away by Hades' dark grip. We are not the first to wonder and ask how we will find the strength to care for the children left behind. But they know, Daphne *mou*. They know what it is to love a man, to love a child, to love another. And they are here to guide us when we don't have the strength left to do so ourselves."

Daphne sipped her wine and glanced again around the empty patio, trying in vain to imagine the women Yia-yia had so vividly described. But it was no use. That was all right for now, at least for tonight. On this night, Daphne had another story in mind.

"Tell me what happened, Yia-yia." She pulled her chair closer. "Yia-yia, tell me the story, the story of you and Dora."

Yia-yia closed her eyes and lifted her face toward the sea breeze, as if summoning her memories from the evening air. "You know, I wasn't supposed to be in Kerkyra that day," Yia-yia began, her hands resting flat on her lap. "I rarely went to the main island back then. Why would I need to? I had no money to buy things with, no husband to shop for. Your *papou* had been missing for several months at that point, and I knew in my bones that he was dead.

"I had a small baby, your mother, God rest her soul." Yia-yia paused a moment, making the sign of the cross, and continued with her story. "Food was scarce back then—we had barely enough to survive. I was terrified that we would starve. There was a war going on around us, Daphne, and as much as the islanders take care of one another, help one another, our friends and family had barely enough to feed their own children—I could not ask them to feed us as well. To make the trip to Kerkyra, I left your mother with my *thea* for the day, and I traded eggs for the *kaiki* ride, since I had no money to pay. Your *papou* left behind many debts when we lost him, and I knew he owed money to the tailor in Corfu. He had told me what a kind and generous man this tailor was, how he had made Papou a new shirt for Easter and told him to pay when he could. I knew I needed to go to him, to thank this man for his kindness and try to repay the debt the only way I could, with eggs and olive oil. The night before the trip, the *agios* came to me in a dream. He called to me, Daphne. He spoke to me. It had been a long time since I had prayed at the *agios*'s side, so I went. I went straight from the port to the church and I knelt beside him that morning and prayed he would protect us, help me find a way to survive with no money and no husband. And then I lit a candle and left the church, walking back through the old city to the Jewish quarter and the tailor's shop, having faith that my prayers would somehow be answered."

Yia-yia stopped once again. Her breath was rapid and shallow. As she spoke, it was as if each word was siphoning the energy from her frail body. But that didn't stop her. She breathed deeply this time and waited, as if her beloved island breeze could breathe new life into her. She began again, her voice stronger this time.

"I knew something was wrong. The streets were empty. There was no one around, nothing but silence. As I walked toward the open door of the tailor, I heard a desperate wail. It sounded like a wild animal, but it wasn't. I looked inside and saw it was a woman, Dora, Yianni's grandmother. I stood in the doorway to see what had happened, what would cause her to make those sounds. I watched her, her dress and hair matted with her husband's blood, screaming for her lost son."

Yia-yia shook her head, her body shuddering again at the sounds and sights of that horrible day. "I pray you never hear the sound of a mother who has lost her child, Daphne. It is an inhuman sound, agonizing . . . I looked down, and there I saw her little girls kneeling on the floor, holding their *baba*'s lifeless body and begging him to wake up. It was like walking into hell, Daphne *mou*. I looked into Dora's eyes, and I swear to you, I saw her being consumed by the flames of hell. And in that moment, everything changed.

"I knew what had happened throughout Greece, I had heard the stories. There was no television—I could not read the newspaper myself, but I knew nonetheless what those animals had done throughout Greece. And I could not let another family be destroyed, murdered. I would not allow it."

Daphne felt her stomach tighten. She clutched the edge of her chair.

"That day, as I stood in the doorway in the Jewish quarter, the breeze kicked up, sending papers and leaves swirling in the empty alleyways. I took my eyes off of Yianni's grandmother and mother for a moment and watched the papers and leaves swirling at my feet. Just as I looked away, tempted to leave that place and forget what I had seen, that is when I heard it. It was faint at first, the softest murmur, like the wings of a butterfly in my ear. But it was there, Daphne *mou*. It was there. At first, I denied that I heard anything. How could it be? But the wind kicked up again, and the voice grew stronger. It was a woman's voice, soft and beautiful. I could hear her crying, I could hear her soft whispers between the muffled sobs. And I knew that my own *yia-yia* had been right. The cypress whispers do exist."

Yia-yia closed her eyes again and sat in silence. The words that poured out of her seemed to have again taken her strength. Daphne held her breath and waited, but Yia-yia remained silent. Then, just as Daphne leaned forward to touch her grandmother, to make sure she was indeed awake, Yia-yia opened her eyes again and continued with her story.

"Daphne *mou*. I listened, and I understood what I needed to do. What my role was. That I had not been brought to this earth to be another forgotten widow, a burden on society, someone to be pitied and plied with handouts. It was faint, the faintest sound I had ever heard, but it screamed, Daphne. It screamed for me to do something. It screamed for me to help this woman, to get her away from there before the soldiers returned. It was the softest possible whisper, but it screamed that this was a good woman, a God-fearing and kind woman. A woman who deserved to be revered and respected, not treated like a gutter animal. I know so many good women, so many good men and their children, were beyond salvation that day, Daphne. I could not help them—I don't know if anyone could have helped them. Those monsters murdered them all. And for what? I still don't understand." Yia-yia shook her head and looked deep into the fire.

"But this woman, Daphne, *this* mother, wife, daughter. She was placed in my hands that day. *My* hands, Daphne. These two very hands. These hands of a poor widow that never held anything of value. That day I held Dora's fate in my hands, and I could not let her slip through my fingers." Yia-yia cupped her hands, palms up toward the heavens as if to save the memories of that day from slipping through her fingers even now, so many years later.

She looked from her hands to Daphne. "The voice told me to save Dora and her children. And so I did. I brought them to Agios Spyridon that day. I knew he would protect them like he protects and loves us all. And he did, Daphne. We hid in the church. The Germans went door to door searching, knowing more Jews were hiding. But even as they hunted more victims, no Nazi entered the church of Agios Spyridon. Not one. I knew they would be safe there, that the *agios* would keep us safe. I knew that even without the whispers in my ear. When I realized there was no hope of finding young David, I brought them back here, Dora, Ester, and poor sweet Rachel. I brought them right here to our home and shared with them the little we had. As you know, we were very poor, and I had only one other dress, my good church dress. I gave it to Dora to wear, so she would look like one of us, Christian Greek, and not a Jew. We did the same with the girls, dressing them in the peasant clothes of our island. As Dora dressed Ester in a church dress I had been saving for your mother, the sweet child turned and asked, 'Is it Purim already, Mama?' Dora's tears ran deeper than the sea that day as she answered 'Yes, my sweet, it is,' and dressed her children to conceal their faith."

The old woman stared again into the fire, as if she could see the frightened mother and the scared, confused children playing out the scene within the dancing flames.

"Rachel's death devastated us all. But after some time, Dora began to speak and eat again. She was a shade of what she had been before—but she managed somehow to carry on. Dora had lost so much, but what little strength she had left, she summoned for her only surviving child, for Ester. Your mother and Ester played together and grew to love each other like sisters. And Dora . . ." She sighed and looked up toward the heavens, knowing her friend was still there with her in some way.

"Dora and I grew to love and trust one another. We spent night after night talking, sharing stories and secrets of our people and of ourselves. They came to church with us, and although they did not believe in Christ as our savior, they respected our traditions and celebrated our holy days with us. They stood side by side with us, and as we said our prayers, they silently said theirs too, knowing that God would hear all of our voices, together, stronger. They respected and honored our traditions as we did theirs. I learned to keep the Sabbath with Dora. Each Friday we would prepare, cooking and cleaning together so there would be no fires lit and no work done in our home. I watched each Friday night as she lit the Sabbath candles, and we fasted and prayed together for their High Holy Days. I learned to cherish those quiet evenings together,

Daphne. We both did. We became a family, and soon, we felt no difference—Greek, Jew . . . we were a family with many rich traditions. On August fifteenth, in fact, as the entire island celebrated Our Blessed Virgin Mary's assumption to heaven, little Ester held your mother's hand and the girls walked in a beautiful procession of all the children. One of the boys snickered at this, muttering under his breath that how could she, a Jew, walk beside Christ's children? Father Petro heard the child and smacked the bad-mannered boy across the head before his father had the chance to do so himself." Yia-yia clapped her hands and laughed at the memory.

"Daphne *mou*—" She pointed her crooked finger toward the sky, toward the heavens. "Daphne, it was Father Petro himself who set the tone for others to follow. I will never forget, Daphne. He would not allow us to bury dear Rachel in our cemetery, saying the laws of the church would not allow it. Saying he was certain as well that Dora's own rabbi would not have allowed it. At first I was angry, so angry with him. How, I argued, how could God not want this poor child to rest in eternal peace, had she not suffered enough? But gradually I understood. Father was bound by the rules of the church. He saw me that day, on my hands and knees, preparing the earth to receive little Rachel's body. Father Petro came and stood with me, helped me prepare Rachel's grave with his own two hands. He prayed over her tiny body, the most beautiful prayers, asking God to take this child into his kingdom and lead her into paradise.

"And each time I heard the warnings—each time the cypresses would whisper to me and tell me the Germans were coming—I would send Dora and Ester up to the dark and difficult side of the island to hide. Each time we did this, Father Petro would take a cross from the church altar and place it on Rachel's grave so the soldiers would not find her and disturb her eternal peace. Again and again the Germans came, searching for Jews, intent on sniffing them out like a dog his dinner. Again and again they passed that poor child's grave, and they never knew that what they were searching for was right below their feet. They never knew a Jewish child was buried right there, her grave hidden in plain sight.

"We lived in fear for six months, until the British solders came and liberated Kerkyra. But even then, Dora stayed with me here on the island, where she felt safest. Several more months passed, and finally a letter arrived from her sister in Athens, saying that she too had survived and that Dora had a home, a family to return to."

Daphne could not sit quietly any longer. "But Yia-yia—how? How did you know all this? How did you know what to do, how to keep them safe, when to hide them? How?"

Yia-yia brought her fingers to her lips as if to quiet Daphne's doubts. "I told you, Daphne *mou*. I have told you, but although you hear the words, you have chosen not to listen. It was the cypress whispers. It was the ancient voices on the breeze, the voices of the gods, our ancestors, my own *yia-yia*—a beautiful chorus of their voices, all joined together as one voice. One voice guiding me, guiding us all."

Yia-yia reached out and took Daphne's hand in her own.

"I know it is hard for you to understand, to believe. I too had little faith once. I was raised by my mother and grandmother, right here in this house. One day, as I was heading to play with the baby chicks, I found my *yia-yia* on her knees, crying under the shade of a cypress tree. I was no more than five years old, Evie's age. 'Yia-yia,' I asked as I came up behind her and wrapped my little hands around her shoulder. 'Yia-yia, what's wrong?' Still on her knees, my *yia-yia* turned to look at me. 'It is decided. You have been chosen.' She cried and pulled me into her arms. 'What has been decided?' I asked. And that is when my *yia-yia* turned to me and told me my fate. She told me that one day I would hear the island speak to me. That many would try to hear the cypress whispers, but only I would understand them. In that moment, in the doorway as Yianni's mother wailed, I finally heard them. And that's when I came to realize why Yia-yia was crying. My fate was both a blessing and a curse."

"Your fate?" Daphne could not believe what she was hearing.

"My fate had been decided before I was born, Daphne. I was destined to understand the whispers. I had been given this gift that others would covet like Midas his gold. And at first I didn't understand why, I didn't know why I had been chosen. But then I brought Yianni's shattered family home with me. Dora was a shell of a woman. We lived in silence for weeks. I shared with her what little I had, and finally, slowly, she began to share with me; stories of her family, their culture, their religion, and the skills she had learned working with her husband in the tailor's shop. She taught me those skills—how to mend a blouse, how to make skirts from the sacks that held our flour and rice. How to make something valuable and beautiful out of scraps and rags. We mended old clothes and sewed new ones, and we traded our sewing for food and supplies. Your mother and I would have starved without Dora, without her guidance. When I saved Dora, she in turn saved me as well. I didn't know that at first; I didn't realize it until much later. Sometimes, Daphne *mou*, when we don't know which path to take, when we feel hopeless and lost, we just need to be still and listen. Sometimes our salvation is right there, just waiting to be heard. The cypress whispers are always there for us, just waiting to be heard."

Daphne remained still, as still as her body would allow. She had sat here year after year and listened to Yia-yia's stories of myths and legends, and once upon a time she had even wished for them to be true. As a child she had wondered what it would be like to sit at Hades' feast beside Persephone, or if she, unlike Psyche, would have had the willpower to resist stealing a glance at her sleeping lover. But that was a lifetime ago. The very words that she'd once dreamed of hearing now made her every hair stand on end. How could this be? How could Yia-yia really hear voices speaking to her from beyond the grave, on the breeze? How was this possible? It was crazy. It was impossible.

She did as she had promised; she listened without interruption, with an open heart and open mind. But now that Yia-yia had finished her story, there was one more question Daphne needed to ask, one final thing she needed to know.

"Do they still speak to you, Yia-yia?"

The old woman didn't hesitate. "Yes, they do. I am still blessed."

A gentle breeze rolled across the patio and between the majestic trees that surrounded them on all sides. Daphne held her breath and strained to listen. Nothing. Nothing but the sound of shivering leaves dancing on the breeze. The silence confirmed what she had known all along. The cypress whispers did not exist.

"What are they saying to you?"

Yia-yia didn't answer.

"What are they saying to you?" Daphne repeated.

The breeze died down. The old woman released Daphne's hand and looked deep into her eyes. Finally, she spoke. "They are saying that this man is not for you. Do not marry him, Daphne. You cannot marry him."

Twenty-nine

CONNECTICUT AND BROOKLYN

2008

Alex's parents had insisted the funeral be held in the Episcopal church where Alex had been baptized. It had always troubled the couple that their son had agreed to marry in the Greek Orthodox Church, with its foreign language and strange traditions. But Daphne had stood firm, insisting that their first steps as man and wife would be taken around the altar of her childhood church, where Alex had sat patiently waiting for her week after week. But as passionate as she had been about every decision when Alex was alive, she was as indifferent in his death.

"He's gone. I don't care," was the mantra she had repeated when the funeral director asked her if she wanted him interred in the blue or the pinstripe suit, when the police reported back that the truck driver had indeed been drunk when he crashed into Alex's car, and when Alex's pale mother asked if she could say good-bye to her son in the church where she had watched him grow up. "He's gone. I don't care," was all she could bring herself to say.

But on the day of Alex's funeral, what had begun as mournful indifference evolved into exhausted gratitude. Daphne sat stone-still and watched as the funeral mass unfolded around her. It was a small, simple, civilized ceremony with no wailing, no lament songs, no women threatening to throw themselves into the casket, as the black-veiled women at Greek funerals so often do. The priest was young and golden-haired, wearing a simple white collar—worlds away from the ornately robed priests Daphne was accustomed to. The priest, in fact, was new to the parish and had never even met Alex. Daphne looked around as he rushed through the mass with his impersonal, monotone delivery. She thought how sterile it all seemed, how devoid of emotion . . . and for that, she was grateful.

After the burial and luncheon at the club, Daphne poured herself into the black car for the drive back home to Brooklyn and the reality of life without her husband. Evie, who had never been one for long car rides, wailed and cried from the moment they hit the parkway.

"Do you need me to pull over, lady?" The driver had looked into the rearview mirror. "Is everything okay?"

"It's fine," she mumbled.

When Evie's cries turned to screams, he asked again, "Lady, do you need me to pull over?"

Still staring out the window, Daphne stuck a fresh bottle in Evie's mouth.

He's gone, and I don't care.

The moment she stepped through the door at home, Daphne placed the baby carrier on the floor. She undid the buttons of her plain black dress and let it fall off her shoulders and down around her feet. She stepped out of her dress and carried Evie to her crib, thankful the baby had finally fallen asleep in her carrier. Getting Evie to sleep had become a nightly battle, one that Daphne had neither the stomach nor the strength for right now. She tucked Evie into her crib and removed the evil-eye medallion from the carrier before fastening it once again on the white ruffled crib bumper. Daphne poured herself a large glass of wine and climbed into bed. Her fingers reached for the phone.

She answered with the first ring. "*Ne* . . ." The tears came again with the sound of her voice.

"Yia-yia . . ." She could barely get the word out.

"*Koukla mou, koukla.* Oh, Daphne *mou.* What a dark day. It's a dark, dark day."

"It's done, Yia-yia. He's gone. It's finished." She sobbed. "I can't believe he's gone."

"*Koukla,* I am so sorry. He was a good boy, a fine boy." The sound of Yia-yia's voice soothed Daphne. Soon, her glass drained, Daphne curled into a fetal position, the phone nestled under her ear.

"You will be all right, *koukla mou.* You are a strong girl. And you will be a good mother to that baby, I know you will."

"I'm trying, Yia-yia. But it's so unfair, and I'm so tired. I'm so tired, Yia-yia, I feel like I don't have the strength to take care of her. How am I supposed to take care of her when I can't even take care of myself right now?" She cried. "I just want to curl up and die."

"I know, *koukla*. I know that is how you feel right now." Yia-yia knew the feeling well.

"Yia-yia, will you do something for me?" Daphne asked as she wiped the tears with the corner of the bedsheet.

"*Ne, koukla mou*. Anything."

"Tell me a story." Daphne could barely get the words out. She reached her arm out to the side where Alex had slept and stroked the pillow with her fingers, just as she used to his hair. She laid her hand flat on the sheet, just where his head would have rested if he were still there lying beside her.

"Ah, *kala. Ne, koukla mou*. I'll tell you a story." Daphne closed her eyes as Yia-yia began to speak.

"I know your heart is broken today, Daphne *mou*, shattered and shredded. But there was once another beautiful girl, just like yourself, who thought her world would come to an end when she lost her love. But it didn't. Life went on for her, Daphne *mou*, as I know it will for you. Her name was Ariadne—she was the daughter of King Minos of Crete." Yia-yia could hear Daphne's muffled whimpers on the other end of the line.

"When the hero Theseus came to Crete to slay the Minotaur, he knew he could not do it alone. Like most men, he needed a woman's help to accomplish this task. And since the Minotaur was Ariadne's brother, the sly prince knew she would hold the secret so Theseus could get close enough to kill him. Knowing this, Theseus whispered promises into Ariadne's ear—promises of love, romance, and endless days of happiness together. Believing Theseus's promises, Ariadne betrayed her brother and her entire family. She showed Theseus how he could slay the Minotaur. Once the deed was done, the couple made their escape. They sailed safely away from Crete and the family and friends Ariadne had betrayed for the sake of love. After a day at sea, they pulled in to the port of the island of Naxos. 'Why are we not going to Athens so I can meet your father, the king?' Ariadne asked. 'We're just going to spend the night here, and we'll make sail in the morning,' Theseus assured his young lover. Ariadne slept under the stars that night, dreaming of Theseus and the children they would have together. The next morning, Ariadne awoke to begin her new life. But she looked around and realized Theseus and the ship were gone. She had been abandoned. Ariadne wandered the island, inconsolable in her grief. She had lost everything: her love, her family, her homeland. She felt she didn't deserve to walk among the living, and she prayed Queen Persephone would summon her down to her dark kingdom. One day, as she slept in the woods; disheveled, dirty hair matted like a wild animal, the three Graces stumbled upon her. They took pity on the girl and noted her fine bone structure, which was now caked in dirt, her once regal gown, which was now threadbare and torn. They knew this was Ariadne, the princess who had been abandoned by Theseus. The Graces gathered round and whispered in her ear as she slept—*Do not worry, young Ariadne. We know your heart has been broken, that you have lost your faith and your will to live, but do not be dissuaded. You have a purpose in life, and soon you will learn it. Do not lose heart, young maiden, for the gods have promised to embrace you and protect you. Just have faith and believe, and everything you have ever wished for will come true . . . for your heart, although broken, is pure and untainted.* The next morning, Ariadne awoke and remembered her dream of the Graces' visit—or was it really a dream? She looked up at the sky and saw a gilded chariot covered with luscious vines and dripping with giant, sweet purple grapes. The chariot glided to earth and touched down next to where Ariadne lay. There, driving the chariot, was Dionysus, the god of wine and revelry. *Come with me*, he said. *We will live a blessed life together, one happier and more fulfilling than you could have ever imagined*. Dionysus reached his hand out to Ariadne, and she took it. She climbed beside him, and they sailed off in his chariot, back up to Mount Olympus, where they married and she was made a goddess herself. Ariadne finally lived the life she was destined to live; not as a Cretan princess, not as the beleaguered wife of Theseus, but as a deity whose days were more intoxicating and blissful than she could have ever imagined."

Yia-yia finished her story and waited for Daphne to speak. But there were no words from the other end of the line, just the soft breathing of her brokenhearted granddaughter, who had fallen asleep with the phone still nestled against her ear.

"Good night, my *koukla*," Yia-yia whispered into the phone. "Sleep soundly, my love, my beautiful goddess."

Thirty

She had never been afraid of the dark, but on this particular night, Daphne welcomed the pale light from the full moon's glow. She walked along the shoreline, the flounce of her skirt gathered in her hand as her toes dipped in and out of the gentle Ionian Sea. The moon's makeshift night-light skimmed across the water, shimmering like an oil slick.

Oh, what the hell. In one fluid movement, her dress was over her head and discarded on the sand. She waded waist-deep into the water. Arms raised, she sprang up and dove under the water as she had countless times before in this very spot. But there was something undeniably different about this moonlit swim. She had been up all night, aimlessly wandering the same island paths that she had roamed year after year since she had first learned to toddle on them. Daphne knew sleep was an impossibility from the moment Yia-yia had announced that she could not marry Stephen and that the cypress whispers had insisted she stop the wedding.

She opened her eyes underwater as usual, but there was nothing to see this time. She knew the fish and other sea creatures were there, as they always were, but this time they were hidden in the darkness. *They're right in front of me, but I can't see them. Like so many other things about this place, about my life.*

She broke the surface and gasped for air, treading water well over her head. The night air was cool and still. She kicked and fanned her hands to turn and face the open sea, whose rhythmic bobbing up and down with the current seemed to match her own breath. She could barely make out the two stone jetties on either side of the cove, but she knew they were there, somewhere in the darkness. Now, more than ever, she needed them to keep her safe.

Daphne flipped onto her back and let the current take her, allowing the pull of the tide to take over. She looked up at the black sky, wishing the pull would take her far away. She wished she could float like this forever, like an ancient sea nymph, carefree and safe in the water, away from the inevitability of what awaited her on land.

How had this happened? Why hadn't she seen this coming? What the hell was she going to do?

There was nothing Daphne loved more than to indulge in the world Yia-yia had cultivated and created for her. She couldn't imagine a more colorful and effective way to teach a child valuable life lessons about hubris, greed, jealousy, and vengeance. But now Daphne was faced with a very real dilemma of her own. For Yia-yia and Daphne, the line between myth and reality had always been murky and blurred. But it seemed that now, this time, the line had not only been crossed, it had been erased—decimated. It was one thing to revel in the possibility of it all, but now, as an adult, with bills to pay, payroll to meet, a child of her own to raise, and a future to contemplate, Daphne found she couldn't afford to lose herself in her imagination.

The inevitability of making this decision had hung over her like a storm cloud from the day Mama and Baba were killed. She was the adult now, the responsible one, the *Amerikanida*. And despite Yia-yia's repeated protests that she would never leave her home or her island, Daphne always knew the day would come when it wasn't safe or smart for the old woman to live here alone. Daphne had dreaded this day's arrival, just as she had dreaded each of the funerals she had no choice but to plan. Last night, Daphne had realized that it was finally time. Fantasy had smothered reality, and reason had been sacrificed in the process. Once again, it had fallen on Daphne to make the arrangements.

The tears came with the reality of what she needed to do. The current carried her farther and farther out to sea, but Daphne didn't care. She wished she could simply vanish, like the tears that slid down her face and disappeared into the water. And now, knowing what she was being forced to do, she knew this place would never again be the same. Their beloved island would no longer be a refuge. From this day forward, this place would be yet another reminder of so many irreparably broken hearts, so many stillborn immigrant dreams.

I can do this. It's for the best. Daphne flipped on to her belly and began the long swim back to shore. *Long, strong strokes. Long, strong strokes.* Her arms sliced into the water with each kick. She just needed to be strong, strong enough for all of them.

She has to come with me. She has to leave this place. There's no other way. Daphne had made up her mind. It was time. She would insist that Yia-yia leave Erikousa and come live with Daphne, Evie, and Stephen in New York.

The tables had now been turned. Once upon a time it was Yia-yia who kept Daphne safe from the monsters who haunted her imagination and invaded her dreams. Now it was Daphne's turn to save Yia-yia from the monsters and vengeful gods who had crept out of the storybooks and into their lives.

When she finally reached shore and got dressed again, Daphne's dress clung to her body like a wet tissue. As uncomfortable as she felt, chilled with every step in the predawn air, she didn't for a moment regret her impromptu moonlit swim. Floating on her back in the darkness, Daphne had finally faced the unavoidable. It was overwhelming and devastating, but at least now she had a plan. Perhaps that was Stephen's pragmatism rubbing off on her, but lately, Daphne always felt better with a plan.

Holding the flashlight in her right hand and spinning her diamond ring around and around with the thumb of her left, she walked the familiar dirt roads into town. As she walked toward the port, Daphne wondered what time it was. *God, it must still be the middle of the night, even the fishermen aren't up yet.* She mapped out her plan for the morning. *I'll watch the sunrise over the port, then go to the hotel to wake Stephen.*

She walked along the dock, watching the *kaikis* bobbing in the water, their white masts reflecting the moonlight and piercing the dark sky like a row of slim fingers pointing toward the heavens. Middle fingers, Daphne imagined, feeling as if she too would like to give the heavens the middle finger for the fate her family had once again been dealt. Besides the bobbing masts, the port was perfectly still and quiet except for the continuing *thud, thud, thud* of the waves against the bulkhead. Daphne stood in the middle of the dock, taking it all in, completely engrossed in the deadly tranquillity of the hour.

"You're either up really early, or really late. Which one is it?"

The voice came out of nowhere, and although she was startled, she wasn't surprised by who had broken the predawn spell.

"Yianni." She strained her eyes to see him in the blackness. "Is it time to cast your nets already?"

"I guess I have my answer. You've been up all night, haven't you?"

"Yes."

"Well, that must have been some party." He laughed before disappearing belowdecks.

The lights in the small cabin flickered on.

"So where is your groom? Don't tell me he couldn't keep up with you and went to bed already?"

"He's back at Nitsa's, sleeping."

"Not a good omen for the wedding night." He chuckled, but just as the laugh escaped, Yianni brought both hands to his mouth in mock horror. "You know I'm only joking, don't you?"

She shook her head and smiled at him. Yes, she knew this time that he was only joking. "Can I ask you a question?" She inched closer to the *kaiki*.

"Of course, anything."

"How has Yia-yia seemed to you lately? I mean really, how does she seem to you? Do you think she's changed at all?"

"Changed? Of course she has—she's never been happier now that you and Evie are here. It's like she is a young woman again."

A fresh wave of guilt overtook Daphne. This was good news for the moment, while they were together, but what would happen after she and Evie left again? "I guess what I want to know . . ."

Yianni reached his hand out to her. She took it without hesitation. He wrapped his callused fingers around her wrist and guided her onboard.

Her chin tilted up, face-to-face with him now on the *kaiki* deck as she finished her question. "I guess what I want to know is, do you see any problems with Yia-yia? I'm worried about her, that she might be losing it, at least a little bit."

"Losing what?"

Daphne inhaled. "Losing her mind, Yianni. I'm afraid she's losing her mind."

They stood in silence as Yianni processed what Daphne was saying. He finally opened his mouth to speak, but when he did, they were not the words Daphne expected to hear.

"Hurry, come with me into the cabin. Now." He grabbed her arm and tugged her toward him. Daphne teetered off balance. She landed chest to chest, virtually on top of the man whom she instantly chided herself for having trusted. He snaked his arm around her waist and pulled her to him. "Come with me *now*." The urgency in his voice panicked her.

What's wrong with me? What was I thinking? She felt the tears well up, furious with herself for being so naive, for thinking for a moment she could trust him. "What are you doing? Let me go."

"I'm telling you"—he moved closer, his breath hot on her face—"for the last time, Daphne, come with me into the cabin."

"No. No," she hissed. "I'm not going anywhere with you." She snatched her arm away and again lunged for the dock. He let her go this time.

"Fine, go. But when the other fishermen see you scurrying away from my boat in the middle of the night, exactly what do you think they're going to say? Exactly what do you think their wives will say when they bring this bit of gossip home along with their fish later this morning? There's nothing like a scandal to liven up a summer, and you, Daphne, with your stubbornness, are about to deliver the biggest one in years."

She froze, still precariously situated with one foot on the *kaiki* and one on the dock. She could hear faint voices coming from the other end of the port and knew he was telling the truth. There was nothing the bored and righteous wives of the fishermen loved more than to dissect a woman's virtue. And a visiting *Amerikanida's* reputation was always a favorite topic. Now, with so much at stake, the last thing Daphne needed was to be fodder for the Erikousa gossip mill. Looking straight ahead into the darkness, Daphne blindly reached behind herself. She felt the familiar callused fingers latch on and in one fluid motion pull her back onboard and belowdecks.

"I'm sorry, I guess I thought—"

"Yes." He motioned for her to sit on the small cushioned bench. "Yes, please, tell me. Tell me, Daphne, what exactly did you think?" It was more a command than a question.

Her mind raced to Nitsa and the story she had shared about Yianni and Sophia falling all over each other that drunken night at the hotel. From the moment Nitsa had told her the story, an image of Yianni and Sophia locked in a passionate embrace had been seared in Daphne's mind. "I, I just thought . . . ," she stammered, not sure how or if to come clean. "All right, I thought you were hitting on me. Trying to take advantage of me."

"Take advantage of you? Another man's fiancée?"

"Yes." The word tasted sour in her mouth.

"That's brilliant, Daphne, just brilliant." He was seething, his hand pulled into a fist.

"Well, it's not like it would have been the first time." In an effort to climb out of the very large and very deep hole she had dug for herself, Daphne was well aware that she had just caused the hole to cave in around her.

"What are you talking about?" Yianni's eyes were wide. She

wasn't quite sure if she was seeing confusion or rage, or perhaps a bit of both.

"I know about Sophia, about what happens after you get drunk with her at the hotel. So, I thought you were trying the same thing with me." She attempted to smooth the still-damp fabric of her dress, but the effort was futile, as was her explanation.

Yianni stared at her. "I gave you more credit than this, *Amerikanida*. You believe those stories?"

"Actually, I don't know what stories to believe anymore. But yes, I heard it was true."

"Sophia is lonely, and her loneliness causes her to drink too much sometimes. I have helped her home many nights, even brought her home to her bed when she was too far gone to stand up. And yes, for my efforts she has rewarded me many times." His eyes were glowing now. "Yes, Daphne. Sophia has thanked me many times for bringing her home to bed."

Daphne inched away from him. Yia-yia was wrong about Yianni, just as she had been wrong about Stephen, wrong about women's voices dancing on the breeze. She wanted nothing more than to escape this cabin, escape this web of lies and get as far away from Yianni as quickly as possible.

He watched as Daphne crept closer and closer to the stairs, and finally he moved aside to let her pass, but not without first finishing what he had to say. "She thanks me with meals, Daphne. Nothing ever close to your or your *yia-yia*'s food, but it's the only thing she has ever offered, and the only thing I have ever taken from her. Food. Not sex. I know your other story was far more interesting, but this one is the truth."

She knew in her bones it was. Daphne sank her head into her hands. "I'm so sorry." Embarrassed, ashamed, and somehow flushed, despite the chill of her still damp dress, she looked at him. The familiar flutter was once again working its way up her windpipe. "I'm so sorry."

"I know." The mischief was erased from his face. It was replaced with a crinkled smile. "But don't listen to those harpies. You're better than that."

The voices on the dock were now clear as day. Yianni stood in the small galley and drew the curtain. He filled the *briki* with water and placed it on the hot plate. "Now, tell me, what were you saying about Thea Evangelia?" Outside, the dawn was finally breaking through the darkness.

Daphne sank into her seat, thankful that he seemed to have forgiven her. "I—I was asking if you had noticed anything about her. If you think she has deteriorated in any way—"

"Actually, I think she seems stronger now, like she saved her energy for you and Evie. Like she is reborn in your presence."

"But what about her mind? Yianni, I feel like she's losing her grip on reality." As much as she wanted to open up and trust Yianni, she couldn't bring herself to tell him what Yia-yia had said about Stephen and the wedding. She fully believed that he loved Yia-yia and had her best interest in mind. It was how he felt about her that she still couldn't quite get a handle on.

"Here, you are shivering." He tossed her a blanket before pouring two cups of the coffee and coming to join her at the table. "What makes you think your *yia-yia* is not well?"

"She's saying the strangest things, Yianni. I know she's always believed the island spoke to her, that she could hear whispers in the breeze. But it's different now. You know, it's one thing to read a coffee cup and tell someone they'll have good luck or that the fish will bite, but it's another thing to listen to these legends as if they were facts. She really believes the island is speaking to her. That it's telling her what to do." She stared into the cup. *Telling me what to do.*

He put his coffee down and leaned in closer. "How do you know it's not?"

Daphne choked on her drink, the hot liquid scorching her throat. "You're joking with me, again? Right."

"No, I'm not." His face was unflinching. "Daphne, when I first came here, to this island, I was coming merely to fulfill my grandmother's dying wish. She had always told me stories about Evangelia. She had always wished to see her old friend one last time, to sit with her and hear one last story by the firelight. She asked me to bring her back to Erikousa, and I always said I would, I promised that one day, one day I would bring her home to Evangelia. But I was too busy. My head stuck too deep in my books, so consumed with the past that I never once stopped to think about the present or even the future."

The picture was now growing clearer. She finally understood. No wonder he was so angry with her for staying away. He knew. He knew because he'd broken Dora's heart. He'd made the same mistake. Like her, he'd stayed away too long.

"When I got the call that she was close to death, I finally left my studies, but it was too late. She passed before my flight landed, before I could tell her how much I loved her. She passed before I could thank her for all she had done and bring her home to Evangelia one last time. I had failed the one person who never asked me for anything—who never did anything but love me. She had fought so hard for her family's survival. Dora had suffered so much, and in my selfishness, I didn't do the one thing, the only thing, she had ever asked of me." He turned away from her, but it was no use. The tearstains on his face glimmered in the dawn's first light.

That morning on the *kaiki*, Daphne had recognized that this was a man crippled by pain. But now, watching as he spoke of Dora, she realized that he was consumed with guilt as well.

"I knew then that although Dora could not sit again by the fire-light with Evangelia, I could, and I would. I would do this for Dora. The day I arrived, I found Evangelia and sat with her. After we drank our coffee, she turned my cup upside down and looked inside. 'Your search ends here,' she said. At first, I thought it was nothing more than a dear old woman having a bit of fun with a young visitor. But then I went back to school, back to Athens to finish my thesis. I had already left Columbia by this time and returned to Greece. I was like a madman, obsessed with my research, at odds with the head of my department, and in jeopardy of being kicked out of school for what they called my frivolous attempt to rewrite history. But I didn't care, I was convinced I could prove my theory."

"What theory?" Daphne was once again confused, wondering what the hell his thesis could possibly have to do with Yia-yia.

"I was just another eager graduate student"—he ran his fingers through his thick tuft of hair—"excited about the beauty and history of the ancient world. I became fascinated and consumed with the image of the Pythian priestess, and how this one woman could sway the hands of man and lead him to war or sacrifice. But in the course of my research, I began to believe that there was more to learn about the oracle, more than what was written by the historians."

"What does that have to do with Yia-yia?" Daphne was confused, her patience disappearing along with the final traces of pre-dawn darkness.

"There have been murmurs for years among classicists that there was a forgotten oracle from ancient times. That there was an oracle so pure, so cherished, that its existence was kept secret so as not to be corrupted like the Pythia. The existence of this mysterious oracle was much debated and pondered but never proven.

"So many years, so much research, but the greatest minds in the classical world could come up with nothing more than a rumor—hearsay no different than your typical island gossip. It was an embarrassment—for the universities, the scholars, and mostly, for the pigheaded professors who claim to know all there is about ancient civilization but are far more well-versed in their own hubris than any in a classical text. But I couldn't forget. I always had a romanticized idea that this place and these women did exist. Years ago, there was a historian who claimed the answer lay somewhere in Homer's *Odyssey*, but it was never proven, and there were so many stops Odysseus made on his way back to Penelope."

At the mention of Odysseus, Daphne thought about her many trips to Pontikonisi, how she would fantasize about him walking the very paths she loved to explore each summer.

"But sitting there with your *yia-yia*, she began to tell me the stories of how she and my family survived, how she heard a voice telling her to save my mother and grandmother and take them to safety. She told me how she always knew it was time for them to go into the hills and hide as the soldiers approached to search the homes for dissidents. And then she read my cup. . . . It wasn't until weeks later, when I was once again poring through old manuscripts, going through all of Homer's writings, that it dawned on me. *Your search ends here*, she had said. And finally, I knew that she was right."

"Oh, come on, Yianni." Daphne stood, not realizing or caring how small and low the cabin was. The hollow thud of her head smashing against a wooden beam reverberated through the small room. "Shit," she shouted. "Shit, *shit*." She brought her hand to her head and rubbed. There was no blood, just a sharp pain followed by a pulsing throb that mimicked the thud of the waves against the boat's hull.

"Sit down," he ordered. This time she did as she was told. "I know it sounds crazy."

"It is crazy."

"Why, Daphne? Why is this so crazy to you? Why won't you open your mind to the possibility that there could be something here?"

"You really have spent too much time in the sun." She got up to leave, but he stood too, his body blocking the narrow passage between the bench and the wall. "I have to go."

"Let me ask you this." He put his hand up, palm facing her face. "Just answer this. You believe in God, don't you?"

"Yes."

"You're a Christian—you believe in Jesus, don't you?"

"Well, yes . . . I . . ."

"And the *agios*, you believe in the *agios*, don't you?"

"Of course I do."

"I know you do. I saw you praying at his side that evening in Kerkyra, while your boyfriend looked around, trying to figure out what was going on."

I saw you too.

"So you have faith. You don't need to see something to believe it. You feel it." He lifted her hand with his fingers and placed it on his heart. "Here. You feel things here." She could feel the pounding of his heart through his shirt.

"Trust her, Daphne. I'm asking you to put your faith in her." She felt her own heart pumping furiously in her chest and wondered if he could hear it too. "Put your faith in both of us."

It was as if there were no oxygen left in the cabin. She needed to get out, she needed to go abovedecks, she needed to escape and to breathe . . . now. *This is insane. I have to get out of here.* She slid past him, her hips turned sideways, brushing his as she passed. *It's the wet dress—I need to get into some dry clothes,* she tried to convince herself as the electricity shuddered through her body like a chill.

He called out to her as she made her way abovedecks. "Did you ever stop to think, Daphne, that it's not Thea Evangelia who is losing her mind . . . but you who won't open yours?"

She didn't stop, nor did she answer. Only once she was safely back on deck did she turn and look down the narrow stairs at him. His eyes were black, wild.

"You're making a mistake, Daphne."

Not as big as the one I'll make if I stay here any longer. She scanned the port to make sure no one was around. Once she saw that all of the fishermen had already pulled out, Daphne jumped back to the dock and ran all the way to the hotel.

Thirty-one

Daphne didn't stop running until she reached Hotel Nitsa. She stood there for a moment, one hand on the sign, the other on her hip, doubled over and trying to regain her breath as well as her composure. *God help me, what is happening here?* She stood like that outside the hotel a little while longer, grateful that it was still early enough that no one was outside yet. *This cannot be happening. I'm getting married. I'm finally getting my life in order. I'm losing my grip on reality, right there along with Yia-yia.*

She had never expected to react that way to his touch. She didn't see it coming, and it had scared her, terrified her actually. When his hand reached out and grabbed hers, the unexpected shivers reverberated through her body. Even here, on solid ground, away from him and his *kaiki*, she still felt unsteady on her feet. She leaned her forehead against the sign and tried in vain to control her breathing.

"Look who it is. Up so bright and early, Daphne *mou*." Nitsa burst through the double doors. "You can't stay away from your man, can you?"

"It's still early—he must be tired from the trip. I don't want to wake him." Daphne tried to compose herself by smoothing her dress but it was no use.

Nitsa looked Daphne up and down. She placed her watering can on the ground and fished a cigarette from her apron. "He is already awake, on his second cup of coffee and working on his computer on the patio. So . . ." She inhaled, lifted her head to the sky, and let out a thin, long stream of white smoke. "So . . . what is this?" She tilted her head back and waved the cigarette in circles toward Daphne.

"What? What is what?"

"You, Daphne—what is wrong? You have a crazy look in your eyes."

"I'm fine," she lied. "I'll just go inside and find Stephen." She leaned in and gave Nitsa a hug as she passed her on the steps. Daphne knew she wasn't quite fine yet—but she would be, she had to be, she had no choice. What had happened with Yianni was plain and simple a repercussion from the difficult conversation she had had with Yia-yia the night before; the sad reality that Yia-yia's age was finally catching up to her, and the fragile state that realization had left Daphne in. There was no other way to explain it. This was all a misunderstanding. In fact, it was as if the three of them—Yia-yia, Yianni, and Daphne—had become entangled in a holy trinity of mixed signals and mistakes.

"Your dress is wet." Nitsa dropped her cigarette and crushed it beneath her foot. "And your cheeks are bright red." She looked over her shoulder to where Daphne had one hand on the door handle, ready to enter the hotel. "I'd be sure to get my story straight before you open that door."

"Nitsa, really there's no—"

"Daphne *mou*, I'm not going to ask, and you don't have to tell me." She turned and faced Daphne. "All I know is, your *yia-yia* has her gift and I have mine. I see it in your face. You look exhausted, like you haven't slept in days, and you have the burden of the world on your shoulders. But yet there is something underneath it all as well. There's a spark in your eyes, Daphne. I remember this beautiful spark from when you were a young girl—but it has been missing from your face. I've been looking for it since you arrived, but it was nowhere to be seen. Gone . . . *poof*, like that." Nitsa waved her cigarette, a puff of smoke rising to the heavens like the incense from Father Nikolaos's scepter. "All I know is, something brought that spark back, Daphne. The light in your face is here again . . . and it happened while Stephen was asleep in my hotel."

"Oh, Nitsa. You do love the gossip and the drama, don't you?" Daphne laughed, trying to shake off Nitsa's comment.

"Yes, yes I do," she admitted with a snort. "But I also love you and your *yia-yia* like my own family, Daphne. And since I do, I will say it again. Think about what you are going to say when you open that door. Think carefully before you piss it all away. Eh?"

"Don't worry. I'm fine." She blew Nitsa a kiss and stepped into the hotel.

She heard him before she spotted him.

"No, small specialty shops. There's nothing like this outside of the islands—I know what I'm talking about here." His voice echoed across the marble foyer. He sat at a corner table with a cup of coffee, his laptop, his iPhone, and Popi.

"Popi, what are you doing here?" Daphne walked over to where her cousin and fiancé sat. Stephen tilted his head up toward her, phone still attached to his ear, and kissed her. She leaned in and gave Popi a hug. Her cousin's soft arms felt warm against Daphne's cool skin. Daphne pulled over a chair and sat down between them. Stephen was too immersed in his phone conversation to notice the quizzical look and arched eyebrow Popi shot at Daphne.

"What are you doing here?" Daphne repeated, thankful for whatever had brought her cousin here this morning.

"Stephen asked me to meet him here. He liked my ideas last night and wants to help me." The room was barely big enough to contain Popi's excitement. "What happened to you?" she leaned in and whispered.

Daphne waved the question away with the swipe of her hand in the air as if it were an annoying fly. "So what's this grand plan?" Daphne asked.

"Frappe," Popi announced.

"Frappe?"

"All right, it's settled. Great. We'll see you in New York." Stephen put down his cell phone and turned to Popi. "Is your passport valid?"

"Yes, I think . . . I'm not sure. Why?" Her voice was trembling, as was every dimple and fold on her body.

"You're coming back to New York with us. I got financing, and we're going to do this."

Popi jumped up and practically jumped into Stephen's lap. "I'm coming to New York. I'm coming to New York." The entire building shook. Daphne placed her hands over the coffee cups to keep them from spilling their contents all over Stephen's electronics. "I'm going to be in business, like you, Daphne *mou*. Just like you.

We're going to open little frappe shops with Greek sweets, small cute little shops—Frappe Popi."

"Seriously?" Daphne looked from a tearful Popi to Stephen.

"Seriously. It can't fail. Not with my business plan." He turned to Popi. "You, my soon-to-be cousin, are soon to be very, very rich. Just do what I say, and this can't go wrong."

"Did you hear that, Daphne *mou?*" Popi reached out and grabbed her cousin. "Very, very rich . . . very, very rich," she chanted as she pulled Daphne close and squeezed.

There he is, the man I'm going to marry. Daphne watched Stephen dive back into his laptop as Popi clung to her. *This is a man who makes dreams come true, who takes care of me and makes things happen . . . and this is the man who loves me. Yia-yia's just confused. How can she think I shouldn't marry him? It makes no sense.*

"Popi, come here. Look at this. They've already wired the money to our account. It's done. You should be proud, Popi. I saw something special in Daphne, and now I see it in you. This, Cousin Popi, is the beginning of great things for you." He reached for Daphne's hand. "For all of us."

Daphne didn't have to look at her cousin to know she was once again jumping up and down; she could hear the slap of her *sayonares* against the marble floor and feel the seismic tremors of her jig. Instead she tilted her head back to look at Stephen, a Cheshire-cat grin splayed across his face.

"I'm telling you, Popi, I know a good business plan when I see it, and this one can't fail. This one is guaranteed to make us all rich. I'm telling you, the three of us working together will be magic. This cannot fail."

Gazing up at her fiancé, Daphne again thought of Yia-yia and what she had said as they stood together and gazed at the gaping hole left by the escaped fly in the spider's web. *See, Daphne* mou, Yia-yia had cautioned. *Hubris is a dangerous thing. Look away for a moment, and your prized possession may escape even the loveliest of traps.* She might have been an old woman who was losing her grip on reality, but Daphne still couldn't get Yia-yia's foreboding words out of her mind.

Thirty-two

"Mommy, where have you been?" Evie rushed into Daphne's arms the moment she heard the gate open.

"Hi, honey." She scooped Evie up. "I had to go to the hotel for a little while." She placed Evie back on the pavement and took her tiny hand in hers. "And I didn't want to wake you."

They walked hand in hand to the indoor kitchen where Yia-yia stood at the counter, mixing warm water with yeast. She wore a white apron over her black dress. Her handkerchief was draped on the back of a kitchen chair, and her gray braids fell down her back to her waist.

"*Koukla mou.* I missed you. Come, sit, have some *kafes.* I'm making *loukoumades* for Evie—you should have some too."

Daphne pulled a chair from the table and sat down. Evie was already off and running, entertaining herself as usual with the animals and bugs that brought the patio—as well as the little girl's smile—to life.

"I saw Popi at the hotel."

"Popi, at this early hour? That girl usually puts the roosters to bed."

"She was with Stephen." Yia-yia didn't respond to the mention of his name. Daphne continued chattering, uncomfortable with the silence. "He's helping her open a business. He thinks her ideas are good and he wants to help her."

"Good for her. She's a good girl. She deserves it." Daphne noted how Yia-yia praised Popi but never once mentioned Stephen. "In New York, Yia-yia. She's coming to New York."

"Ah, New York," was all Yia-yia said in reply. "You didn't sleep, did you?" she asked, changing the subject as she added the dissolved yeast to the flour along with raisins, more warm water, and a pinch of nutmeg. When it was mixed, she covered it with a clean dish towel and placed it inside the oven to rise.

"No. I didn't sleep," Daphne answered as Yia-yia sat down next to her at the table. She knew she couldn't lie to Yia-yia—she never had, and she wasn't about to start now. "No, I didn't. How could I?"

"You should go lie down."

"I don't want to lie down. I want to talk to you." She reached across the table and covered Yia-yia's hands with her own. "I don't understand why you said what you did last night—why you wouldn't want me to be happy, Yia-yia."

"I do want you to be happy, *koukla mou*." Her head shook up and down, her eyelids heavy with the weight of her granddaughter's accusation. "No one wants you to be happier, no one." Yia-yia reached for her kerchief and knotted it below her chin.

Another widow's tradition, Daphne thought as Yia-yia's

gnarled fingers looped the fabric through and secured the sheer black triangle on her head. *Cover your hair, wear black, sing and wail about your sadness, and never marry again.*

"Things are different now, Yia-yia."

"Things are never that different, Daphne. Young people always feel like things are so different for them. But they're not. It is all the same. Generation after generation, it is all the same."

"But Yia-yia, this is going to be a fresh start for us. For me, for Evie . . . for you." She couldn't look Yia-yia in the eye as she said it. She knew that she would soon be forced to tell Yia-yia that she had made up her mind—that for her own good, Yia-yia would have to leave Erikousa and come with them to New York. Soon she would be forced to tell her, but not yet. There was too much to sort through before they dealt with that drama.

"Yes, but how can you be so sure that this is the right start? Are you certain this is your fresh start, your correct path, Daphne *mou*?" Yia-yia stroked Daphne's hair.

"How can you be so certain it's not?" She sat up, terrified that maybe Yia-yia somehow knew about the jolt she felt when she brushed past Yianni.

"What is the point of living your American dream, Daphne *mou*, if you are sleepwalking through life?"

Daphne sat silent.

Yia-yia paused, placing her hands flat on the table in front of her, leaning heavily for support. "I know what this man has offered you, and I know it's tempting. But you and he are very much different. We are different from those people."

We are different from those people. They are not like us. Keep your culture and traditions intact. Don't pollute your heritage, don't con-

taminate the bloodline. They were the words Daphne had heard over and over again as a child as she sat on the kitchen counter, watching Mama make *loukoumades,* or as she bounced on Baba's knee while he read the Greek newspaper. But that was so long ago—she never imagined the very same chorus would come back to haunt her as an adult, as a grown woman making her own decisions about her life, her future . . . her daughter's future.

"Yia-yia, I'm not you." The words spilled out, sounding harsher than she meant them to. "I don't want to sit alone year after year. Don't condemn me to a life of loneliness because Alex died. It's not my fault Alex died. I've been punished enough; I don't want to be punished anymore."

"Is that what you think? That traditions matter to me more than your happiness? That I don't want you to get married because you are a widow?" Yia-yia's eyes were even heavier now, red and tinged with sadness.

"Well, isn't it?" Daphne whispered.

"No, *koukla,* it's not. No one wants to see you happier than I do, *koukla mou.* No one. Have you been away so long that you've forgotten that?"

Silent, Daphne shook her head. She knew in her heart that it was true. She had never before doubted Yia-yia's devotion, and she hated herself for doubting it now.

Without another word, Yia-yia stood and made her way to the oven. She seemed tired, shuffling along the floor, never quite lifting her feet off the ground and leaning on the counter the entire time. She opened the oven and took the glass bowl out. She lifted the edge of the dishcloth and peered into the bowl, the sour smell of yeast and dough wafting through the kitchen.

Daphne remained seated, arms crossed on the tabletop, chin resting on them as she watched her grandmother. After a few moments, the old woman dropped a tiny drop of the dough into the heated oil. The frenzy of bubbles on the surface told her it was ready. Daphne stood and walked over to where Yia-yia was preparing to fry the *loukoumades*. She rarely allowed herself to indulge in such decadent treats as fried dough anymore. But even in this state, as mentally and physically exhausted as she was, she couldn't pass up the opportunity to watch how deftly Yia-yia's hands worked to make perfect pillows of dough. As a child, carefree and complete in Yia-yia's kitchen, it seemed all Daphne could ever desire in life began and ended with those very hands.

Daphne hoisted herself up on the counter. She could now peer directly into the bowl and watched as Yia-yia immersed her left hand into the thin beige batter. Yia-yia held her hand upright, opening and closing it slowly, the perfect amount of dough escaping from the top of her fist, near her thumb. As it emerged from her hand, Yia-yia swooped in with her other hand and scooped the dough up with a spoon before dropping it in the simmering pot of oil. The wet dollop rolled around and around in the oil, joined by another and yet another as the pot filled with perfect little doughnut balls that bobbed and browned alongside each other. When they were cooked perfectly, Yia-yia scooped them up with her slotted spoon and placed them in a large bowl that was lined with a dishcloth to absorb the excess oil.

Yia-yia worked silently until the final small doughnut was retrieved from the hot oil, then sprinkled the pile with sugar, knowing Daphne preferred this simple method to the traditional topping of honey. She pierced a warm ball with a toothpick and handed it to Daphne before wiping her hands on her apron and resting her hands on Daphne's knees.

"Daphne *mou*. I know you are trying to make sense of this all. The last thing I want is to make you unhappy. And I won't. I know you think age has clouded my judgment—I can see it in your eyes. But I won't judge you, Daphne *mou*. I want you to be happy. All I ever wanted is for you to be happy."

"But Yia-yia—"

"No, it's all right. You'll find your way, just as I did."

"But what about what you said last night about the cypress whispers, about what they told you? About me and Stephen?"

"They're quiet now, Daphne *mou*. They're tired, just as I am. Maybe they're resting and telling me to do the same."

"I want you to be happy for me." Daphne felt the familiar tingle of tears. "I want your blessing."

"*Koukla mou*. I am a simple old woman who loves you. I'll give you everything in my power, the blood from my veins. But I don't have the power to give blessings. That is not for me to decide."

Daphne jumped off the counter and wrapped her arms around her grandmother. It wasn't fair; the one thing Daphne needed from Yia-yia right now was the one thing Yia-yia couldn't or wouldn't provide.

Thirty-three

With Stephen's help, Daphne laid the red-and-white-striped blanket out on the sand. She made certain it was far enough from the shoreline so the incoming tide wouldn't ruin the picnic she had prepared back at home.

"Come on, Evie, lunch is ready," Daphne shouted at Evie, who had ridden Jack to the beach.

"So what's on the menu?" Stephen lifted the aluminum covering from the bowl of *loukoumades* and popped one in his mouth. "Delicious."

"I thought you might like that." She smiled at him. It felt good to be here, talking, enjoying each other's company and the relative quiet before the wedding. Since his arrival, Stephen had been immersed in plans for Popi's coffee bars. It was nice to be here beside him, without an iPhone or computer competing for his attention. The silly incident with Yianni seemed like a lifetime ago, although it had been just a few hours since she had run away from him and his boat. It was probably just the lack of sleep. I was delirious and tired, she thought as she lifted the lid off a bowl of tiny fried meatballs.

"Evie, honey, please come," Daphne shouted, waving at Evie, who seemed to be taking an incredibly long time getting off Jack's back and down to the picnic. "The *keftedes* are getting cold."

"The plans are really coming along," Stephen said as he popped a *kefte* in his mouth. "Everyone wants in on this thing. I'm telling you, it's like one of your perfect little recipes"—he lifted a *kefte* into the air, twisting it around between his fingers, examining it—"it's like all of New York knows that if you mix my business acumen with an incredibly talented—"

"Not to mention beautiful," Daphne chimed in.

"Yes, of course. Not to mention very beautiful Greek woman, it makes for a perfect business opportunity, a true success story." He tossed the *kefte* into his mouth and reached for another.

"Hey, slow down on those things, save some for Evie." She shielded her eyes from the sun with her hand and again shouted toward her little girl, who was still playing with Jack. "Evie . . . Evie, come on, honey. Time to eat."

Evie finally made her way to the blanket and curled up against the velvety soft fabric of her mother's red dress. She reached first for the *loukoumades* and managed to get three in her mouth before Daphne stuck her own hand out and redirected Evie's fingers toward the bowl of *keftedes*. The little girl shoved a handful in her mouth.

"Can I be excused?" she asked through a mouthful of ground meat, parsley, and breadcrumbs.

"Are you sure you ate enough?" Daphne twirled her daughter's curls.

Evie nodded, her eyes big and pleading.

"Have a piece of spanakopita—you need some vegetables." Daphne handed Evie a piece of the spinach pie, which she shoved in her mouth.

"Can I be excused now?" Evie asked again.

Daphne planted a kiss on the little girl's forehead. "Of course, honey." Evie couldn't get off the picnic blanket fast enough.

"Hey, remember what they say, wait a half hour before going in the water," Stephen shouted toward Evie, laughing. If the little girl heard him, she didn't bother to turn.

"I wish." Daphne snickered as she wiped the corner of her mouth. "Don't worry. She won't go in the water at all. She still won't go in past her knees."

"Are you serious?" Stephen turned to watch Evie as she climbed back up on Jack's back.

"I wish I wasn't. She won't do it. I've tried and tried, but for some reason she's terrified." Daphne helped herself to a healthy portion of tomato salad.

"We'll get her in. You'll see, by the time we head back to the house, she'll be swimming like a fish. I bet if we both go in with her, she'll feel safer. We'll get her swimming in no time."

"I hope so."

"I know so. And if not, then, well, we just won't leave here until she does." Stephen smiled at Daphne, waving his fork around like a scepter.

"She's a child." Daphne laughed. "Not a project with a deadline."

"I know. But it's a challenge, Daphne." He stabbed the salad with his fork. "And you know how I love a challenge." He ripped the tomato off the fork with his front teeth.

"Yes, yes, I do." She nodded, thinking about how they first met. This is what had first drawn her to Stephen, the fact that he would not take no for an answer; neither in business nor in life. She had loved his tenacity. Tenacity made things happen. But Daphne was beginning to realize that there was a time and a place for such single-minded stubbornness, and this was not one of them. She knew her little girl responded to whispers, a soft touch, and gentle, thoughtful suggestions, not commands and deadlines.

"Stephen, I've been thinking." She put her plate down and turned to face him, finally speaking the words she had always dreaded saying out loud. "I think Yia-yia's getting too old to live here herself. I'm worried. I don't think it's safe for her to be here alone anymore."

"Yeah, I can see that." He nodded in agreement. "I'm actually amazed that's she's been able to stay here this long. As beautiful as it is here, it is not an easy place to maneuver. I think you're right, honey. It's probably a good idea for her to go someplace easier, safer."

Daphne exhaled, a wave of relief washing over her. *He noticed too. He knows we have to take her away from here to bring her home with us.* She smiled. Everything was going to work out just fine.

"I'm so glad to hear you say that." She reached over and hugged him. Up until now, Yia-yia had always been right—but about Stephen, Daphne was convinced, Yia-yia could not have been more wrong.

"Of course, honey." That whisky voice had soothed her once again—until he opened his mouth once more. "So where's the nearest nursing home? On Corfu?" He reached over and stabbed another meatball with a toothpick.

"Nursing home? Why would we need a nursing home?"

"I'm sure there's one on Corfu. Or maybe we should check Athens. I bet they have better facilities in Athens, but they're probably a lot more expensive. It's up to you. When we get back to the hotel we'll do some research, crunch some numbers, and we'll figure it out, okay?" He grabbed a cold beer, threw his head back, and took a long sip. "You have nothing to worry about, Daphne. I promise, we'll figure this out and we'll take care of her. We'll find the best fit for her."

Her cheeks were blazing; she could feel them hot and tingling, as was her entire body. He was speaking, but she could not, would not, comprehend what he was saying.

"Nursing home? Why would we need a nursing home? I'm not putting Yia-yia in a nursing home."

"Why not? It makes perfect sense." There was that pragmatism again.

"Not to me it doesn't. Not at all."

"Daphne, come on, be realistic. It's not going to be easy to find a home health care worker to come here and spend winters on this island." He drained his beer and placed the empty bottle on the blanket behind him. "I just don't know if that's realistic or even smart. Especially as she gets older, she'll need more care, easier access to doctors and a hospital. When my grandfather got too old to take care of himself, we put him right in a nursing home. It was the best thing for him."

"That was him, Stephen. This is Yia-yia. *My* Yia-yia. I don't want her to live in a nursing home." She took a moment to lean in closer to him. "I want her to come live with us." There, it was done.

He sat straight up, shaking his head, a nervous laugh escaping his lips. "Come on, Daphne." He squinted at her. "You've got to be kidding me. Are you serious?"

She stared back, wordless.

"Daphne." He stood when he realized she wasn't joking. "Daphne, seriously. How do you think we can take your *yia-yia*, as wonderful as she is, and bring her to live with us in Manhattan? I mean, seriously. How is that going to work?" He took both of her hands in his.

"It'll work."

"Honestly, honey. I don't see how, I really don't see how we could ever make that work, on so many levels. I would do anything for you, you know that. But I need you to think about this, really think about this with reason and logic, not just your emotions."

There was no discussing Yia-yia without emotions. Every memory, every moment, everything about Yia-yia was tied to Daphne's emotions. There was no separating the two. It was impossible.

"It will work. It has to. There's no other choice." She dropped his hands and stared out across the water. "She's coming to live with us."

They retreated to opposite edges of the shoreline, Daphne standing by the water and Stephen storming away to the top of the beach, where the sand meets the brush. Neither spoke. Only the sounds of Evie's squeals could be heard above the gentle ripples of the surf.

Eventually, Stephen could take the silence no longer. "Explain exactly how, Daphne. How?" He walked toward her again. "Millions of people put their parents and grandparents in nursing homes every year. I don't understand what the problem is." He stopped just before the waterline, making sure the sea never touched the hem of his pants. "We'll make sure she has the best care, I promise you. She'll have everything she needs."

"We're all she needs."

The water was now midway up Daphne's calves, the hem of her red skirt twisted in her hands. She didn't turn to look at him; she just stared out into the sea. "We don't do that here, Stephen. People don't send their family away. We take care of them ourselves, the way they took care of us when we were little." She released the fabric of her skirt into the sea and watched as it drifted on the water's surface, surrounding her like a pool of blood. "Everything comes full circle, Stephen. Can't you see that? I can't send Yia-yia away, I just can't." She turned and walked toward him on the dry sand.

"But you're forgetting one thing." He reached his hands out and placed them on her shoulders, holding her squarely in front of his face. "We don't live here, we live in New York. Different country, different rules . . . *our* rules, Daphne. Yours and mine."

"Not when it comes to this."

"So now all of a sudden you're this traditional good little Greek girl? When did that happen? You've told me millions of times how embarrassing this all was for you when you were growing up. How backward this place is, with its arranged marriages and old widows' covens." He threw his hands up in the air. They landed again at his side, rigid and in two tight fists. "So explain to me how is this going to work, Daphne, when I entertain clients at home, when we throw dinner parties in our fabulous new apartment. I can see it now. . . . Sure, come enjoy a dinner made by my very own four-star chef wife. Eat the best food, drink the best wine, revel in our witty conversations, but pay no mind to the babushka-wearing *yia-yia* all dressed in black and shuffling along our parquet floors in her plastic slippers. What's she gonna do, Daph? Come out at the end and read their coffee cups, tell them if they should go through with the deal or not? Now that's something no other banker in New York has, his very own live-in witch. That'll be great for business, Daphne. Just great." He was walking in circles now, his face as red as hers.

She had seen Stephen in attack mode only twice since they had known each other. Both times it was when an important deal went bad. Both times it was when he lost millions of dollars in potential revenue. Perhaps, Daphne thought, this was the third time.

"This is our family, Stephen. Not business, family."

He walked toward her. "I'm sorry, honey. I'm so sorry. I know how important this is to you, how important she is to you. But Daphne, I just don't see how. It doesn't fit with our lives." He threw his hands up again and hunched his shoulders, as if merely dissecting and analyzing the problem would be enough to make it go away. "It doesn't fit, Daphne."

She stared up at him for as long as she could, but finally dropped her head. It hurt to look into his emotionless eyes anymore.

Then we don't fit.

The breeze kicked in, stirring up the air of what had been a typically hot and stagnant afternoon. Daphne ran to the picnic blanket and reached out, trying to keep it and the remnants of their lunch from floating away on the wind. Her eyes spilling over with tears, she watched as the zephyr lifted a plain white paper napkin—lifting, looping, and twirling in the air, as gracefully and beautifully as a Greek bride dancing on her wedding day.

Thirty-four

That night, after Stephen stormed off to the hotel, Daphne took comfort in the warmth of a quiet night at home with Yia-yia and Evie. She needed the reassurance of Yia-yia's gentle touch to quiet the uncertainty of what her own future held for her.

Daphne held her palms out to the fire. It was still mid-August, but a hint of early-autumn crispness had worked its way into the air. She wrapped a crochet blanket around her body and hugged her arms around herself to keep warm, willing the gentle bite in the breeze away. It was undetectable to most, but Daphne had trained herself to feel it, to smell the change in the air. Even as a young girl she had always been keenly aware of early warnings that one season was coming to an end and another would soon begin. Unlike most people, Daphne took no autumnal pleasure in a palate of rust and amber leaves crowning a forest of trees. The sight of a woolen sweater or the slightest whiff of crispness on the breeze was enough to send her spiraling into a fit of melancholy. For Daphne, these were signs that the summer was ending and she would soon have to go back to her life in New York; a life of hiding in the back booth of her parents' diner instead of running free here in Erikousa. Now, as she once again felt the ever-so-slight change in the air, the same brooding feeling washed over her. But this time she knew there was more at stake in the season's change than ever before.

"Look at our *koukla*." Yia-yia motioned to Evie, who held a tree branch in either hand and was spinning and dancing in the corner of the patio. Yia-yia reached out and handed Daphne a freshly steeped cup of chamomile tea. The tiny yellow-and-white flowers grew all over the island, and picking them had been a yearly ritual for the grandmother and granddaughter, just as harvesting the oregano had been. The sweet aroma of the herbal tea emanating from the hot mug had always had a soothing effect on Daphne, and tonight was no different.

"She looks like a little wood nymph dancing in the grotto." Yia-yia smiled as she steadied herself against the stone wall of the fireplace and lowered herself into her chair. Daphne reached out to help, but Yia-yia shook her arm away and settled into her seat.

"She's happy," Daphne replied as she cupped both hands around the mug and watched Evie skip across the patio while her kitten swatted at the hem of Evie's dress with her paw.

"Are you?" Yia-yia asked. "Are you happy, Daphne *mou*?"

Daphne turned and faced her grandmother. She looked into Yia-yia's red eyes, gazed at the crags and creases that lined her face and the brown spots that dotted her olive skin, physical markers of time passed and lessons learned. This was the face of the person she loved and trusted most in the world. It had always been that way.

"I'm not so sure anymore." She felt lighter just saying the words.

"How did you know?" she asked, her voice soft, her eyes pleading for answers. "How did you know Stephen was not for me?"

"I knew, Daphne, I knew from even before I saw him." She sighed, a deep mournful sigh that emerged as if escaping from her guts. "You don't belong together. It wasn't meant to be."

"How is that possible? How did you know before you met him?"

"I've told you, *koukla*, but you chose not to hear. You chose not to believe."

Daphne brought the mug to her chest. She felt her heart thumping faster and faster. "I'm ready to listen, Yia-yia. I'm ready to." Faced with so many new questions, Daphne had now resigned herself to seeking answers.

"I knew this day would come, *koukla*. I just wasn't sure when it would be. I hoped it would be soon—I hoped it would be before you left me again."

Daphne placed the mug on the floor and leaned in, grabbing Yia-yia's hands with her own. "I won't leave you." Her laugh masked the sob that attempted to escape her throat. "I'm not exactly sure what that means yet, but I won't leave you, Yia-yia. Not again."

She knew it was true. She could never leave Yia-yia again, even if that meant losing Stephen in the process.

Yia-yia closed her eyes and began to speak. "I told you that when I was a little girl, just about Evie's age, my *yia-yia* sat with me and told me my fate. She told me that I would hear the island speaking to me, that I would one day be privy to its secrets. I didn't understand what she meant until that day when I saw Dora in the Jewish quarter, and then I heard it and I understood. But even then, Daphne, even then, I didn't understand why. Why had I been chosen? What did it mean, and why was I the one? I had done nothing special. I was in no way extraordinary. I was no different from any of the other girls on the island who had been brought up to be wives and mothers. But then one night, not long after I brought Dora here, I fell asleep with your mother in my arms as she nursed. I awoke with a start, thinking I heard your mother crying for more milk, but there she was, still asleep and nestled in the crook of my arm. I squinted in the darkness and thought I saw someone in the corner of the room, but I wasn't certain. And then I saw her." Yia-yia's face softened at the thought of that night. Her eyes took on a faraway, longing glow, as if she could still see the image of this person so many years later.

"It was my *yia-yia*, my own beloved *yia-yia* who cared for me and loved me so tenderly and completely, just as I have loved you." The tears began to fall down Yia-yia's face like slow, lazy rivers that over time carved the very creases and wrinkles they disappeared into. "As she walked toward me, I wanted to jump up, to hold her, to hug her and kiss her, I missed her so desperately. But she put her finger to her lips and held her arm out toward me. 'The baby,' she said. 'Stay there, my Evangelia, and don't wake the precious baby.' I lay there, cradling your mother and watching as my dead grandmother walked to the foot of the bed. But I was not afraid, not at all." Yia-yia shook her head, her scarf slipping away, exposing her braids.

"This was my *yia-yia*. She had come to me, and I felt nothing but love and gratitude. 'The island has spoken to you, Evangelia,' she said. 'You are blessed. You are a good woman with a clean soul. The spirits know they can trust you, my granddaughter, just as they trusted me and my grandmother before me. Years ago we were chosen because our hearts are clean, not tinged with selfishness and darkness like so many others. But this honor comes with a burden as well, my *koukla*. As in ancient times, the blessed oracles who could hear the gods' whispers were virgins or widows. We are not virgins, but all widows instead. We are blessed, my girl, but also cursed. It is easy for a broken heart to turn black, bitter, and filled with rage. But not yours—yours stayed clean and pure even after it was shattered. And that is why you have been chosen. The world is different from when this gift was bestowed upon our ancestors, my child. But even so, we still need divine guidance to help us see sometimes what is right before our eyes, to decide which path to choose, to help us hear sometimes what is being whispered on the breeze.' "

Daphne trembled as Yia-yia spoke. Is this what Yia-yia had meant? That this was their family's curse, their history? Was this her fate then too—to be a widow, to live her life alone, full of unfulfilled dreams, as she helped others fulfill theirs? She thought she had a decision to make, a decision that would lay the path for the rest of her life; but from what Yia-yia was saying, it seemed the decision had already been made for her.

"And then, Daphne *mou*," Yia-yia continued, shifting her gaze from the faraway setting sun and back to Daphne, "and then my *yia-yia* was gone. It was the last time I would see her, although I have heard her voice thousands of times in my mind and even on the breeze." Yia-yia lifted her trembling hand to sip her tea. The cup shook between her fingers, the wavering liquid spilling over the rim and falling onto the black fabric of Yia-yia's dress.

"So you see, Daphne, I knew this young man was not for you. I heard the whispers. I heard them telling me that if you committed yourself to him, you were destined to a life of unhappiness, another broken heart. This man does not see you for who you truly are, all that you are worth. He thinks he knows you, but he knows only what he sees on the surface, afraid to look deeper. You deserve someone who will look deeper, Daphne, who loves you for what you have been and who you are, not just what you can become. A man who cannot look deep into your heart will break your heart. It will happen little by little and over time. But he will break your heart. And your heart has been broken enough already."

Daphne looked up into the black night sky. A shooting star exploded across the heavens. Persephone, Ariadne . . . Evangelia, Daphne. Different women, different times. But their stories, so much alike. Their stories, so much more than myths.

Daphne promised Yia-yia she would listen, and listen she did. Daphne stayed up most of the night, listening to her stories of the island and how she had learned so much in life just by stopping, sitting still, and listening. In the end, Daphne realized there was nothing old-fashioned or closed-minded about Yia-yia's beliefs and the way she lived her life. Yia-yia explained that she did indeed pray and hope that Daphne would once again find a man to love and share her life with. That while the cypress whispers were true, the tradition of widows never marrying again was simply because there were never any men left on the island for the women to marry. There was no stigma, just not enough men. But if she did marry again, Yia-yia made Daphne promise that it would be for love—not security, not money, not even physical pleasure—for true love, like the love she had known with Alex.

When they finally went to bed just before dawn, Daphne kissed her grandmother's wrinkled cheek and thanked her. "Do not thank me, Daphne *mou*. I have done nothing but love you. And that, my *koukla*, is all I have to give, and all that has ever mattered to me in this world; that you know how much you are loved."

As her head hit the pillow that night, Daphne knew she was at a crossroads in her life, and that she needed more time. She needed more time with Yia-yia, more time to devote to Evie, and more time to figure out exactly how Stephen fit into her life, if at all. She made up her mind to walk to the hotel the next morning and tell him that she had realized it was just too soon, that she was not ready to make such a huge commitment again. He was a product of his environment, just as she was of hers. And nothing, not a new bank account or even a newly refined nose, could ever change who she was.

IT COULDN'T HAVE BEEN LONG after she had fallen asleep; it was still dark in the tiny bedroom, and outside the window Daphne could barely make out the first sliver of light weaving its way into the blanket of night that still covered the island. At first she thought it was the creak of the bedsprings beneath her body. But she lay perfectly still, and she heard it again. Daphne sat up in bed, squinting into the predawn darkness. There, at the other end of the room, stood Yia-yia. Her braids were unbound, her hair freely flowing down to her waist, her feet shuffling under the hem of her white nightgown. "Yia-yia—why are you still up?" Daphne asked.

"I wanted to say good night to you one more time, my Daphne." Yia-yia stood at the foot of the bed. "I need to be certain that you know just how much I love you and our beautiful little Evie. I never doubted you for a moment, Daphne, even when you doubted yourself. I never did. I love you with all my heart, my *koukla*.

You'll find your happiness again, when you are ready to finally follow your heart again, just close your eyes and listen. A beautiful life awaits you, and those of us who love you will always be by your side. When you need strength or guidance, promise me you'll just close your eyes and listen."

"I will, Yia-yia. I promise." There was no more doubt left in Daphne. It was gone, exorcised from her life like the possibility of living someone else's dream, of fulfilling someone else's destiny and not her own.

"Good night, my *koukla.*" Yia-yia turned and shuffled out of the room. As she did, Daphne rolled over on her side and fell instantly asleep. She slept peacefully and soundly that night, confident that she would make the right decision and that she would never again lose sight of what she valued most in life: her family and her history—as well as her future.

DAPHNE FOUND HER THE NEXT morning, her lifeless body lying in the single bed where she had slept alone every night since her young husband was lost at sea. She sank to her knees beside her grandmother's motionless corpse and leaned in to kiss Yia-yia's hollow cheek, tears cascading down her face and onto Yia-yia's gray skin. She pulled the bedsheet up to Yia-yia's chest and covered the still-warm remains of the woman who had taught Daphne so much about life and love. Stroking the soft flannel that covered her arm, she lifted Yia-yia's hand to her mouth and kissed the thin skin of her gnarled fingers, praying there were some way to breathe life into the veins that protruded from her hand. She knew she would have to leave her there and go explain to Evie what had happened, alert Father Nikolaos, make the arrangements, and share the news with their friends and family—but she couldn't pull herself away just yet. She needed another moment alone with her beloved Yia-yia before she could face the cold reality of what would come next.

Finally she stood to go, leaning down and kissing the top of Yia-yia's head. She traced her finger along Yia-yia's lips and tucked a stray gray hair behind her ear, just as she had so many times before. Her fingers lingered down the length of Yia-yia's gray and black hair, still fastened in braids.

"Tell me a story, Yia-yia, one last story." She could barely get the whisper out. Her vision blurred as the tears fell down Daphne's face and spotted the white flannel of Yia-yia's nightgown. But there was no story this time. Yia-yia lay silent.

Daphne turned to leave the room. She stopped, remembering the image of Yia-yia at her bedside, her final promise to her grandmother. Daphne lifted her head and closed her eyes, her hands braced against the door frame. There, standing in the doorway, struggling to find the strength to stay upright, she fulfilled her final promise to Yia-yia. There, standing in the doorway, Daphne finally stopped to listen.

It was no louder than a soft murmur, like the sound of a hummingbird's tiny wings flitting on the breeze. She stayed there, afraid to move, afraid to breathe, forcing her sobs to quiet down so she could hear.

And finally, she did.

Even as the tears continued to spill down her cheeks, a broad smile spread across Daphne's face. She was amazed that in the midst of such despair, such sorrow, there could also be such beauty and joy. She clutched her hands to her chest, sobbing and laughing simultaneously. The voice she heard was not the booming baritone of some great and powerful God, nor was it the ethereal mutterings of some nameless, faceless deity. The voice that greeted Daphne on the breeze was a familiar one. It was the voice of Yiayia; soft, comforting and loving—singing softly to Daphne now, just as she had so many years ago, so many times before.

> *I love you like no other . . .*
> *I have no gifts to shower upon you*
> *No gold or jewels or riches*
> *But still, I give you all I have*
> *And that, my sweet child, is all my love*
> *I promise you this,*
> *You will always have my love*

Thirty-five

Wearing the black uniform of mourning, Nitsa, Popi, and Daphne worked side by side all morning preparing Yia-yia for her funeral. There was no mortician to summon for such duties. Here, in death as in life, families took care of their own. Daphne searched the closet and found Yia-yia's nicest black dress, the one she had planned on wearing to the wedding. She hand-washed the dress in the basin out back and placed it on the clothesline, infusing the fabric with the island breeze that had meant so much to the old woman.

The three women worked together through their tears. They laughed, thinking of all the wonderful times they'd shared together, and cried, thinking that Yia-yia would no longer be waiting for them by the fire. Together they bathed Yia-yia's lifeless body, but Daphne insisted she be the one to braid Yia-yia's hair for the last time. They lifted Yia-yia into the simple wood casket and placed her hands on her chest. In her hands they placed a single red rose plucked from her garden along with an icon of her beloved Agios Spyridon.

"So you can always tell me your stories," Daphne whispered into Yia-yia's ear as she tucked a cypress sprig beneath her grandmother's body.

Daphne had toyed with the idea of holding the wake in the church, but instead she chose to honor the island tradition of a home wake. She wanted Yia-yia to spend her final moments in the simple and sparse home that had provided them all with immeasurable riches. At first Evie was frightened by the sight of Yia-yia lying still and silent in the middle of the living room. The little girl could not understand why her *yia-yia* was lying in the brown box and would not get up to see the newly hatched chicks, as Evie so desperately pleaded with her to do.

"She's gone, honey," Daphne tried explaining as she stood next to the casket, stroking Evie's hair. "She's up in heaven with your daddy and your other *yia-yia* and Papou. They're watching over you, sweetheart."

"But why won't she get up, Mommy? Tell Yia-yia to get up," Evie cried as she stomped her feet. Seeing her little girl in tears brought them once again to Daphne's eyes as well.

Stephen stood perched in the doorway as if death were contagious. He had never seen anything like this in his life and wasn't quite sure how to process it. Back home, there were people who dealt with this sort of thing. For Stephen, death, like cleaning the tub or doing your taxes, was something to be outsourced.

"Don't you think we should move her to the church?" he asked as he first walked into the house. He didn't wait for Daphne to answer. "I really think we should move her to the church."

It seemed the entire island filed in to the little house to pay their respects to Yia-yia. One by one they entered the living room, knelt at Yia-yia's side, and spoke to her, sang to her; caressed her face, kissed her hands, and showed her the same reverence, warmth, and affection in death as they all had in life. For a full day and night the entire island gave up their own homes for the sake of keeping Yia-yia company as she left hers.

Sophia was one of the first to arrive. She brought with her a tray of homemade *koulourakia*, simple braided cookies. "I thought you could serve these to everyone as they drank their coffee." She smiled at Daphne as she placed the tray on the table. "Your *yia-yia* was always so good to me, Daphne. I know we don't know each other well, but I want you to know how much she meant to me. There were so many afternoons spent here, drinking coffee. Thea Evangelia would comfort me and tell me to be strong, not to lose my faith, not to care what the gossips say about me. Her friendship meant everything to me. She told me to have faith when I had lost mine. She told me that despite what the gossips said, Petro had not forgotten me. That he still loved me and would send for me. And she was right." Sophia squeezed Daphne's hand. "He has sent for me, Daphne. He's saved enough money, and I am finally going to join him in New York. We're going to have a new life together, Daphne. Just as Thea Evangelia told me we would."

"She was always right." Daphne brought one of the *koulourakia* to her lips. She was surprised to realize just how hungry she was, that she had forgotten to eat all day. "I am so happy for you, Sophia. Really I am. Yianni speaks very highly of you as well."

"He is a good man, Daphne. I feel lucky to call him my friend."

Me too, Daphne thought. Me too. "Excuse me," she said as she turned away from Sophia. She heard the gate creak open and was surprised to find Ari standing there, holding a small cluster of wildflowers.

"Ari?" Daphne couldn't help saying his name as if it were a question. She'd known everyone on the island would come say his or her good-byes, but for some reason she had not envisioned Ari showing up.

"You sound surprised to see me." He held out the flowers for Daphne to take. "Here, these are for you. Well, for you and Thea Evangelia."

"Thank you."

"I just wanted to say good-bye to her. She helped me, Daphne. Even though I know she meant what she said that time about using her machete—" Daphne and Ari both laughed at the memory of Yia-yia hunting Ari down and threatening to cut off his manhood. "Even though she owed me nothing, she helped me, Daphne. I never told a soul, but somehow she knew that I was going to lose my house—that I had no money left; that I had gambled and drunk it all away. I went to the bank to turn in my keys, and by some miracle they told me my debt was gone, that it had been paid in full. A few days afterward, your *yia-yia* and I passed each other on the road to the port. She reached her walking stick out and blocked my path. 'You scare the young girls,' she said to me. 'Leave them alone and let them be. Our young girls have enough to worry about without you lurking in the shadows. You've been given a second chance, a fresh start in your home. It's only right to give a gift back. It's time to give our girls the gift of peace.' Then without another word, she removed her walking stick from my path and went on her way. And so I made a promise that day. I never bothered another girl again. I keep my hands and my eyes to myself. I know it was Thea Evangelia who paid my debt. I made a promise to her, and I will never break it."

Daphne put her hands on her hips. "Come on, Ari. Save your stories for someone else. I saw you, Ari, remember? I was there that day on Big Al, the day you mauled that blond girl. Her boyfriend would have killed you if we let him. Don't try to tell me you've changed. Not when I've seen you with my own eyes."

"I promised never to look or bother another *island* girl, Daphne," he insisted. "That girl was German."

As she stared at Ari grinning back at her, Daphne heard a piercing wail coming from inside the house. She left Ari standing there and ran inside to find Nitsa laying her rotund body across the casket, covering Yia-yia's with her own.

"Daphne *mou*, Daphne, my child." Nitsa sobbed and pounded on her chest with her fist, her black slip tangled up between her legs, exposing her knee-high stockings, her fat knees bulging over the elastic that dug into her flesh.

"It is a black day that you have left this earth, Evangelia. A black, black day. One last hug—one last hug from you, my friend." Daphne didn't know whether to laugh or cry as Nitsa hoisted her skirt up farther between her legs so she could lean in to give Yia-yia another hug.

Daphne looked from Nitsa over to Stephen, who was still hovering in the doorway, watching with a mix of wonder and disgust on his face. Surely, Daphne thought, he had never seen anything like this in the proper funerals he had attended back home. But as confused as Stephen seemed to be by the overt displays of grief, Daphne was surprisingly comforted by them. In all these years, she had hated the dramatics of wailing lament songs. But this was different. This time Daphne was just as overwhelmed herself. She too would have beaten her chest, pulled out her hair, clawed at her face, or thrown herself on the casket, if it would only bring Yia-yia back. Daphne finally understood that for these people, mourning was not a contest. There was no prize for the person whose grief outshone others, the one who cried the loudest or beat her chest the hardest. This was emotion, pure unfiltered love and emotion, and it was all they had to offer. They had no money for large charitable donations in Yia-yia's name; there were no monuments to be built for the simple old woman, no full-page obituaries to buy so everyone could read about her virtues. This was the only way they could honor her; with their emotions, their voices, and their grief. And these things, Daphne realized, were far more precious and meaningful than anything she could imagine.

"Daphne *mou*. Oh, Daphne, I am so sorry. What will we do without her?" Popi fell into Daphne's arms. "Look at you. You were supposed to be wearing white, the white of your wedding dress, not dressed in black for mourning."

"It's okay, Popi. Don't worry about me." She meant to say more, to tell Popi that there would be no wedding, but the touch of a hand on her shoulder made her turn around before she could continue.

"Yianni." She swayed ever so slightly. Perhaps no one else would have even noticed, but he did. He placed his arm around her waist and steadied her.

"I am so sorry, Daphne." He looked tired, as if he hadn't slept himself.

"I know." She looked up at him, his disheveled hair, his gray stubble. She felt comforted by the touch of his hand, as if she knew those hands could support her, could keep her safe. "I know you loved her. She loved you too. You were very special to her." She made no effort to move away.

"I feel blessed to have known her, Daphne. She changed my life. She gave it meaning." His dark eyes closed for a moment. When he opened them again, Daphne noticed how red they were, how dark the circles under his eyes appeared. She also couldn't help but notice that his hand was still around her waist. That fact was not lost on Stephen either, who for the first time that morning entered the room where Yia-yia's body lay.

"Daphne." Stephen finally moved from his perch outside the door and entered the room. "Are you all right, honey?"

As if on cue, Yianni dropped his arm from Daphne's waist. "Excuse me," he said as he walked to the casket. Instantly, the comfort was gone.

Daphne watched as Yianni walked over to Yia-yia and knelt beside her body. He closed his eyes as if in prayer. When he was finished, he leaned in and touched Yia-yia's hand before whispering something into her ear.

"So are you?" Stephen was speaking to her, but she was so immersed in what Yianni was doing that she didn't hear what he was saying.

"Am I what?"

"I said, just come spend the night at the hotel with me. There's no one left to judge you, Daphne." He put his arm around her waist just as Yianni had done. "Come stay with me." He tugged her closer.

"Honey, I'm sorry," she replied. "I want to stay here. I need to be here." She pulled away from him just slightly. "I need you to

understand. I really need you to understand why this is so important to me."

"I know. But I thought I was important too," he said before
dropping his hand from her waist and walking over again to his
perch in the doorway.

Daphne didn't follow him. She stood and watched as Yianni
reached his hand out and lay it on top of Yia-yia's, smiling down at
his dear friend. He leaned in and kissed her one last time. Finally
he turned away from the casket. He bent his head to put his cap on,
the glistening streak of a single tear sliding down his face.

After a few more hours, the house slowly emptied out. As she
walked around the patio, Daphne was struck by how clean and
orderly everything was. Each of the women had helped; washing dishes and sweeping the patio so Daphne could focus on her
grief and not be distracted by mundane tasks like cleaning and
housekeeping. That was the way of the island women. Sure, they
might gossip about you behind your back, but when it came to
matters like weddings, deaths, and births, they would go to the
ends of the earth to help each other, knowing that one day their
friends and neighbors would be there for them in their time of
need as well.

Daphne walked over to the garden wall, where Evie and Popi
sat looking through a stack of old photos.

"You see, Evie," Popi said as she lifted a faded and yellowed
picture and handed it to Evie. "That is your mommy when she was
a baby, and her mommy and Yia-yia. Three beautiful and special
women."

Evie and Daphne both leaned in to get a better glimpse of the
picture. It was a photo of Daphne in her cradle, Yia-yia and Mama
hovering over the sleeping baby with broad, proud smiles on their

faces. The picture was taken in the very spot where they sat now. It was just as Yia-yia had described it.

"Can I have this, Mommy?" Evie snatched the photo from Popi's hand and waved it at her mother. "Can I have it so I can put it in my room? I want to look at it every day so I can remember Yia-yia. Is that okay?"

"Of course you can." Daphne picked Evie up, balancing the little girl on her hips. "I think that's a great idea, a perfect idea. So we can both remember Yia-yia and my mama. They were special women, you know, just like you'll grow up to be." Daphne hugged Evie closer.

"Just like you, Mommy." Evie wrapped her arms tighter around her mother's neck. The photo shook in the breeze that worked its way across the patio.

"Now, honey," Daphne said as she placed the little girl on the ground once again. "Gather your things; you're going to spend the night at Thea Popi's so I can get everything ready for tomorrow, all right?"

"All right, Mommy." Evie disappeared into the house to grab her bag.

"Cousin, is Stephen going to stay here with you?" Popi asked as she motioned over to Stephen, who was once again talking on his phone on the other side of the patio.

"No, he'll go back to the hotel. I want to be alone. I need to be alone with Yia-yia. One last time."

"Of course, Daphne." Popi reached out to hug her cousin as the tears began again. "I understand, of course you do." Popi released Daphne from her embrace as Evie came out of the house, carrying her suitcase.

"Ready, honey?" Daphne asked as she kissed her daughter good night.

Popi and the little girl walked hand in hand across the patio. Once they reached the gate, Evie reached her little hand out to pull it open—but suddenly released it. The gate slammed shut as Evie raced across the patio and fell again into her mother's arms.

"Evie, honey." Daphne tucked a curl behind Evie's ears. "Evie, what is it?"

"Thank you, Mommy." Evie hugged Daphne tighter. "Thank you for sharing Yia-yia and her island with me, even if it was for just a little while."

Thirty-six

Daphne pulled a single chair from the table and placed it beside the casket. The room was aglow with the soft golden light of a dozen or so candles scattered about. As Daphne looked down at Yia-yia's still face, she noticed how the light of the candles cast a warm glow on Yia-yia's skin. She looked alive, healthy, sleeping. Daphne prayed the luminosity of Yia-yia's complexion could be more than a mere optical illusion. But she knew that once the flames of the candles were extinguished, so too would be any illusions that the blood in her veins ran warm, that her beloved Yia-yia was merely resting.

She sat like that for a long time, never taking her eyes off her grandmother, conjuring up cherished memories of their time together, each remembrance more precious than the last. Time seemed to evaporate in the haze of candlelight, reminiscences, and tears. She didn't know how long she had been sitting there, but she had just gotten out of her chair and reached for another tissue when she thought she heard a noise. She stopped, sat silently, and waited. Within seconds she heard it again. It was a soft tapping on the door, as if someone wanted to knock, but was unsure if they should intrude. Daphne stood and walked toward the door. She didn't have to open it to know who she would find on the other side.

She smiled, pulling back the door to reveal him standing there. "Yianni."

"I don't mean to intrude." He removed his fisherman's cap. "I imagined you would stay with her. And I wanted to make sure you were all right, that you didn't need anything," he explained, still standing just outside. "But I see that you are, so I should just go," he stammered as he took a small step backward.

She leaned out across the threshold and grabbed his arm before he could go. "No. Stay. Here." She released his arm and moved aside to let him pass. "Come inside."

"I don't want to disturb you, Daphne."

"You're not disturbing me. She'd want you here. Please, come in." She motioned him into the room and closed the door behind him.

They sat silently at first, each lost in private thoughts and favorite memories of Yia-yia. After a while, Daphne was the first to speak. "I didn't know what to make of you at first, Yianni. I mean, there you were, this menacing madman with a *kaiki*." She turned toward him and laughed. "But then I saw you with Yia-yia, and I saw something else. I saw how much you meant to her. I saw how much she loved you." Daphne bit her lip to keep from crying again. "I never said this before. But thank you—thank you for taking such good care of her, even when I couldn't. Even when I didn't."

He removed his right hand from his jacket pocket and placed it on the edge of the casket, clutching it with such strength that Daphne watched his fingers turn red, then white.

"I loved her like my own grandmother, you know. I failed my own family, Daphne. I was too selfish, too caught up in my own dreams to realize that my grandmother had hers as well." He nodded toward the casket and then turned to face Daphne. "She worried about you, Daphne. She told me many times how she was afraid that you had lost yourself in your grief. That losing your young man and your parents had weighed down your heart with far too heavy a burden for a young girl to manage. She understood why you couldn't come back, even if I could not. She understood how you became a prisoner to your loss, how debilitating it was for you. But she knew you would come back. As sick as she was, Daphne, she knew she had to wait for you to come back."

"She waited for me?"

"She told me once, Daphne. One night, when she was so frail and sick that I carried her in my arms to the *kaiki* and brought her to the doctor in Kerkyra in the middle of the night, she told me that the angels were calling for her, but she refused. She told them she was not ready. She told them she would not leave until you returned to the island. She would not leave this earth until she could see you again—no matter how long it took for you to come back."

"What are you saying?"

"I'm saying she knew she was dying. But she refused to let go until she'd spent one final summer with you. The doctors never expected her to make it through the night, let alone get well enough to come home. But she did. She waited for you."

Daphne stood. She walked over to Yia-yia's casket. Clutching the wood, she leaned in to touch her grandmother's folded hands.

"You waited for me." She stroked her grandmother's cool cheek. "I'm sorry, Yia-yia. I'm so sorry I took so long."

Yianni ran his fingers up and down his beard, uncertain of what to say or do next. He looked lost and out of his element, like a fish that had escaped from his very own net and now sat helplessly flopping on the *kaiki* deck. Daphne had a sudden urge to make him feel at ease, to comfort him, as he had done to her.

"Yianni, I have to tell you something." She closed her eyes and took a deep breath. "I heard it."

She turned to face him, but he was already gone. Yianni had slipped out of the door and into the night.

Thirty-seven

The following morning, the entire island gathered once again, this time to say a final good-bye to Yia-yia. The tiny church was packed. There were no pews or air-conditioning in the old Greek Orthodox church. But Daphne didn't mind standing side by side, shoulder to shoulder in the oppressive heat with the friends and family who had loved Yia-yia so deeply. Today, it felt like an honor.

Daphne stood at the front of the church, holding Evie's hand, Stephen beside her. She watched as Father Nikolaos shook the incense burner back and forth over Yia-yia's open casket, filling the old church with the familiar musky scent. Wearing his black robes, trailing smoke as he waved the censer in the air, he sang the traditional funeral chant with such passion and intensity that she knew he was living the prayer, feeling it in his soul and not just reading it off the page. "*Eonia oi mnoi oi-mnee mnee.* May your memory be eternal. Memory eternal. Eternally in our memories."

Daphne felt the tears spill over again as she opened her mouth to join in the singing. She meant it. She meant every word. Although her body felt weak, her legs trembling beneath her, Daphne's voice was steady and strong.

She looked around her and watched as the entire church, this sea of black dresses and moth-eaten, ill-fitting suit jackets, stood together, singing, crying, and vowing never to forget Yia-yia. She looked up at Stephen. He stood dry-eyed and stoic in this pageant of tears; not a hair or emotion out of place. In that moment, the church heavy with incense and sorrow, Daphne looked at Stephen and realized that like her fiancé, she too felt nothing. She looked deeper into the eyes of the man she had promised to marry, to spend the rest of her life with, to raise Evie with—and felt nothing. Daphne realized that this was the day she would be laying more than just her grandmother to rest.

Yia-yia was buried in the overgrown cemetery next to the church. As was customary, each mourner stepped up to the casket as it was being lowered into the ground and tossed a flower on top of the closed coffin to say good-bye. Daphne's last vision of Yia-yia would be of her wooden casket covered in a blanket of red carnations, tossed to her by those who loved her most.

After the service ended, one by one the mourners began to file out of the cemetery and toward the hotel for the postfuneral luncheon. But Daphne lingered behind. "Take Evie." She motioned for Popi to go ahead. "I'll meet you at the hotel."

Standing alone next to Yia-yia's open grave, Daphne watched as Popi walked over to Evie, who stood by herself just outside the cemetery gate, gazing out at the sea in the distance. Evie had been quiet and withdrawn all morning, not even stopping to pet the kitten that had followed her down the dirt path from the house to the church. Popi bent down and took the little girl's hands in her own. She leaned in farther and whispered something into Evie's ear. Evie smiled for the first time that day as Popi kissed the tip of her little nose. Popi then scooped Evie into her arms and hugged her close. Evie wrapped her arms around her aunt's neck and nestled her head on Popi's shoulder. Popi carried her the entire way to the hotel, Evie's tanned legs crossed at the ankles around Popi's thick waist.

Daphne stood alone, looking down on Yia-yia's casket, a single red carnation in her hand. She wanted one last solitary moment with her grandmother, but this was not good-bye. She knew better than to say good-bye. She lifted her hand to drop this one final flower, but just as she was about to release it from her fingers, she stopped.

Still clutching the carnation, she walked just to the other side of the cemetery gate. It took a moment, but then she found it. She dropped to her knees, and with her hands she swept away the leaves that had fallen on the simple stone marker from the olive tree above. Finally, when she was satisfied, she said one last prayer before laying this final flower on Rachel's grave.

Thirty-eight

Although she had not eaten anything since Sophia's *koulouraki* the day before, Daphne had no appetite when Nitsa placed the traditional mourning meal of fried fish with rosemary and vinegar sauce before her. "Eat, Daphne *mou*. You need to keep up your strength. Evie needs you, you cannot afford to make yourself sick."

"Thank you, Thea." Nitsa's concern had a medicinal effect on Daphne. She instantly felt stronger, steadier, as she used to merely by being in the presence of Yia-yia.

"Daphne *mou*. Who would have known it?" Nitsa dug into her apron and pulled out a cigarette, using the burning tobacco stick to gesture around them. "Who would have known it—who knew that instead of a wedding, we would be hosting a funeral feast? No dancing. No joy. Just the sorrow of life, knowing that my friend Evangelia is no longer with us." Nitsa looked around the room. "Where is Stephen? His fish will get cold."

"He went back up to his room to make a phone call."

"Still working? Even on a day like today?" Nitsa took a deep drag, exhaling above Daphne's head. "Ah, Daphne *mou*. Does your young man ever stop working? Does he ever stop to enjoy what he has built? What he has accomplished?"

She shook her head while picking at her fish with her fork. "Ah, *kala*. I understand." Nitsa stood to leave, but not before leaving Daphne with one final thought. "I knew your *yia-yia* for many many years, Daphne *mou*. You come from a long line of strong, incredible women. Don't ever forget that."

"Trust me, Nitsa. I know it well." Daphne looked up at Nitsa. "I know it very, very well."

"All right, then, you sit here, and I will finish serving the meal." Nitsa turned to go, but as she did, she stumbled, her knee giving out beneath the weight of her body.

"Nitsa!" Daphne shouted, jumping up to grab her before she fell to the ground. "Are you all right?"

"Ah, damn. My knee has been bothering me. Not now." Nitsa slapped at her knee with her dishrag as if she could shoo the pain away.

"Here, you stay. You sit. Let me help you serve." Daphne was instantly up on her feet.

"No, no, no." Nitsa lurched forward and tried to stand but fell back into the chair with a thud. "*Gamoto, poutana . . .*" The torrent of Greek curses streaming from her mouth caught the attention of many of the mourners, including Yianni.

"Nitsa *mou*, what happened?" Yianni asked. "What could have caused the mighty Nitsa to fall?" He knelt at her side and held his hand out to her.

"Nothing, it is nothing." She took Yianni's hand and again attempted to stand. He placed his arm under hers for support, but it was no use. The moment Nitsa put any pressure on her knee, she sank back down into the chair, writhing in pain. The cursing continued. "*Gamoto, malaka, poutana*—"

By now the entire patio full of guests had come over to see what was wrong, including Father Nikolaos, who despite being known for his warmth and sense of humor, was not amused by Nitsa's choice of words.

"*Ella*, Nitsa. Such language, on such a day?" Father chided.

"Father, you know my friend Evangelia is looking down on us right now, laughing about how I can't get my big fat ass out of this chair." Nitsa took a deep drag, exhaling the thin stream of smoke up toward the heavens. "Eh, Evangelia, look at me. I am too fat for my old knees. Evangelia, put on some *kafes*, eh, I may be joining you sooner than you think."

The entire room erupted into a chorus of laughter. Daphne looked around her and committed the vision to her memory; the threadbare clothes, the weathered skin, the callused hands, the signs that these were simple people who lived simple lives. But watching them all come together like this, supporting each other, helping each other through their grief with a simple hug or a naughty joke, Daphne could see how much they all meant to each other, how they all sustained each other. Daphne finally understood what Yia-yia had meant all these years. Despite the poverty, the isolation, and the lack of material goods, this truly was the richest place on earth.

"Nitsa, sit. Stay here. I'll finish up for you. You have to take care of yourself, or you will be joining Yia-yia." Daphne joked, but there was an undercurrent of seriousness that even stubborn Nitsa heard loud and clear.

"Ah, *entaksi*. All right. If you insist," she finally concurred.

As Daphne got up and headed toward the kitchen, she felt a hand wrap itself around her wrist. "I'll help you. It's my fish, after all—it will only reflect badly for me if it's not prepared properly." Yianni spoke directly to Nitsa, but he continued holding Daphne's hand. "*Ella*, let's go."

They walked toward the kitchen in silence. Leaving the chatter of the dining room behind, they entered the kitchen through the swinging double doors. Once inside the kitchen, he turned to face her and finally let go. She looked down at her arm where he had held her, where she could still feel the imprint of his hand.

"It's been a difficult day for you, hasn't it?" he asked.

"Yes." She looked up at him. "It's been awful, but not just for me. For everyone." She paused, biting her lip. "And for you."

There was silence for a moment, neither one knowing what to say or do next. He turned from her and opened the oven, where Nitsa had placed the large platter of fried fish. He pulled it out and placed it on top of the stove, ready to start plating the fish that he had caught in his nets just yesterday.

"I did it, you know," she blurted out.

He turned to her again, cocking his head as if he didn't quite hear or understand what she had said.

"I did it," she repeated. "I tried to tell you last night, but you were gone. You left."

He winced as if he had been caught in a lie or stealing, instead of merely walking out a door and into the night.

"I finally stopped to listen, like Yia-yia told me to do."

He sucked the air from his cheeks before taking three steps toward her. "And . . ."

"And I heard it." She was trembling now, uncertain if it was the heat, the fact that she was hungry, or because he was once again

inches away from her, and she could now feel the electricity emanating from his body without the necessity of his touch. "I heard
Yia-yia, Yianni. She spoke to me. I heard her in the cypress whispers. I could barely hear it at first, but it was there. It was her. I
know it was."

He watched her cry and didn't speak a word. He didn't reply. He
didn't move to comfort her or wipe the wetness from her cheek.
Nothing. He stood staring at her, as if his feet were cemented to
the floor just inches from where she stood, just inches from where
she had spoken words he had waited so long to hear. But now it
seemed even these words were not enough to draw him closer.

"On your *kaiki* that morning, you asked me to put my faith in
Yia-yia . . . and I did. I finally did." It was she who inched closer
to him. "You also asked me to put my faith in you." She stood
chest to chest with him now, his breath warm on her face as he
looked down at her. "I'm ready to. I'd like to. I'm ready to believe again." He still had not moved, but she didn't wait for him
this time. Wrapping her arms around his back, she placed her
head on his chest. This time, it was his heart she felt racing in
her ear.

He lifted his arms and placed them on her slim shoulders. They
stayed like that for no more than a few seconds before he took the
three fingers of his right hand and put them under Daphne's chin.
She was surprised by their light, delicate touch. They could now
clearly see each other's faces, his left hand still embracing her
shoulder, her arms still clasped around his back.

"Daphne, I don't . . . But you are getting married . . ." Her chest
swelled as he began to speak, but before he could finish, the double doors burst open.

"Here you are. Look, I—" It was Stephen. He burst into the

room but stopped short as he spotted his fiancée chest to chest with Yianni, her arms around him. "Daphne?"

She didn't know how to answer him—or simply didn't care to.

Yianni was the first to speak. "I was just saying good-bye to your fiancée." He removed his arm from her shoulder and took two steps backward.

Daphne felt her blood run cold, a wave of fear washing over her body. *Good-bye*—what did he mean, good-bye? And she wasn't Stephen's fiancée. Well, not for much longer, anyway—she just hadn't found the right way to tell him yet.

Yianni didn't look at Daphne, but spoke directly to Stephen this time. "I whispered my plans to Thea Evangelia before we laid her to rest, so now it's time to tell everyone else, I suppose."

"You're leaving?" Stephen asked, the corners of his mouth lifting in a smile.

"Yes. With Thea Evangelia gone, there's really nothing keeping me here any longer. She was the reason I stayed. Without her, I have nothing here." He finally turned his head and looked again at Daphne, who was steadying herself against the kitchen counter. "Nothing."

But I'm still here, I haven't gone. I'm still here. The words screamed inside her head. But when she opened her mouth to speak, all she could say was, "But where will you go?"

"Maybe back to Athens. I don't know. Maybe Oxford. I'm going to hang up my nets and get back to my work. I've been running away for so long, it's time for me to run toward something again. It's time for me to reignite my passion. I've seen so much here, learned so much. But it's finished for me here now. I suppose the two of you have something to look forward to. I imagine you'll have your wedding back in New York."

Stephen was now beside Daphne. He reached his arm around her waist, but she pulled away. He shot her a sideways look, his thin lips in a tight line across his face.

"Well, I guess it's good-bye, then." Yianni turned and held his arm out to Stephen. "Good luck to you. You are a lucky man."

"I know." Stephen shook Yianni's hand using the most forceful grip he could muster.

"Good-bye, Daphne." Yianni leaned in and kissed Daphne one time on either cheek. She didn't care that his stubble felt like hundreds of sea urchin spikes digging into her skin. The pain was proof that he was still there.

"Good-bye, Yianni." She grabbed his arms and stared into his face, desperate to memorize every detail. She dug her fingernails into the cotton of Yianni's shirt until he pulled away from her.

Thirty-nine

Daphne took Popi up on her offer to spend the night with Evie so Stephen and Daphne could have some much-needed time alone. Everyone imagined the couple would want a little quiet time together after the whirlwind of the past few days. They all figured the wedding would be postponed for at least the forty official days of mourning, No one yet knew it was Daphne's intention to call it off altogether.

"Here, Daphne *mou*, *ella etho*," Nitsa summoned her from the sofa in the lobby area where she had been convalescing since her knee gave out earlier that afternoon. It was not quite eleven. All the guests had stumbled off into the night, their bellies filled with Nitsa's food and wine and their minds filled with their favorite Yia-yia stories, which they had all taken turns sharing and toasting to.

"Come, my Daphne. Come sit with me for a moment." Nitsa patted the tiny space beside her on the couch, the only space not taken up by her ample assets. "You need to know something. Daphne *mou*, your *yia-yia* knew she didn't have much longer on this earth. She knew I would do anything for her, but there was only one thing she asked me to do. One thing I promised her I would do when she was gone."

Daphne straightened her back. "What was it? What did you promise?"

"I promised her I would remind you to keep living. We both saw the difference in you since you arrived. When you came, it was as if the light had gone out of you. But then we saw the change. After just a few days here, you were once again filled with life, with color and light. I know you think that we don't understand these things. How could we, old widows dressed in our black, know about color? How could we know about life when we never leave this tiny island of ours. But we do know these things, Daphne. We do know how precious it all is. Every moment is a gift, Daphne *mou*. Every moment, every breath, even every tear, is a gift. Without our tears, how can we truly appreciate the laughter? Women like your *yia-yia* and me, we shed many, many tears, Daphne. And all of that sadness, all of that sorrow, all of those scars and difficult times—they only help to make our time here, surrounded by the ones we love, so much sweeter. Your *yia-yia* and I lost the men we loved, but we still had love in our lives, Daphne. We still found happiness. And now it is your turn to find your happiness. Whatever that means for you."

Nitsa stopped and took a long, hard drag. Never at a loss for words, she exhaled before finding just the right ones to finish her thought.

"Find your happiness, Daphne. This is something you must do

for yourself. This is something you must bring to a marriage, not something you take from a marriage. Your own happiness. Your *yia-yia* and I both learned this lesson, and now you must too. You owe that to yourself . . . and to my friend."

Nitsa looked up to the heavens and waved her short, fat fingers toward the ceiling as if saying hello to Evangelia. Still smiling, she leaned in and pulled Daphne to her humongous bosom.

"Daphne *mou*, sometimes the loneliest people are the ones who never know a moment's solitude, and the most fulfilled are those who stand alone but can say that they were loved. That at least once in their lives, they knew what it was to be truly loved."

It was the one certainty in her life right now. Daphne knew beyond a doubt that she was indeed loved. She hugged Nitsa back with all of her might.

"Thank you. Nitsa, thank you." She kissed Nitsa good night and headed to the room where Stephen was waiting.

She entered unnoticed as he sat on the bed, typing on his computer. She had no idea what she would say or how she would say it. All she knew was that she wanted out. Finally, he looked up.

"Daphne. How long have you been standing there?" He walked toward her. "Honey, I know how hard this is for you. I know how much you loved her. The stress has been too much for you . . . and now, now this . . ."

He took one more step toward her, but she did not move.

"We just need to get back home, and everything will be back to normal. Once we get home you'll see. All of this will be like a distant memory. We'll go to Santorini like we planned. Let's get away, just the two of us. We'll move forward, we'll get married in New York—and everything will be like we planned it. We just need to get home."

But this is home.

His voice had lost its anesthetic effect. That deep whisky rasp did nothing to dull the memory of their impasse on the beach. It did nothing to soften the frustration of having her faith questioned and the reality of knowing that he would never understand the depth of her bond with Yia-yia, this island, or her people. And without that, she knew he could never truly understand her or love her for who she really was.

He took two more steps toward her, pleading. "I want you to forget about it. Let's just forget all of this. We'll put it in the past and just focus on the future."

"Stephen, there is no future without my past."

"What are you saying?"

"I'm saying I am my past."

As the words left her lips, the sea breeze charged into the room through the open window. As if bestowed the gift of breath, the white curtains filled with air, inhaling and exhaling up and out. Daphne watched as the two lace panels performed their frenzied *sirtaki* side by side, dipping, jumping, and spinning in unison, as gorgeous and as graceful as Daphne and Popi's dance had been on the flower-filled patio just below.

She stood taller now, knowing the breeze had bestowed a gift upon her as well. She smiled as she spoke, the zephyr's kiss upon her cheek confirming again what she already knew to be true.

"I am my past."

He sat on the bed and buried his face in his hands.

She watched her fiancé sitting there, confused, deflated, and defeated. She didn't want to hurt him. But she didn't want to spend the rest of her life with him either.

She had meant well; she had entered into this relationship with the best intentions. She knew he truly was a good man, but she now realized that he was not her man. It wasn't his fault that he didn't understand her. Like Daphne, he couldn't erase who he was or how he was raised. It is an unspoken rule that one should never ask a woman to choose between her child and her lover. Daphne now knew she could never and would never be made to choose between her past and her future either.

She had enjoyed their talks, his company, and the idea of no longer being alone. But Daphne didn't want just a companion, a business partner, or someone to take care of her. She wanted a husband—a friend, a lover. She wanted a man who was willing to open his heart and believe, as she had once upon a time and so long ago believed, that love can defy the laws of man and that angels can be summoned by the power of a kiss.

"I'm not in love with you," she said. "I'm so sorry, Stephen. But I'm not in love with you."

She slipped the ring off her finger and placed it on the bureau before turning and walking out the door.

Forty

Her voice came from across the darkened lobby, as if from the shadows. "So it's finished, then."

"Nitsa?"

"Yes, Daphne *mou*. I'm still here."

Daphne squinted into the darkness. All she could see was the glowing red tip of a burning cigarette. She pressed her hands along the wall until she felt the light switch. The lights flickered on to reveal Nitsa, right where Daphne had left her, lying on the couch in the middle of the lobby. "What are you still doing down here?"

"I was waiting for you."

Daphne walked over to Nitsa and once again sat on the small space at the edge of the sofa. "Me—why?"

"Because I promised your *yia-yia* I would look after you. And I knew when you went up to that room that you would be coming back down, alone."

Daphne was silent for a moment. There were a million things

she could say, a million things she could ask, but right now there was only one that mattered. "How did you know?"

"I had my suspicions when I met him, Daphne, just like Evangelia did. He can't ever be what you need him to be. And you are so much more than he wants you to be."

"More than he wants me to be." Daphne laughed, repeating the words.

"But then I saw you tonight, at the dinner. Your heart was heavy with the loss of your *yia-yia*, and there has been nothing that anyone could do or say to lift this blackness from you, Daphne. But then, tonight, I saw your face. I watched you, and in an instant I saw the spark, the life come back in you, just as I saw it that morning when you showed up wet and out of breath at the hotel. Something or someone changed you, Daphne, changed everything about you in an instant."

"Yianni." His name rolled off her tongue before she could will it back. She knew the answer was Yianni.

Nitsa smiled and remained silent for a moment, allowing Daphne to digest what was happening, what she was saying— what she was finally admitting to.

"I saw you, Daphne. I saw what a man's touch can do to you, how it changes you. There was no mistaking it, even with these tired old eyes. I prayed you would see it yourself and not sacrifice yourself to a life spent living with the wrong man's touch."

Daphne felt as if the wind had been knocked out of her. She never expected these words from Nitsa, never. How was it that Yia-yia and Nitsa, the two women Daphne never imagined to have had much passion in their lives, seemed to be the ones who understood it best?

"Daphne *mou*, listen to this old woman. There is so little in life that really matters. Look around you. Think about what you need in your life—it's all right here at your fingertips. You've been searching for something, for a reason to smile—and it has been in front of you the whole time."

"What are you saying?"

"*Ella*, Daphne—an educated *Amerikanida* like you—how can you be so stupid, eh?" Nitsa again looked up toward the heavens. "Evangelia, what happened to our girl? Too many books, don't you think?" She put her hands down on her lap and spoke directly at Daphne this time, deadly serious. "It's time for you to stop thinking about your life and start living it. Don't think—just live. Do what your heart tells you to do for once."

Daphne knew there was only one place that would lead—right to the man whose touch made her feel alive again, the man she felt she could talk with for hours and hours and never run out of things to say. The man who for the first time in a long time had asked her to believe that magic could indeed exist.

It was as if Nitsa could read her mind, and at this point, Daphne thought, she probably could. "Go to him, Daphne. Find him and talk to him. Find him before it's too late."

She looked at Nitsa and knew that once again, her old friend was right. Yianni had said that he was leaving the island, that with Yia-yia gone he had nothing left to stay here for. She had to show him that he was wrong, that she was here and he needed to stay for her, for each other, at least a little bit longer.

"Nitsa—" Daphne began to speak but the old woman cut her off.

"Save your words, Daphne. Just go." Nitsa swatted at Daphne's behind with her hand, shooing her away from the couch and toward her new life.

"Thank you, Nitsa. Thank you."

She ran all the way to the port. It was pitch-black outside. She raced down the concrete causeway, the moonlight shimmering on the sea's surface providing just enough light to guide her way. She scanned each of the boats moored in the port and spotted Yianni's tethered at the far end of the dock. Daphne jumped onboard and unlatched the doorway that led belowdecks. She lurched down the stairs, trying not to think about what she would say to him. *No more thinking, just living.*

He looked up at her. "Daphne, what are you doing here?"

She didn't answer. This was not a time for stories. She dove into his arms.

He held her face in his hands, just as he had in the kitchen. "What about Stephen?" he asked.

"He's gone. Forget about Stephen." She lunged at his lips, inhaling his breath.

He kissed her back, deep and hard. His whiskers dug into her cheeks, like the spikes of a thousand sea urchins. But she liked the way they hurt.

They made love all over the boat, all night. There was nothing safe or quiet about their lovemaking, as it had been with Stephen. The sex was raw and primal—and she was ravenous. Daphne had forgotten what it was like to give in to lust, to let it take her away and consume her. She had forgotten what it was to be guided by emotions and pleasure instead of duty and pragmatism. And it felt wonderful.

Daphne woke up with the rooster's first call. She lay facedown in the bed, her back exposed to the early-morning air. The faintest breeze kissed her skin. She didn't move or even open her eyes, not wanting to wake him. She didn't want to talk, not just yet. She just wanted to lie quietly, to breathe in the stillness. She lifted her chin ever so slightly and listened, wondering if she would be there.

It was soft and distant, but she could hear it. There was no mistaking the voice, or the story.

He will bring such great joy and love back into your life. And you will walk side by side with him for all the rest of your days.

Forty-one

BROOKLYN

ONE YEAR LATER

She knew she should be sleeping. It was four a.m., and the alarm was set to go off again at six. But she didn't care. As tired as she was, she just lay in bed watching him sleep. She loved how his chest bobbed up and down with each breath, how his black hair shone like silk, and how his lashes fluttered as he dreamed. But she loved nothing more than to reach her hand out across the bed and feel his heart beating beneath her fingers.

She inched closer to him. His drool smelling sweet on the pillow. She inhaled his scent, feeling as if her heart would burst with love. She couldn't stand it any longer. She had to touch him.

Daphne reached her arms out and scooped him up. "Come here, my love," she whispered. It was amazing how fast he was growing. It had only been three months since she had given birth, but already he seemed much heavier, so much bigger.

She covered him with the crochet blanket Nitsa had sent as a gift and carried him into the living room, stopping only to peek at Evie, sleeping peacefully in her bed, and Popi, snoring loudly in hers. Daphne knew Popi would be up soon; it was her turn to prepare for the lunch rush at Koukla while Daphne took Evie to school.

"We're just like Yia-yia and Dora, aren't we?" Each night the cousins would look at each other and laugh at how history was indeed repeating itself. They never imagined they would be living together here in an old Brooklyn town house, working and raising the children together. But Daphne knew Popi would be the perfect business partner, as well as a surrogate parent for Evie and Johnny. For Popi, moving to New York had been the fresh start she had always craved. But above all, the cousins knew they would love each other, take care of each other and the children, like no others would or ever could.

She settled into the cozy chair by the big bay window. Nuzzling Johnny closer, she kissed his forehead and gazed out across the yard. The cypress trees swayed ever so slightly in the cool fall air. She closed her eyes and listened, waiting for Yia-yia's morning lullaby.

> *I love you like no other . . .*
> *I have no gifts to shower upon you*
> *No gold or jewels or riches*
> *But still, I give you all I have*
> *And that, my sweet child, is all my love*

I promise you this,
You will always have my love

She never imagined when she had the cypress trees planted in the yard that they would sing for her here in Brooklyn. She had simply wanted the comfort of watching them dance on the wind in the garden of their new home. But then she heard Yia-yia's soft serenade, and she knew that everything was going to be all right. Yia-yia continued to watch over them, even here.

She looked down at little Johnny's face as he slept cradled in her arms. He was the image of his father, handsome and dark. She lifted his soft, tiny fingers with her own—and wondered if one day they, like his, would be callused and hardened by his love of the sea.

"Maybe you'll meet him one day," she whispered to her son. She wondered if she too would ever see him again. She thought back, as she often did, to their time together on Erikousa. After that first night on the boat, they spent every moment together as days spilled into weeks. They swam, fished, and explored the island with Evie, who finally learned to swim by jumping off Yianni's boat into the sea and into Daphne's waiting arms below. Every evening they feasted on fresh fish captured in Yianni's nets and stayed up talking well into the night after Evie had fallen asleep and the fire died down to mere embers that would float between them on the breeze. Yia-yia's house once again came to life with the sound of their laughter, their soft lovers' whispers blending with the murmurs of the cypresses rustling on the wind. For the first time in a long time Daphne felt that when she spoke, she was heard, and when she was touched, she was alive.

And then it happened.

As summer gave way to fall, there was no mistaking the difference in the air or the one in Yianni's eyes. Just as she had trained herself to sense the subtleties in the change of seasons, so too did she sense the one in him, or perhaps this time it was a change in her, she couldn't be sure. She noticed how the light illuminated his face when she walked into the room and how he stood taller when she was near. She could feel his eyes lingering and following each time she walked away again. And then she realized why it all seemed and felt so familiar. It was the way Alex had looked at her. It was the way she had looked at Alex.

Yianni began to speak of the future, of we and us and family. He asked what she thought of London and Athens and said he would consider moving to New York again for her, for them. He used the word *forever*. He used the word *love*.

At first she embraced it, relished what was happening, what he was proposing. But then she began to realize that it was all moving so fast. There was so much she loved about Yianni. It was as if he had woken her from a long sleep and opened her eyes to a new appreciation, a new clarity. But with that new clarity, she now realized that loving someone is not the same as truly being in love. To be certain of that, she needed more time.

She tried to tell him once, as they lay in bed listening to the distant sound of the incoming tide. "We should strongly consider London," he said. "You would fit in beautifully with the culinary scene, Evie's school would be English, and perhaps I will give Oxford a chance."

"I'm not ready to think about that yet." She turned to face him; but before she could continue speaking, he placed his fingertips on her lips.

"Shhhhhh," he said. "Daphne, I will come with you wherever you lead." And then he kissed her, and she said no more.

Again and again Popi told her how lucky she was, how wonderful that all her dreams were coming true. Again and again she agreed and told herself the same, but the gnawing in her stomach began to tell her otherwise. And then finally, so did the cup.

It happened one afternoon, as Yianni knelt under the lemon tree, mending his nets, and Evie sat nearby, teasing her kitten with his leftover twine. Popi and Daphne sat by the garden wall, sipping their coffee just as they had countless times before. Only this time was different. This time as they turned their cups over, laughing in anticipation of the usual muddied mess Daphne assumed she would see, she was greeted instead by something unexpected. The picture in the grounds was clear and cloudless, just as the sky above had been that beautiful mid-September afternoon.

"What do you see?" Popi asked, leaning in closer.

"I see two figures," Daphne replied, turning the cup this way and that. "I can't tell what they are, men or women, but I see two people clear as day. The first one is flying, soaring high with big, wide wings. But the one on the ground doesn't have wings. It looks like this one has both arms raised up toward the sky, holding on to the one that's flying."

Popi leaned in closer to get a better look. "I wonder what that means," she said as they both contemplated the picture.

Daphne sat back in her seat. She looked up at the bright blue sky and then again at Popi. "I think it means that sometimes when you love someone so much, you can be terrified of losing them. Of being left alone."

But as he listened from across the patio, Yianni realized Daphne was wrong. He could translate the cup's meaning without even a glance. The picture Daphne described spoke clearly to Yianni, just as the cypress whispers had to Daphne and Yia-yia. This was an image not of someone being held down, but of someone being released.

The next morning, as Daphne woke and pulled a blanket around her body to ward off the morning chill, she turned over in bed and found that he was gone. Once again, he had slipped out the door and into the night. In that moment Daphne realized that Yianni had not been blind to her hesitation and growing uncertainty. That morning, as she pulled the blanket tighter around her body, Daphne realized what Yianni had done, what he had sacrificed by saving her the pain of walking away first.

He loved her enough to let go.

She was grateful then, as she was grateful now. Grateful they had shared a beautiful summer together and that he had given her the gift of a son. She had tried to find him, first when she returned to New York and learned she was pregnant and then again when Johnny was born. She knew that one day she would try again, that he deserved to know he had a son and maybe, together, even a second chance. But when that day would be, she still wasn't certain. There was still so much for her to digest, to contemplate and comprehend. For now it was enough to know that Evangelia and Dora were united again, this time eternally, by the sweet baby boy asleep in her arms.

She kissed Johnny's head and inhaled his baby scent. "Let me tell you a story, little man," she whispered.

"A long, long time ago lived a young wood nymph named Daphne. She lived in the forest with her friends, and they spent their days climbing trees, singing, swimming in the streams, and playing. She loved her life among the trees and animals and her other wood nymph friends. Every day she prayed to her father, the river god, and asked that he protect her and always keep her safe. Well, one day the god Apollo was walking in the woods, and he spotted Daphne playing with her friends. He instantly fell in love with the young nymph and vowed to marry her. But Daphne had other ideas. She didn't want to be the wife of a god, stuck up on Mount Olympus with all the other fancy gods and goddesses. She wanted to be left alone, to stay where she was happiest, in the grotto with her friends, the ones who understood her and loved her best. But the god Apollo refused to take no for an answer. He ran after poor Daphne. He chased the terrified young nymph across the woods, through the streams, and over mountains. Finally, when she was so exhausted that she could run no more, Daphne prayed again to her father, the river god. She asked that he save her from a fate that she was not meant for, from a life not meant to be hers. Suddenly the young nymph stopped running. Just as Apollo caught up with her and reached out to grab her, her feet sprang roots that burrowed deep into the ground; her legs became dark and rough, like bark. Daphne stretched her arms up toward the sky. Branches and leaves sprang from her fingers. Apollo held her tight, but the god would not have his way. Daphne was no longer a beautiful young wood nymph. Her father had turned her into a tree. From that moment on, Daphne stayed rooted in the place that she loved, surrounded by those who loved her most."

Daphne nuzzled Johnny closer and kissed his chubby pink cheek. She gazed out the window as the cypresses danced on the breeze, their dense leaves shivering in the predawn quiet.

ACKNOWLEDGMENTS

My deepest gratitude to everyone at HarperCollins; especially Jonathan Burnham, Brenda Segel, Carolyn Bodkin, Hannah Wood, Heather Drucker, and Miranda Ottewell.

There are not enough words or pages for me to adequately thank my editor, Claire Wachtel. Your insight and careful guidance have transformed this book, and me, in the most wonderful ways.

My Greek partner in crime, Publicity Goddess Tina Andreadis. Working with you has been the sweet cherry on top of it all . . . or should I say baklava?

My agents, Jan Miller and Nena Madonia. It was indeed An Invisible Thread that brought us together. I am so lucky to have you both in my corner. Nena, you are a valued and trusted friend and one of the most beautiful people I know, inside and out.

Our invisible thread would not be complete without Laura Schroff. Look at the ripple effects from just one act of kindness. Thank you for sharing your thread, and your friendship.

To Dr. Spyros Orfanos, for filling in the blanks. Also, Isaac Dostis, whose documentary, *Farewell My Island*, allowed me to hear the stories of the surviving Jews of Corfu in their own words. And to Marcia Haddad Ikonomopoulos of the Kehila Kedosha Janina Museum and Synagogue for her support and tireless commitment to telling the stories of the Greek Jews of the Holocaust.

I'm blessed with the most incredible circle of friends and soul sisters. Bonnie Bernstein, my confidante and cohort whom I will never tire of talking to. Joanne Rendell, who kept me writing, page after page. To Karen Kelly, Kathy Giaconia, and the LPW Dinner Club; the Woods, Wettons, and Brycelands—Kelsey too. And of course, to Adrianna Nionakis and Olga Makrias, who taught me at the earliest age that you don't need many friends in life, just the right friends.

Thanks also to my *Extra* family, the best producers and talent team in the biz. Special thanks to Lisa Gregorisch, Theresa Coffino, Jeremy Spiegel, Mario Lopez, Maria Menounos, A.J. Calloway, Hilaria Baldwin, Jerry Penacoli, Marilyn Ortiz, Nicki Fertile . . . and of course, Marie Hickey, the best boss, friend, and reader, a girl could ask for.

Everything I know about faith, family, strength, and kindness, I learned from my own family, especially my parents, Kiki and Tasso and my brother, Emanuel . . . aka Noli. My own *yia-yias* and *papous* set the bar so very high. To this day, my *yia-yia* Lamprini tells me that all she has to give me in this life is her blessing . . . and that's all I've ever needed or wanted.

Like Daphne, I spent magical summers in Greece surrounded by a glorious posse of aunts, uncles, and cousins. This book is about you and for you, every single last wonderfully crazy one of you. Special thanks to Effie Orfanos, my Frousha, for answering endless questions and for all those candles you lit for me at Agios Spyridon. Once again, he answered our prayers.

To Christiana and Nico, every day you inspire me and make me so very proud. Mama loves you more than you can imagine. And, of course, to Dave. There would be no Alex without you. There would be no book without you . . . there would be nothing without you.

While this book is a work of fiction, it is inspired by my father's birthplace, the real life island paradise that is Erikousa. During WWII, the islanders came together to hide a Jewish man and his daughters from the Nazis. Everyone worked together to save the family, not one person gave up the secret of Savas and his daughters, even as the Nazis searched house to house. The islanders shared what little they had and risked their own lives without hesitation because they were good people, and it was the right thing to do. There were no awards, accolades, or honors for the people of Erikousa after the war, the Jewish family survived and life on the island simply went on. I hope that in some small way, this book can finally help others recognize the beauty and bravery of the people of Erikousa. It's a story I'm honored to tell, and an island family I'm proud to be a part of.

MUSKOKA LAKES PUBLIC LIBRARY
P.O. BOX 189; 69 JOSEPH STREET
PORT CARLING, ON P0B 1J0
705-765-5650
www.muskoka.com/library

ABOUT THE AUTHOR

YVETTE MANESSIS CORPORON is an Emmy Award–winning writer, producer, and author. She is currently a senior producer with the syndicated entertainment news show *Extra*. With more than twenty years' experience in television news, Yvette has written and produced for the most celebrated names in broadcasting and interviewed the most iconic newsmakers and celebrities of our time. In addition to her Emmy Award, Yvette has received a Silurian Award for Excellence in Journalism, and the New York City Comptroller and City Council's Award for Greek Heritage and Culture. She is married to award-winning photojournalist David Corporon. They have two children and live in New York.

MUSKOKA LAKES PUBLIC LIBRARY
P.O. BOX 189; 69 JOSEPH STREET
PORT CARLING, ON P0B 1J0
705-765-5650
www.muskoka.com/library